VEIL OF SHADOWS IV

OMNIBUS SPECIAL EDITION

M. R. PRITCHARD

First Edition
2025
Midnight Ledger
Paperback ISBN: 978-1-957709-62-8
Hardcover ISBN: 978-1-957709-63-5

VEIL OF SHADOWS IV

About Veil of Shadows IV

**A collection of the Veil of Shadows Series
Books 11-13.**

This omnibus edition begins with "Echoes of Treachery", book 11 in the Veil of Shadows Series. Do not start here. You must begin this story at the beginning.

When the Veil grows thin, the shadows grow hungry.

Step into a world where the boundaries between the living and the damned are dangerously thin, where angels and demons wage wars, and where love and sacrifice blur the line between light and darkness. *The Veil of Shadows* series plunges readers into a dark fantasy realm where nothing is as it seems, and every decision comes with a cost.

Follow the journey of Meg, a fierce heroine caught between her mortal ties and her fated role in Hell's power struggle. With her children's lives on the line and the weight of Lucifer's legacy on her shoulders, Meg must navigate treacherous alliances, deadly enemies, and a love that defies the heavens and hell itself.

From the ominous halls of Hell to the fragile sanctuary of the Earthen plane, each book in the series reveals deeper secrets, more twisted fates, and the relentless pull of destiny.

For fans of dark fantasy, paranormal romance, and epic battles between good and evil, *The Veil of Shadows* series is an unmissable journey into a world where the Veil grows thin, and the shadows grow hungry.

———

If you want to immerse yourself further in the Veil of Shadows, visit the blog for Veil of Shadows discussions, previews, and spoilers.

———

Echoes of Treachery (Veil of Shadows 11)

Meg has finally found love, family, and a life she never thought she deserved. But just as she begins to embrace it, chaos looms on the horizon.

The Safe Houses are burning, the horde of the dead swells, and the Veil between realms is thinning. The Deacons, once protectors of order, are falling one by one. And the man who nearly killed her years ago—**the one who haunts her darkest nightmares**—may be returning to finish what he started.

Meg has spent her life deceiving Demons and Angels, outwitting even the most powerful beings in all the realms. But as her kingdom teeters on the edge of annihilation, her greatest weapon —her lies—might also become her greatest weakness.

With everything she loves on the line, **Meg must decide: will she face the truth or continue weaving the webs that could destroy her?**

Love, betrayal, and war collide in a battle for survival where secrets have the power to kill—and Meg may have to pay the ultimate price for hers.

Temptations of Fate (Veil of Shadows 12)

Lucifer's return looms, his voice calling from beyond the grave, driving Alastor to the brink of madness. With the realms teetering on the edge of chaos, Meg finds herself held captive by the one person she never imagined.

As the veil between worlds weakens, darkness threatens to consume everything—and time is running out to stop it.

Omens of Darkness (Veil of Shadows 13)

The Throne of Hell Awaits. The Final Battle Beckons.

Meg and Sparrow have faced insurmountable odds, but nothing could prepare them for the final descent into Hell. With Lucifer resurrected and chaos gripping the realms, they must rally their allies for one last battle to reclaim their kingdom and save their family.

But as the war unfolds, Lucifer delivers a shattering revelation: the curse Meg always believed marked Sparrow was hers to bear all along—a dark legacy that now threatens their daughter's life.

The stakes have never been higher, and as Hell's throne hangs in the balance, Meg and Sparrow must summon every ounce of strength, love, and sacrifice they possess. Because this time, the fate of more than one world rests on their shoulders.

The epic conclusion to the *Veil of Shadows* series will leave you breathless.

———

I was hooked from the get-go..." -ABNA Expert Reviewer

"It's unfortunate that one can't predict or be a part of aiding which books go viral, as Sparrow Man by M.R. Pritchard is certainly worthy of such reward ... this novel took me by complete surprise. What I thought was a simple zombie story morphed into something wild and completely unforeseen. Yet it fit perfectly within the world Pritchard has created, mysteries unfolding into fantastical developments. The eclectic characters were a joy to follow and the romance

unfolded without being forced."-TheBehrg, KindleScout winning author of Housebroken

"Whoever thought a trip to Hell could be so interesting! Pritchard does a good job balancing humor and thrills—hell, it's mostly funny —and delivering the reader a cast of characters so unbelievable that you can't help but love them." - Charles, Vine Voice

"Another great fantasy ... with humor, edginess, childlike joy, and the frailty of love. Pritchard reminds us to nurture those we hold dear as we root for her characters to have a happily ever after." - Muddy Rose Reviews

"This is the story of being there for someone who is going through a tough time, of love and trauma with strong characters that you can't help but like. Meg, and Sparrow, stand out in a well told tale. I am not normally into fantasy but this one grabbed me as it is so much more." -Misfits Reviewer

ECHOES OF TREACHERY

Echoes of Treachery
(Veil of Shadows 11)

M. R. Pritchard

Meg has finally found love, family, and a life she never thought she deserved. But just as she begins to embrace it, chaos looms on the horizon.

The Safe Houses are burning, the horde of the dead swells, and the Veil between realms is thinning. The Deacons, once protectors of order, are falling one by one. And the man who nearly killed her years ago—**the one who haunts her darkest nightmares**—may be returning to finish what he started.

Meg has spent her life deceiving Demons and Angels, outwitting even the most powerful beings in all the realms. But as her kingdom teeters on the edge of annihilation, her greatest weapon —her lies—might also become her greatest weakness.

With everything she loves on the line, **Meg must decide: will she face the truth or continue weaving the webs that could destroy her?**

Love, betrayal, and war collide in a battle for survival where secrets have the power to kill—and Meg may have to pay the ultimate price for hers.

ONE

MEG

I'M SITTING on a soggy dock, feet dangling in cool, dark water, watching the loons floating in the morning mist. Nightingale runs toward me, sprinting on water, arms outstretched, terror etched on her face. The loons scramble away, their wings flapping against the water as they soar low. I want to yell at Nightingale for ruining my fucking peace. She promised to stop, but this must be something serious because she hasn't come to me in a dream like this in years.

"What is it?" I ask.

"Wake up, Meg." She's shaking my shoulders. "Get up! Get up now! Wake up! You must save your children!" she screams in my face.

My eyes flash open. I sit up in bed, smelling acrid creosote. It's familiar but too intense, too fresh. The window is open; no birds chirp, no owls hoot. There's fresh smoke drifting inside, the hammering of stone and metal, shouting echoes.

Skeele shifts, moving closer, smoothing his hand over my hip.

Someone howls like a creature of night out on a hunt. There are footsteps in the hallway.

"Wake up!" I yell to Skeele, launching myself out of bed.

He's on his feet, naked, ready to fight, a speck of dried blood on his lip. We wake to chaos. There's no slow morning stretches with our limbs rubbing together, no savoring the memories and ache of last night.

"Get dressed." I throw him a pair of pants and a shirt.

"The babies." His eyes are wide, terrified. "Get them." Skeele's shirt gets caught on his horns. He tugs hard, tearing it in a rush.

He calls them babies still but they are much older, too old to be called that. They're teenagers now, but he's never stopped. I guess compared to him, they will always be babies. Young, innocent, his–something he never thought he'd have. Skeele never thought he'd have a family. Neither did I. He was bred to serve the throne but took on so much more. I have always lived a life of chaos and destruction and never thought I deserved the love of a real family. Raised on the Earthen plane by a Demon who killed my mother, I knew nothing but feat and mistrust and hate. It took a long time to get to where I am now.

Dread spreads through my gut. Teari warned me of something terrible coming years ago. I threatened to kick her out of my realm because she didn't give me details. She just had a feeling, a premonition. She was right and now I'm thankful she told us. Otherwise, I wouldn't have a bugout bag packed and ready, or a plan.

I grab clothes and throw them on. I get my bag, my blade, and other weapons.

"Here." Skeele tosses me the jar of Snowy Owl feathers from my bedside.

Poof. I leave the room.

"Children," I whisper, shaking them awake. "Wake up right now."

Remington launches up straight with a deep intake of breath. Rue wakes quieter. Green eyes flash open, her arms jerk to the sides, gripping the sheets. "Are we going to die?" she asks.

"Get moving." I throw her blankets back and don't answer her question. I can't answer because fear is more than a flood threatening to overtake my body. It's a tsunami, an earthquake, something thoroughly consuming that clogs my throat and traps my words. My children will not die. Not again. But I might.

This is not new. I have been attacked by evil before, but that was when my world was small. The stakes are higher than ever now. I couldn't protect the seed in my womb then, but now... now I could lose everything I didn't think I deserved. Fate has been cruel and unfair, but I don't have time to dwell on it.

Remington and Rue scramble out of bed, and when they smell the smoke that seeps under their door and hear the commotion echoing in the hall, they move quickly and meet me in their closet.

"Get clothes," I say. "Boots, knives, leather jackets, and pants."

They know what to do. Everything is within reach for a quick exit.

Clea arrives, wisps of white swirling into her ethereal form. "Let me say goodbye," Clea's voice breaks through before she's fully formed. "I must say goodbye to them."

My mother's lips are deep red, her transparent skin a ghastly white, but she doesn't scare them. This is all they know of their grandmother. She died the day I was born, so it is all I know of her as well.

"Hurry, Clea," I warn, collecting more clothing and tucking knives into Rue's pockets.

"Oh, children," her form turns solid, "be safe." She hugs them together, one on each arm, hugged so tight they might complain that they can't breathe, but instead they embrace her just as fiercely.

"What have you seen?" I ask Clea, tossing a pack to Remington. He straps it on and pulls the clips tight.

"Demons from the mountains. Lesser Demons from the south. Bugs and snakes and roaches coming in droves." Clea shivers with disgust. "The dark energy is strong, familiar."

"Did you see a face?" I ask, helping Rue tighten her pack so she can run if she needs to without it flopping around on her back.

"Not yet," Clea says. "I had to stop and say goodbye." She squeezes the children one last time. "I'll go back."

"Be careful," I warn.

"Hide them well," Clea says with a warm smile, patting each child on their cheek then pinching them. "I wish you could take my bones so I could go with you and have more time. Our women are cursed with losing children."

"They won't be lost," I say. "They'll be in hiding."

Clea nods and straightens her back. "Hurry." She turns toward the door. "Something is coming."

I nod. "Help the Hellions. Skeele is in charge while I'm gone."

For a split second, I wonder where my grandfather, Lucifer, put Clea's bones after I found them all those years ago. I make a mental note to add it to my to-do list then curse myself for not thinking of it sooner.

I take Rue's hand then Remington's. *Poof*–we're gone.

Two

Before the attack on the Castle in the Burning Caves

Alastor trekked from his hovel in the mountains to the Black River of Hell's Adirondacks. He had one goal: secure a Basilisk. He didn't have a castle to defend–yet– but he'd need the creature to get there. Lucifer had told him. Get the Basilisk, demolish the Deacons, feed the horde, storm the castle, kill everyone but Meg. Find his bones.

Alastor drove to Old Forge, taking Interstate-81 but avoiding all of Pennsylvania. He passed herds of the walking dead, a smirk crossing his face as he counted them and calculated how large his army would become. He didn't desire the throne, but the thrill of power was something Alastor couldn't ignore. He'd been thriving on it since growing the skin trades bigger than they'd been before Shay and that half-breed scum Jed had tried to take him down.

Yes, the intoxicating rush of power swelled within Alastor now; it swelled with need; more, more than ever before.

Alastor turned off the exit toward Interstate-481 north, then turned onto Interstate-90 east. He passed farmland and dense forests. He saw signs for the Safe House nearby. He made a mental note to have those taken down. Soon there would be no need for a Safe House or repenting because all souls would stay in Hell and *he* would dole them out to a realm or a Kingdom using his own deal with the Archangels.

Alastor merged onto 365 E and veered off onto Eastern Rock Road. The Jeep jostled across the busted parking lot, pavement cracked and sunken into the soft ground. He turned onto Moose River Road and drove past old houses and grocery stores. The Black River roared from nearby, the waters turbid and angry and the slick serpentine backs of the Basilisk blending in with the motion of the water.

They were spawning. Perfect.

Alastor parked his vehicle, tires snapping pine needles and releasing their scent. He got out and made his way to the edge of the riverbank. Standing on a giant rock, he planned the next move. There were plenty of ways to fish for a Basilisk. He needed the biggest one, though. Nothing small or weak. He needed a giant Basilisk that could consume an army.

Alastor jumped down to the lower rocks and made his way toward the shallow pool of baby Basilisk.

A giant head rose from the surface of the river, watching with a sinister gaze. Rows of sharp teeth flashed and a warning hiss echoed.

"Come on ya slimy bitch," Alastor said, pulling a knife from his belt.

He crouched, reaching into the pool of babies. The mother swam closer, teeth bared. Alastor reached into the water and grabbed a small one. An ear-piercing squeal signaled the mother. Alastor cut the baby in half and tossed the body back into the water, turning it a murky red. The mother moved closer, jaws gnashing, threatening. It didn't scare Alastor–he had a plan. Alastor jumped in the dark water and made quick work of slaughtering all the baby Basilisk. Within minutes, he was saturated in bloody river water. Alastor rubbed the pieces of Basilisk on his body, dipping his head and coating his hair and clothing in their blood. He bathed, rubbing their blood on his arms and neck.

The Mother Basilisk slithered closer, confused. Her children were dead, but Alastor smelled just like them. She glanced to the blood bath then the Demon. He smelled like them, like hers. He must be her child, the only one, the very last one. Being a creature of darkness, she would protect him until the very end.

Alastor tucked pieces of bleeding Basilisk into his pockets so the smell remained fresh. He emerged from the river, covered in blood and bits of flesh and bone. His clothing clung to his skin and bloody water dripped down his body in dark rivulets. He walked back to his Jeep, smiling as the Mother Basilisk followed him, a menacing shadow at his back.

THREE

Meg

PEABODY LIBRARY IS DARK. When we arrive, it sets off every ward in the building. After all these years Jed *would* ward his home against me. Typical Jed.

The horse shows up to investigate first. A shallow whinny greets us.

"Nero! Come clear this rune." I motion to the circle of salt and chalk that's trapping us.

Nero shakes his head in a firm response of "no."

The damn horse doesn't even trust me. Perfect. I can't blame Jed or Shay, I've gotten them in plenty of trouble over the years. They probably don't want any surprises.

"Go get Shay," I say. "And hurry."

Before the giant black stallion gets himself turned around, footsteps echo down the hall.

"Meg?" Shay's voice calls.

"Shhh," Jed shushes her.

"Come free us," I holler. "I don't have much time." I do my best to hide the panic in my voice. I have to get out of here, return to Hell and defend the castle.

"What shit-fuckery did you bring us this time?" Jed asks, rounding a bookshelf. He stops short when he sees the children behind me. His eyes go wide, knowing. "What's happening?" He moves closer but doesn't clear the rune.

"The castle in the burning caves is under attack." I shift on my feet, eager to get out of the circle in the middle of the room. I feel too exposed like this, trapped with my children. I want them hidden. I want them away from the door.

"You mean *your* throne is under attack?" Shay clarifies.

I nod.

Jed takes a few quick steps forward and scuffs his boot over the runes on the floor.

I take a deep breath and step away, dragging the children with me. I go to Shay. She helped me many years ago with a search and rescue. Then again, when the Deacons imprisoned me, she impersonated me to keep the throne of Hell safe.

"I need you to take them," I say, desperate.

"Are you sure about this, Meg?" Shay's voice breaks through my thoughts, concern clear in her eyes.

I nod, trying not to fall apart at the thought of handing my children over for someone else to ensure their safety. "I have to go back. The attack on the castle needs to be stopped, and I'm the only one who can do it."

"We'll take care of them," Jed says, stepping closer.

I swallow hard, fighting back the tears threatening to spill over. Turning, I face Rue and Remington, trying to ignore the ache in my heart. This might be the last time I see them. "Listen to Shay and Jed. They'll keep you both safe." I grip their hands and squeeze. "Promise me."

"I promise," they reply in tandem.

"A promise is a promise, remember?" I grip them in a tight hug.

"A promise is a promise," Remington repeats, the sound and tone of his voice too familiar to someone else's. Someone from my past. The one person who is probably on their way to kill me.

Rue's eyes well with tears as she clutches me with both arms. "Don't go," she pleads.

"I have to. I'll come back for you, I promise." I say, hoping it's not a lie.

Barely able to speak past the lump in my throat, I turn back to Shay and Jed. "Thank you," I muster.

With a last glance at my children, I turn and walk away, each step heavier than the last. The weight of my decision presses down like a boulder on my back. This is the right decision. It must be.

"Wait," I say. "One more thing." I drop my bag off my shoulder, unzip it, and pull out the jar of snowy owl feathers. "Put this somewhere safe. Please."

Shay reaches for the jar. It's small, not much more than a jelly jar; etched glass and a steel lid. These are the remains of my dead daughter, Elise. I swallow hard, tamping down emotion, afraid that this night might leave me with three jars of feathers and no children. I'm not sure I can go back to that person. Empty, filled with fear and hate. Three jars of feathers would most certainly release the monster inside me.

There. I have left everything that I care about in the Peabody Library. Everything I never thought I'd have, I've left in the hands of others.

Jed and Shay are good. They will do what is right. They will protect my children. Jed has been on the run his entire life, he knows all the tricks. Shay was raised a prepper on a Montana ranch; she's the strongest woman I know–even stronger with the Demon poison that's embedded in the scar on her leg. Yes, mild relief flushes over me. This is the best place for them.

FOUR

Shay took the jar of mottled white and brown feathers, blinked, and she was immediately transported back to a memory from a Crossroads Demon deal.

The air crackled with an ominous energy as the figure approached the crossroads, their steps hesitant yet filled with a sense of desperate determination. They bore the weight of something heavy upon their shoulders, their gaze haunted by the specter of tragedy that loomed over their existence.

It was a Deacon.

Nero backed up.

Shay tensed.

Deacons were the gatekeepers of balance between the Seven Kingdoms of Heaven, the Earthen plane and Hell. Why did one summon Shay and Nero?

"What is it that you seek, Deacon?" Shay asked.

The Deacon hesitated, their gaze flickering with uncertainty before they spoke, voice tinged with a mixture of power and desperation.

"No one can know that I'm here," the Deacon said.

Shay nodded. "Is that your deal?"

"No." the Deacon folded his hands. "This deal will be a great burden for both of us."

The Deacon kept looking over his shoulder and to the desert beyond. He'd drawn them to a crossroads in the middle of nowhere. They could see for miles even with only moonlight.

"There is a great darkness coming," the Deacon warned.

"That sounds like a warning, not a deal. Why did you call me here?" Shay didn't want to return to Alastor, but she didn't want her time wasted by this creature.

The Deacon paused and closed his eyes, finding calm and choosing his words carefully. "The deal is, you must take the children to safety and tell no one where they are. You must hide them until Clea's prophecy comes to fruition."

"What children?"

The Deacon held up a finger. "They are not born yet. When the time comes, you will know. You must agree to this now, before it's too late."

"What are you wishing to give me?" Shay asked, knowing that what the Crossroads Demon would take was not negotiable and typically unknown.

"I will give my life. Sooner rather than later."

Shay blinked again before glancing at Nero. His ear twitched with recognition. He remembered the deal.

"They'll be safe here. We won't let anything happen to them," Shay said.

Meg nodded, and Shay noticed the slight quiver in her bottom lip. Meg wouldn't fall apart though, never did. She always kept her feelings in check unless it was *anger*. That was a feeling she wasn't afraid to let out. She'd kept it tamped down since the children were born. Now love... That was a feeling Meg kept under wraps and Shay could understand why. Meg had let her love escape once; she'd loved the Raven King and he nearly killed her. He ruined her, wrecked her, let others clean up what was left of her broken heart and bleeding body. Meg was right to have trust issues. Last time she trusted someone heart and soul, she'd nearly died. Shay would never forget the moment Jed arrived, covered in blood, and panicking that they'd die in Hell along with Meg. When she had *poofed* back to Hell at Skeele's feet, the Hellions tried to save her and failed, so they dragged Jed into the mess. Jed did what he could, but he wasn't as strong a spell caster in those days. It was Teari's knowledge that brought her back to life. Since Meg would no longer get blood from Sparrow, her first in Command, Skeele, had to give her blood and it forced a bond that resulted in children.

Shay focused on the children standing behind Meg. They seemed despondent, didn't show a speck of fear. They'd never been to the Peabody Library, never been to the Earthen plane as far as Shay knew. Shay and Jed had known them their whole lives, spent time with them during the holidays and Sunday dinners that Meg held. Shay and Jed attended, both having no other family and feeling compelled since Meg bought the library and let them live there.

Shay reached out to Rue first and hugged her. She gripped Remington's shoulder and gave him a little shake as a greeting and a promise.

"We'll take good care of them, for as long as you need," Shay promised.

Rue didn't say a word, but Shay noticed the slight tremble of her bottom lip, exactly like her mother. She'd have to learn how to hide that better. The girl swiped at long dark hair that had fallen across her eyes.

Jed was there, taking Remington aside and whispering to him, no doubt warning him of the Earthen plane and what the boy could and could not do while he was here.

Shay shook Meg's shoulder, "If you've got to burn it all to the ground, then let it *burn*."

A chill passed through Meg as Shay's eyes flashed black. It was a side-effect of the Demon poison in Shay's leg. She was tethered to the Crossroads Demon Nero, her horse. As a result, Shay had the ability to transform into something wraithlike and make deals that transcended all the realms.

Shay tipped the jar to the side, watched the feathers drift, and realized that they looked very much like Meg's wings.

Meg nodded, tucking her wings tight against her back.

Shay hugged her, worried that Meg might fail. No. No. Shay wouldn't let that thought out into the wild. Never wanted it to become true. Meg was the strongest person Shay had ever met. Shay squeezed Meg tighter, easy not to pinch her wings.

"Burn it all, Meg," Shay whispered in her ear. "You are formidable."

Meg wiped her eyes; she wanted to tell the children goodbye again, but she'd been here too long. She needed to go back.

"One last thing," Meg said as she pulled a small piece of paper from her pocket and tucked it into Shay's hand. "No one knows about this place. Only myself and Skeele."

Meg raised a hand, gaze meeting her children's as she waved goodbye to them. Meg never prayed because she couldn't worship a God who'd allowed such violence and pain in her life. She couldn't see the worth in a being who allowed everything that had happened in her life. No, she'd never prayed but in that moment she did, and she prayed that it wouldn't be the last time she ever saw them.

Poof – Meg returned to Hell.

FIVE

BEFORE THE ATTACK ON THE CASTLE IN THE BURNING Caves

ALASTOR MOVED through the darkness of Hell with a singular purpose, his eyes burning with the intensity of his mission. The landscape of Hell, with its familiar chaos and torment, mirrored the turmoil within his mind as the voice of Lucifer drove him. Each step he took left scorched earth in his wake, a testament to the power that coursed through him. He distorted Meg's realm with each step.

The Safe Houses were his next target; sanctuaries for the lost souls to find their final resting place and the only place they'd find refuge from eternal torment. Within those walls balance was kept, and Alastor intended to snuff it out completely. No souls would leave Hell.

The Safe Houses began falling one by one.

Alastor began with the ones furthest away. Those that

wouldn't be noticed until it was too late. It would upset the balance and sorting of souls, but the Seven Kingdoms of Heaven would blame Meg as they always did. She was an easy scapegoat and none would figure out the truth until it was too late.

Alastor found the eldest of the Deacons at the Safe House; he looked like no one and everyone, nondescript, neither short nor tall, neither fat nor thin.

"You won't win, Alastor," the Deacon spat, as his even voice held a hint of defiance. "We keep the balance."

Alastor laughed, a sound devoid of humor. "There will be no more balance. Tell me where his bones are."

The Deacon clammed up, his lips sealed, he refused to release any information. The location of Lucifer's bones was a secret few were aware of.

Alastor leaned in, whispering the final words the Deacon would hear. "Your hope is a lie. Your fight for balance is meaningless." He shook the Deacon by his shirt. "Lucifer's bones. I need them."

The Deacon shook his head. "No."

The Deacons fell. Alastor slaughtered them one by one. None would release the location of Lucifer's bones. With the Deacons dead and the Safe House reduced to rubble, Alastor surveyed the destruction he had wrought. The fires burned brightly, casting a hellish glow that illuminated his path to the next Safe House. He felt a dark satisfaction knowing he'd eradicated yet another point of defiance against Lucifer's rebirth. He had a greater mission to fulfill, and nothing would stand in his way. Hell would belong to Lucifer once again, and Alastor would rule with an iron fist, crushing any who dared to oppose.

———

THERE WERE twelve Deacons in the room reserved for questioning at the Elmira Safe House. Three sat behind a table as though waiting to hand down a sentencing. They were all plain faced, dull, brown hair and brown eyes, they were anyone and everyone. If a Deacon walked down the street not a soul would recognize or remember them. This was the way of the Deacons.

"Forty Safe Houses have been demolished," a Deacon said.

"Survivors?"

"None of us survived. Only survivors are the souls that were there for sorting."

A Deacon seated at the table nodded, thinking.

"The destruction will come to us, we knew it would."

The Deacons all replied in monotone chatter, each with an idea or a plan for survival.

"We leave now. Go into hiding."

"No. We cannot leave the newly dead souls to linger and turn."

"Once they destroy us all none of that will matter."

"We need to hide."

"We need to get out of here."

"We cannot abandon the souls. It will upset the balance."

"There will be no balance on any realm once we are all dead."

The room went silent as the Deacons considered their fate. A world without Deacons was unfathomable.

———

AS THE DAYS PASSED, more Safe Houses fell. The Deacons did their duty and processed newly dead souls from the Earthen plane as though nothing were happening.

———

"It's here," Deacon announced.

One grabbed a Newcomer uniform from the supply cabinet. The maroon jumpsuit identified newly dead souls for processing. Or at least it used to, because after today none of that would exist.

Two Deacons grabbed a third by his elbows and directed them toward a supply cabinet.

"Put this on," they demanded. "Hurry."

The building shook with malice as Alastor's army of Demons, dark creatures, and the dead broke down doors and walls. They slammed thru windows and gates, killing every Deacon in sight.

The Deacon who had been pulled into the supply cabinet closed his eyes, feeling the change in the air as brethren were slaughtered under this roof.

"Hurry!" they ripped the white collar off and tore the buttons of the Deacon's shirt. "Change before it's too late."

They moved faster, kicking off shoes and pants and stepping into the Newcomer uniform. It had been ages since the Deacon wore anything besides the black suit and Roman collar. They zipped the Newcomer uniform, stepped into a pair of nondescript white shoes, and mussed their hair.

"You are no longer a Deacon."

The Deacon nodded.

"You have no duty other than to survive."

The Deacon nodded.

"It has been decided." The Deacon giving instructions pointed to the mess hall where detainees were gathering. "Go with them. Abandon everything you've been taught. Survive. Find water. Go to safety and wait."

"What do I wait for?"

They didn't explain; while the Deacons were many, they were also one—one soul that shared debts and prosper, one soul that was bound by a deal with the Crossroads Demon.

The Deacon nodded before being shoved in the direction of the detainees. He stumbled as he filtered between the bodies and became invisible in the crowd. Faces watched him but would never remember him, they could never point him out in a crowd because he looked like everyone and no one.

The other Deacons stayed in the supply cabinet. One collected the uniform, rolled it into a tight ball and hid it behind boxes and bins of cleaning supplies. When they were done, they stepped out into the hall and headed toward the entrance to face their fate. They ignored the Deacon in the Newcomer uniform, knew that they were so nondescript no one would recognize him. He would find safety in obscurity.

The closest body of water was the Nightjar's pond. He could make it there in time. He had to.

———

ALASTOR KILLED every Deacon in the building then left the Safe House with its doors wide open. The nondescript man exited the building at nightfall and ran into the nearby forest.

The Nightjar's pond was a good twenty miles away. As the Deacon ran, he did his best to avoid the dead sleeping in the dark forest. He crushed a leg, tripped over a whole person, fell, and landed with his elbow against a head. It crumpled under his weight and stained his uniform with gore. The Deacon stood and composed himself. The dead slept at night, that was the only good thing, but he had miles to go then the sun would rise and the dead would walk once again. He considered running on the road but decided that would make him too visible. God forbid Alastor noticed him and realized who he was. He shuffled to the side and let his vision adjust to the wavering shadows created by the forest canopy. The ochre Hellsky didn't provide much light, but he could see the bodies lying on the ground now that he took a moment to observe his surroundings.

The Deacon stepped to the side, making his way around the sleeping horde, easy not to step on anyone and damage them further. He still had hope that these souls could be saved and go to their rightful resting place. It wasn't right that they were trapped. These souls didn't deserve to turn and rot here in Hell–not all of them at least.

The Queen had done well to ensure the newly dead made it to a Safe House–better than Lucifer ever had. As a result, the numbers of walking dead had subsided to nearly nothing. Now it was different, now they'd came from the west and filled the forests. Now, if the Deacons ever recovered from this slaughter, they'd have their work cut out for them because there were too many souls. The balance would be tipped further than ever. The Veil between Hell and the Earthen plane just might shred.

Deacon made his way around the sleeping horde and began running again. Twigs snapped and leaves rustled with his movement. He felt the solid ropes of snakes underfoot, the gentle crunch of crushed bugs. Too many creatures had crawled out of the dirt to follow Alastor. He paused every few hundred yards to listen and make sure he wasn't being followed. Deacon ran through the night, while the moon was high in Hellsky until it sank to the horizon. He ran until the Newcomer uniform was torn by branches and bramble, the shoes were stained with dirt, mud, and blood.

He ran until he heard the mournful song of the Nightjar. The creature knew something was happening in the realm of Hell. The ochre sun began to rise.

Moans filled the forest.

The Deacon's heart began to beat rapidly and dread flooded his chest. With the sun rising, so would the dead. They'd follow his noise. They'd follow the snakes and the bugs and the rustling creatures that were after him. He made his way out of the forest, and began running on the road to avoid sounds of snapping sticks and rustling leaves. The deep inhale and exhale of his breaths and the padded footsteps were the only noise for miles.

Only once did Deacon glance over his shoulder to see slithering ropes in the road and scuttling legs. He couldn't control the shiver that sped up his spine and propelled him to run faster than ever.

He ran until he could see the shadow of the Nightjar's cabin from the road. He paused to catch his breath before jogging down the ditch and into the forest again. He stumbled, landed on low branches with a grunt and snapping of rib bones.

"Dear God," he groaned.

That was all the noise the walking dead needed.

The Deacon heard the guttural groans of the dead, but their footsteps weren't shuffling, no, they were *running*.

Memories of the Fast-Zombie War were easy to come by. It was a tragedy for all involved. The Deacon never thought he'd see something like it again. But the horde he'd stepped around delicately were coming full force now. He could hear their footsteps. They were moving faster than the Deacon ever thought he could.

Running and running and running and...

"Grrr," a rotten toothed man leapt at the Deacon, smashing him to the ground, jabbing broken ribs into his lung.

Teeth snapped. The Deacon struggled; he wasn't trained in combat. His kind hired out force when they needed to. He was weak, muscles burning with the effort it took to keep the snapping jaws from grabbing his skin.

There were more running toward him. Soon he'd be the bottom of the pile, consumed to nothing but toothpicks and gore.

The Deacon twisted to the side, pain searing though his

ribcage. He found a moss-covered rock, fingers stretched and clawing to get ahold of it. Fingernails scraped and tore. When he finally gripped the rock, he slammed it into the side of the dead man's head.

It fell away, skull caved in. Ichor dripped.

The Deacon scrambled to his feet, recognized the Nightjar's pond in the distance. He also noticed the dark outlines of the fast dead coming toward him.

He ran; chest heaving, ribcage burning, lung collapsing, and blood filling his mouth. He'd never tasted the sweet tang of his own blood before. He choked on it, stumbled, fell to his knees before finding some strength inside of him to get up.

Get up. Get up. Get up. It was the chanting in his head as though every Deacon that ever lived was urging him on. They might all be dead, but they were compelling him to *move*.

He made it to his feet. The fast dead were not far behind– they'd outrun him. Just a few more heartbeats and they'd be gnawing on his spine.

The lights were off in the Nightjar's cabin, and her sad warbling had stopped. He imagined she was watching from the dark windows, hoping for a child sacrifice, and losing interest when all she saw was a slowly dying man.

The Deacon ran like he was running from the law for a crime he did not commit, he ran for freedom, he ran for balance, he ran for hope, he ran for–

He tripped in the slick mud, dropped, rolled and rolled and rolled, broken rib stabbing further into his lung. The pond was there, and wetness touched half of his body. Cool dark water.

Get up. Get up. Get up.

He stumbled to his feet and fell face first into the deep water of the Nightjar's pond. The soft current carried him away to safety.

Six

Then

Alastor didn't have wings. Lucifer had made him with a lesser-Demon female, much like Clea. He dropped his seed in the wind and left it to grow without guidance. He was nothing more than an errant weed to his father. Alastor wasn't raised in the castle in the burning caves, no, he was raised in a dirt floored hovel of the mountains. The only thing he had to acknowledge his heritage was the Basilisk tooth blade that was gifted to him and the voice in his head that wouldn't stop. It was incessant. What started as a dream, a desire, now was full blown screaming in the voice of Lucifer, his father, demanding he find Lucifer's bones and revive him.

Alastor couldn't fly, but he could run and drive and hide in the shadows. All of this came in handy as he led the Fast-Zombies back to the castle in the burning caves.

Find my bones, the voice in his head demanded.

"I'm trying," Alastor replied, rubbing his temples, wishing the voice would stop. He'd been in the middle of a collection on the Earthen plane when the voice started. Alastor had to leave his second in command in charge of the skin trades. The business was bringing in loads of souls, which he split between himself and the Raven King. Alastor didn't hold a throne in Hell – yet– but he'd regained power with the skin trades. It had taken years to rebuild what Shay and that half-breed Angel had cost him, but he'd gotten there. He'd gotten there and stayed under the radar by paying off Hellions and making promises and slithering in the dark.

Alastor traveled between realms using an illegal portal constructed in the West. During Meg's reign she'd destroyed most of the portals during the Fast-Zombie War and left them demolished, forcing the movement between realms to a trickle. This made the Deacons happy, and others livid.

Find my bones, the voice in Alastor's head demanded.

"I'm coming," Alastor promised.

Kill them all, the voice insisted.

"I will."

Kill her.

Alastor rubbed his face, wishing the voice would stop.

"Promise me you'll stop when it's done," Alastor said. "You'll leave me alone."

The voice was unrelenting and its now silence made him uneasy.

Alastor stood on a cliff ledge of a crumbling highway. The dead from the west were bottlenecked. He took a knife, cut the soft skin of his wrist, and held it out over the horde.

Alastor learned something important from the Fast-Zombie War: if the dead consumed the blood of Archangel royalty, they became *fast*. He figured the same was true for a bastard son of the original fallen Archangel Lucifer. The dead lapped at his blood as it dripped, and it didn't take long for the dead to convert. They became faster, easier to control, especially with the giant Basilisk that followed.

Still covered in rotting gore and dried blood of the baby Basilisks, Alastor didn't look that different from the dead. Didn't smell much different either.

It was all coming together, Alastor chuckled to himself. The laughter was awkward and weak because all he wanted was the voice in his head to stop. He even prayed it would stop.

Find my bones. Find my bones. Find my bones. Find my bones. Find my bones!

SEVEN

POOF – I travel to the front stoop of the chapel in the graveyard. For a moment, I enjoy Hellbreeze as it covers my face and bends the reedy grass that has grown up around the safety fence. The chapel in the graveyard is peaceful. It's been a safe place for those I consider close as family. Noah and Nightingale and Thrush have lived here for years. Two ghosts and their son in the only place where they could find peace in the realms, strangely. I think back on my life, to a time when I thought I was simply human on the Earthen plane. The idea of ghosts raising their living child would be absurd, but now it's just another day amongst supernatural beings in the realm of Hell.

There's commotion outside the fence. Bodies shuffling, the whisper of snakes slithering, the chatter of bugs. The castle in the burning caves isn't far from here, and the sound of battle echoes. A chill slides up my spine. I need to get back there.

I knock, wanting to storm in and make my demands known but I can't do that to Noah and Nightingale. Ages ago I promised to do better, to be better, so here I am trying. However, Nightingale should be expecting me since she woke me up not long ago to warn me of the attack.

The door cracks open.

It's Noah, looking at his wrist like he's checking the time, but he doesn't have a watch. "Sun's barely up, woman, you never eat this early."

"We have an emergency," I say.

Noah pauses, hearing the commotion in the distance. "What is it?" His eyes widen with concern.

"Let me in." The idea of telling this truth in the wide open causes a chill to roll up my spine. I don't want anything else hearing this. Noah and Nightingale may be ghosts but they are formidable in their own way, with their own astral magic. But this is something new and I don't want them surprised.

Noah steps back and opens the door further. "You all must leave. Now." I close the door behind me.

"I can't leave you," Noah says.

I hold up a hand, stopping him from saying more. "Today you will. Today you will take your family and go."

"What's happening?" Nightingale walks into the room, dark hair mussed from sleep.

Their son Thrush isn't far behind. He's nearly grown, fifteen now. With dirty blonde hair and blue eyes, he looks just like Noah did in high school. Thankfully there aren't many girls his age down here or there'd be plenty of broken hearts.

I close my eyes and search for the tether that joins my soul to Noah's. My wings feel heavy. My heart like a stone. It all feels so *wrong*.

"Don't, Meg," Noah warns.

"Get out of here," I warn. I reach deep inside, using the power I'd found once to the gather the tether. I cut it for the second time, the final time. If he asks to link our souls again, I won't. Noah deserves more. He's done his duty taking care of me all these years. He deserves freedom in his afterlife.

Thrush is staring. "Make them listen," I warn. "Make them go to save you," I take it a step too far. "You know who this is. He'll string you up and skin you. He'll make you wish you were never born. You saw what he did to the others. You know what he's been doing for years."

Thrush has trained with the Hellions and they've taken him out in the field. After all, Thrush will be required to serve his time as a Hellion when he comes of age. All the children of Archangel lineage do and will. If not, the family will suffer a curse. Memories of Sparrow's tics and Nightingale's antics before their family curse was lifted flash through my mind. None of us will let that happen again.

Thrush's eyes widen. He knows we've been living with a monster in our backyard. He's found the bodies and been on the hunt for the illegal portal with the Hellions. Thrush turns to his parents. "I want to go. Now."

"Rue and Remington?" Noah asks where they are.

If I learned anything from my father, the Archangel Gabriel, never tell a soul where you hide your people, not even family. I shake my head. "They're safe," is all I reply.

Noah is standing still. Stone still. Deathly still. Unbelievably still. I guess Nightingale didn't warn him. Good to know I'm not the only one who sucks at relationships.

"Go," I say.

There's no movement except in Thrush's bedroom as he gathers his belongings.

"I banish you from the realm of Hell. You are untethered. Go." I point to the sky.

Nightingale touches Noah's arm. "We will be safe in my family's realm."

I turn, not wanting to hear about Sparrow's realm. He promised a truce since Nightingale was living in Hell with me. But once she goes back, I know Sparrow will lift the truce. He nearly killed me once already, with his sister out of my realm, he'll be back with a vengeance. I'm sure Babylon will strike all treaties, even the one about not totally decimating another realm's policing force. The thought sinks in my gut as I consider how shitty things are about to get.

"Goodbye," I say over my shoulder, running for the door because I can't bear to look at them even though it might be the last time. I owe Noah more, a better goodbye, he's been the best friend a girl could have all these years since we were children. He saw me at my lowest; skipped school together, stole cars and went on joyrides together, fed me when my fake-father didn't. No, I can't look at him.

"You don't get to do that," Noah's suddenly standing in front of me, lopsided grin and handsome features. "You don't get to walk away after everything we've been through without a real goodbye." He runs a hand through shaggy blonde hair.

"I don't like touching people," I remind him.

"I don't like seeing you hurting." He opens his arms, and I step into them in an instant. "And I'm not people."

"I'm going to miss you," I say, pressing my face to his chest and swallowing down the sob that's sticking in my throat. "You must protect your family. Nightingale's world is brutal. Those Angels in the Seven Kingdoms of Heaven are assholes. There is nothing nice about them."

Noah squeezes me and I hug him tighter.

"Goodbye," I say, knowing that I am sending them to live with my mortal enemy. Nightingale is Sparrow's sister, the only place she can go in the Seven Kingdom's of Heaven is the Raven King's lands. I'm sending my best friends to my enemy.

"No. It's never goodbye. Wasn't goodbye when you found my newly dead soul down here. Wasn't goodbye when you ran off to college and left me in that Godforsaken town alone. It's never goodbye." Noah is still smiling. He whistles a light trill like a jay.

I smile, nod and whisper, "Never." I whistle back, a little chickadee chirp, because I must. This is what we do, what we inherited from Nightingale and Sparrow, a greeting or goodbye with birdsong is life.

"We'll see you soon. I'll bring the orange soda and fried chicken."

"Thanks. I really miss ice cold Diet Pepsi though." It was my favorite.

"Haven't been able to find that in ages," Noah smiles sadly.

A sob escapes my throat. I'm not sure why, I've never been afraid to run into danger alone. I knew that letting my guard down all these years would make me weak. Make me soft and emotional. I've spent too long holding close the ones I love. My wings feel heavy, my heart cracks. "I gotta go."

"Go get 'em, killer. Remember, Meg, you're north country trash, you burn *hot*." Noah gives me a wide smile, and everything is right in the world for just a moment... *Suddenly we are sixteen and Noah just showed me how to hotwire a Chevy and he's sitting in the passenger side of that car we stole. I'm driving ninety-five miles an hour down State Route 104 headed for Six Flags, high on life and freedom knowing I don't have to spend another night on that dirty mattress on the trailer floor. The music is blaring, and his arm is stretched across the backrest, and I'm wondering how I got the most handsome boy in school to be my best friend...*

Tears prick my eyes. I don't know if I should be insulted or... *Poof* –I leave.

EIGHT

MEG

I KILLED SEVEN HELLIONS ONCE. Back then I was alone and broken. I can handle one Demon. One will be easy. One will be nothing.

I fly home. I could have just *poofed* the rest of the way there, but I need to see what I'm walking into. It feels good to stretch my wings and feel the Hellbreeze between the mottled feathers.

The doors to the cave are open. Demons and creatures and the dead wander inside. There are dead Hellions on my lands. Other battle at the driveway and the barracks and the empty stables.

I glide to the balcony outside my bedroom. Landing softly, I crouch and listen. Glancing through the glass it looks like the bedroom door is closed.

Poof. I go inside. It's silent, probably a trap. *Poof.* I go to the windows outside the infirmary. It's trashed. *Poof.* I go to the ballroom balcony. I grip my blade and it hums to life, ready to slice. It was the only good thing Lucifer gifted me; a blade forged in the fires of Hell that only cuts in my grip. The Hellions have similar blades.

Klaus is here, his white beard coated in blood splatter. I jump down from the balcony railing and kick the door open.

They come running.

Klaus curses. "I had them," he shouts. "Go to safety."

I slash, cutting a kidney-red Demon in half. Bugs crunch under my boots. Klaus raises his blade and cuts down more of the attackers. I make my way toward him, cutting at the snakes that slither across the floor.

"Where are the rest?" I ask.

"The lair," Klaus says.

I hold out my hand and wiggle my fingers until he grips my palm, his giant hand slippery with gore. I wrinkle my nose in disgust.

Poof – we land in the Hellion lair. I wipe a slippery palm on my jeans.

Chel is busted up, his wing cut and face bruised. Tukka looks uninjured but it's hard to see blood on his dark red skin. He's wrapping his wrists for support, must be preparing for a lot of hacking away at intruders.

Skeele starts to move toward me. I pause him with the slight rise of my palm. His lips press into a grim line. He probably wants to talk about the children or Noah. He probably wants to ask me if I'm okay. I'm not. But I can't talk about it right now. This is not the time.

Klaus grabs a towel from behind the bar and uses it to clean the blood off his horns.

Clea arrives in a whisp. "They're fast, child," she warns. My mother can only do so much as a ghost, and I'll take the intel over another body fighting alongside us. She's wringing her hands and making the room cold.

"Fast means Archangel blood," I say.

"Babylon truced," Skeele says.

"They deceive." I move toward the wall of weapons and select a pistol and ammo, and another small blade that fits nicely in my belt. "We get the Basilisk and start clearing the castle."

"Noah?" Chel asks.

I shake my head. "He's gone. It's just us." I circle a finger in the air. "No one else but us."

Skeele is watching me, waiting for weakness, waiting to see me crack–because I warned him I would. I warned him I am not as strong as I used to be. I've controlled the wrath that put me in this throne for too long. My children have never seen their true mother, they've never seen my rage. I couldn't disappoint them like that.

Skeele holds out his hand. "We go to the Basilisk together."

The air in the room feels thick, heavy. I've controlled the rage for so long I'm not sure I can remember how to let it flow, how to let it win. It's tamped so far down; a flattened nail head imbedded in wood, difficult to pull out. I put my monster in a box and entombed it in chains.

"This will be our stronghold," Skeele tells the others. There's a door in the back of the room that leads to private quarters and the new recruit barracks. "Meet here if things go awry. You three, gather what's left of the new recruits and the others."

I take Skeele's hand and shiver. He squeezes with urgency. *Poof* – we go to the old office where the Basilisk are kept.

"Shit," Skeele mutters as he slips on a puddle of slime.

The door creaks as bodies shove against it, trying to get inside.

"Come on, babies." I motion to the slithering bodies in the shadows of the ceiling. "We've got a snack for you."

The Basilisk babies grew too big for the castle. We kept two and released the others. One protects Noah and Nightingale's chapel. Two went to Demore's pond. The others went back to the dark waters of the black river in the Adirondacks of Hell.

We slowly brought them back to the castle in the burning caves as Hellion intel worsened.

Eight heads dip down from above, hissing at the door. Sharp, long, dripping teeth ready to chomp peek from their mouths, eager to consume.

Years ago, I was blamed for the Fast-Zombie War, I was blamed for bringing the Basilisk to the Seven Kingdoms of Heaven. If Sparrow sent this War, I have enough grown Basilisk to end all of Heaven and Babylon.

Skeele is bracing the door, waiting for me to send them into action.

"Now," I say.

He opens it and the Basilisk slither out the door, mouths open, eating everything in the hallway, everything that moves that isn't a Hellion or me.

We follow, killing what they miss, crushing bugs under our feet. We make our way through the castle, and room by room the Basilisk eat the Fast-Dead.

We clear the second floor, then the third, leaving a Basilisk at the stairwell to catch anything that comes up. It's going to stay here and guard the dungeon. If those creatures get out we'll have a shit-fest on our hands and I get the feeling we don't need the distraction with what's waiting for us outside.

On the first level we clear the kitchen. I notice the dead have demolished my snack pantry. Twinkies are crushed, brownies half-bitten, two-liter bottles of soda leak onto the floor.

"We'll get more snacks," Skeele says, searching the room.

"It's just utter bullshit," I say. "You know how long Noah

worked stocking that stash." I shake my head, and a new anger bubbles up inside me. You don't mess with the Queen of Hell's junk food stash.

It's probably better this way, I don't need the sugar during battle. I sigh and move on.

We make our way to the ballroom, then the infirmary, then we head toward the main entrance, passing the Hellion lair on the way.

I send a Basilisk inside to wait for us. It paces near the door like an anxious dog.

We head toward the giant wooden doors at the end of the hall. They're secured with a large beam that locks into place. The Hellions must've gotten them closed.

The door surges forward like there's a hundred bodies on the other side.

Skeele glances at me. "You should go to safety. I can do this."

"You won't be doing it alone," I say. I grip my blade and gather the attention of the remaining Basilisk. "Eat everything," I instruct. They hiss at the door, ready, so big there's barely enough room for them lined up in the hallway. Skeele stoops down to avoid scraping their bellies with his horns.

I reach for the beam. Skeele is at my side, lifting. The door blasts inward, knocking us onto our asses.

"Blade ready," Skeele shouts.

I want to tell him I fucking know that this isn't my first battle for my life, but the fast dead trample me, stepping on my arms and stomach. I hold in a few screams of pain and roll out of the way. Glancing at Skeele, I see him slicing at legs and necks. He's on his feet already. Damn I'm slow.

A Basilisk hovers over me, protectively, eating every fast-dead that comes for me. I scramble to my feet. These dead are the things of nightmares, moving faster than ever. Just like the time they licked Sparrow's blood off that rock wall on the earthen plane.

Each one I kill, I imagine I'm slicing the Raven King's neck. If their blood weren't rotten, I'd bite them and drain them just like I did to Lucifer and the others. Unfortunately, there is no power in drinking from the walking dead, only gut rot. Not that I've tried it; I asked once, for a friend.

Where are all of these dead coming from? This is so much more than the Fast-Zombie War. What have the Deacons been doing?

I think back to the last time I saw one or spoke with one. It's been months, maybe even years. Things were going so well with them not meddling in my life that I lost track.

A woman with ragged clothing and a lopsided face comes running at me. I step forward and cut, her head falls off. Something concerning comes into my line of sight. There's a Basilisk near the dead tree in the courtyard. And it's huge.

"Skeele?" I shout.

"What?" his voice is strained as he fights.

"Who else would have a Basilisk for a pet in Hell?"

"Only you." His voice is closer as he makes his way toward me.

Two of my Basilisk have their heads halfway out the door, catching as many of the fast-dead as they can.

"Oh shit," Skeele says as he notices the Basilisk near the tree. "That's enormous."

The giant Basilisk snaps forward, grabbing one of my Basilisk by the head and eats it. The remaining four squeal in protest at the death of their sibling.

I notice the most concerning scene. Something more so than a ginormous Basilisk slurping at mine like they're angel hair spaghetti. A cluster of the dead, all wearing black, with white Roman collars. The Deacons, they're dead. Too many of them, maybe even all of them. Behind them, it's not the Raven King like I expected.

It's Alastor.

"We should retreat," Skeele suggests.

"No, we must kill them." I can't bite the dead but I can bite Alastor.

NINE

In the heart of Babylon, where the golden city's splendor melded the Seven Kingdoms of Heaven, stood the Fountain of Eternity–a shimmering pool of iridescent light that served as a portal between realms. As the Archangels left the courthouse, unaware of the secrets hidden beneath the surface, a disturbance rippled through tranquil waters.

Gabriel noticed though. Meg's father was hyperalert to movement while walking through Babylon. He was once the most powerful of all the Archangels, his vote holding the greatest power. He trusted no one in Babylon after they'd imprisoned him and blamed his daughter, Meg, for the Fast-Zombie War when it spilled into the Seven Kingdoms of Heaven.

So when the rest of the cocky and righteous Archangels left their evening meeting with no worries of the dark, Gabriel was the only one to sense the anomaly. His keen eyes narrowed as he approached the fountain, his wings casting a shadow over the sacred waters to shield the activity from onlookers.

With a sense of foreboding, Gabriel reached out and plunged

his hand into the fountain, his fingers tingling with the power that pulsed below the surface. Between the shadows cast by his wings, he could see the outline of a maroon jumpsuit. A Newcomer uniform. His heart banged against his ribs as he gripped the cloth and pulled. What he found sent a shock through his very being–a Deacon, half-alive and gasping for breath, struggling against the vortex-like current of the fountain as it threatened to pull him under. Gabriel could not deny the ancient power and aura that enveloped the man. It was much stronger than he'd ever witnessed.

Without hesitation, Gabriel reached in with another hand and pulled the Deacon to safety, his movements swift and decisive as he lifted the man from the fountain and set him on wobbly feet.

The Deacon's eyes fluttered open and he focused on the large Archangel. "Oh, thank God it's you," he coughed out as water and blood dripped from his mouth. "Hide me, please!" the words came out as a strangled gasp.

Gabriel kept his wings open and used his wide robes to shelter the Deacon, half-dragging the man to a Cadillac Escalade parked nearby.

Something was very wrong, and it was nothing like the bull-shit story he'd just heard in the courthouse. The balance between realms was shifting, he could feel it.

Gabriel gathered the injured Deacon and set him in the back seat of the Escalade.

"Lay down," Gabriel ordered. "Do not let anyone see you."

The Deacon nodded, water dripping from his clothing and pooling on the leather seats of the vehicle.

Gabriel quietly closed the door and got behind the wheel. He glanced out the window to ensure no one had seen them before driving toward his lands.

"Tell me what happened," Gabriel said. "Why are you dressed like that?"

The Deacon coughed, and between chattering teeth stained with blood he replied, "The others changed my clothing and forced me into general population so I wouldn't be noticed during the attack."

Gabriel watched the man in his rearview mirror, accelerating the vehicle with an urgency to get home quickly.

"Why?" Gabriel asked.

"All the Deacons are dead. I am the last one."

Gabriel couldn't deny the ache in the Deacon's voice. His story would account for the dwindling number of souls that had reached the heavens.

"What about the Safe Houses?" Gabriel asked.

"Burned or abandoned."

Gabriel entered his lands, hit the button on the console to lock the gates and kept driving past the house and the training grounds for his Legion. He drove to a trail in the forest shrouded in shadow. There was a path only identifiable by a few oak trees and moss covered rocks deep under the canopy. Only Gabriel knew of this place, he'd never shown a soul.

Gabriel got out of the vehicle, went to the back door, and dragged the Deacon out. The man was shivering and pale.

"Can you walk?" Gabriel asked.

The man nodded but stumbled. The Deacon hissed in pain.

Gabriel looked down and noticed the shimmer of blood. "You're injured. I'll carry you."

"Thank you," the Deacon whispered.

Gabriel carried the man through the forest to a hidden door behind a curtain of vines.

"What is this place?" the Deacon asked between labored breaths, ignoring his slowly deflating lung.

"Safety. Not another soul knows about it. You'll be safe here." Gabriel set the Deacon at a table and dragged a chair closer to prop up the man's foot. He began removing the man's shoe and pulled up the pant leg of his uniform.

Red teeth marks stared back.

Gabriel turned quickly to the Deacon, "This must go," he warned. There were already black lines seeping up the Deacon's leg.

The Deacon nodded in agreement. "I must stay alive."

Gabriel gripped the blade at his side, it glowed to life. He used the tip to cut a strip of material off the Deacon's jumpsuit, then tied it tightly above the man's knee.

The Deacon was watching him with wide eyes. Blood dripped from his mouth and nose as he coughed then paled considerably.

Gabriel whispered a prayer before placing his free hand on the Deacon's forehead, unsure if he could outpower the man. But fear and pain won. The Deacon closed his eyes and went unconscious. In one swift movement, Gabriel cut off the man's leg just below the knee.

Poof – Gabriel went to Teari.

———

Teari was folding gauze and resetting her workspace after a long day of healing Gabriel's Legion warriors who had minor injuries from sparring and training.

"I need you to come with me," Gabriel boomed.

Teari startled, spilling a container of cotton balls. She didn't like the sound of Gabriel's voice. "Prepare me a little for what I'm about to see," she warned. As Gabriel's personal healer, she'd been dragged into a lot of shit shows.

"An amputation," he replied.

She sucked in a breath. "I'll get my things." Her hands quickly collected gauze and suture strings... she paused, stared at her own hands for a moment, remembering there was a time that she didn't have hands. They'd been cut off during the Fast-Zombie War, but Meg had saved her and made her whole again.

She turned with her bag. Gabriel was holding out his hand. "So we're traveling like that?" she didn't like the way Gabriel could *poof* from place to place. It made her dizzy, but that wasn't terrible, she'd seen others vomit from it.

Gabriel brought her to the secret cave in the forest. Teari knew the inside, but not how to get there. It was the place Gabriel had hidden his people during the Fast-Zombie War.

Teari turned to find a man in a maroon jumpsuit, his left leg cut off at the shin and bleeding all over the floor. Worse was the blood seeping between his lips and the gasping sound he was making. He smelled like brimstone. She moved quickly, staunching the blood flow. Her hands hovered over the wound, magic stitching together veins and arteries. She sealed the muscle and secured lose tendons and fascia. She removed bits of rotten tissue, recognizing what she was dealing with. She'd felt that rot in her own body before. "How long ago was he bit?" she asked.

Gabriel shrugged. "I'm not sure. I found him less than an hour ago. Cut off the foot then got you. I could wake him up and we can ask the precise time he was bitten..."

"No," Teari was shaking her head, remembering what it felt like after a limb was cut off. "Keep him unconscious for as long as possible." She glanced at his face. He looked like no one and every-one. "Who is he?" she asked.

"A Deacon." Gabriel's reply was flat, serious.

Teari's shoulders sagged. "It's started then." She moved to her feet, lifted the Deacon and laid him on a nearby cot. She needed a moment to right her words. "Where is Meg?"

Gabriel's face was stone. "I don't know."

"You just came from a council meeting in Babylon. They had no information?"

"They only had bullshit to spew. They know nothing. I don't think they know precisely what's going on in Hell."

"Did they see the Deacon?"

"No," Gabriel assured her. "He's the last one. They're all dead. I believe him."

Dread filled Teari. She knew something terrible would be coming to Hell. She didn't want to believe that the time had come.

"Was Sparrow at your council meeting?" Teari asked.

Gabriel sighed and ran a large hand through black hair that went to his shoulders. Bright blue eyes locked on Teari. "I cannot speak of it, you know this."

Teari nodded. "You have family in Hell," she reminded him. "You once desired heirs to your throne."

"Do not fucking remind me of my own aspirations." He stepped closer to Teari and reached out a long arm, flicking her in the forehead. "This is the deepest pile of shit I've ever seen in my life, and I get the feeling we're only seeing a small portion of it."

"You must worry about Rue," Teari said. "You must wonder if she's safe."

Gabriel rubbed his face, thinking.

Teari wanted to say more but she couldn't because very few knew about Remington and who he really was. As far as the other realms were concerned, Meg only gave birth to one child that day. Remington was a shadow heir. Never spoken about, never announced, never discussed. No one knew he existed besides those closest to Meg.

Teari glanced at the sleeping man, ensured his bandaged leg was dry then stepped further away. "He is the last of the Deacons?"

"Yes," Gabriel nodded.

"Can you feel the archaic energy bound within him?" she asked.

Gabriel's lips pressed into a line. He didn't want to admit anything.

"Maybe you are already aware of this but the Deacons have held the balance of power for ages. They have the ability to cross realms and do as they wish to maintain the balance." Teari took a deep breath, afraid of what she was thinking.

"This man is the last, all that power is harnessed within him. He is a walking time bomb. Stronger than anything we've ever met." She pointed at Gabriel. "Stronger than you, than Sparrow. A collection of souls won't make a difference against him. He might even be stronger than... God."

Gabriel rubbed his beard and contemplated the words of his healer. He waved a hand, dismissing her concern, "Well, he's missing half a leg now, so that might change things."

TEN

FIND MY BONES. FIND MY BONES. FIND MY BONES. FIND my bones. Find my bones...

The voice echoed in Alastor's head as he watched the Fast-Dead overtake the castle in the burning caves. He smiled when he saw the Queen and her Hellion Commander at the door. She should have an army out here. But, he'd seen the bodies of the other Hellions littering the grounds. Saw them flying down to capture the dead one by one. They were too fast and the Hellions clearly weren't skilled in fighting creatures like this. If they had trained, they were terrible at it. Lucifer would be rolling over in his grave if he could see how far the throne had fallen since his days. Hellions of Lucifer's time would have shredded anything within a five mile radius. The dead and the rest of Alastor's army would have never gotten this close.

The Queen and her Hellion Commander weren't completely alone, they had a handful of Basilisk, but Alastor's was bigger and stronger. He moved closer and the Basilisk followed, protecting him. The scent of her dead children pooled in his footsteps.

Alastor's Basilisk snapped forward, grabbing another one of Meg's Basilisk and eating it, head first. Then another, then another. Until there was only one.

Meg shouted, tried to run outside and attack Alastor head on. Skeele grabbed her across the middle and dragged her inside, slamming the doors closed.

Alastor moved closer and knocked on the large wooden doors. "Honey, I'm home!" He shouted as a greeting. "I'm home to take my throne! I'm home to free the true King of Hell!"

He motioned to the Basilisk and it began butting the door with its head. Wood cracked, stone crumbled and fell from the walls above. Alastor took a few steps back as his Basilisk destroyed the entrance. The doors snapped and fell inward. The Basilisk slammed against the stone walls until the opening was large enough for it to move inside.

Alastor stepped through the threshold of the castle in the burning caves and it felt like he'd come home. He spread is arms wide and sucked in a deep breath. Ah, woodsmoke and pine and true blood. This was the smell of home. This was the home he never got to visit, never got to live in; it was so much better than the hovel in the mountains.

Find my bones. Find my bones. The voice of Lucifer was louder here, pounding in his head until he could barely hear anything else. Lucifer's voice was so loud Alastor didn't hear the shrieking of Meg's Basilisk as it defended the door to the Hellion lair, only to die by one of its own kind.

Eleven

"It's dead," I say, glancing to the Basilisk slithering against the ceiling.

"There's one at the stairwell, guarding the dungeon," Skeele says.

"That thing will kill it." I pace the lair, rubbing at the small cuts on my arms and smearing the blood inadvertently.

Skeele has a deep cut across his thigh and one on his cheek. I can't stop my mouth from watering at the smell of his blood.

As though Skeele could sense my hunger, he rounds the bar and pulls every bag of blood out of the fridge.

"Eat," he says, ripping open a bag for himself.

He knows better: fresh blood will make us stronger. But we don't have time for that.

I cross the room and start drinking. It quells the hunger to a

59

dull hum in the background. I glance up and find Skeele watching me. Both of us wish my teeth were biting into his neck.

Something slams against the door to the lair.

Footsteps and shouting come from the hall at the back of the room that leads to the private quarters and barracks. Tukka and Klaus blast through the door with a few of the newer Hellions.

"What's going on out there?" Skeele asks as I drink.

"There's too many. Too fast." Klaus squeezes blood and gore from his beard. It's no longer white but completely stained rusty red.

"Where's Chel?" Skeele asks.

"Gone." Tukka grips his blade, grimacing.

"Brace that door," I say. I glance to the bar, moving to place what's left of the bagged blood in the fridge.

More heavy footsteps echo.

"Wait!" a familiar voice shouts. It's Chel!

Tukka grabs Chel's arms, pulling him inside the room before Klaus slams the door closed. "We thought you'd been killed."

"Ya fucks didn't look too hard for me," Chel grumbled, swiping gore off his arm.

Chel glanced at the bag of blood. Then me. Then the other Hellions.

Simple math. One Queen of Hell with a blood bond to her Hellion Commander, two Hellions that I know well, and three whom I am barely acquainted with. If I learned anything from Jim besides sturdy boots and a good gun–it was prep food for the long haul. There's barely enough bagged blood to make it two days between us all. We'll be starving in about twelve hours. If Alastor lets us live that long.

The Basilisk turns and looks at me.

Damn. Another mouth to feed.

———

THERE'S a knock on the door to the Hellion lair. Skeele moves forward like he's going to answer it.

"Let me." I step in front of him and tip my ear toward the door. Skeele flashes me an irritated look.

"What do you want?" I ask.

There's a chuckle on the other side.

Clea arrives in the room, wringing her hands. "It's another child of Lucifer. A halfling." Clea motions to the side of her face, dragging her hand down it. "He's scarred."

"You never told me I had an uncle," I say, watching Clea.

"I'm sure I have plenty of brethren but I was never formally introduced. Lucifer wasn't the Sunday dinner and family holiday type." Clea glances at the door. "That Demon out there; he's big, powerful. I think it's the one your Hellions have been watching."

"We've known about him for a long time. It's the one who kidnapped Shay." I remind her. "Should have killed him a long time ago. Truthfully, I was expecting someone else to show up today."

"Sparrow?" Clea asks.

"Yes," I say.

"This is a surprise that the Raven King didn't come for you. Does that mean the Seven Kingdoms of Heaven are upholding their truce?" Skeele asks. "Or are they blind to this upheaval?"

I shake my head. "I haven't spoken to any of them."

"Not even Gabriel?" Clea asks, biting her lip.

"Some things are better left avoided," I say.

Hours pass and the threat outside the door remains. Our hunger grows with the passing of time. The bagged blood has been shared but what little remains isn't enough to sustain a Hellion for an entire day, especially a day thick with battle.

The Basilisk shifts anxiously at the ceiling.

There are footsteps at the back door to the lair. Something is coming up the hallway.

The room is thick with tension and a palpable anxiety settles over everyone like a suffocating blanket. Klaus paces back and forth, his footsteps echoing off the walls of the dimly lit lair.

I could hear my own heartbeat, the rhythmic thud in my chest a stark reminder of what was at stake. Chel stands beside me, his usual smirk replaced with lips pressed to a line and stress wrinkles. Skeele and Klaus are positioned strategically around the room, their eyes sharp and focused.

Suddenly, a crash shatters the silence and the door threatens to splinter under the force of the impact.

"Open the door, don't let it break," Skeele says.

Klaus moves closer, hitting the latch.

A crash shatters the silence as the door slams open under the force of the impact. I feel a cold rush of adrenaline as I recognize the dead, the grotesque forms spilling into our holdout.

"Here we go," I mutter under my breath, gripping the weapon in my hand tighter.

The smells hit us first, that rancid stench of decay and death. It was almost overpowering, but I force myself to focus.

Chel is the first to react, moving with a fluid grace that seemed unnatural after a lifetime of Hellion training. His blade slices through the air, connecting with the first zombie's neck, sending its head rolling across the floor.

"Keep them back," Skeele shouts, his voice cutting through the chaos.

One comes running toward me. I swing my weapon, the impact jarring my arms. The creature staggers back but I don't stop. I can't afford to. I kick one in the back, throwing it off balance. Klaus finishes in with a swift strike to the head.

To my left, Skeele is a whirlwind of motion, his blades a blur as he cuts down anything that comes through the door. My Hellions are methodical and precise, each movement they make calculated and deadly.

"That's all of them," Klaus calls out, his voice steady despite the bodies littering the floor.

Someone slams the door closed and we drag the headless bodies to a pile on the far side of the room. I gag a little at the stench.

"Being locked in here with this is not optimal," Klaus says with a groan of disgust.

There is another knock on the main door to the Hellion lair. It turns into a repetitive pounding.

Chel is standing there looking distraught for the first time ever. "We can't do this alone."

"We have each other," I say.

"We need more!" he shouts.

"Stop," Skeele holds up a hand. "We can do this. It's just *one* Demon."

"That thing is more than a simple Demon. We all know it. He's been on our radar for years. We should have killed him when we had the chance at the Black Mansion. Should have chopped him to bits before setting fire to the place. And we should have killed whoever brought him back to life." Chel's eyes land on mine. "I've fought him before. He's stronger."

Chel and Jed battled Alastor long ago to save Shay. Alastor kidnapped her. Jed stabbed him with a Basilisk tooth knife to immobilize him, then Nero set him on fire. It should have ended him, Alastor should be nothing but ash. But *someone* brought him back, with a vengeance.

"We couldn't risk upheaval of the higher Demon caste." Skeele paces. "This was a delicate situation."

No, it was a straightforward one. But I didn't want more death in my realm. It's hard admitting I was wrong, that's why I can't say it out loud.

"Chel, you're going to take the back corridor out of here. Go to the portal, any portal. You might just have to find water. Get to Babylon. Get to Gabriel," I say.

"You'll all die if I leave," Chel argues. "He's too powerful."

I shake my head.

"Do as your Queen instructs," Skeele says.

"You really want to involve Gabriel?" Chel asks, looking concerned. "He hasn't helped. Where is he now?"

"He is bound by the rules of the Seven Kingdoms of Heaven. If he is not here now, he has good reason. You need to go to him." I hope my words are true. My father has helped me before in Hell. A long time ago he snuck through the Veil to seek vengeance and help rescue me; I'm sure he'd do it again.

Chel rests his hands on his hips and glances at the wall of weapons. He closes his eyes, paces slowly and takes a deep breath, considering my orders. "Fine," he says with a nod. "I'll go."

"Good." I turn toward the door to the Hellion lair as something thuds against it, causing the wood to bend.

The last Basilisk is watching warily.

"You go with Chel," I tell the Basilisk, waiting to see if it understands.

"No, Meg…" Chel's voice is demanding. "I don't need it."

"Then send it back when you've escaped." I try my best not to glance at Skeele, sensing he does not agree with this plan. "You're not doing this alone."

Chel rubs his face. "This is a bad idea."

"We are out of good ideas," I say. There are no good ideas. We must get out of this room. We can't go out the back with Chel;

that will cause too much attention. No, Chel is going to run and I'm going to open that door and let the Demon in.

Chel takes a few weapons off the wall, then I give him the last bag of blood.

"No–" he argues.

"Eat it and go." I walk toward the door to the Hellion lair. "Go now."

Chel turns tail and whips open the door at the back of the lair. The Basilisk goes first, eating whatever dead roam. Chel follows.

"Hide that door," I tell Klaus, motioning to furniture that's big enough to conceal it; a large bookshelf and a bureau with wide doors.

I reach for the door handle of the lair. The door bulges again. I rip it open and face my fate with open arms.

TWELVE

MEG

"AH, Queen Meg, it's about time we formally met." Alastor walks into the lair like he owns it.

His Basilisk slithers in the hall, going still before darting away.

Stones sink in my gut. I hope it's not going after Chel and my last Basilisk.

"What do you want?" I ask.

"I'm looking for something and you just might have it." Alastor wags a finger in my face. "The bones of Lucifer. Where are they?"

My body goes stiff. My mind goes blank. "I don't know."

"Don't play dumb, now." Alastor paces the room, inspecting.

Skeele walks closer to me, like a lion sizing up its prey.

"Uh uh," Alastor warns Skeele. "Step away from her."

The look on Skeele's face is nothing less than murderous. The veins in his arms bulge with rage at Alastor's threatening tone.

"So you don't know where Lucifer's bones are? Tragic." Alastor inspects what remains on the wall of weapons. A few daggers, a nail bat, a few swords.

"I was unconscious for weeks," I say. "I never asked."

"Hm. You should have." Alastor brushes a hand over his dark hair, smoothing it back so he doesn't look so disheveled. The movement revealed melted skin on half of his face. "This is going to be harder than I thought." Alastor selects the nail bat and swings it a few times. "I need those bones." He shivers, his eyes glazing over like he's mentally gone somewhere else for a moment. He blinks and comes back, shaking his head like he's chasing away a bad dream.

Something isn't right. I wonder if he's possessed by something right now.

"We don't have the bones," Skeele says. "Leave us."

Alastor chuckles before skipping a few steps toward the nearest Hellion and slamming the nail bat into his head. Blood splatters and the Hellion drops to the ground, skull crushed.

"I can do this all day," Alastor says with a shuddering of his body. "Feels good, killing things. I've suppressed it for too long."

He points the bat at me. "The bones." Ichor drips from the nails.

"I don't have them," I say, a sickening feeling crawling up my throat.

Skeele inches closer to me. I want to tell him to stop looking suspicious. I have sharp teeth, I can protect myself. I think. It's been years since I had to draw upon the rage that seated me in the throne of Hell. I think I can do it again.

Alastor wags the bat and black blood drops off the nails, spattering the floor. "Tell me, Queen."

"I can't, I don't know where they are." I keep my chin high, my body still. I have been a very good liar throughout my life, this is no different. No different than all those other lies I spewed.

Alastor points the bat at me, the gore-covered end scraping my arm. A strip of skin breaks open.

"Who would know?" Alastor asks.

I stare, search my thoughts. "The Deacons."

Alastor's face is impassive for a moment before it crinkles in pain, dropping the bat, both hands fly to his ears, covering them. "I need the bones!" he screams like a madman, eyes wide and burning, hair matted to his face. The room goes silent, not a breath echoing on the stone walls; only his tormented voice fills the void as he screams.

THIRTEEN

Find my bones. Find my bones. The voice of Lucifer was louder than ever. Alastor's scream brought silence, but only for a moment as he could feel the whispers of Lucifer in the back of his brain, threatening to overtake his mind.

Alastor chanted in Hellspeak and the floor opened up. Lesser Demons and strange creatures began crawling out. Cockroaches and spiders and black beetles swarmed the group, biting and scratching, bringing chaos and destruction.

Skeele stepped closer to Meg. Klaus followed. Tukka was too far away to get closer without making a scene.

A knowing look passed between Tukka and Skeele. There was another Hellion with Tukka.

The creatures scrambled toward them, bugs skittering and snakes slithering. Skeele, Klaus, Meg, Tukka, and the remaining Hellion recruit begin slicing at the creatures and stomping them.

Alastor waited, letting his creatures do the hard work. Slowly picking up the nail-bat, he gripped it and shook away the voice in his head.

The fighters' blades were dripping with ichor, their boots slimy with bug guts. Lesser Demons are thrown against the wall, slapped across the room. They bite. One hung from Klaus's arm, teeth sinking deep as the Hellion roared and tore the creature off, ripping out a good chunk of skin. Klaus gripped the little Demon with two hands and tore it in half, throwing the pieces in defense as more came crawling out of the hole.

The silence that followed was deafening, a stillness that belied the imminent threat. They stood ready, weapons in hand, eyes locked on the gaping hole in the floor that seemed to breathe malevolence.

Meg glanced at Skeele, his eyes gleaming with predatory focus. Klaus stood tall, his stance disciplined, his blade glinting in the dim light. Tukka, ever the wild card had a manic grin on his face, twirling a chain with restless energy.

The ground trembled, a low rumble sending a shiver down Meg's spine.

Tiny Demons and creatures of chaos clawed their way out of the darkness, their eyes glowing with unholy light. They moved with primal ferocity, their growls and roars filling the air, a cacophony of madness and rage.

"Here more come," Klaus muttered, his voice steady but laced with tension.

The first lesser Demon lunged at Klaus, who was closest, a twisted mass of muscle and teeth. Klaus moved instinctively, his blade slicing through the air with a satisfying thwack as it connected with the creature's head, sending it crashing to the ground.

"Stay focused," Skeele said, swinging his blade to keep the next one at bay. "We can't let them overwhelm us!"

Skeele was a blur of motion, blades slashing through the Demons with brutal efficiency. He fought with a focused intensity, each strike fueled by a deep-seated rage. "Just keep them coming," he growled at Alastor, his voice a guttural snarl.

Tukka laughed manically, his chain spinning faster and faster as he waded into the fray. "This is what I've been waiting for!" he shouted, his eyes alight with a wild excitement. "Let's show these bastards what we're made of!"

Klaus was a pillar of strength, his movements precise and controlled. He fought with a calm efficiency, his sword cutting through the chaos with deadly accuracy. "Watch your flanks," he called out, his voice carrying over the din of battle. "Don't let them surround you!"

Meg could feel adrenaline coursing through her veins, sharpening her senses and dulling the pain of each new scratch and bruise. They fought as one, a seamless unit, each covering the other's weaknesses, their movements perfectly synchronized.

The creatures kept coming, a seemingly endless tide of darkness and fury. Tukka lashed out with his chain, feeling the satisfying crunch of bone as it connected with a Demon's skull. "Just keep fighting," he gasped, barely pausing to catch his breath.

Skeele let out a triumphant roar as he tore through a mess of Demons and bugs and snakes. His blade dripped with black blood. Meg glanced to him, just once to make sure he was okay, and his eyes were ablaze with determination.

Meg swung her blade, splitting heads, chopping necks. The scene was all very bloody and gory and disgusting. Alastor was impressed. He didn't know much about Meg, had never seen her in action, but this was a tiny bit impressive. He was slightly disappointed that she was going to die immediately.

"Get back," Skeele warned.

"I'm fine," Meg shouted back, stomping on a giant cockroach. "Everything is fine," she muttered under her breath.

But then it wasn't. Alastor was headed for the duo on the

opposite side of the room. Klaus and the other Hellion didn't see him, too busy with battling the creatures. Alastor swung the nail bat at the other Hellion, piercing his shoulder, then his stomach, then the back of his neck. The last hit took him down.

Tukka noticed and raised his chain.

"What will it be, Queen Meg?" Alastor shouted. "Tell me where the bones are or I kill your Hellion."

"You've already killed enough," Meg shouted back.

"What's one more?" Alastor said as he swung the bat toward Tukka.

The Hellion moved fast, swinging his chain blocking the nail-bat before it had a chance to crush his skull.

Tukka and Alastor swung weapons, barely missing each other. Metal slammed against wood. Alastor lurched forward, hitting him in the knee. The Hellion roared as nails pierced his leg and his knee gave out.

A sickening squelch echoed in the room as Alastor pulled the nail-bat out of Tukka's leg.

Tukka let out a breathless laugh, his chain finally still. "That was one hell of a fight," he said, a note of satisfaction in his voice.

"Bleed her out. Bleed them out until they confess where my bones are," Lucifer's voice shouted in Alastor's mind.

Alastor swung the nail-bat, circling the air until there was enough momentum then he whipped it in Klaus's direction.

Klaus didn't see the nail-bat coming, he was too busy tearing apart lesser Demons and tossing their body parts aside. The nail-bat hit him in the back, embedded in his shoulder blade.

Klaus roared as blood dripped out of his skin. He struggled to bend his arm behind his back and pull it out. When he finally reached the handle, he tugged and the nails tore his skin; blood trickled down his body and pooled at his feet.

Alastor smiled, knowing that the two Hellions would die quickly without blood to heal their injuries. He glanced to the Commander, the one named Skeele. He needed to get that one next. Alastor chanted in Hellspeak. Suddenly the ground beneath Skeele seemed to ripple and a dark, writhing mass of small demons, bugs, and snakes emerged from the cracks in the floor. The deluge ascended upon Skeele with an unholy fervor, their eyes glowing with malevolent intent. Snakes wrapped around his legs, tripping him. Spiders and cockroaches and giant beetles bit him.

Skeele snarled, his claws flashing as he slashed at the oncoming tide. He managed to tear through several of the creatures, but for every one he killed, ten more took its place. The sheer number of them was overwhelming. He felt a sharp pain in his leg as a snake's fangs sank into his flesh, its venom spreading through his veins like wildfire. He stumbled, swatting at the bugs that had crawled up his arms, their bites searing his skin. The small Demons leaped onto him, their claws digging into his flesh, their teeth tearing at him with relentless ferocity.

The creatures swarmed until Skeele was a writhing figure on the floor, not an inch of his skin could be seen.

Meg tried to get to Skeele, kicking and chopping at the creatures. She'd never killed so many spiders or beetles in her life. Still, she could barely see him under the creatures.

Alastor called upon his Basilisk next; the giant creature slithered into the lair and it started toward Tukka.

"No," Meg shouted as she tried to clear Skeele of the deluge of creatures that were consuming him. "Leave them alone." Meg was glaring at Alastor. "Leave them. You want me, take me."

"I want the bones," Alastor said.

"I already told you," Meg was out of breath, panting as she fought and bartered, "I don't know where Lucifer's bones are."

"*She's lying*," Lucifer roared in Alastor's mind.

The Basilisk darted forward and gobbled Tukka in one bite.

"No!" Meg shouted.

A dark smile quirked Alastor's lip. "You've only got two Hellions, Queen." He shrugged. "Well, what's left of them."

"Stop!" Meg shouted, pleaded. Panic pricked through her limbs as she took in the shit show erupting around her.

Alastor chanted and his creatures receded to the hole in the floor, the Basilisk slithered to a corner and waited.

Meg inhaled a sharp breath as the creatures scattered away from Skeele. His right leg had no skin, chunks of flesh were missing from his body, a hole had been bit in his cheek. Dark eyes flashed open and focused on her. She'd spent enough time with him she could read his face, or what was left of it. He was in agony, nearly eaten alive.

"Commander," Klaus started to say as he dashed across the room to offer help.

The Basilisk darted from the ceiling, consuming Klaus in one bite.

Skeele tried to turn his head, a gasping breath echoed.

"No," Meg whispered, grief flooding her body like a tidal wave, cold and unrelenting. Every piece of her threatened to crack, as if her bones had become fragile glass, splintering under the weight of the moment. Her knees trembled, wanting to give in, to collapse under the crushing sorrow. She stared ahead, unblinking, as reality set it. This couldn't be real. Not him. Not now. It was too early in the fight.

Meg's heart screamed to shatter, to weep, to let the agony consume her—but she couldn't. Not here. Not now. This was not the time to fall apart. She forced herself to breathe, each inhale shallow and ragged, her chest tightening as if bound by iron chains.

Meg bit her lip, the taste of copper filling her mouth, a feeble attempt to keep the flood of emotion from breaking through. She couldn't afford to fall apart–not when danger was watching her from across the room, not when others still relied on her.

But inside, the fracture lines spread.

FOURTEEN

MEG

SKEELE TRIED, fought with all his might. I knew he would. Skeele always said his duty was to serve the throne. I never thought he'd serve it with his life.

Alastor shoves me and I drop to the ground.

"No," the word falls from my lips like a prayer. I scramble to him. "No. No. No."

"Shh." A broken hand touches my face. "Feed." It's his last word before his chest stops moving and his eyes go glassy.

There's blood everywhere. Bones sticking out of his skin. His wings tattered, torn and broken, wings that once enveloped me in privacy, in trust, in tenderness.

Feed. Echoes in my mind. His last wish. His last breath.

I kiss him. His lips feeling cooler than ever. No, I can't feed. I can't take the last of him right now. He deserved so much better than me and I can't take any more from him. I press my lips to his cheek, to his shoulder.

"I'm sorry," I whisper. "I'm sorry I couldn't save you." I should have sent him to the Peabody Library. He would have never gone though. He would have never left me alone.

"Pathetic," Alastor sneers.

I hear bone crunching, don't feel the pain until it's too late as Alastor slams his boot down on my wing, breaking it. I cry out easily, giving in like I never have before. Heavy sobs shudder from my chest and I remember why I was so guarded all those years ago. I remember why I let no one touch me. I remember why I never trusted a soul.

It's all falling down, crumbling to nothing. I didn't start with much to begin with. I only took the throne of Hell because I lost my temper and killed my grandfather Lucifer. But watching everything shatter around me is a real downer.

Now, I am nothing. Just a murderer like John Lewis always said. *You killed her and don't you forget it.* Every terrible memory comes flooding back.

I've killed Skeele. It's my fault in the end. I'll never forget it. Something heavy sinks in my chest and shreds to bits.

FIFTEEN

Chel ran full bore down the dark passageways, boots slipping on blood and gore. He was following the Basilisk, the creature slithering fast through the hallways, eating the dead and offering him safety out of the castle in the burning caves.

They turned left, then right before coming to the Hellion barracks. They were on the edge of Meg's lands here, past the sparring grounds and the stables. The Basilisk cleared the room of the dead. No one had survived. The Fast-Zombies were too fast. No Hellions remained here.

"Wait," Chel warned the Basilisk. They watched out the windows to be sure no one was nearby. All bodies were on the ground or re-animated and headed toward the castle. "Okay," Chel nodded, motioning to the door.

The Basilisk nosed the door open and the duo slithered into the nearby forest like shadows.

Chel stuck to the cover of the tree canopy while the Basilisk hovered above the nearby road. They ran as fast as they could toward the portal closest to the castle. It was a good thirty miles away; easy to reach by Jeep, but the trek was another story on foot.

They slowed, coming upon a horde of the dead ambling through the forest. Chel breathed a sigh of relief when he realized they were not fast, but the typical stumbling slow. Still, there were so many of them.

The view of the dead Deacons came to mind. Chel was connecting the dots, the rumors of the past few years, and the intel. If there were this many souls trapped and roaming Hell then the Safe Houses were gone.

Chel ran faster, glancing to the Basilisk as it kept pace. He swerved around the dead, felt dread tickling his shoulders when he realized they'd follow and expose him. He cleared the canopy of Hellforest, ducked under the Basilisk as he crossed the road and made it to the cover of the forest again. They were making good time, but Chel was thinking of the scene he'd left behind; he hoped to Hell everyone was still alive. It was the only way. With all these souls collecting, Babylon would come looking for answers. Chel didn't want to serve another throne, he didn't want to go back to the days of Lucifer.

The sun peaked in Hellsky as the duo kept moving. The portal wasn't far and Chel was sure he could get there alone. He made his way to the road and motioned to the Basilisk.

"Go back to the castle," he told the creature.

―――――

THE BASILISK SLITHERED HOME, past Hellforest and crumbling roadways. It kept to the shadows, afraid of coming across the giant Basilisk who'd eaten its siblings.

The Basilisk digested as it moved, looking forward to a rest in the cozy office which had become home. It would be alone though, the thought came to the creature. There would be no other Basilisk family waiting for it. The Basilisk trembled, mourning its siblings. But, Meg would be there. Meg would take care of it. And there was Noah the ghost man, he'd still feed the Basilisk. The creature was unaware that Noah had left the realm with his family.

The Basilisk made it to the royal grounds, slithered to the open door of the Hellion barracks and took the tunnel that led to the Hellion lair. It sensed no dead wandering, no Hellions. As it slithered slowly, it came to a stop at the closed door. It nudged, hearing the scraping of furniture. The Basilisk pushed harder until the furniture tipped over.

A hiss echoed through the sliver of an opening. The Basilisk could see into the room. Meg wasn't there. It sniffed. The Hellions were dead.

Sadness overwhelmed the Basilisk as it realized everyone was dead or gone. It began backing up as the threatening hiss of Alastor's giant Basilisk echoed in the emptiness.

It moved away, slithered as quickly as it could out of the hallway, then out of the Hellion barracks, then away from the castle grounds. The Basilisk took to the sky, avoiding the dead and anything else it might come across. It slithered to the only place it knew where to go, the Black river in the Adirondacks of Hell. The Basilisk went home.

Sixteen

Thrush grabbed the small blade Chel had given him during training and tucked it into the pocket near his belt. He picked up his bag and secured it on his back. There was only time to grab a few things from his room; a few books he'd taken from the castle, clothes, small weapons, and snacks. His parents were pacing the living room when he finally left his bedroom.

Noah glanced at the clock, "We gotta go. It's getting closer."

Nightingale was standing near the door. "Now, son. Quickly and quietly." She opened the door, careful that the hinges didn't squeak. They crossed the lawn and paused near the gate to the high fence that protected their sanctuary in the graveyard. Past the chain link, they saw snakes and bugs and small creatures of havoc headed toward the castle in the burning caves.

Noah mouthed, "Follow me."

Thrush nodded.

The gate opened silently, not drawing attention from the creatures on the ground.

Thrush ran as fast as his legs would carry him, his heart

pounding in his chest like a war drum. He glanced at his mother beside him, her face set with grim determination. Since his parents were technically dead, they could flash where ever they wanted, but they stayed by his side. Thrush was grateful for it. They had their limitations being spectral beings and all, but they did their best. They still functioned as though they were very much alive.

"Stay close, Thrush!" Noah called out, his voice strained but firm.

Noah glanced back and Thrush could see the worry etched on his father's face. Nightingale's eyes darted around, scanning the Hellforest for any signs of movement. Escaping during the day hours meant the dead would be wandering.

The castle in the burning caves loomed to their right, a sinister silhouette against the ochre Hellsky. The cries of Demons echoed through the air, growing closer. And... there was another sound...

"No," Noah muttered, slowing to run by Thrush's side. He pointed to one of the dead. It wasn't ambling around looking lost like they usually were, this one was running toward the castle.

"Fast-dead," Nightingale warned. "Stay clear of them."

They ran faster, further.

"We are almost there," Nightingale said, her voice a mix of hope and desperation. "The portal is just ahead."

Thrush's legs burned with fatigue, but he pushed himself harder. He'd trained hard for this day. The portal was their only chance. It shimmered faintly in the distance, a beacon of hope in the darkness. But as they drew closer, he saw the dark shapes moving around it.

"Demons," Thrush said just loud enough for his parents to hear, pointing toward the portal.

Noah's jaw tightened. "We have to get through them. There's no other way."

The three skidded to a halt, hiding behind a jagged outcropping of rocks. Thrush peered around the edge, counting the Demons. There were five of them, grotesque creatures with leathery wings and claws that gleamed in the hellish light.

"We need a distraction," Nightingale whispered, her eyes narrowing as she formulated a plan.

Thrush's mind raced. He looked down and spotted a loose, heavy rock. It wasn't much, but it might just buy them the time they needed.

"I'll throw this," Thrush said, hefting the rock. "When they go to check, we make a run for it."

Noah nodded. "On my signal."

Thrush took a deep breath, trying to steady his trembling hands. He waited for his father's signal, the tension stretching out every second into an eternity.

"Now!" Noah hissed.

Thrush hurled the rock with all his might, watching as it arced through the air and crashed into a distant pile of debris. The Demons' heads snapped toward the noise. They moved to investigate.

"Go!" Noah urged, and they sprinted from their hiding place, making a beeline for the portal.

The Demons saw them and let out enraged roars as they ran back toward the portal.

Thrush's heart pounded harder, adrenaline coursing through his veins. The portal shimmered tantalizingly close, but the Demons were closing in fast.

Nightingale reached the portal first, her hand outstretched toward the shimmering surface. "Thrush, hurry!"

Thrush pushed himself harder, his feet barely touching the ground as he raced toward safety. Noah was right behind him, glancing back to see the Demons almost upon them.

"No!" Nightingale shouted. She waved for Thrush to run around the portal. "The fast-dead are coming."

"Change of plans," Noah said, grabbing Thrush by his shirt.

The fast dead didn't pick favorites, they went after whatever moved, whatever was closest, and the Demons had their attention.

"Keep running," Nightingale said, waving, "this way."

Thrush lunged with a final burst of speed following Nightingale as she changed course.

"Where?" Thrush asked between heavy breaths.

"The pond is the closest." Noah was running by Thrush's side.

The sounds of hundreds of feet running echoed through Hell-forest. Thrush glanced from side to side, didn't notice the branches on the ground and tripped.

Noah was lifting him to his feet harshly. "Keep going," he urged.

Thrush limped for a few steps before swallowing down the pain in his ankle and resuming his previous speed.

"It's not far," Nightingale said.

Thrush knew better; it was a good distance away and he wasn't sure he could keep running at this pace, but he'd try his hardest. They ran across empty roads and through forests littered with wandering dead.

Nightingale finally slowed near a shallow stream. "It's up here." She motioned toward the dark pond in the distance. "We're safe, Thrush. It's not much further."

Noah placed a hand on Thrush's shoulder, his expression a mix of pride and exhaustion. "You did it, son. We're out of here."

Thrush allowed himself a small, weary smile. They had almost escaped Hell but he knew their journey was far from over. There were still dangers ahead, still battles to be fought–

A fast-dead was running toward Thrush. He acted quick, not

ready for the speed at which the fast-dead ran. His parents didn't notice in time. Thrush gripped his knife and slammed it into the skull of the fast-dead as it knocked him over.

Thrush groaned, trying to shove the zombie off him but it was the corpse of a rather large man.

"No!" Nightingale shouted, grabbing at the zombie, and trying to get it off Thrush.

"It's dead," Noah said, dragging Thrush out from under the corpse.

Gore and blood stained Thrush's clothing. He shuddered, thankful for his training with the Hellions the past few years. He wiped his knife on his pant leg and secured it again. "Let's go," he said, making a beeline for the pond.

"The Basilisk," Nightingale warned. "There's two."

Noah pointed to the still surface of the pond. "They're not here."

"Go," Nightingale urged.

The trio ran for the pond.

Thrush dove under, a cold sensation washing over him as the soft current pulled them away.

SEVENTEEN

ALASTOR DRAGS me to the dungeon. Broken, bleeding. I can't *poof* and travel, my injuries making me too weak. I need blood. I catch a glimpse of my Basilisk that was guarding the stairs. It's dead and dark creatures are eating its flesh. Something worse than dread floods me.

"Plenty of unseen creatures down here," Alastor says as he drags me. "Things I haven't seen in ages."

My broken wing twists and rolls against the stone floor as he drags me through the dark, labyrinthine corridors of the infernal palace dungeon. The only light came from flickering torches casting eerie shadows on the stone walls. The air was thick with the scent of brimstone and tormented wails.

I haven't been in the dungeons in years, never felt the need to. Seems I'm about to become closely acquainted with the creatures that snarl and hiss from behind solid doors. Sharp talons scrape against the stone floor. The creatures howl and screech and pound on their doors sensing the Queen of Hell in their presence. Or maybe it's the Demon dragging me like a sack of shit. A door slams and Alastor wrenches my leg, dragging me into a cell. I should fight. I should try to stand. I should drain every last drop of blood in his body. Confusion and grief bombard me. There's a sickening feeling in my chest, a lurching in my stomach when I smell the rotten blood dried to the floor.

I should stay regal even like this, I should struggle against Alastor as he grips my wrists and wraps rusted chains around them.

Alastor kicks me. "Tell me where the bones are," he shouts, his voice echoing off the stone walls. He kicks me again, stomping on my broken wing. I cry out. The creatures detained down here howl and heckle, excited for their potential release with the changing of the crown.

The room turns cold.

"Child," the voice of Clea echoes in the room. "You must fight him," she begs, dropping to her knees to face me. "Get up. You must get up."

"Get the fuck out of here," Alastor shouts, grabbing a rusted iron rod from the floor and whipping it at Clea. Her wavering image disappears.

"You're a bastard," I say. "She didn't do anything to you." I don't like it when people threaten my mother. She might be dead, but she didn't deserve what was done to her. A rage swells inside me. A long time ago, Lucifer sparked my rage by being cruel to my mother.

"You dare lay hands on me," I hiss, my voice a mix of fury and command.

Alastor's lips curl into a cruel smile. "The days of your rule are over, my dear. It's time for a new order in Hell." His voice is a low growl, dripping with venom.

I fight against the chains, ignoring the sharp pain in my ribs and broken wing. It's too late. Clea needed to give me that pep talk about fifteen minutes ago.

Alastor chuckles with his newfound sense of power, the iron doors of the cell screeching in protest as he closes them.

"You will pay for this treachery, Alastor. Hell will not bend to your will so easily."

"You overestimate your influence, Queen," Alastor sneers, watching me through the barred window in the door.

I am left with the icy chill of the cell, the musky air from damp walls. There is no window to the outside, only a few slivers of light shining past the door. There is something rust colored dried on the floor. Memories surface: this was Sparrow's cell when he was bitten. That's his dried blood on the stones. Ironic.

THE AIR GROWS COLDER, the darkness more oppressive. Clea arrives again in wisps.

"No," she mutters as she takes in the scene. "No this can't be happening."

Tears dry on my cheeks as I struggle to get to my feet.

"Can you break these chains?" I ask.

Clea is shaking her head. "Not the iron." She reaches forward but her hands hover over the chains surrounding my wrists. "The iron will just send me to the Astral plane."

"Damn." I jerk the chains and find where they are secured against the wall. The room is barely more than a stone box, dank and reeking of despair. The chains are secured to a metal ring on the wall.

Something shifts in the air, the castle creaks, the prisoners howl louder then go stunned silence. If there were a Hellion here, they'd no longer intervene. The power dynamic has shifted, the unthinkable has come to pass: the Queen of Hell is now a prisoner.

EIGHTEEN

Nero whinnied and nodded toward the back hallway of the Peabody Library. There was a long, underground hallway that exited near the Patapsco River. An empty plot with overgrown shrubbery and abandoned buildings, Jed had been warding the area for years, doing his best to provide an outdoor living space where Nero could roam freely for a few hours a day. He typically went out at night, when the chances of being seen were low and he could no longer suppress the urge to run.

Nero glanced at the two teenagers lounging in overstuffed high back chairs, reading. They weren't supposed to leave the building, but Nero needed to go out. He didn't use toilets and he couldn't very well leave a pile of horseshit in the hallway. Jed would never forgive him.

Shay and Jed had gone to get food and the supplies needed for housing the kids. They'd promised to be back soon but it had been hours. Nero didn't want to let the children out of his sight. The fresh air might do them some good, he figured. It wasn't healthy for any creature to be locked indoors for days and weeks at a time.

———

Under the silvery glow of the moonlight, Nero led Rue and Remington through the quiet corridor and riverfront surrounding the Peabody Library. The night air was cool and crisp, carrying with it the faint scent of earth.

As they walked, Rue and Remington clung close to Nero. They spoke in hushed tones, their voices a mixture of excitement and longing.

"I miss mother," Rue whispered, her voice tinged with sadness. "I miss Thrush too. I wish they were here with us."

Remington nodded in agreement, his expression mirroring his sister's melancholy. "Me too," he replied softly. "But we have to stay here where it's safe."

Rue frowned, her brow furrowing with confusion. "I think she was wrong, separating everyone. We should be fighting together. We could help her."

Remington chuckled before saying, "Not you, you're too small."

Rue gave him a dirty look. She was tired of everyone protecting her. She'd spent years watching Remington and Thrush train with the Hellions and the most she got was self-defense and knife wielding. She could do more, she just knew it.

Nero paused from nibbling the dry grass near the riverbank and nudged Rue with his snout. He didn't know how to comfort the children, but he knew the dangers of Hell firsthand. He wished he could tell the children something, anything... All he could offer was a soft whinny of comfort.

Rue and Remington exchanged a knowing glance. They looked up at Nero, a sense of trust and reassurance filling them. Rue reached out and pet Nero's neck and that urge to return home which had flared inside her dampened.

"Shay said there are a lot of kids on the Earthen plane. Plenty our age." Remington rose up on his toes to get a good look across the river.

"More than three is a good number of kids," Rue said, wandering away from Nero.

Could you imagine seeing a whole bunch of kids our age every day?"

Remington made a sound that didn't convey excitement. "You've heard mother's stories." His hands gripped the metal railing and he leaned forward, looking into the dark river. "Kids on the Earthen plane are not all they're cracked up to be."

"They could be nice," Rue said.

"They could suck." Remington turned and leaned his back against the railing, his heels stepping just outside of the markings Jed had made on the cement curbing.

A strange noise came from the murky water.

"What was that?" Rue asked, moving closer to her brother.

Nero whinnied a warning and walked closer, trying to nudge the children away from the edge of the protective runes and markings on the ground.

Rue and Remington together, both with a half a foot outside the runes of protection, lit the skies above with a silvery ethereal light like nothing ever seen before. Two rays blasted to the sky and illuminated the night clouds. Every illegal creature that didn't belong on the Earthen plane saw it.

Without the Deacons to keep the balance, creatures slid between the Veils separating realms. Good and bad, dark and light, they all seeped to the Earthen plane, drawn by forbidden fruit. A tempting aura that begged for inspection, a light that hadn't been seen in eons, curious creatures and those looking to slay the unknown, those looking to consume, made their way toward the river.

JED AND SHAY returned to the library only to find it empty. They juggled bags filled with clothing, food, and supplies, twice as much as they usually brought home. Shay wasn't sure it was enough. They'd have to go back out again soon. These kids ate a lot, especially the boy. Jed kicked the door closed and enhanced the spell of protection before turning to face Shay. Concern wrinkled her brow.

"Rue?" Shay called. "Remington?" No one replied. "Nero?" There was nothing. Silence. The library was empty.

"I told you it wasn't a good idea to leave a horse in charge of two teenagers," Jed muttered.

Shay felt a nudge down the tether that linked her to Nero. "They're outside," Shay said, dropping her bags and springing toward the back corridor. "Something is happening." Shay's eyes went wide and she shoved blowtorch blue hair out of her face. "Nero is worried."

"Shit," Jed echoed and followed.

Footsteps boomed as they ran hard and as fast as they could.

"Why would they go outside?" Jed muttered between breaths.

"They're kids," Shay said as she shoved open the door.

"No!" Jed pushed Shay aside and sprinted ahead of her, toward the riverbank walkway. "Stay back!"

The runes and spells that Jed and Shay had been working on for years were meant to shield the outside world from the secrets that the Peabody Library and surrounding empty lot held, but it did nothing to shield those inside from what they could see beyond the wards. Jed's gut punched, he'd never seen so many Demons in all his life. A familiar panic surfaced, one reminding him to run and hide and stay alive. He couldn't do that anymore. Too many relied on him.

Nero whinnied, grabbed Rue's shirt with his teeth and tugged her away from the edge of the riverbank. Rue was smaller and easier to move, Remington was going to be harder, the boy was twice his sister's size, lean and built like a warrior.

"Get away from the river!" Jed shouted as he ran toward them, arms waving.

Creatures big and small had collected along the edge of the property. Strange Demons Jed had never seen before lingered, inspecting, trying to get a glimpse of what had sparked the light. The scene was like a cake drawing children to the table. The Patapsco River had become a cesspool of Hellspawn.

Jed's heart thumped against his ribs as he recognized the cloud-like Demon who'd killed his friend Declan. There were more creatures, things with teeth and feathers and tails. But the worst was the Angel hovering in the shadows, squinting, blade drawn, wings exposed.

Shay saw it and panic burned through her body.

Nero saw it and shoved Rue to the ground. He raced forward and grabbed at Remington by the sleeve.

The boy laughed and pushed Nero away. "Stop it," he said, unaware of the danger lurking behind him.

Nero's eyes went wide as Remington leaned back, breaching the wards again.

The Angel's head snapped toward the light and it began to move closer.

Jed saw the light the boy emitted and every warning from his mother, every battle he fought as a child, every dark cloud he ran from came flooding back, a tsunami of will to fight and survive.

"Get away from the river!" Jed shouted, hands out, magic pouring from his fingertips. He shouted words to knit the wards back together and strengthen them, his words sounded like thunder cracking and ocean waves splitting on rock.

Nero reared up, shocking Remington. The boy leaned back again, anticipating getting kicked.

A hand from outside the runes reached for the top of Remington's head. Drawn by the delightful energy of the Shadow Heir. Creatures from all realms loved something forbidden, they loved something unknown, they loved something consumable that they could exploit. They might not have belonged on the Earthen plane but the boy emitting the light belonged even less. Without the Deacons, the Veil was ready to fracture, chaos was about to win.

Nero threatened to turn into the monster. It had been a long time since he'd released fire of vengeance from his throat. He was ready and eager to create ash if needed. He'd burn them all. He'd burn that Angel to a cinder if it reached for Remington's head one more time.

"Don't Nero!" Shay shouted, sensing the change. She didn't know what Nero changing inside the wards would do to him... or her. Worse, she feared he'd breathe fire and burn the wards away and then they'd be completely exposed to the creatures and people of the city.

Nero lurched forward, grabbed Remington's arm between his teeth, the bite sunk into skin drawing blood. He tore Remington away from the edge of the property and inside the wards, dragging him halfway to the door that led inside before finally releasing him.

The creatures moved closer. All of them. They pressed their faces against the protective layer created by the wards like shoppers pressing their noses against a store window. Eager, interested, and ready to *take*. It was a frightful scene; so many dark creatures in one place, hunting the same prey.

Rue backstepped and knocked into Shay.

Shay grabbed onto the girl and ran to the door. Jed went to work, fixing the wards. Nero headbutted Remington. The boy turned and shock slammed across his face as he saw the mountains of Demons searching for what had created the light. Nero whinnied darkly and nodded to the side. Remington followed his gaze and saw the Angel, searching, his face scrunched like he was looking through a waterfall and couldn't focus.

"Inside!" Jed shouted as he backed away from the warded lot. He grabbed Remington's arm and took off running.

Nero galloped after them.

Everyone clamored inside the door. Jed closed it gently, trying not to draw the creatures to the noise, then he locked the door with heavy chains and strengthened the wards. Jed took a Sharpie out of his pocket, drew new runes, and considered sealing the door completely.

———

"THAT WAS the worst idea in the history of ideas," Jed said, leading everyone back to the main lounge in the library.

"It was the horse's fault," Rue said.

Everyone glanced to Nero and he hung his head ashamed. Nero lowered his eyes to the floor before gazing back up at Shay like a hurt puppy.

Shay reached out and patted Nero.

Jed was muttering something under his breath as he strode to a bookshelf and pulled off a box.

Shay's gut clenched. She knew what he'd planned to do before he even said a word.

Jed grabbed Remington's arm and dragged him over to a table. "You've seen your mother's tattoos?" Jed asked, sweat dripped down the side of his face and he was breathing rapidly.

"Yes," Remington nodded.

"You see these?" Jed held out his arms and ripped off his shirt.

He pointed to a marking on his chest, "This protects me from Demons." Pointed to another, "This protects me from Angels. And this," he chuckled as though it was absurd because Jed thought his blue aura was bright but it was nothing compared to this kid's, "this one dims my aura." His finger pointed to a black rune tattooed at the base of his throat. "You can never be too careful."

He paused to open his tattoo case and chose a greenish-black pot of ink. "Take off your shirt," he ordered the boy.

"I don't have an aura," Remington said.

Jed laughed out loud. "Oh, you sure do, boy. And we must hide it if you're going to stay in seclusion on the Earthen plane because that was bright as fuck." Jed was high on magic and this discovery as he assembled his tattoo gun and set up. "Do you have an aura like that, Rue?" he shouted across the room absently before shaking his head in disbelief.

Nero whinnied in response, he'd seen Rue's light but pulled her away before Jed and Shay came running out the back door of the library.

"Wait," Shay warned, "shouldn't we ask Meg?"

"You want permission?" Jed asked. The words came out rougher than he wanted to speak to her but he couldn't help it. Adrenaline was coursing through his veins and it was a high he hadn't enjoyed in a long time. "You want consent? We haven't heard from Meg in weeks. Who knows how deep of a shit pile she's in. This can't wait. We're doing this tonight."

Rue's chin trembled as she watched.

Shay pulled her closer. "He doesn't mean that. We don't know where she is."

Jed was shaking his head as metal clicked. "Sit," he told Remington.

The boy plopped down in a chair then pulled his shirt off.

"Christ," Jed muttered. "Aren't you like fifteen?"

"I'll be fourteen soon," Remington said.

"What have they been feeding you down there in Hell? Last time I saw you, you were this big." Jed held his hand level with the floor and to his shoulder. "It wasn't that long ago."

Remington shrugged. "My dad said it was a growth spurt."

"It must've been something." Jed flicked the button on his tattoo gun and it buzzed to life. "I said I'd never tattoo a kid…" Jed shook his head, felt like he'd been doing that a lot the past hour.

"What if she's dead?" Rue asked.

"No." Shay was shaking her head, trying to shake out the thoughts she'd been struggling with for weeks, but she wouldn't let the girl know. "There is no way she's dead, Rue. Give her time."

"I'm afraid. What if she's afraid right now?" Rue asked. "What if our mom is somewhere alone and afraid and hurt?"

Shay gripped her shoulders. "Your mother is never afraid. *They* should fear your mother." She searched the girl's eyes for understanding. "She is something to fear. Not the other way around."

The noise of Jed's electric tattoo gun echoed through the corridors of the library.

Remington hissed as the needle penetrated and inked his skin.

"You want a spell for the discomfort?" Jed asked Remington.

The boy hesitated before saying, "It doesn't hurt."

Rue focused on Shay, an unspoken question in her eyes.

"Yes," Shay said, exhaling a breath of knowing. "Yes, you're next." Shay was nodding, doing her best to soothe the girl. "You can do this. Jed is right. We need to protect you both." Shay held out her arm to show Rue her tattoos.

Jed decorated Remington's skin with three runes before stopping. One for the aura, one for protection, and the last for strength.

"Come now, Rue," Jed called as he cleaned his machine and retrieved new pots of ink.

Remington went to sit on the dark green couch near the fireplace. Nero joined him, sniffing at the boy's hair and nipping his shoulder in an attempt to comfort him. Nero knelt and curled up next to the couch.

Remington held out a hand and pet Nero between the ears. "Thanks for getting us in trouble, horse," he muttered.

Jed sighed as Rue sat in the chair. "You have to take off the shirt."

Shay started to say something but Rue interrupted her, "It's okay. I have a bra on."

Jed raised his palm and whispered words that sounded like the soft petals of a rose rubbing together in a summer storm. A coolness coated Rue's skin.

"What was that?" Rue asked.

"For the discomfort of the needle," Jed said as he scooted closer. "I must touch your chest and your bare skin." He pressed his lips into a line and glanced at Shay, unsure of how a teenage girl would feel about his hands and forearms leaning on her body.

"It's okay," Rue said. "You forget, I grew up in Hell."

"Your mother kept you close to her. As she should have," Jed said.

"That doesn't mean I didn't see things. I watched movies. I hung around Hellions." She straightened her back. "I know you're only touching me to tattoo the runes." She tipped her chin up. "Just do it."

Jed nodded and scooted closer. Shay sat opposite Rue and watched the girl in case she changed her mind.

Jed inked Rue's skin with three runes; one to dull her aura, one for protection, and the last for strength. Because of her small size and gender, he doubled the rune for strength.

Jed clicked off his tattoo gun and pushed his chair away from the girl. "Go to bed, both of you," he said to the children.

"But... we haven't eaten dinner," Remington said from the couch.

"And you won't. Maybe that will be a reminder to never go outside alone again." Jed slammed the cover of his tattoo kit.

"We went with Nero," Rue said, eyes large and face pale.

"That doesn't count–" Jed started to say but a loud nicker interrupted him. "You go to bed too." Jed pointed at Nero then arced his arm toward the hallway that led to the bedrooms. "Go."

The boy, the girl, and the horse all stood and walked away, heads down and shoulders slumped. After hearing the doors close–Nero's slammed especially loud–Jed turned to Shay.

"What the fuck," Jed said.

Shay moved to him. "Of all the time we've spent with those two children, I have never seen an aura like that come from them."

Jed ran his hand through messy hair then searched his pocket for a tie. "It must be this plane. That's all I can think." He rubbed his mouth and glanced to the corridors of books. "We'll have to research it."

Jed and Shay had spent plenty of time visiting Hell over the years. After everything they'd been through, Meg was like family and even though she was the Queen of Hell, she still insisted on weekend family dinners and holidays together. Of the few Jed and Shay had missed, Meg had shown up and guilted them into never wanting to miss another. Deep down, Jed and Shay knew that the time together was important, it was normal, it was... human.

"They should have eaten before bed," Shay said, looking toward the dark hallway.

"They'll get over it." Jed was tucking his box away on the shelf.

Shay moved closer, reached up on her toes and wrapped her arms around his neck. "When I saw you running out there, magic streaming from your fingers," she inhaled the scent of him and a quiver hit her center, "it was really hot."

Jed chuckled and tugged her closer. "Oh yeah." He kissed her mouth, then her jaw, then the soft skin of her neck.

"You smell like magic." Shay sucked in a breath as he nipped her shoulder. "I like it."

"I didn't realize it had a smell." His hands gripped her backside and lifted her.

Shay's legs wrapped around his waist and blue hair fell over her shoulders as she leaned into him. "I like it when you go all combat mode."

"I could say the same about you, but I never get to see it." Jed's eyes darkened as he watched her.

Shay giggled. "Maybe Nero could take a picture for you."

Jed carried her behind the bookshelves to a private corner. He pressed her back against the shelves and ground his hips against her center.

Shay's blood heated and she tugged at her shirt, tossing it aside. Jed's mouth lowered to her neck and chest as he pressed open-mouthed kisses to her heated skin.

"You didn't have to jump in there and take over," Shay said. "I could have done it."

"You promised to watch over those children," Jed said. "I will not let you fail. I will not let you do this alone." He kissed her harder.

Nineteen

Meg

Alastor steps inside the dungeon, closing the heavy door behind him. He grabs the iron rod from the floor and grips it, testing its weight.

I watch him with half-lidded eyes and try to give myself a pep-talk. *I am Meg, Queen of Hell, Granddaughter of Lucifer, Daughter of the Archangel Gabriel.* My chest still feels empty. Hollow. I think I am nothing and I cannot hide it from myself.

Alastor pokes me in the stomach with the iron rod. I roll away and move to my knees, ready to stand. The chains rattle and go taut.

"What do you want?" I ask.

Alastor smiles and for a moment I am shocked by how handsome he could be if he weren't my uncle and trying to kill me. His eyes flash red. I shake my head and draw on that empty feeling in my center.

"Just tell me where the bones are," Alastor says, jiggling the rod.

I shake my head. "No clue, buddy." I shrug and do my best to look like an innocent, misunderstood girl.

He steps closer, just close enough for me to make the first move. I'm hoping to surprise him with my strength, instead I surprise myself with my lack of. I'm slow. Weaker than ever. I scrape my nails across his skin. Alastor dodges my attacks with ease, his movements fluid and practiced. He grabs my wrist, twisting it, forcing me to my knees. With a swift motion, he drags me against the wall, wrapping the chains tighter.

I pull against them, my skin tearing and bleeding.

Alastor admires his work. "Comfortable?" he taunts, eyes glinting with sadistic pleasure.

I spit at him; there's no other way to communicate my hatred. "You may have me in chains but you will never break me."

He leans in close, his face inches from mine. "We'll see about that," he whispers, hot breath against my skin, eyes black as night. "Welcome to your new kingdom, Queen. Get used to it."

He clears his throat before turning away and wandering the cell. "Now, about the bones."

"I don't know where they are. I told you." I exhale a breath as the chains sag.

He tests the balance of the rod. "Did Clea tell you about me?" he asks.

My gaze roams his face, focusing on the shadows that seem to swirl and move under his eyes and the hollows of his cheeks.

"Have you been wondering where she went?" he asks.

I say nothing.

"Banishing something like her wasn't terribly difficult. Lucifer told me where her bones were." He sighs as though banishing my mother from her home was a boring task.

If I could burn him to ash with my eyes I would. My steady breaths echo in the dungeon as the faint, distant screams of the damned seep in from the open door.

Alastor swings the rod a few times, testing its weight again and his swing arc, lining up the strike.

My stomach clenches, anticipating. I've been hit with random objects before, and I wonder if Alastor knows anything about my upbringing on the Earthen plane. I wonder if he knew John Lewis or Jim? He seems the type, they probably bullied kids in high school together.

He pauses, his head tips to the side. "Tell me where Lucifer's bones are."

"I can't," I say.

"I don't believe you." Alastor swings the iron bar like a batter at the plate, the end of it barely an inch from my nose.

I don't flinch. I prepared for this for twenty-five years. I spent more time as a punching bag for John Lewis and Jim than I have spent as a Queen. It's a training that is hard to break. I'll never forget how to still my body, how to loosen my muscles so the ache doesn't linger afterwards, how to tense my abdomen but nothing else. I've already died once—maybe even twice—nothing Alastor could do to me would compare to that heartbreak. Not sure I ever really recovered from Sparrow's deception.

Alastor snorts and wanders. "I can do this all day. All night."

"You must be bored," I mutter. "Lucifer will use you just like he used my mother. Did he tell you why I killed him? He sent the Basilisk after her. He'll do the same to you. He'll kill you once he's used you up." My stomach growls.

"Oh," one dark brow rises in interest. "You hungry, girl?"

"No," I lie.

"That sounded like hunger. You want some blood?" his smile

is sinister and now I can see the resemblance to Lucifer in his features.

I close my eyes, focusing on the remaining flicker of strength. A tiny flame in my center threatened to extinguish.

I lurch forward, teeth bared, ready to bite. The chains snap taut: he's just out of my reach.

"Ah, you are hungry."

"Nope," I lie. "I'm never hungry." My stomach clenches, I'm so hungry I could eat five pizzas or five guys. "I just want you dead."

"Where are Lucifer's bones?" Alastor asks. "Tell me and I'll set you free."

"The Deacons took them." I shudder. "I wanted to burn them but I was overruled." It's a partial lie.

"I need the bones to make the voice stop!" Alastor's eyes are wild. "Tell me where they are!"

"Go ask the Deacons," I shout back. "Oh wait, you killed them all didn't you? Dumb ass!"

He swings the iron rod, hitting me in the ribs. I hiss. "You fuck."

"That's no way to talk to your King," Alastor seethes.

I go still, trying to compose myself and ignore the throbbing in my side.

He swings the rod and hits my other side. Pain shoots through my body as more ribs crack. I hold in a groan, imagine my teeth sinking into his neck and killing him.

"Bow," he orders. "Welcome to your new kingdom, Meg. Get used to it."

"Never," I say. My heart is beating hard against my broken ribs, my sides ache. The chains around my wrist are feeling incredibly heavy.

He taps the top of my head twice with the iron rod. I know

better than to fuck with a head injury and no fresh blood in my future. I hate him, I hate this, but I must keep my brain in its rightful place.

I tip my head.

"As you should." Alastor turns and leaves the cell, the heavy door slamming shut behind him.

My mind races with thoughts of escape and vengeance. I close my eyes. This is not the end. The battle for my throne has just begun.

TWENTY

ALASTOR FELL TO THE GROUND OUTSIDE MEG'S CELL. The voice of Lucifer roared in his mind.

Find my bones. Find my bones. Find my bones!

He'd almost fallen apart in front of the throneless Queen. Sweat dripped down his back as he struggled to hold himself together. The voice of Lucifer was too much. It was driving him mad.

A breeze sifted through the dungeon, carrying whispers of anguish and misery. Alastor clenched his fists and pressed his knuckles to the stone floor, hoping the pain of bone on stone would help him drown out the demanding voice echoing in his mind.

Find my bones...

The voice softened to a whisper, still relentless, a constant presence that gnawed at his sanity. Alastor pressed his palms against his temples as if he could push the voice away. Lucifer's demands grew louder, more insistent.

Find my bones. Find my bones. Find my bones.

Alastor's breaths came in ragged gasps. He felt like a puppet, pulled by strings he could not sever. Lucifer's demand felt like a crushing burden.

Alastor moved to his feet, stumbling forward, boots scraping on uneven stone floor. Each step felt like an eternity. Alastor's mind raced with memories of before. He'd finally gotten the skin trades back on track, he was making millions, selling souls, and securing a future at the table with higher Demons.

He'd finally dragged himself out of the downfall from dealing with Shay and her half-breed boyfriend. He never considered the throne of Hell, it was never on his list of goals. But Lucifer's demands changed everything. Now the Raven King was breathing down his neck because he wasn't making the soul quota and the Higher Demons of Hell had been promised skin, neither of which Alastor could focus on while dealing with this mess.

Alastor's jaw tightened as he mentally checked off the places he'd searched. He'd interrogated Demons, followed every whisper and rumor, and it all led him here to the castle in the burning caves. The bones remained elusive, a tantalizing prize just out of reach. Frustration burned within him, threatening to consume him. He made his way out of the dungeon and climbed the winding stairs. He passed the rotting body of Meg's Basilisk, bones and flesh from the war he'd brought here. He walked down the hall, passed the Hellion lair, and shoved open the doors to the courtyard. He sprinted a few quick steps before jumping into the dead tree in the center of the courtyard. He gripped branches above his head and pulled himself up. Alastor climbed until he could see over the canopy of the nearby forests. The depths of Hell seemed endless, a labyrinth of torment and darkness. Just the way he liked it. Somewhere in that infernal maze lay the remains of Lucifer, and with them, the power to be free.

You are nothing without me, Lucifer's voice said. *Remember that. Your strength, your purpose all stem from my will. Find my bones and you will be rewarded.*

With a roar of frustration, Alastor leapt from the tree branch. The winds howled around him but he welcomed the chaos, it matched the turmoil within his soul. He fell like a cat, landing on two feet with a heavy thump. The only reward Alastor wanted was freedom from the voice in his head. He began searching the grounds himself. He would find the bones, restore Lucifer and then... he would wrest his destiny from the clutches of his sperm donor.

While he searched, he contacted the Hellion families and called upon the next batch of Hellions bred to serve the throne.

TWENTY-ONE

MEG

THERE IS NOT much sense of time in this cell, but from the cramping in my stomach, I know it's been a few days. The cold stone walls press in on me, their dampness seeping into my bones. A single torch flickers in the hallway outside, casting erratic shadows through the small, barred window on the door.

Footsteps echo in the corridor, a constant reminder of my captivity. I've heard the changing of the guards, new Hellions taking their place, their guttural voices muttering as they pass by. It didn't take Alastor long to replace the ones he killed.

One Hellion sits outside my door now. I can hear his breathing; a harsh rasp that grates on my nerves. I wonder if he's bored or if he's waiting for something interesting to happen. But then, nothing about this place encourages curiosity or hope.

My stomach growls loudly, a painful reminder of my situation. I wonder if they'll ever feed me in this prison. Alastor has many ways to break a person, and starvation is one of the simplest–the easiest with me. It's a slow torment, gnawing away at strength and resolve. He knows I'm starving. Food has always been a hot point for me. Raised on starvation, it became worse when the need to consume blood overtook me all those years ago.

I shift slightly, the chains binding my wrists clinking softly. My thoughts wander, trying to focus on anything other than the hunger. I wonder if anyone will be looking for me. The chances of them finding me here, in this forsaken dungeon, feel terribly slim.

My throat is parched, each swallow a reminder of the thirst burning within me. I need a warm body, heck I'd suck on a blood popsicle right now, that's how low my standards are. I glance to the dried blood on the stone floor... No. Not that low. But... maybe.

My thoughts keep drifting to Skeele and his torn body on the floor of the Hellion lair. I've never let regrets run my life, but it's grim to not think about all the things I could have done differently when Alastor breached the castle walls.

The Hellion outside shifts, his armor clinking. I open my eyes, staring at the door. If he comes in, maybe I can overpower him, take his weapon. But even in my thoughts, the idea feels desperate and foolish. I'm too weak, my strength sapped by days of hunger and thirst.

My fingers trace the rough stone beneath me, feeling each crack and crevice. This cell, this tomb, feels like it's swallowing me whole. I can't let Alastor win. I have to hold on, have to believe that there's a way out of this nightmare. I've spent too much of my life locked up. Bitches always seem to want to lock me up. It started with John Lewis, then the Sheriff in Gouverneur, then those fucking Deacons, then Remiel, the Archangels... Damn the list goes on and on and makes me wonder why in the hell I didn't lock more people up in my dungeon. I put a pin in that shit for when I get out of here. Everyone who's ever looked at me sideways is going in a cell. I'll cage them and starve them and see how they like it.

The footsteps in the hallway continue, a grim symphony of my imprisonment. Each step is a reminder of my helplessness, each pause a punctuation to my despair. But the horrors persist and so do I. I must. For my children, for the memory of Skeele, for the chance to make Alastor pay for what he's done.

As the torchlight flickers and the hours drag on, I cling to that thought. I will survive this. Somehow. I'll find a rat or a... spoon. I've done that before, spooned my way out of lockup. I move my arms and tap the metal chains to a tune. After a few jangles I settle on Michael Jackson's *Beat It*.

I lean my head back against the wall, closing my eyes briefly. I won't be getting food while I'm here. Maybe I can get that Hellion to come closer to me and I can bite him. Yeah, that's my next plan. Bite the monster. Become the monster. Fuck shit up.

Twenty-Two

Sparrow always knew where Alastor was, it was part of the deal with the Crossroads Demon or Demon*s*, Shay and Nero. If Alastor were a needle in a haystack, Sparrow would find him. No matter what plane he was on Alastor was tracked, Earthen or Hell or Seven Kingdoms of Heaven–not that any Demon would be caught dead in Heaven.

Sparrow had been inside the castle in the burning caves before, knew it quite well after being Lucifer's Hellion for all that time he was trying to free his family from the curse of his father, the Archangel Remiel. It was a burden left for Sparrow. Remiel never did his required time as a Hellion, and as a result, his children were a bit crazy. Sparrow did his time–against Meg's wishes–in an effort to cure himself, Nightingale, and any future children of the curse.

A Hellion met Sparrow in the hall. The fucker was disgusting, definitely Hellions of a different time. Menacing, feral, trouble. These were the kind that killed first and asked questions later. These were the Hellions of Lucifer's reign returned. Sparrow wondered what happened here. Judging from the rotting flesh in the hall, and the destruction and smell, Alastor had taken the castle by force.

"Alastor, now," Sparrow told the Hellion.

The creature grunted and began walking. They passed the Hellion lair, the stairwell, the kitchen. The Hellion brought Sparrow to the ballroom, opened the door and grunted with the motioning of his hand. Sparrow entered.

The ballroom had been transformed into a disaster. There was broken furniture, holes in the walls, papers littering the floor, food rotted on tables. Haphazard blankets had been hung over the floor to ceiling windows letting in streaks of ochre light.

The sound of water sloshing echoed in the giant room. Sparrow followed the noise, footsteps making hollow noise as he rounded a mountain of broken chairs piled ten feet high. Alastor was kneeling at an out of place tub, his head underneath the water.

Sparrow walked closer, waiting to see if the Demon was possessed or looking to die. He glanced at the time, at the slow bubbles rising from the tub. Either Alastor had more self-control that he'd ever seen or something else was holding him under. Sparrow would give him a few more seconds before intervening. He didn't want the Demon dead–Sparrow had too much to collect from him. They had a deal for a transaction of souls to rebuild Sparrow's kingdom and power. Sparrow was nearly there; his seat in Babylon had grown by leaps and bounds, he had a say in plenty of decisions these days. He had more power than his father ever dreamed of having. No, Sparrow couldn't risk the death of Alastor, he'd have to pull the Demon out of the water soon if the guy didn't do it himself.

Water flew through the air as Alastor whipped himself upright, his neck arching back, dark hair flying and spraying more water as he took a giant gulping breath. Water speckled the room and Sparrow's clothing.

"Are you stupid?" Sparrow asked.

Alastor laughed, water streaming from his hair, soaking his shirt. His chest expanded as he breathed deep, wiping off his face, then stood.

"More than stupid," Alastor finally said. He wasn't going to tell the Sparrow that the only way to stop Lucifer's voice was a near death experience. "What do you want?"

Sparrow wandered the once grand ballroom, taking in the desecration.

"I already sent the souls," Alastor said.

"You were short. A hundred less than last month." Sparrow scraped his heels as he walked, enjoying the sound against the elaborate tile flooring. "We have a deal."

"I have been preoccupied with this," Alastor said as he walked to a table with a map laid out.

"Questing?" Sparrow asked.

Alastor slammed his fists down on the table. "Lucifer wants his bones." He glanced at Sparrow, dark eyes desperate. "Do you know where they are?"

Sparrow clicked his tongue. "Afraid not." He smirked. Poor shit, Sparrow wasn't going to get involved in that horror show. "The souls."

"I'll get the numbers up again. Just as soon as I'm done here." Alastor moved to another table littered with glasses and liquor. He poured a half glass of bourbon like one would pour a glass of orange juice. He took a long swig before turning to Sparrow again. "I worked too hard to watch everything crash and burn again."

"We have a deal," Sparrow reminded Alastor.

"I know." Alastor paced, glass in hand. "You think I like being here? I don't. I want out. I want to be gone but I need those damn bones. No one has them. No one knows where they are." He pressed the glass to his forehead.

"I'm sure someone does," Sparrow said, biting his cheek. "Have you tried the Deacons?"

"They're all dead."

"Well that was a stupid decision." Sparrow tapped the map, rounded the table, and noted the markings. There were X's and scratches all over the parchment. It looked like Safe Houses and Hellion camps had been searched and checked off the list.

"Heard a rumor you caught Meg," Sparrow said, keeping his eyes on the map.

Alastor chuckled wickedly. "Wasn't that hard." He downed the rest of the bourbon. "Killing everyone around her was easy. She barely put up a fight."

"You killed everyone?" Sparrow's brow rose in interest. "Even her child?"

"There were no children in the castle. Searched every corner. Empty. Not even Shay nor that half-breed abomination."

"Haven't seen those two in a very long time," Sparrow muttered as he feigned interest in the map in an effort to distract him from the possibility of Meg's child being dead along with everyone else. The kid couldn't have been very old, barely a teenager by now. What a waste.

"But Meg's alive?" Sparrow asked.

"You could say that." Alastor headed toward the tub of water again.

"Babylon will be very interested in her."

"She's mine to deal with. I can't get rid of her until she tells me where Lucifer's bones are."

"She was unconscious when they were collected," Sparrow said.

"She knows where they are." Alastor knelt at the tub, ready to worship the silence. "He told me she knows."

Sparrow kept his tone even, relaying nothing in his words. "She is a trophy, one that Babylon would pay highly for."

Alastor took a deep breath, steadied himself on the edge of the tub and said, "Give me a minute."

Sparrow's brow and cheek ticked in curiosity. Once Alastor went under, shadows drifted from under Sparrow's black wings and around his feet. He paced the room, knowing he probably had a just a minute or two before Alastor came up for air and more conversation.

The sound of water splashing echoed. Sparrow mentally calculated Meg's worth in Babylon, nudging a pile of papers on the floor and controlling the tick that threatened to escape.

Alastor was drying his face with a towel this time as he walked toward Sparrow. "You want to see her?" he asked. "Meg in chains is a spectacle."

"Isn't she your niece?"

Alastor shrugged. "It's just a fact. Didn't say I wanted to screw her."

Something like rage flooded Sparrow's body at the thought of Alastor touching Meg. He had half an urge to wrap his hands around Alastor's neck and force him to retract the statement. Sparrow shivered. He couldn't lose his cool. Not now. Not after everything.

Alastor threw the towel across the room and it landed haphazardly on a chair. "Lucifer says hello."

Sparrow nodded. "Show me Meg."

He wanted to make sure she was alive and would remain alive. She'd be worth a lot to Babylon. Sparrow calculated the souls she'd be worth, the power he could get for brokering her delivery to Babylon.

Sparrow followed Alastor as he itched his scalp and muttered to himself. The poor fuck was losing his mind. Maybe Sparrow should help him find the bones and put the Demon out of his misery so he could get back to the skin trades and delivering souls to Sparrow's kingdom.

TWENTY-THREE

MEG

THERE ARE footsteps outside my cell. I don't have the energy to roll over and see who it is. The lack of blood has made me weak. Too weak. What I wouldn't do for a slice of pizza right now or a bag of blood. The dried blood on the floor is starting to look more appetizing by the minute. I glance at the dried blood and consider licking it off the floor.

The hinges of the door scream as it opens. Footsteps, a studder step. It's Alastor. I've recognized he can't walk more than a few steps these days without scraping his left foot across the floor. Something is wrong with him. He reminds me of a dog with fleas, always scratching his head and talking to himself. It seems the new King of Hell might have mange.

A small knife falls to the floor, landing in front of my face.

"Cut it off," Alastor says.

"My nose?" I ask, holding in a laugh, feeling as crazy as he is. Delusional even. I blame the lack of nutrition.

"The birthmark."

I roll to my back. "Not a tattoo or a scar or a limb. A birthmark." I look up at him and move my hands so the chains scrape across the stone floor.

Alastor's pointing to my upper thigh. "The birthmark. Cut it off," he demands. "I have a task for you and can't risk you disappearing on me."

My stomach clenches. I can't travel at will without fresh blood, I never considered the lack of the birthmark. It's small, looks like a snake eating its own head. The ouroboros gave me the power to flash between realms, but so did my father's blood. I am still Gabriel's daughter. Still the granddaughter of Lucifer. I take a deep breath, losing the birthmark might be nothing. Or, it could be *everything*.

Alastor kicks the knife closer to me. "Do it now. Stop wasting time." He paces a few steps. "Do it or I'll have one of my Hellions do it."

There's a growl from outside my cell. Something sinks in my gut. It sounds like the Hellions of old, the Hellions of Lucifer's rule. Those Hellions broke me, nearly killed me. Panic starts to rise in my chest, my throat feels full, and it's hard to swallow.

"Do it!" Alastor shouts.

"Fine." I sit up and grab the knife. What have I got to lose? My back aches from my broken wing. Only one side will fold in and lay flat, the other is twisted, the bone too far broke to reconnect and heal. If I had some blood it might heal itself. I grip the knife. Even if I make it out of here, I wouldn't get far with a broken wing and no blood, no ability to *poof* and travel at will. I'll be nothing but a mortal traipsing through Hell. I've been there once before.

"You gonna watch me take off my pants, you sick fuck?" I ask.

Alastor kicks me in the back, sharp pain erupts up my spine. "Do it. Or I'll stomp your good wing."

I shimmy out of my jeans, press the tip of the knife to the soft skin of my inner thigh, blood leaking. This is going to hurt like a bitch. But, I'll have a knife. It seems like a decent tradeoff considering my current situation.

I hiss at the pain of slicing my own skin. *This is nothing*, I tell myself, *you've lived through worse*. The birthmark is no bigger than a quarter but the hole in my thigh bleeds all over the floor.

"Give it," Alastor says.

I throw the skin at him and it lands on the floor by his shoes. He mutters something guttural as he bends down. Hellspeak. His fingertips ignite, burning the scrap of flesh in a minute.

"What was the significance of that?" I ask.

"Some thought it made you special. The ouroboros mark brings power. Now you're nothing special, no different than the rest of us monsters." Alastor looks down his nose at me. "Tragic, I could have made a killing off you in the skin trades, even with all those tattoos and scars. The higher Demons go feral for the trashy ones."

I'm paralyzed as he mouths off about how much he could sell me for, how many times, and to who. I try to remember their names so I know who to lock up first when I get on the other side of this ordeal.

Alastor waltzes out of the room. "Had you told me where his bones were..."

He never finishes, simply slams the door closed.

I tear a strip of fabric off my shirt and wrap it around the bleeding wound on my leg.

"Throw the knife toward the door," the Hellion says. "Stop the bleeding." The Hellion's tone changes and I know why. Fresh blood is difficult to ignore.

I was hoping they'd forget. I throw the knife overhand like a baseball and it lodges in the door, far from my reach. It stays there. No one opens the door to retrieve it.

I lay back on the stone floor and distract myself with memories of my children and consider where it all went wrong. Probably the moment I met Sparrow and trusted him with my life. Probably the second I fell in love with him.

Twenty-Four

Alastor sat on the old leather club chair, his fingers drumming rhythmically on the armrest. The disheveled ballroom was eerily silent, save for the occasional crackle of fire and the distant wails of the damned drifting up from the dungeon. The air was thick with the stench of brimstone, and shadows danced on the walls, cast by the flickering torches.

The grand doors creaked open and Sparrow strode in, his eyes scanning the room before settling on Alastor. He was relieved that the Demon wasn't kneeling before the porcelain tub attempting to drown by baptismal bath again. A smirk tugged at the corner of Sparrow's lips as he approached the throne, his steps echoing through the cavernous space.

"Each time I come here I am impressed by the disarray," Sparrow said, his voice laced with mock admiration. "Suits you well."

Alastor's lips curled into a thin smile. "It's good to see you. Finally someone who understands Lucifer's incessant nagging."

Sparrow chuckled, his eyes glinting with mischief. "Just

thought I'd drop by and see how the new King of Hell is settling in. And of course, I'm curious about your progress with Lucifer's bones."

Alastor's expression darkened slightly, but he maintained his composure. "The bones are... elusive. But I'm making progress. Every day I get closer to finding them."

Sparrow raised an eyebrow, his smirk widening. "Elusive, you say? I suppose it's not easy tracking down pieces of the devil himself. Any leads?"

Alastor's fingers stopped drumming, and he leaned forward slightly. "I will find them. It's only a matter of time."

Sparrow nodded thoughtfully, his gaze never leaving Alastor's. "And when you do, you'll have your freedom."

"Babylon wants her," Sparrow said, watching Alastor closely. The Demon looked like shit and that was unlike him. Alastor was always dressed well, groomed, and styled like a Wall Street businessman. Now his suit was tattered, dress shirt untucked and buttoned wrong.

"No," Alastor said. "They can't have her, not until she tells me where Lucifer's bones are."

"After all this time," Sparrow took a deep breath, "if she hasn't told you after everything you've done to her, she doesn't know."

"You pity her," Alastor said.

"Not her." Sparrow crossed his arms over his chest, annoyed. "You owe me souls. Another month has passed and the soul count dwindles." Sparrow tipped his chin down. "Meg is a valuable asset. Her soul could pay off quite a few debts, don't you think?"

Alastor's gaze hardened, and he leaned back in the leather chair. "Don't play games with me, Raven King. I know the value of her soul. But she's more than just a bargaining chip. She's a thorn in my side and I will deal with her accordingly."

Sparrow raised his hands in mock surrender. "Of course, of course. I wouldn't dream of questioning your methods."

Alastor's hands tore through his hair. "Lucifer won't release me until I find his bones and bring him back."

"We have a deal," Sparrow reminded him. It was more than a deal and Sparrow had yet to show Alastor the hold he had over the Demon thanks to Shay and Nero. He was saving that for when it was really needed, for a dire situation, for when Alastor was so far out of place he needed a full reset. "Maybe get her out of the dungeon, that might help," Sparrow suggested. "You need more portals, stop bottlenecking the influx." Sparrow strode to the map that Alastor had been studying. He pointed to the one portal that remained about thirty miles to the west. "If you built even two more, it would be like Lucifer's days. Free trade, free movement. With the Deacons gone, the Earthen plane is yours to pillage. More souls for all of us. You need to catch up."

Alastor shook his head to stop the voice and moved to the table. He should set up Hell to function smoother once Lucifer took over again.

Sparrow noted new Xs on the map. There were only two more Safe Houses that hadn't been checked for the bones.

Alastor was nodding in agreement to Sparrow's recommendation. The Demon didn't heed advice but his mental state was subpar these days. He'd probably jump out the window if Sparrow told him to.

"More portals are good. Meg destroyed most of them during the Fast-Zombie War." Alastor was nodding as he spoke, he rubbed his palms together. "I think I have an even better idea."

"If you need any assistance, I'm always here." Sparrow stepped back, ready to leave.

Alastor chuckled. "You're only slumming it down here

because you want your souls and that's it. Why don't you help me find the bones?" Alastor slammed his fist on the table.

"I don't know a thing about his bones. I wasn't here for that." Sparrow backed away.

Alastor watched him go, a mixture of suspicion and determination in his eyes. The ballroom fell silent once more, the weight of their conversation lingering in the air like a dark, unspoken menace.

TWENTY-FIVE

THE STRIP of fabric wrapped around my thigh has finally dried. I'm afraid to remove it. Afraid what little blood I have left will leak out and the Hellion outside my door will come inside looking for a meal.

I pick up my jeans and shake them. A few spiders scurry away. A shiver rolls up my spine. I could eat the spiders. I've eaten rats to survive. The thought leaves me as the dungeon door opens.

"Get dressed," Alastor orders. He crosses the room and releases my chains from the wall.

I stand and put my filthy jeans on, easing them over the wound on my thigh.

"Follow me," Alastor says, holding the chain like a leash.

"Where are you taking me?" I ask, stepping across the threshold of the cell for the first time in weeks. I get a glance at the Hellion standing guard and immediately wish I'd never looked.

He's pug-faced and warty with a headful of horns and sharp teeth curling out from his bottom lip.

I am led up the stairs and toward the door to the courtyard. The pug-faced Hellion follows closely and his presence makes me feel like I'm being chased by a boar.

Alastor opens the door to the courtyard. I see Hellsky for the first time in weeks. I raise a hand to shade my eyes against the ochre sun. It's not even that bright but my vision is acclimated to weeks of darkness.

I am taken to a Jeep and told to sit in the back, the chains around my wrists secured to a bolt in the floor. Alastor gets behind the wheel and pulls away from the castle. I turn, noticing another Jeep following. He drives down crumbling roads and past hordes of the dead, more than I've ever seen in this realm. I think of all the dead Deacons Alastor brought when he overtook the castle. I'm not one for worrying but these people don't deserve to be lost to Hell, they deserve their time to repent, for their souls to find peace in death. I scan the road and the forests, every turn, and every crumbling building. I wonder if Babylon has figured out what's going on here. What's taken them so long to investigate?

Alastor drives to a familiar place, a field where there used to be a portal. I destroyed it years ago with Skeele to prevent more of the Fast-Zombies from entering Hell.

Alastor stops the Jeep and gets out. He rounds the vehicle and opens my door, tugging me out by the chains.

"I have a little chore for you," Alastor says. He motions to the piles of blasted stone. "Fix it. Once you're done with this, there's more. All of the ones you destroyed. Maybe the physical labor and fresh air will help you remember where your grandfather's bones are buried."

"You want me to rebuild a portal, alone, with no food or drink?" I ask.

"No, you won't be alone." Alastor motions to the Jeep behind us.

A Hellion exits the driver side, walks to the back of the vehicle, and opens the door. Someone gets out and there's a sinking in my gut. I'm worried that it's someone close; one of the children or Shay. Alastor has always had a thing for Shay. Or Jed. He's always had a hard on to kill Jed. The door slams.

Breath catches in my throat as the figure rounds the Jeep. It's Chel. His wings are tattered, he's thin–too thin–and haggard. There are cuts to his face and chest, scars etched into his arms and legs.

The plummeting realization hits me that he never made it to the last portal when the siege on the castle began, he never found help.

Chel is chained around his wrists just the same as I am and now I wonder if those cries of torment I heard in the dungeon were his. He is the last of my Hellions. The last of anyone who might be on my side in this realm. I try my best to tamp down the small flutter of hope.

Alastor unlocks one of my shackles and one of Chel's, then connects the chains together.

"There ya go. Help." Alastor turns to look at me. "Big strong Hellion to help you lift the heavy rocks." He points to the road. "When you're done here, there's more to piece together."

There's shuffling in the forest.

"You're going to leave us out here with no weapons and the dead wandering? I am no longer the Queen of Hell, they'll come for us," I remind him.

Alastor shrugs. "You'll figure it out."

Alastor and his Hellion retreat to the Jeeps and drive away. I barely believe it. Fresh air, sunlight, near freedom.

Chel comes at me. His face is hard to read. I backstep. A sad smile escapes his lips as he folds both arms around me.

"I'm sorry," Chel says.

"Don't be sorry," I say. "We tried." I always hated being touched but nothing has ever felt more wonderful than Chel's arms squeezing me.

"I failed." Chel releases me, setting me on my feet.

I look away, ashamed. "I failed bigger. The biggest."

Chel sniffs the air before his eyes zero in on the blood soaking through my jeans. "You're injured. Did they…" his face drops. "What did they do to you?"

I force an uncomfortable laugh. "I'm fine. It's just… a wound. He made me cut off the birthmark."

Chel makes a face, not understanding.

"It helped me *poof*," I say. "I'm not sure if I'll ever be able to travel like that again."

Chel shrugs. "You're alive at least. That's all that matters."

"I'm not so sure." There's shuffling in the nearby forest. "Maybe we should be quiet until nightfall. Work when the dead are asleep."

"That would draw less attention." Chel scans the grassy area and the tree line. "I'd rather run away. Get to safety." He moves his arm and the chain clangs. "The other portal is not far."

I shake my head. "We are no longer safe in Hell. Did you see Alastor's Hellions?" I swallow hard, remembering. "Those are the worst kind."

"I know," Chel says. "My father was one."

A moment passes between us. He glances at my left wing. "What happened there?"

"Too broken to heal." I look away, trying to ignore the throbbing in my leg and my back, my head and my heart.

"Want me to do something for it? Do you want my blood?" He holds out his arm.

I glance back at him, lifting my arm so the chain connecting us clatters. "Nah, we got bigger fish to fry." I move closer to the giant pieces of cement and rock that were once a portal to cross into other realms. "How long do you think it will take us to do this?"

"A few days." He glances at me. "How weak are you?"

"I'm fine," I lie. The thought of drinking from him, of risking the bloodlust, of risking a blood bond, makes me want to vomit. I can't do that again. It's too dangerous. I'd rather die or be eaten by the dead than go down that road again.

We sit in the tall grass and wait for nightfall. Nearby a horde of the dead all fall with a *thump*, asleep at last.

"Let's get to work," I say, moving to stand. My left wing falls, grinding bone against soil, stretching the thickly scarred skin. I hiss in pain.

"You gotta fix that," Chel warns.

"Someday. If Alastor doesn't kill me first."

I start moving rocks, arranging them in the arch and matching up the runes like a giant puzzle.

"Alastor won't kill you, Meg," Chel says. "You're worth too much to all the realms." He groans, lifting a large chunk of the portal and moving it into place.

"I think you're wrong." I'm glad for the darkness so he can't see my expressions.

TWENTY-SIX

Sparrow treaded cautiously through the shadowed corridors of Babylon, his footsteps echoing softly against the stone walls that delineated his realm from Gabriel's. Once, he and Teari had been allies, bound by friendship and a shared purpose. But that was before Sparrow's betrayal, before he'd chosen a darker path that led him away from those he once called friends.

Teari approached, walking instead of flying. Sparrow's heart raced with uncertainty. He knew he was treading on dangerous ground, seeking aid from someone he'd wronged so grievously.

Sparrow announced his presence with a heavy foot fall, his voice barely more than a whisper. Teari startled, her expression a mask of cool indifference.

"Raven King," Teari greeted, her voice tinged with a hint of disdain. "To what do I owe the pleasure of your visit?"

"I need your help."

Teari's eyebrow arched in skepticism. "My help?" she

repeated, her tone laced with sarcasm. "I went to you for help and you slammed the door in my face."

Sparrow stepped back, remembering the day Teari sought him out. The Raven King had plenty of dark days in which he struggled to step into the light. Unfortunately, she had approached him on one of those days.

"I have a question," Sparrow said.

"Okay." Teari's gaze softened slightly, though suspicion still lingered in her eyes. "I have places to be," she warned. "Hurry up."

Sparrow met Teari's gaze. "What is the treatment for drinking blood from the walking dead?"

"Who would do that?" Teari asked, unbelieving he'd have the audacity to ask her such a thing.

"Consider it a hypothetical."

"Did you do that?" Teari's eyes went wide as she inspected him closely. "Did you?"

"Not me."

Teari didn't like where this conversation was going. If it wasn't Sparrow then it was someone he knew or wanted to poison.

"Do you know the cure?" Sparrow asked again.

"You could ask your kingdom's healer," Teari said.

Sparrow exhaled an annoyed breath. "I don't have one."

"Sounds like a problem," she scoffed. Teari glanced over her shoulder, hoping no one caught her speaking with Sparrow. She didn't want Gabriel to know and lose his trust in her. She'd worked too hard for Gabriel to do that. "Look, I'm busy. I have to go."

A hand reached out to stop her. "What do you want for the information?" Sparrow finally asked.

"Where is Meg?" Teari asked.

Sparrow's lips pressed together in a tight line. "Who is that?"

"You should do better," Teari warned.

Sparrow rushed towards her, his face an inch from her nose, shadows and anger swelled around his body. "You know nothing," he seethed. "Not a single thing. Don't stand there with your white wings and pride and think you are so much better than me." His hands had curled into fists and he shifted his big body, wanting to strangle her where he stood.

"No, Sparrow," Teari replied flatly. "It's you who know nothing." She turned on her heel and stepped across the boundary to Gabriel's kingdom. Guilt flooded her when she realized someone might actually be suffering. "Tincture of time is your answer," she shouted over her shoulder. "There is no other cure."

TWENTY-SEVEN

Nightingale, Noah, and Thrush exited the fountain in the center of Babylon. Noah turned, taking in his surroundings.

"Do ethereal creatures belong here?" Noah asked.

"I don't care," Nightingale replied. "Follow me." She skated over the water, turning to a stop before stepping down from the fountain.

"Why you always gotta skate all fancy-like?" Noah asked Nightingale, appreciating the short shorts. "Why can't you just walk like the rest of us schmucks?"

"Because it's boring," Nightingale replied with an unimpressed tone.

Thrush stepped over the ledge of the fountain, his soaked clothing leaving puddles as he walked. His parents were dry, like they'd never been submerged. Thrush followed the two toward a stone walkway. The lingering Angels of Babylon began noticing them and moving closer.

What Thrush couldn't see was the steam rising off his body like smoke, he didn't notice the smell of woodsmoke and pine. He didn't smell like Heaven, he smelled like Hell and everyone within a certain radius noticed. He didn't belong there and it was blatantly obvious.

Thrush took in every motion of the surrounding crowd that had gathered to watch them. Thrush hadn't been to the Seven Kingdoms of Heaven since he was an infant. He wasn't sure what to expect, but he'd been trained by the strongest Hellions in Meg's court so he didn't miss one hand movement, one step fall, or one motion in his periphery. He gripped the small blade at his hip and adjusted the bag on his shoulder. He wondered if they'd try and attack. Sure that he could take out a handful of them by himself, he worried if anyone would come to their rescue if an Angel attack overwhelmed him. He glanced at his parents. They'd have to draw on their Astral magic to protect him. Thrush hid his limp, not favoring his sore ankle that had twisted during their escape. He didn't want the Angels to notice any weakness.

"How far?" Noah asked.

"Maybe twenty minutes," Nightingale slowed to walk next to Thrush, his clothes drying quickly under the heat of Heaven's skies. The sun was intense.

They stopped at the gates leading to the Raven King's lands.

"Brother," Nightingale called. "Let us in, please."

Sparrow appeared in the distance, walking down a long winding driveway, toward the gate. Nightingale was shocked at the sight of her brother. It had been years since she'd last seen him. He'd given them peace in Meg's realm, promised ceasefire. The smirk on his face led Nightingale to believe that everything was about to change.

Sparrow stood at the gate, his hand resting on the lock.

"Shouldn't you both be in the Ethereal realm?" he looked from Nightingale to Noah before his eyes landed on Thrush.

"Let us in," Nightingale said.

"Just send the boy," Sparrow's eyes narrowed on Thrush. "He's due for training. He needs to be prepared for his future now that you've changed sides. He's been away from his rightful home for too long."

Nightingale called upon the same ethereal power she used to defeat the Nightjar. She began to illuminate, drawing light from the sun until her body glowed brightly.

"Neat trick," Sparrow said as he unlocked the gate and pushed it open.

"Raven King," Nightingale said. "This land is as much his as it is yours. This is family land. We are refugees of war."

Sparrow stepped back and motioned for them to enter. "What happened to Hell?" Sparrow glanced at her scarred cheek.

"We've been banished," Nightingale said, her voice cold. She had an urge to remind her brother that the scars came from her death, bitten in the neck and face by the Fast-Dead.

Noah glared at Sparrow. "I remember a time when you weren't such a dick."

The corner of Sparrow's mouth tipped up in a half smile. Noah took that as a good sign. Maybe under Sparrow's dark façade he wasn't so different. Noah had seen the masks Meg had to wear as the Queen of Hell. There was a time that Sparrow and Noah were friends when Sparrow was doing his time as a Hellion and remained devoted to Meg. Times had changed. Still, it was hard for Noah to understand what Sparrow had turned into after all these years. He'd went from quirky and fun to dark and serious.

The lock to the gate clicked closed. Nightingale turned. "Thrush, this is your uncle Sparrow," Nightingale motioned to the Raven King.

Sparrow held out a hand toward Thrush. "Haven't seen you since you were a baby. You're practically grown now."

Thrush placed his hand in Sparrow's, wary with his free hand on the hilt of his hidden knife.

Sparrow glanced to the boy's hip and noted the weapon. One brow rose in interest. "Seems you've had some training."

Thrush smiled and it was just as dark as Sparrow's. Thrush wouldn't hesitate to draw a weapon, didn't want his uncle to think he had the upper hand, King or not.

"Don't mind Sparrow," Nightingale warned. "He went crazy a few times. But you can thank him for breaking the family curse." Nightingale touched the back of Thrush's head. "He's the reason why you aren't cracked in the head like the rest of us."

"Jury's still out on if it was a curse." Sparrow released Thrush's hand and began walking, black wings scraping the road in a constant *shhhhhh*.

Nightingale gave Sparrow a dirty look, and Noah stayed protectively close to Thrush.

A house appeared in the distance. These were not the family lands Nightingale remembered. Their home was gone, destroyed in the Fast-Zombie War. That was also where Nightingale died, bit in the neck by the dead. Then Jack, Noah's brother, was bit. Meg rescued Thrush–kidnapped him really–and brought him to Hell.

Nightingale held back emotion. Returning to this place brought back too many memories and the realization of missed time after she'd died and strangers were left to raise her child. Nightingale moved closer to Thrush as they neared the house.

"I wasn't expecting guests," Sparrow said as he opened the door to the house. "Wait here while I have one of the surrounding cabins prepared."

Nightingale noted it wasn't as grand as their father's house.

There were fewer levels, it reminded her of a large cabin. She wondered if the underground levels where their father had kept her locked up for most of her life remained. Nightingale decided she wouldn't ask right now, maybe later.

Noah got Nightingale's attention. "Do you think this is safe?" he mouthed.

"It's all we've got." She focused on Thrush. "We can't take our son to the Ether and the Earthen plane is too dangerous." Nightingale shuddered at the thought of going to Babylon and begging another Archangel to give them sanctuary. She might be dead but she had some pride still.

———

Sparrow led them to a small cabin not far from the main house. "Make yourselves at home," he said as he opened the door and entered. "Some things are similar to the way father ran the kingdom. The fridge will remain stocked. Clothes cleaned." He turned to look at Thrush. "You can start training with the Legion in the morning."

Thrush nodded. His ankle throbbed and he couldn't wait to put it up and rest.

"Are the training grounds in the same location?" Nightingale asked.

Sparrow nodded. "Welcome home, sister and family." He closed the door and left them alone.

Noah exhaled a large sigh. "Jesus Christ," his eyes were wide as he focused on Nightingale, "is it always this suffocating here? Everything is so quiet and proper and stoic and hot." He ran hands through shaggy blonde hair. "How did you survive this most of your life?"

Nightingale smirked. "Now you see why I was so eager to follow Meg to Hell. And don't worry, it will only get worse. You've only met one person so far."

"Yeah but there's a *vibe*." Noah rolled his eyes before nudging Thrush. "You doin' okay with all this?"

Thrush shrugged. "The Raven King sees me as a threat."

"No, no," Nightingale soothed. "He's just had his brains scrambled too many times." She rubbed Thrush's arms trying to calm him.

"Maybe we should have taken our chances with Alastor," Thrush suggested before saying, "I'm gonna find my room."

Thrush walked away from his parents to explore the cabin.

"He's just a teenage boy," Noah said to Nightingale. "We just took him away from the only home he's ever known. And the only friends he's ever had."

Nightingale never had any friends as a child so she couldn't relate much, but she nodded remembering the joy she felt when Meg visited that first time.

———

THRUSH FOUND a room in the back of the cabin. There was a large window that faced the forest and a private bathroom. He threw his bag on the floor before bending to unpack his things. He pulled out the books, wishing he'd wrapped them in something waterproof. The pages were soggy and limp. He set them out to dry and hoped they'd regain their original shape. He shook out his clothing and hung them to dry. Opening a small, zippered pocket, he took out a charcoal pencil and a pouch of salt and a small notebook with spells. The notebook hadn't fared so well after getting wet. He gripped the charcoal pencil and flipped through the pages, landing on a rune he knew quite well. He closed his eyes, remembering the door casings of their home in Hell. Then he began to etch the door and the window casings with charcoal. When he was done, he took out one of the small blades given to him by the Hellions and began carving runes into the wood of the cabin. Thrush wasn't about to risk his life to the Raven King's lands.

TWENTY-EIGHT

WE FINISH the portal in two days. Just as Chel is fitting the keystone into place, the sound of tires crunching on concrete approaches.

Chel groans as he drops the stone into place. The runes illuminate for a moment and a transparent sheen wavers between the arch.

"Strong work," I try to joke with Chel, but it comes out sounding patronizing. "Sorry, I'm tired."

Chel nods, understanding. Neither of us have eaten. We found crabapples at the tree line but they were sour and hard to bite. Neither of us wanted the gut ache that would come from eating them.

We turn and watch the vehicles approach. They park nearby and Alastor and one of his Hellions walk toward us.

Alastor slow claps. "You did it in record time. Keep up this pace and we'll have all the portals up and functioning again." He reaches in his pocket and pulls out two vials. "A reward for your hard work."

I glance at Chel. Alastor is holding out two vials of blood. My mouth waters. I don't even care where the blood came from, I'm so hungry I'd drink blood from a worm, if worms had blood. I don't know if they do, but if they did, I'd drain them.

We each take a vial.

"Drink up," Alastor says. "You'll need your strength for the next portal."

We both pop the top off the vials, thirsty, hungry, parched beyond what we've ever been in a long time. It's not a lot of blood for either of us, just enough to wet our tongues and keep moving.

Chel drops his vial, his hand moving to his throat. He turns to look at me, panic in his eyes. "It's from the dead," he chokes out.

Dread hits me. I already drank mine, threw it back like a shot of whiskey. My stomach punches and bile rides up my throat. I bend over and vomit. Thin blood drips on the dirt. I rub my face and feel wetness as blood runs from my nose and eyes and ears. My head feels foggy and full. I drop to the ground, and easy on my left wing I force myself to fall face first into the grass. The ground vibrates as Chel drops, both of us gagging and choking and bleeding from our eyes.

Alastor laughs. "Are you ready to tell me where your grandfather's bones are now?"

I can't speak, can't make a noise. I can only gurgle and decide it's not worth trying to reply to him.

Alastor watches us writhe in pain. And when the worst of it has passed, Alastor's Hellion drags us to the back of his Jeep and tosses us in.

WE ARE DROPPED at the next broken portal site still barely functioning. My head feels like exploding, my throat is on fire, my stomach is churning. I didn't really believe it when I was told blood from the dead would make me sick.

"Get this done," Alastor motions to the rocks on the ground.

Not long after they leave, Chel is able to sit up, still gagging and retching. He takes deep breaths, apologizes when he lifts his arm and it jerks the chain attached to my wrist.

"It's okay," I mutter, moving to sit.

There are shuffling footsteps moving closer.

"They must like the sound of me puking." Chel stands, ready to fight.

I move to my feet, still feeling woozy. There's three of the dead headed our way. There's no way we can run.

"I got them," Chel says, "you stay behind me."

I reach for my blade, cursing when my hand comes in contact with my jean-clad thigh. My blade was lost after the battle in the Hellion lair.

A dead man wanders closer, mouth open and ready to bite. Chel steps forward and punches the man in his throat so hard his head snaps to the side and he drops to the ground.

He does this twice more and I think of how nice it would have been to have Chel around last time I was wandering Hell as nothing but a lost soul all those years ago. He makes killing the walking dead look easy.

"Look," I point to one of the corpses on the ground. The guy looks like he was a lumberjack or something with his flannel shirt and Carhart pants. "He has a hatchet."

Chel crouches down, grabs the hatchet and rips it free of the zombie. "This could come in handy."

"Yeah," I nod in agreement. "I'd like to chop off Alastor's head with it."

Chel chuckles. "Maybe." He turns to look at the ruins of the portal then glances at the chain linking us together. "Let's do this now, faster."

"What are you thinking?" I ask.

"Thinking like I'm already over this shit."

"Same."

We make fast work of the portal. Thankfully the chunks of rock are bigger. We finish by the time the moon is high in Hellsky. Then we stand side by side, watching the portal come to life.

Chel bends and picks up the hatchet from where he set it while we were working.

"What are you doing?" I ask.

"We can't stay chained together like this," Chel says, gripping the handle of the hatchet.

I lift my arm, jingling the chain. "Not possible. I don't have a key."

He crouches, laying his arm on the ground, his other hand gripping the hatchet. "In a moment it will be."

In a swift movement, Chel cuts off his hand.

"What the fuck!" I shout at him. "You could have warned me."

He stands, groaning, blood spurting. "You would have told me not to." He nods toward the portal. "You go first."

I hold up my arm and his lost hand falls from the shackle. "Do you want your hand?"

Chel picks it up and tucks it in his pocket as his arm bleeds profusely. He stumbles.

"You need to go first," I say. "You need to go to the Earthen plane. To the Peabody Library."

"What's there?" he asks.

"Friends." I lay a hand on his shoulder and push him toward the portal. "Go. I'll follow."

"You go next, Meg." He's watching me closely. "As soon as I'm gone, you better step through this portal."

I nod. "I will."

He glances at me one last time, a sickly pallor taking over his skin.

"Go," I urge.

"You did everything you could do," Chel says and then he steps through the portal.

I shiver, pushing away the thought that this was too easy. The sound of wings flapping fills the night sky. A Hellion hovers nearby. I catch a glimpse of its shadow.

I stand alone, moving away from the portal, the weight of the chain attached to my arm a constant reminder of the battles to come. The air is still, the eerie silence a prelude to the chaos that's about to hit me head on.

The sky darkens further, the Hellion's shadow eclipsing the ochre sun. I look up, squinting against the glare. The Hellion plummets from the sky, wings spread wide, moving with terrifying speed.

I brace myself, twisting my wrist to wrap the chain in my palm. It clinks ominously as I wrap it tighter in my grip. The Hellion lands with a thunderous crash, the force of its impact sending a shockwave through the ground and nearly knocking me off my feet. Dust and debris swirl around us creating a momentary veil obscuring the Hellion's form.

Memories of Lucifer's Hellions rush me and a cold shiver of fear runs up my spine. I never stood a chance against those monsters, and definitely not now. This Hellion is massive, easily twice my height with skin like charred stone and eyes that burn with a hellish fire. It roars a sound that reverberates through my bones. It takes a step toward me, blade ready and claws extended, ready to rend flesh.

I don't give it a chance, I strike first with a swift motion I swing the chain in a wide arc, aiming for its kneecaps. The chain whistles through the air like a deadly serpent of iron and fury. It connects with the Hellion's knee, hitting that soft spot in the back of the leg, causing the Hellion's leg to give. It stumbles but quickly regains footing, snarling with rage.

"You're going to have to do better than that," I taunt, yanking the chain.

The Hellion lunges at me, claws and blade slashing through the air. I duck and roll to the side, narrowly avoiding its deadly strike.

I spring to my feet, using the momentum to swing the chain again, this time aiming higher. The chain wraps around the Hellion's arm. I pull with all my might but I'm not much of a match for the beast. It's muscles bulge and it snaps sharp teeth in my direction.

With a roar of defiance, the Hellion yanks its arm free, the force of the motion sending me sprawling to the ground, knocking the wind out of me. I struggle to catch my breath and taste blood as my lip splits against the rough terrain.

The Hellion is on me in an instant, blade descending in a deadly arc. Guess Chel was wrong, they don't mind me being dead.

I roll to the side and the Hellion's blade hits dirt. I swing the chain again, aiming for its neck. It wraps around his throat and I pull with all my might, using the chain to leverage myself to my feet.

The Hellion chokes, eyes blazing with fury.

"You're strong," I say, tightening my grip on the chain. "But I once fought a dog for a peanut butter and jelly sandwich; this isn't much different. I've had practice."

The Hellion stops clawing at the chain around its neck and smiles at me before reaching for the chain.

My eyes go wide and a sickening feeling rushes my stomach as I see his wings spread wide. He bends his knees and launches himself into the sky, dragging me along.

I only have one functioning wing and this Hellion is fast. He wraps his wrist around the chain and swings me to the side. Soon it's like I'm on a carnival ride and ready to lose my lunch, except I never ate lunch and this is absolute bullshit.

The Hellion's wings flash up and he starts dropping. He's ready to smash me onto the ground. My stomach flip-flops. I spread one wing to lessen the blow. I try to stretch the other, groaning against the pull of broken bone, damaged tendons, and aching muscle. I'm not fast enough.

The Hellion yanks the chain and slams me onto my back next to the portal. My vision blurs as I look up at Hellsky. Blood drips from my lip and ears. I steel myself for whatever comes next as I hear the Hellion drop the chain to the ground with a heavy thud. Yes, Chel was very wrong. This Hellion is going to finish me.

There's a noise beside me, a whisper. My vision blurs and I see blobs of black. I think I have a concussion, maybe even brain damage because I see a hand reaching through the portal, wrap around my wrist, and pull me through just as everything turns to black.

TWENTY-NINE

Shay stood in the grassy plains of Montana, the vast expanse of open sky stretching endlessly above her. The air was crisp, it smelled like wildflowers and pine and snow, a stark contrast to the scent of creosote and woodsmoke of Hell's atmosphere. Shay felt the familiar reins in her hands, and beneath her, the powerful, steady presence of Nero.

She urged Nero into a gentle trot, the rhythmic thudding of his hooves a soothing melody. The landscape rolled out before her, serene and untouched, a haven of peace that she longed to hold onto. In the distance, she recognized the family ranch, warm and inviting. So unlike the way she'd left it; saturated with blood and gore, zombies and her parents buried in shallow graves in the pasture. This was another memory. This was how her parents would want her to remember their home. The sun cast a golden glow over everything, making the world shimmer with warmth and light.

As they rode, Shay felt a deep sense of contentment wash over her. This was home, always would be, a place where her worries seemed to dissolve into the gentle breeze. She leaned forward, running a hand along Nero's strong neck, feeling the smoothness of his coat and the strength of his muscles.

"Good boy," she whispered.

But as they rode further, the dream began to shift. The sky darkened, clouds gathered ominously. Shay felt a chill creep into the air. Nero's ears flicked back, sensing the change. Shay glanced around, trying to pinpoint the source of her unease, hoping that the dead nor Alastor's Demons were coming to infect her dream.

It was then Shay saw her–Nightingale–standing alone in the middle of the field, her presence both startling and familiar. The ethereal glow that surrounded her cast an eerie light, making her stand out against the darkening sky.

Nero disappeared and Shay was on her feet. Her boots crunched on the dry grass as she approached Nightingale.

"What are you doing here?" Shay asked. "This is my dream."

"You gave me permission a long time ago. And... I need your help. I'm searching for Meg." Nightingale's gaze locked onto Shay's and the dream world seemed to hold its breath.

"Meg?" Shay asked.

The dream began to collapse, the world around them faded into darkness. There was a pounding sound that echoed.

Shay woke, startled. Jed was already moving out of bed and pulling a shirt on.

"Someone is at the door," Jed warned. His fingertips flexed and sparks flew.

The pounding continued, more frantic now. Jed approached the door cautiously, sparks flying from his fingers, a battle spell on the tip of his tongue. He motioned for Shay to stay back, then bent and made a marking on the floor.

No one had come to the door of the abandoned Peabody Library since they'd lived here. The building was warded with protection spells, even more since they'd taken Meg's children into hiding.

"Who is it?" Jed asked, unsure if the person knocking could hear him through the hundred's years old wooden door.

"Chel," a gruff voice replied.

Shay's eyes went wide. "Open it," she said.

Jed pulled the heavy door open, and a shadowy figure, hunched and clutching something to his chest, lingered a moment before stepping inside.

"Holy shit," Chel said. "This is where you two have been hiding?"

Jed slammed the door closed, locking it and drawing new runes. It was the first time they'd opened the door and he hoped the last. Jed didn't want the humans of the Earthen plane noticing that the library wasn't really abandoned.

Chel stumbled and fell to his knees inside the rune circle on the floor, stuck. Blood dripped from his right wrist. His hand was missing and there was no bandage to stop the bleeding.

Shay gasped, rushing to Chel's side, "What happened?"

Chel's face was pale, pain and fear etched into every line. "Alastor chained us together. He made us rebuild the portals. It was the only way to free Meg." He glanced at the door. "She should have been right behind me."

Jed broke the rune circle on the floor, releasing Chel. The Hellion tipped over on his side and rolled to his back with a groan.

"Um," Shay picked up the giant hand that had fallen out of his pocket. "Is this your hand?" she asked with a gulp.

"Oh yeah," Chel chuckled faintly. "I used a hatchet to cut it off. You should've seen Meg's face."

"Alastor didn't do this to you?" Jed asked.

Chel made a noise of exasperation. "Hell no. I did it." He was staring at the door, expectantly. "She was supposed to be directly behind me. She made me go first." He closed his eyes.

"There's blood everywhere," Shay said.

"The castle is overrun. There's no one left," Chel said, blinking slowly.

Jed kneeled next to Chel, he took the severed hand and lined it up with Chel's wrist, then he chanted words that sounded like beach sand sifting between rocks and shells on a cold night. Tendrils of healing magic sprung from his fingertips and began mending Chel's severed limb. It staunched the bleeding and began knitting the blood vessels, muscle and bone back together.

Chel winced in pain.

"Sorry," Jed muttered between words.

Shay took Chel's free hand, her touch gentle but firm. "You're safe here, for now," she assured him. "We'll figure out the next move together."

Jed looked at Shay, their eyes meeting in silent understanding. This wasn't just about Chel or Meg, the war in Hell was spilling over into the Earthen plane, and they couldn't ignore it any longer. They had precious cargo to keep safe. More creatures were on the Earthen plane than ever before now that word had spread about the double auras. And now there was a Hellion, battered and broken. Shay glanced at his tattered leathery wings. They shouldn't be visible on the Earthen plane, but Shay was looking right at them which meant the Veil was thinning considerably.

"Can you get the med kit?" Jed asked Shay.

She nodded and got up to retrieve it, her mind racing.

Chel closed his eyes, finally allowing himself a moment of respite. He took deep breaths, opening his eyes again when Shay settled next to him and passed Jed items from the med kit. Jed wrapped Chel's wrist and hand then splinted it. Chel gave him a questioning look.

"The magic is good, but I've never done that before." He folded Chel's arm against the Hellion's chest. "Just to be safe. You'll be sore."

Chel wiggled his fingers. "Seems to have worked."

Light footsteps shuffled from behind a bookshelf.

"Who's there?" Shay asked, squinting in the darkness.

The girl walked out; Rue with her dark hair mussed and pajamas wrinkled. "I heard voices."

Chel's eyes went wide and he struggled to sit up. "Are they both here?"

Jed pressed a hand on Chel's shoulder, preventing him from getting up. "Easy."

"You shouldn't be out here," Shay warned. "What if it was a Demon, one of the bad ones?"

Rue stared at Chel. "But I know him. He's not bad."

Tears glistened in the old Hellion's eyes as he reached toward Rue. "Your momma hid you well. Is your brother here also?"

Rue nodded. "He's asleep. He'll sleep through anything."

Jed made a face. "The only problem is, now you're stuck here too."

"No," Chel argued. "I have to get back out there and find Meg."

Jed shook his head. "No, you're not leaving until we have some more answers. Meg didn't want a soul to know about this place. Now you're here."

"She sent me here. She said I'd find friends." Chel rubbed his face with his good hand.

"Can't risk it," Jed said, magic crackling from his fingertips. "We don't have the resources to fight Hell's war here. We'll find another way to get Meg."

Chel nodded, understanding.

Jed placed a reassuring hand on Chel's shoulder. "Rest. Recover."

————

SHAY SAT in a quiet corner of the Peabody Library, the soft glow of the lamp illuminating the pages of the ancient tome spread out before her. Across the table, Jed was meticulously organizing a stack of scrolls by order of spells, his brow furrowed in concentration. Chel, meanwhile, paced back and forth near the window, his eyes scanning the darkening street outside.

"It's too quiet," Chel muttered, breaking the silence. "I don't like it."

Jed looked up, a flicker of concern crossing his face. "We can't afford to let our guard down," he agreed. "Especially not now." He glanced at the children sitting near the fire.

Shay sighed, closing her book with a thud. "I just feel like I'm waiting for the next disaster," she said, her voice tinged with frustration.

Chel paced closer to the table where Shay was reading, paused, and watched Rue and Remington near the fire, engrossed in their own studies.

"Shay," Chel began, his voice low but insistent. "What's with the tattoos on the kids?"

Shay looked up, her brow furrowing. "What about them?"

Chel lowered his voice. "They didn't have tattoos the last time I saw them in Hell. Those are powerful runes, not something to be used lightly, especially on children."

"We had no choice," Shay said. "They went outside and their auras drew the attention of every Demon nearby. It was like a beacon, alerting every dark creature to their presence on the Earthen plane."

Jed had moved closer, hearing the conversation. "The runes are the only way to protect them, to dampen their light enough to keep them hidden from those who seek to harm them."

Chel frowned, crossing his arms over his chest. "Do they know the significance of the runes? Do they understand why they were marked?"

"They understand," Jed replied. "They're okay."

Shay turned the page of her book. "Just because they're smaller than you does not mean they're babies. They understand. If they lived here they'd be away from their parents more than half the day at school and activities. Heck, you helped train them and took Remington on missions."

Chel's gaze softened slightly as he looked at the children, who were oblivious to the weight of the conversation happening around them. "You're right. They just look so small."

"They're not," Shay reminded him.

Chel exhaled a breath. "If the runes fail or the Demons find another way to track them, we'll need more than just tattoos to keep them safe."

Jed nodded, his expression grim. "For now the runes are our best defense. We'll do whatever it takes to protect them, even if it means facing down every Angel and Demon that crosses into this plane."

Chel's gaze lingered on the children for a moment longer before he turned back to Shay and Jed. "Let's hope it doesn't come to that. But if it does, you'll have my support. We'll protect them together."

Rue was suddenly standing next to Chel. He jumped, startled at her presence.

"Did you see my mother before you came?" Rue asked. "Is she alive?"

Chel kneeled so they were eye to eye. "I did see her." He held Rue's hands, remembering how small they once were, recognizing that she was indeed older and sturdier than the toddler he'd held upright while she learned to walk. "She is alive. We'll get her back," he promised.

Rue was staring into the Hellion's eyes, searching for truth like children do. "Is she hurt?"

"A tiny bit. Just a scratch." Chel shook his head. "She's strong. She'll be better soon."

"How do you know?" Rue frowned. "We should go find her together."

"Well, our friends here are going to keep you and your brother safe." Chel was running out of things to say. He was a Hellion after all, not gifted in the use of neutral language.

Rue released Chel's hands and walked away, muttering something about not being a baby anymore.

"Haven't felt that in a while," Shay said, glancing to Jed, her expression resolute.

Jed and Chel exchanged a worried glance.

Jed reached out and grasped her arm, his eyes filled with concern. "Be careful, Shay-baby," he urged, his voice a whisper to the children couldn't hear. "We don't know who or what we're dealing with."

Shay nodded, her heart pounding in her chest. "I will," she promised. With one last look at her friends Shay and Nero were pulled away and disappeared, the library's warmth replaced by the chill of the unknown.

———

SHAY AND NERO stood at the crossroads in a dark forest, the moon the only light. Shrouded by mist and shadow, the oppressive silence was broken only by the distant howl of a wolf in the mountains. As if on cue, a sudden chill spread over Shay and the faint smell of sulfur wafted through the air. Shay's eyes widened as a dark figure materialized outside the rune circle that had drawn them. A Demon appeared with eyes like burning coals and a sinister grin that sent shivers down her spine.

The Demon hissed, its voice like nails on a chalkboard.

"Who summons?" Shay demanded, her voice steady despite the fear gnawing at her insides. She didn't like when Demons called her. She was reminded of her time with Alastor and the feelings of helplessness and it chipped away at the confidence she typically presented at the Crossroads.

The Demon's grin widened. "A new player in the game," it replied cryptically. "One who wishes to discuss matters of great importance. Alastor's debts are of particular interest."

Without another word, the Demon vanished. Shay gripped Nero's mane, her jaw set with determination.

As the mist cleared, a figure became visible. Standing in the center of the road was a Demon unlike any she had seen before, tall with dark, leathery wings and eyes that glowed like molted gold.

"Hello, Shay," the Demon greeted, its voice smooth and malevolent. "I remember you from the black mansion. Lost my bid to that blubbering fool Krelp." His eyes roamed her body. "I should have bid higher. It's been too long since I laid my eyes on something so delectable."

The mere mention of Krelp made Shay want to vomit. She shivered, remembering his slimy tongue on her body and his teeth piercing her flesh. Shay squared her shoulders, refusing to show any sign of weakness. "What do you want, Demon?"

The Demon chuckled, a sound that sent a chill down her spine. "I am Asmodeus," it replied. "And I seek to take over Alastor's skin trades. He is behind on his deliveries and his failures cannot go unpunished."

Shay's eyes narrowed. "And why involve me?"

Asmodeus stepped closer, his eyes piercing into hers. "Because you can help me and in return I will ensure your safety *forever*."

"That's not how this works," Shay said. "You ask for something, we make the deal."

Nero whinnied in reinforcement of what Shay had said.

Asmodeus stepped closer, the toes of his wingback shoes uncomfortably close to the rune. He leaned forward and whispered. "I heard a rumor about an aura–two auras really– that could be seen between realms." His hands flashed open. "Lit up the sky. The creatures who crossed the Veil can't stop talking about it. There's so much excitement and questioning and *want*!"

"I don't know what you're talking about," Shay said as Nero tipped his head down, ready to breathe fire and burn up Asmodeus for merely mentioning the auras.

A sinister smile split Asmodeus' lips. "Your Demon horse walks the Earthen plane, I'm sure not much happens there without you both knowing."

"The Earthen plane is quite large," Shay said as Nero fidgeted, moving two steps within the rune circle. "Plenty goes on without our knowledge."

"If you say so," Asmodeus said.

"Present your ask or we're leaving." Shay was fed up with the amount of time the Demon was wasting.

"I want the skin trades of Hell."

Shay shook her head. "Can't do that. Alastor and the skin trades are tied up with another Crossroads deal."

Nero whinnied in agreement, wary of the Demon.

Asmodeus's brows rose with this revelation. The gold rings

and chains of the Crossroads Demon glinted and caught Asmodeus's eye.

"How did you become the Crossroads Demon?" Asmodeus asked. "It's a powerful position for a human."

Shay stroked Nero's neck. "Nero is the real Demon. I'm simply his sidekick," Shay said.

Asmodeus studied the duo and Shay didn't like his gaze one bit. "We'll be in touch," Asmodeus said, scuffing his shoe across the markings on the road to release Shay and Nero, before walking backward into the mist and shadows.

Shay leaned down, doing her best to maintain composure. "Run," she whispered to Nero.

Nero shivered, controlling the urge to turn into something else knowing that the threat of Asmodeus was still nearby. He turned and galloped away.

Shay didn't like the prying questions from Asmodeus. And while she typically didn't tell Jed details about their Crossroads deals, she just might have to discuss this with him. If Jed was going to ensure she didn't fail at keeping Meg's children safe, he needed to be aware.

THIRTY

Alastor's hands clawed at the scorched earth outside the castle in the burning caves, his nails breaking and fingertips bleeding as he dug deeper into the dirt. Flames danced around him, casting eerie shadows on his twisted, sweat-soaked face. He'd set the grass on fire burning blade and root to make the excavation easier. His breath came in ragged gasps, his heart pounding with desperation and madness.

"Where are they?" Alastor muttered through gritted teeth, his voice a hoarse whisper. "Where are the bones?"

Find my bones. Find my bones. Find my bones! Lucifer's voice in his mind was a relentless torment that had plagued him for too long. *Find the bones and release me!* Lucifer's voice echoed in Alastor's mind, dripping with malice.

Alastor's neck twitched and he longed to dunk his head under water to make his father's voice stop. His focus resumed by the frantic search. He had spent weeks combing all of Hell, driven by the singular need to find Lucifer's bones. His fingers scraped against something hard and unyielding, and Alastor's heart skipped a beat. With trembling hands, he brushed the dirt, revealing a small, gnarled bone–a little finger bone, barely longer than an inch. Easily missed when the Deacons collected Lucifer's bones after Meg had drained him of blood and he dropped to the ground as nothing but a skeleton.

A triumphant laugh escaped Alastor's lips, a sound that echoed across the castle grounds with a manic intensity. The Hellions working alongside Alastor stopped their digging and focused on him. As Alastor held the bone in his hand, a shiver ran down his spine. There was something unnerving about the bone, something ancient and powerful that seemed to pulse with a promise of life. Alastor's grip tightened, his knuckles white with exertion and anticipation.

You found it! You found something of me. You must find the rest! Lucifer chanted over and over again.

Alastor stood, a crazed grin twisting his lips as he made his way toward the castle. He shoved the bone into his pocket, the weight of it pressing against his chest like a talisman of power. A promise that this hunt was almost over.

———

IN THE DIMLY LIT BALLROOM OF the castle in the burning caves, Sparrow's eyes narrowed with suspicion as Alastor crouched beside the bathtub.

"I heard a rumor that you lost something," Sparrow approached Alastor as he rubbed a towel over his face. The poor Demon had just finished nearly drowning himself, again. Sparrow wondered how long the guy was going to go on like this.

Alastor scoffed. "I lost nothing." He paused to shake a finger in Sparrow's direction. "I take that back. The only thing I've ever *lost* has been Shay."

Sparrow rolled his eyes. "You never deserved that creature." He made his way to Alastor's map. "You lost Meg. Heard she was rebuilding a portal and went missing."

"No biggie," Alastor shrugged. "She won't come back. If she ever steps foot in Hell again, I'll make her wish she was never born." He patted his pocket. "I've found a bone. I'm nearly there. I just need the rest of Lucifer's bones and I'll be released from this chore."

Sparrow tapped the map with an index finger. "Your numbers linger further. You are far behind in delivering souls to me."

"You're not the only one who keeps bringing that up," Alastor snapped, his eyes wide and black, water dripping down his face. "I have quotas to reach but I carry this burden." His arms stretched wide as he motioned to the castle around him.

Sparrow's brows rose. "You know, Meg's soul would be worth a lot. A damn lot. Shame she's missing."

Alastor's body stilled as he stared at Sparrow. He finally moved, crossing the room to lounge casually on a leather chair, a smirk playing at the corners of his lips as he regarded his ally with cool detachment.

"Ah, she is a precious little plaything, that Meg." Alastor reached for a bottle of whiskey that was near the chair.

Sparrow's jaw clenched in frustration. "You owe me souls. I'm tired of waiting." Sparrow's eyes narrowed, a spark of anger igniting within him. "Her soul could be used to pay off your soul debts. Her soul is worth more to you than anything else."

Alastor's demeanor shifted, his eyes glowing with interest. "I am not some lesser Demon to be threatened," Alastor said.

Sparrow met Alastor's gaze head-on. "We are bound by more than the soul trade," Sparrow reminded him. "You're a creature of greed and ambition. You'll do anything to get what you want." He motioned to the ballroom. "Look at you here. This is not a hovel in the mountains. Focus on a clear decision and stop making mistakes."

A tense silence fell over the ballroom as Alastor considered Sparrow's words, his expression unreadable. Then, with a slow, deliberate movement, he rose from the leather chair and stepped closer to Sparrow, his gaze piercing and intense.

"Lucifer is nothing more than a fallen Archangel," Sparrow said. "He is not God. He is merely bone and dust. His granddaughter killed him once already. She's killed other Archangels. Take a lesson from your niece and stop listening to that voice in your head."

"You may be right," Alastor conceded, his voice low and dangerous. "But remember this, Sparrow, I am the standing King of Hell," he patted his shirt pocket, "and Lucifer will heed my word when he takes the reins."

It was a good threat, maybe even a great one. But Sparrow had a history with Lucifer, and he wasn't afraid of the old crone. Sparrow knew things–better yet, he had a plan.

"If I help you find Meg, it will be on my terms, not yours. And you will owe me a debt." Alastor rubbed his chin, contemplating Sparrow's words.

Sparrow's jaw was set with determination as he took a step closer to Alastor. "Just tell me where she is."

With a smirk, Alastor leaned closer, his breath hot against Sparrow's ear. "She's in Hell," he whispered, his voice sending a lick of fire down Sparrow's spine. "And if you want to find her, you'll have to go through me first."

Sparrow's hand curled into a fist and he refrained from punching a hole in Alastor's chest and ripping out his still beating heart. He could do it. He should do it. Shadows gathered at Sparrow's feet and his wings pulsed open.

Alastor smirked and backed away. "The Hellions will find her eventually. But you are more than welcome to search."

Sparrow gathered himself and backed away. "Be careful, Alastor," Sparrow said from the shadows. "One day you might dip your head in that tub and it will be flame, not water."

THIRTY-ONE

Nero stood at the opening of the corridor that led to the back exit of the Peabody Library. He was waiting for Jed to follow and unlock the door. But, Jed kept turning pages on his damned book and holding up a finger. Nero had half a mind to piss where he stood. Instead, he stomped his hooves and pawed at the floor, threatening to scratch it to pieces. He didn't care if the floor was painstakingly laid with turn of the century salvaged bricks sourced from Spain or hand scraped Elm wood. He'd destroy it in an instant if Jed didn't get off his ass. Nero finally released a whinny of annoyance. Maybe he'd blow fire from his throat, just a little bit, enough to burn the book Jed was reading.

"Jed!" Shay shouted across the room. She was holding a spatula and had stepped out of the kitchen.

Jed pushed his chair back and stood. "Fine. Fine."

"You wanted a dog while we were living in Hell," Shay said. "You can't even let out the horse when he needs to go. A dog needs to go out even more frequently." She shook the spatula at him.

"Who the hell has the chore of *letting the horse out to pee* in the history of ever?" Jed snapped back.

"Be thankful you're the first." Shay stood, eager to fight. She was antsy and they'd all been cooped up inside for too long. Everyone was getting on each other's nerves. The horse, the adults, the kids... the Hellion who was currently rearranging boxes in the attic.

Nero turned as Jed got closer and nodded toward the corridor over and over again, huffing and snorting and tapping his hoof on the floor.

"Yes. Yes," Jed said, his fingertips tingling with energy. He passed Nero and strode down the corridor.

Nero trotted after him, nickering and whinnying. He was making a fuss and he knew it. How dare Jed make him wait, Nero was a Crossroads Demon for Christ's sake!

Jed cursed as he unlocked the door that led to the empty lot and scraped his foot over the runes and lines of salt so Nero could pass. The horse was, after all, a Demon. He didn't belong on the Earthen plane. But since he was tethered to Shay, he had to stay. He wanted to stay because each time Nero was gone, Shay managed to get kidnapped by a Demon.

Jed shoved the door open and walked out first. Nero followed close and bit Jed's shirt, snapped his teeth together and made a hole. That was for making him wait.

Jed swatted at Nero. "Hey. Hey!"

Nero whinnied lightly and trotted away. Jed would find the hole when he changed his clothes. Nero whinnied to himself in laughter; serves Jed right. Next time, Nero might kick over the table.

"Stay close," Jed warned.

Nero wandered the empty lot, wary of the shadows beyond the property and swell of the river. Jed began patrolling the exterior of the lot, checking his wards, and stooping to draw new ones.

"Stay away from the perimeter," Jed warned.

Nero glanced at him, then the markings on the cracked pavement next to him. He needed to get out, he needed to make it back to Hell and find Meg. A long time ago Nero had decided most humans were good for nothing and stupid. No wonder they couldn't find her. Nero wanted nothing more than to see Rue and Remington happy again. The children needed their family, they didn't belong trapped indoors for all this time. He could find Meg and help put an end to this, he just knew it.

Nero stood at the edge of the property. He glanced at Jed. The man wasn't paying attention to him.

Nero found a stick and picked it up between his teeth. He walked to the edge of the lot and scraped the stick over the runes, breaking the wards.

"Hey!" Jed shouted, the shift in the protective dome was like a cool breeze blowing across the lot. "Nero," Jed warned. "What are you doing?"

Nero whinnied sadly, wishing he could have told Shay goodbye and promise he'd be back, but there wasn't time for that. He needed to go so Jed could fix his destruction on the runes. Nero leapt off the lot.

"Nero!" Jed shouted. "Where are you going?"

Nero ran down the street, his hooves clopping on pavement. He galloped around a truck, rounded a brick corner store, then made his way to a nearby park. He needed space to leap through the Veil.

There it was. He could see a sliver of reality wavering like heat waves on a sidewalk.

Nero found the split in the Veil and leapt through. The scent of woodsmoke and pine was faint. Nero glanced from side to side, the Patapsco River of Hell was eerily silent, a dark reflection of the Earthen plane. His eyes quickly adjusted to the ochre light that bathed the infernal landscape. He took a breath, steeling himself for the task at hand: finding Meg.

Nero tipped his head down and galloped. Hooves moving faster than lightning, he crossed empty cities and towns and crumbling roads until the once-familiar sight of the castle in the burning caves loomed in the distance. Smoke rose from the castle grounds. Nero's senses were on high alert. The distant sounds of wailing souls and the crackling of infernal fire filled the air. Nero slowed his pace coming through the surrounding forests, not wanting to be seen. He creeped his snout just beyond the shadows and saw the castle grounds were smoldering and lumps of dirt were everywhere.

Hellions, hunched and snarling, were scattered across the grounds, digging feverishly in the ashen dirt.

Nero's eyes narrowed as he recognized the figure overseeing the excavation. Alastor, the rat bastard. Nero held in a whinny of disgust, trying to stay hidden amongst the shadows. His throat ached to set the Demon on fire.

Alastor was barking orders at the new Hellions as their claws and makeshift tools tore into the ground with frantic energy.

Nero moved closer, careful to stay hidden in the shadows cast by the twisted, gnarled trees that dotted the landscape at the edge of the forest. His heart pounded in his chest as he observed the scene, trying to make sense of what he was witnessing. Alastor's voice carried through the air, harsh and impatient all while he patted his shirt pocket as though something special were hiding between the cloth.

Nero would remember this. Whatever the Demon held in his pocket was important.

"Faster! We don't have all eternity!" Alastor snarled, his eyes blazing with manic intensity. "I need the bones! Keep digging!"

Nero's mind raced. So what the others had said was true; this was what Alastor was after, the remnants of Lucifer. Nero had never met the original fallen Angel, but he'd heard stories from Meg's Hellions. If Alastor succeeded, his power would be unimaginable.

Nero scanned the grounds, searching for any sign of Meg. He edged closer, staying within the cover of the shadows. He hadn't seen Meg since she arrived early that morning months ago to leave Rue and Remington at the library. Nero hadn't returned to Hell since before that time. The realm had a different vibe now, Nero could feel it in his bones. His teeth mashed together. He had to find Meg and get her out of here before Alastor's plan came to fruition. He took a step back, ready to slip away and continue his search, but a dry twig snapped under his hoof, echoing loudly in the still air.

Alastor's head snapped in his direction, his eyes narrowing as he scanned the shadows. Nero held his breath, pressing himself against the trunk of a tree, praying he hadn't been seen, not that the tree could hide him.

"Who's there?" Alastor growled, his voice dripping with menace. "Show yourself!"

The Hellions paused their digging, their grotesque heads swiveling toward the source of the noise. Nero's heart pounded in his ears as he remained perfectly still, his eyes locked on Alastor.

After a tense moment, Alastor turned back to his minions. "Get back to work," he snapped. "We don't have time for distractions."

Nero exhaled slowly, relief flooding his veins as he backed away, deeper into the shadows under the cover of the trees. He had to find Meg, and quickly. Every second in this Hell was not good.

He didn't want to be there himself. This was worse than when the Raven King was walking the Earthen plane. Whatever Alastor was, unseating Meg from the throne was causing a massive disturbance.

Nero backed out of the forest and turned as he reached the road. One hoof hit the pavement and the sound echoed louder than he'd ever remembered. He stepped down with as second hoof and the ground reverberated as though he'd stomped with all his strength. Yes, Hell had changed. Before the realm had welcomed him with open arms, let him swim in the shadows and meld with the ochre sky, now it rejected him. It was as though with the changing of the throne Hell required its inhabitants to be *revealed*.

Alastor shouted in the distance.

Nero heard the sounds of dozens of footsteps running. He turned. Now, Nero had seen the dead walk in Hell, it was just the way this realm functioned, but they were typically slow and meandering. Nero looked toward the footsteps. These dead were not slow, they were fast.

Nero turned tail and ran. He felt a sharp tug as something grabbed his tail. Nero whinnied, eyes went wide as he turned and found one of the Fast-Dead gripping his tail and reaching for his rump. Nero kicked his back legs and bucked, trying to loosen the dead creature that was hanging on for dear life. He felt the bones of the dead man crack and break but it didn't let go.

Nero wasn't one to panic, but he'd never seen dead like this before. As he struggled with the clinger, more darted toward him. Nero's mind raced–he needed to escape the dead.

He took off galloping at a rapid pace, swinging his backend and kicking, trying to release the grip of the dead that had a hold on him. As Nero ran, he kicked and the body flopped like a crash test dummy, shredding it at the hips as the lower half of it dropped onto the ground. Nero glanced back, relieved that the fast-dead's mouth had been damaged and its jaw was missing. He wouldn't be bitten, he just needed the damn thing to get off his back. The creature reached up with its free arm and gripped the base of Nero's tail, dragging himself up. Nails bit into Nero's backside as the Fast-Zombie tore at his skin and dragged his body up more. Nero shook as he ran, trying to get the dead thing to drop off him but it was holding tight.

Nero ran harder, faster, rubbed against tree trunks to try and scrape the thing off. Soon the rushing of water distracted him. This was a familiar place. Thunder rumbled in the sky and raindrops fell. Hellsky was shrouded in storm clouds. Past the rows of trees he recognized the pond in the forest.

Plip plop, plip plop. Nero recognized that dreaded sound. The hallowed call of the Nightjar. He was in Demore's forest and she was nearby.

Nero wished the Basilisk was still in Demore's pond. He would consider jumping in there to get free of the dead man crawling on his back.

The creature slammed its nails into Nero's flank. Nero whinnied in pain as the zombie dragged itself up his back. He sideswiped the trees, bouncing side to side trying to scrape off the half zombie like sidewalk gum on his hoof. But the creature swung with his movement. I crawled further up his back, nails digging into the sensitive spine at the base of his neck. Nero reared up and whinnied violently.

The plip-plop sound was closer, hovering nearby. Nero looked up to see the wraithlike blackened tendrils of her figure gliding toward him.

"My precious. My baby. My gift," her voice whispered in mournful melody. "What have you brought me?"

Nero scraped against the widest tree trunk he could find, ready to drop to the ground and roll to get the creature off.

"My precious. My baby. My gift." Demore was closer now.

The rainfall intensified until Nero could see her clearly. He whinnied in both pain and begging.

"A horse, of course a horse, my baby," Demore sang to a tune of her own. "What have they done to you?"

Abruptly, Demore's wailing cry turned into a scream as she reached down and grabbed the dead man clawing at Nero's back. She tore the creature off Nero, flew above the treetops and flung the half of a dead man across the forest toward the castle grounds, releasing a wail of disgust as she did it.

Nero slumped against trees and lowered himself to the ground. The Fast-Zombie had torn his back open and he oozed blood. He held in all sound for fear of getting the attention of more of the fast dead.

Demore drifted down from the forest canopy. *Plip-plop, plip-plop*, her hallowed call softened as she approached the injured horse. "What have they done to my baby?" she lowered her wraith-like form to the ground and draped her shadows over him. "I'll take care of you my baby," Demore purred, rubbing her face on his neck.

Doom flooded Nero, he didn't have time for this creatures' shenanigans. But... his body did hurt and he was bleeding. Maybe she could help him, just until the wounds were a little better.

Thirty-Two

Two things happened that caused Jed to rethink every decision he'd ever made these past few weeks. Jed ran toward the break in the wards, sliding on his knees, crumbling cement tearing his skin, chalk in hand, ready to restore the runes. Then the door to the Peabody Library swung open. Rue stepped out. Her aura—although dimmed—shone through the break in the wards.

A shadow shifted beyond the runes of protection, paused to focus, and then flew over Jed's head into the warded lot, heading straight toward Rue.

Rue screamed at the top of her lungs as the bat-like Demon flew to her, slender arms and legs and talons out, ready to scratch and grab. Long teeth were ready to bite.

With one arm, Jed attempted to replace the rune. With his free hand, arcane magic rushed from his fingertips as he spat words that sounded like a semi-truck smashing into a bridge. Before he could finish the rune, something slammed into his shoulder and sent him rolling onto his ass.

"Run, Rue!" Jed shouted as he scrambled to his feet. More Demons were coming. They were rushing the break in the wards.

Rue turned and ran for the door. With both hands she pulled hard and the heavy door squealed open. The Demon grabbed it with both hands and ripped it off its hinges, tossing it aside before following the girl. Bright light shined from the corridor with the door off its hinges, drawing Demons from the river and surrounding city. They'd been lying in wait for a moment to slink in and sink their teeth into children.

Demons of all kinds rushed the lot, trampling Jed and each other. Undulating clouds and burnt-looking creatures never seen on the Earthen plane before advanced toward the opening to the library. Jed could hear Rue screaming, then he heard the aggressive roar of Chel.

Jed's heart pounded against his ribs as he stood. The wards that had protected them were shattered, and Demons poured through the broken defenses, their eyes gleaming with malice as they homed in on the light from the doorway.

With a determined snarl, Jed drew on archaic energy and lightning left his fingertips, striking the nearest Demon. The creature lunged at him, its claws slashing through the air. Jed ducked, rolling to the side before delivering a swift, upward strike that severed the Demon's head. The body crumpled to the ground, but there was no time to celebrate. More Demons were already closing in.

Inside the library, chaos reigned. Chel, Shay and the children were surrounded. Bookshelves lay toppled, and the floor was littered with torn pages and broken furniture. The library, once a haven of knowledge and safety, was now a war zone.

Chel fought fiercely, his eyes blazing with determination. His Hellion blade had been confiscated by Alastor, so the broken chair leg would have to do. He cut down each Demon that dared come too close to Rue and Remington. Shay stood beside him, her eyes glowing with an unearthly light as she brandished a fire poker from the nearby hearth.

Rue and Remington's faces were pale but their eyes fierce with determination. They weren't afraid to fight, they just didn't have any weapons on them. The children each picked up broken table legs, ready to use them as clubs.

Jed ran down the corridor, fighting his way through the Demons that were filtering in, his muscles burning with exertion. He could hear the sounds of battle inside the library, the shouts and screams of human and Demon and Hellion. Desperation fueled his every move. He couldn't let the Demons take Rue and Remington. He'd promised Shay she wouldn't fail.

Finally, Jed broke through the opening of the corridor and burst into the library, tendrils of dark magic oozing from his fingertips. Devastation greeted him. Chel was bleeding from a deep gash on his arm, but still fought with determination. Shay was a whirlwind of power, her dark energy cutting down Demons left and right. But there were too many of them. Jed joined the fray, his magic taking out a cluster of Demons.

"Where's Nero?" Shay asked, knowing the horse could fight with them, could burn them all and stop this madness.

"He ran off," Jed said with a grunt as he turned a batlike Demon to ice. Chel slammed it with his wooden chair leg and it shattered, dead and gone.

"More like that," Chel urged. "It's working."

"Get back," Shay shouted, swiping her fire-poker toward a cloud-like Demon that was hovering over Rue.

The Demon said something to her in garbled Hellspeak and for a moment Shay wished she'd taken the time to learn the language.

Chel backed into Shay and began moving her and the children

back toward the main entrance of the library. They were being overwhelmed, it was as though the Veil separating realms had split open inside the library with the number of dark creatures that were flooding in from the back corridor.

"We must run," Chel said. "Shay, take the children. We'll stay here and fight."

"No," Shay argued.

"There's too many," Jed agreed. "Run, Shay-baby." He paused and leaned into her, dropping a kiss on her head. "Run!"

"I won't leave you!" Shay argued.

Jed was using so much magic his blue aura was lighting up the room. He had a few more spells in his pocket, but he didn't want to hurt Shay or the children if he used them. He needed them to go.

"I'll find you," Jed promised. "Please, run!"

"Now," Chel shouted. "Before it's too late."

Shay had a sickening feeling in her stomach. She didn't want to leave either of them. They were in this mess together. Emotion swelled in her chest. She didn't want to go.

Rue screamed as a tiny Demon clung to her leg and tried to bite her. Shay stabbed the creature through with her fire-poker, then flung it aside. It hit the wall with a splat. Shay herded Rue and Remington toward the door.

Just as it seemed they'd be overcome and have to separate, a blinding light filled the room.

An Angel descended, his presence commanding yet puzzled. His wings spread wide, casting a golden glow over the chaotic scene. With a wave of his hand, the Demons were obliterated, their bodies disintegrating to ash. The Angel's eyes swept over the room, taking in the devastation and those who remained standing.

"What do we have here?" the Angel asked. "A Hellion. A Nephilim." He leaned to the side and focused on Rue and

Remington. "Those two are something different." Then he stared at Shay. "And you're *barely* human."

Magic prickled in Jed's hands. He drew on it, ready to blast the Angel to another planet. He had zero trust for Angels of any kind. They'd only hunted and tried to kill him his entire life. He wouldn't let this one do the same.

"These children," the Angel said, his voice resonant and powerful, "who are they, and why do they bear such auras?"

Jed took a deep breath, his voice steady despite the turmoil and urge to kill. "They are under our protection. Their mother left them with us to keep them safe. We will protect them from everyone and everything, including you."

The Angel's eyes narrowed, his gaze shifting to Shay. Recognition flickered in his gaze and he took a step back. "You," he said, his tone wary, "are part Crossroads Demon. Somehow. But you weren't born that way."

Shay lifted her chin, her eyes defiant as she swiped blue hair away from her face. "Yes, I am."

The Angel took a step backward. "No deals." He shook his head.

"This is not a crossroads," Shay clarified. "But that doesn't mean I won't kill you." She tapped the fire poker on her palm menacingly.

The Angel crossed his arms and he gazed quickly around the room. "You're all leaving?"

"That seems the smartest choice," Jed said.

"Can I stay here if you're leaving?" the Angel asked. "I need a place to hide." The Angel was surveying the library. "And I get the feeling you all can't stay here, not after this." He opened his arms to the piles of ash all over the floor.

"We don't own this place," Jed warned.

"I'll take care of it," the Angel promised.

"I have never met an Angel that I've trusted," Jed said. "Why should I trust you?"

"I've already fixed the wards." The Angel moved his hands to his hips, real proud of himself.

"I think we should take the deal," Chel suggested. "This piece of flying garbage could fend off more Demons who come here looking for us."

"Hey!" the Angel shouted. "I offer help and you insult me?"

Chel shrugged, unafraid and unbothered.

"I apologize for my friend," Shay said. "But we have yet to meet an Angel who hasn't tried to kill first."

The Angel toed a pile of ash before focusing on Jed. "Not all Angels are of the old ways. Some of us just want peace, just like God intended."

"You can stay here," Jed finally said. "We'll collect our things."

The Angel smiled with relief. He turned his back to the grouping and began picking up pieces of the broken chairs and tossing them in the fireplace.

Jed turned to the others. "Pack. Quickly."

Chel didn't have much to bring besides clothing and he stole some knives from the kitchen.

Rue and Remington had their bags ready, they always did. They'd grabbed them off the foot of their beds and waited outside Jed and Shay's door.

Shay hefted her pack and pulled out a crumpled piece of paper from her pocket. She stared at Meg's handwriting.

"I don't know where we should go," Jed was saying as he collected bundles of sage, bags of sand and bones, and his notebook of spells. "I can't think of what would be the safest, maybe the mountains?" he sighed. "We are just so far away. It might be a battle to get there."

"Jed..." Shay began.

"At least we have a Hellion with us. He'll help. He's already helped." Jed ran hands through disheveled hair before opening a drawer and pulling out a knife carved with runes. "I'll have to make more of these. One for everyone."

"Jed..." Shay was reading the note over and over again, an idea blossoming.

"We can avoid the big cities, but the Veil is thinning. The dead might start walking again like they did when Sparrow was wandering this plane." He sighed and closed his eyes, memories of the zombie apocalypse coming; the Lame Deer Casino, seeing Shay for that first time, French toast. His eyes flashed open.

"What if we went somewhere sunny?" Shay asked. "You know, a place where the sun was so bright it would be hard to see Rue and Remington's auras. The tattoos and the sunshine might be enough to hide them."

Jed contemplated. "I guess it could work." He turned to face Shay.

She was holding up Meg's note with an address written on it. "How do you feel about Florida?"

THIRTY-THREE

I DREAM OF SKEELE. Of his bare skin sliding against mine, fingers pressed into my hips, gripping horns in ecstasy, the feel of him inside me as I take what I want, my mouth pressed to his neck, sharp teeth biting. The smooth taste of his blood, the deep moan in his throat as he lets me take my fill before sinking his teeth into my wrist. He likes it like this, watching me ride him while he eats, blood dripping down my lips, the motion of us. It's always been like this, slow yet frantic. His patience, my lack.

It all ends too quickly and I wake up with my teeth pressed to something soft, searching for blood. My eyes flash open as cotton fills my mouth.

I've bitten a pillow.

A pillow?

I scramble upright, kicking the blanket off myself. My feet hit the floor and I back away from the bed until my spine hits a wall.

Where am I?

I blink rapidly, clearing the sleep from my eyes and give my brain a moment to catch up. The sharp pain of my broken wing pressing against the wall helps bring me back to reality.

Where am I?

There are no windows, stone walls, and a solid door. I cross the room and try the handle. It's locked. There's another door. I cross the room again and open it. A bathroom. A real bathroom with a shower and everything.

I turn and stare at the bed. There's four pillows and heavy white linens. Like a hotel. This can't be a hotel. How did I get here? I scan my body, my arms and legs. I'm clean and wearing black sweats and thick socks. Who washed me? Who dressed me?

No no no, this can't be good. I tap my knuckles on the walls, trying to get a sense of weakness or something hidden. There are no decorations, just white paint. I notice a dresser. I open all the drawer and find clothes. Crazy person clothes, just sweats and granny panties and sports bras. What the fuck who dresses like this? I try the door again, remembering the stories Shay told me about the black mansion and rich Demons searching for blood and sex. Maybe that's where I am; bound for destruction, locked in this room, awaiting a fate worse than death. I should have killed Alastor the moment Shay told me the Demon was still alive but I was trying to be better. I was trying to channel compassion. Look where it got me.

There's an ache in my thigh and I remember cutting off the birthmark. I pull my pants down and get a look at the healing wound. I'm surprised that it didn't fester since the knife was probably dirty and my makeshift bandage was nothing but filthy clothing. There's just bright pink skin where the ouroboros used to be. I stare, never having seen my thigh without the strange birthmark.

Something shifts in my stomach. Wetness drips from my ears. My hands come away covered in dark blood that smells putrid. I stumble to the bathroom and vomit. This is the feeling I had after drinking the old blood that Alastor gave us. I search the bathroom cabinets for towels and wash the blood out of my ears and off my face. Then I crawl back into bed and close my eyes. I curl up and wrap my arms around my middle, hoping it will help the ache in my gut.

————

I've decided I miss Florida. I miss hot summer days and sleeping in and eating fruit and bacon and drinking rum and cokes for breakfast, taking naps and staying up late into the night watching the stars and the moon as a hot breeze blew in off the Gulf. There was plenty of blood in Florida, plenty of homeless men and crackheads that no one would miss. I could eat forever in Florida.

"Those thoughts are what got you on Heaven's naughty list," I mutter to myself since there's no one else to speak to in this room.

I'm not sure how much time has passed, but I've slept most of it as the feeling begins to consume me again. It's easy to drift into darkness here; the bed is soft, the sheets are warm, and the more I sleep the better the ache in my stomach feels. But not the ache in my heart. Nothing can help that. I'm beginning to wish Sparrow had just cut it out of me so I'd never have to deal with it.

This time when I close my eyes, someone is waiting for me. She has long brunette hair cascading down her back and her eyes are bright and just as green as they ever were. She whistles a light melodic trill.

I purse my lips, ready to whistle back, but she interrupts me.

"I spoke with Shay," Nightingale says. "Chel showed up wherever they are, missing a hand." Her head tips to the side, a very birdlike quirk. "Where are you, Meg?"

"I don't know." I tell her about the room, about being dragged through the portal and going unconscious. "I have no idea who has me but they gave me a bathroom and a..." Hot tears prick behind my eyes. I don't know how I feel about it after all those nights laying on the stone floor in the Helldungeon.

"A what?" Nightingale presses.

"A bed. Like a queen sized bed with pillows and blankets. It's like a hotel but I haven't seen a single soul. There's no clock. I have no idea how long I've been here. All I do is sleep. I haven't had blood since Skeele died. I'm just so tired all the time."

"Oh, Meg..." Night's hope-filled expression drops. "I'm so sorry. I didn't know he died."

My chin quivers. Crying in my dreams feels just as real as crying in real life. I let the tears flow and the anguish come out in breathy sobs.

Nightingale feels solid in my dream as she wraps her arms around me and holds me close. "I know you had a bond with him," she says, soothing.

"He deserved better," I say with a hiccup and wipe my face. "He was all duty and tradition."

"He loved you." Nightingale grips my hands and gives me a little shake.

"I know," I whisper because it feels so wrong that I let him love me like that. "I took everything from him... his life. He died because of me."

"Tell me the truth," Nightingale is staring into my eyes. "You did not kill him. Who killed him?"

I nod and tell myself to agree with her. "Alastor did it."

"Are you in Hell?" she asks.

"I don't know."

"What do you feel?"

"Nothing. It's not hot or cold. I smell nothing. I feel nothing. I hear no sounds in this room, only my own heartbeat."

"Are you being fed?"

"I can't remember." I smooth a hand over my stomach. "I can't remember eating anything."

"That's probably why you're so tired and sleeping so much." Nightingale rubs my arms. "You need to eat. You need blood."

I stifle a chuckle. "There's nothing in this room."

"Did you check under the bathroom sink?" Nightingale tips her head to the side, oh so birdlike.

"Who in their right mind keeps food under the bathroom sink?" I ask.

Nightingale shrugs. "I used to hide food there when my father locked me up."

"Sure, I'll check when I wake up."

Nightingale nods with a smile like we've just decided on something really important.

"Did you make it to safety?" I ask. "Is Thrush safe?"

Night nods. "Sparrow let us into his kingdom. We are safe. As safe as we can be now that Babylon thinks we've swapped alliances."

I pause. "Why would Babylon care? Do they know what's happening in Hell? Do they know about the Deacons?"

Nightingale's image fades and she looks away, behind her like someone is approaching. "I have to go, Meg." She hugs me quickly. "We'll find you."

My eyes flash open. The room is dark but there is a sliver of light shining under the door. And... two shadows, like feet. Someone is standing there, in front of the door, waiting patiently for me to open it. Jokes on them, it's locked from the outside. A dreadful sensation floods my stomach. Shit, *it's locked from the outside*. I sit up and brace myself for an intruder.

THIRTY-FOUR

Nightingale observed from a distance as Thrush practiced with Sparrow's Legion, his battle movements fluid yet determined. She didn't trust anyone in this realm to leave Thrush alone for long. She knew what it was like to be a teenager in the Seven Kingdoms of Heaven, but at least her son wasn't locked away in a basement. She couldn't help but feel a swell of pride in her chest as she watched her son, his determination to learn the way of the Legion's Angel warriors, although he did look a bit out of place. As though the darkness of Hell clung to him, plenty stared. He was starting to change; his hair had lightened to a white blonde in the weeks that they'd been in Sparrow's Kingdom.

The sun was starting to dip lower on the horizon, casting long shadows across the training grounds. A faint noise caught Nightingale's keen ears, drawing her attention, a distant sound that sent a shiver down her spine.

Leaving Thrush to his training, Nightingale moved swiftly through the darkening forest, her senses alert for any sign of danger. As she rounded a bend in the path, she nearly collided with a figure emerging from the shadows–Sparrow.

"Raven King," Nightingale greeted him, her voice tight with concern.

"What are you doing roaming the forests this late?" Sparrow asked. He seemed agitated, his face flexed in concern.

The moment she recognized it, he set his expression placid.

"Whatever I'd like. I thought I heard something suspicious." Nightingale glanced behind Sparrow but it appeared he'd come out of the darkness and not off a veering path. "Can't be too careful with the Fast-Zombies on the loose again."

Sparrow's expression remained unreadable, his eyes betraying nothing as he regarded his sister.

Nightingale took a deep breath. "Have you heard anything about Meg?"

Sparrow's brow twitched.

"She's been missing for weeks now. No one knows where she is." Nightingale crossed her arms as the forest darkened. "Have you heard a whisper or a rumor of her whereabouts?"

"I haven't seen her. Don't think she'd enjoy seeing me much after... everything." His black wings twitched.

"We've lost touch. We used to be closer," Nightingale said, eager to get information from him.

"You chose Hell," Sparrow said.

Nightingale frowned, unconvinced by Sparrow's dismissive tone. "Something doesn't feel right," she insisted, her instincts screaming at her to trust her gut. "I haven't seen a Deacon in a long time. It just feels like... the *balance* is off. Can you go check on her? Maybe just from afar. She doesn't have to know."

But Sparrow merely shook his head, his gaze drifting as if he were already miles away. "I'm sorry, Nightingale," he murmured, his voice barely audible above the rustling of the leaves. "I have my own matters to attend to. You'll have to search for Meg on your own."

With a sinking feeling in her chest, Nightingale watched as Sparrow disappeared into the darkness, leaving her alone with her fears. She knew she couldn't rely on him for help, not when he was so intent on keeping his own secrets. Not when he was so intent on Meg's death.

Determined, Nightingale squared her shoulders and set off into the night, her heart heavy with worry. She would find Meg and help get her to safety, even if it meant facing the darkest corners of Hell itself.

———

Nightingale returned to the training grounds to find Thrush collecting his belongings.

"You don't need to watch me so closely," Thrush mumbled as Nightingale approached him.

"I don't trust them," she said.

"They're harder on me when you are here." Thrush's body ached from the training he'd endured. He was sure there would be plenty of bruises coming to the surface. He felt like a punching bag. "I need you to stop hovering. I'm not a child anymore." He stormed around Nightingale, avoiding her and began jogging toward the path that led to the cabin.

It was hard enough learning how to fit in among a Legion of Angel warriors. Everyone knew that Nightingale had chosen Hell over Heaven. And there were no other kids in this realm. Thrush and Rue and Remington had been the first children born in a long time.

Thrush raised his arm and pulled a leaf off a branch overhead. He missed his cousins, hadn't spent a day without them since they were born. Now they were somewhere else and he was stuck in the Seven Kingdoms of Heaven. He couldn't even contact them since Meg had never disclosed their location. He hated it. He hated every second of this place. Thrush felt different here, and he could see it every time he looked in the mirror and saw his white-blonde hair.

Thrush tore up the leaf in his hand, shredded it to a hundred pieces.

"Did the leaf deserve that?" a dark voice asked from the shadows.

Sparrow stepped out and Thrush came to a stop.

"It looked at me wrong," Thrush said.

A smile quirked Sparrow's lip. "Stupid leaf." He motioned for Thrush to follow him. "Training is going well I hear."

"Yeah," Thrush replied, glancing at the tall figure walking next to him.

"I told them to take it easy on you."

Thrush scoffed. "Tell that to my liver."

Sparrow's brow rose in question. "I also told them you might've been trained by the Hellions and to keep you on your toes."

"How do you know that?" Thrush asked.

"I was a Hellion." He paused for dramatic effect. "All males of the Archangel families are required to do their time as a Hellion. Did your mother not discuss this with you?"

Thrush shook his head.

"When the time comes, you must go. You must learn true darkness to rule in the light. You must see bad to do good. I have no children of my own. As the next in line for this kingdom, you must prepare."

"And if I choose not to go?"

"You will curse this bloodline again. You will go."

"Why?" Thrush pushed. "There are no more children. My mother told me that I was the first in decades. It was a miracle." Thrush didn't want to go back to Hell with Alastor in charge. He'd seen enough of Alastor's damage when on patrol with the Hellions. He'd heard the stories of what Alastor had done to Shay and Jed. "Doing time as a Hellion didn't make you good."

Sparrow turned to his nephew and found the boy glaring at him.

Shadows pooled at Sparrow's feet, threatened to go after the boy and drain air from his lungs, make him eat his tongue, make him listen to reason. Sparrow glared down at the boy. "You should go home. Now," he warned.

Thrush turned and ran.

THIRTY-FIVE

MEG

I DON'T THINK I'll ever get out of here. My throat is dry, my body weaker than ever. It's disorienting not having sunlight or a clock.

I know I will die soon. I will rot away. I will wake as a walking corpse, stuck like all the others now that the Deacons are gone. And if that happens, I will forfeit ever seeing my children again. My soul will be trapped. There is no balance any longer.

Crawling out of bed, I stumble into the bathroom. I open the cabinets under the sink again, checking for food like Nightingale suggested. There's nothing. There has been nothing for a long time. Not even a bug or a rat that I could eat.

I turn on the water and drink from the faucet. Water does nothing for me. I need blood. Fresh blood. Holding up my hand, I only see skin and bone. I trace the hollows of my cheeks in the mirror before staring. Dull eyes stare back at me.

This must end.

My eyes trace the edge of the mirror, could whoever trapped me in here be this stupid?

It's been a long time since I've given up completely, but I think my time has come. I have no one left. I scattered them all or they've died. This is not giving up though, this is taking control. I will not have my soul wander eternity in Hell, lost. I will not be one of the walking dead.

I punch the mirror over and over again until cracks form and it shatters, pieces fall on the countertop and into the sink. I pick up a large shard, testing its sharpness with my fingertip. It slices and blood blooms. I touch it to my wrist, press in and hiss, tears well in my eyes. The only way I'll ever see my children again is as a ghost, like Clea. At least I'll have that. Hell is lost and so am I.

I press harder until a stream of blood drips down my arm.

The door to the room slams open and heavy footsteps echo. Someone rushes in–a blur of black in my periphery. Strong hands grab both my wrists, shaking my right hand until I drop the shard of mirror. It shatters in the sink as blood drips off my elbow.

"It's kind of hard to be invincible together if you're dead, Meg," a familiar voice growls in my ear.

Sucking in a sharp breath, my blood runs cold. *No!*

-until next time-

Temptations of Fate

About Temptations of Fate

M. R. Pritchard

Lucifer's return looms, his voice calling from beyond the grave, driving Alastor to the brink of madness. With the realms teetering on the edge of chaos, Meg finds herself held captive by the one person she never imagined. As the veil between worlds weakens, darkness threatens to consume everything—and time is running out to stop it.

ONE

THEN

SPARROW WAS A FALLEN Angel turned Hellion turned walking dead turned Raven King. It wasn't all for nothing. He'd cleared his family curse by sacrifice. He'd done as instructed by the remaining Archangels. If he wanted his family land, he had to purify his blood. And hers. So he did it the only way he could; he killed her. He stabbed her in the heart with a blade that made her bleed out every drop of his blood she'd ever consumed; it erupted from her body and killed her for twenty-four minutes. Their bond was severed.

Two

Now

Sparrow held Meg's wrists; no more of her blood would be spilled. Not in his Kingdom. Nowhere else if he had a say in it. Meg's expression was one of horror and shock, as though she couldn't fathom a worse person to stop her from ending it all. Her body had turned to stone beneath his grip. Wide blue eyes stared up at him. Disheveled dark hair stuck to her lips and she was breathing erratically.

Sparrow released her wrists and stepped back, his hands up in surrender to show her he was safe. He wasn't sure she'd ever believe it, but the thing he'd done, he'd done for her–for *them*.

Meg moved faster than he'd expected in her weakened state. She grabbed another piece of the broken mirror and held the sharp fragment to his neck.

"What the fuck?" she finally spit words like hate. "Where am I?"

Sparrow stepped back until his spine and wings hit the wall. She looked equally as though she might devour him with rage and collapse on the floor from exhaustion. It was the dead blood Alastor had fed her. Clearly it hadn't dissipated from her system even though she'd been sleeping for weeks.

"You're safe," was all Sparrow said.

"If you are here, I am not safe," Meg sneered. She'd cut her hand with the shard of glass she was holding to his neck and blood dripped down her thin wrist. "Let me go," she demanded.

"Can't do that." Sparrow took a side step toward the bathroom door. "I think you should lie down."

"Let me go," Meg demanded with rage in her eyes.

"Go lay down, Meg, before you fall flat on the floor."

Blood dripped. Sparrow stilled and did not lick his lips. Instead, he scowled at her, annoyed that she didn't move, irritated that she wouldn't listen to him.

"I will kill you," she threatened.

"Why would you want to do such a thing?" Sparrow took another step to the side.

Meg took a step forward. "Because you deserve it. Because of what you *did*." She stumbled and fell into the doorframe, her broken wing scraping the wall, and she hissed in pain. "Because you *hurt* me." A broken heart was more than hurt. He'd scarred her to the core.

Sparrow didn't move to help her. Understood if he moved a muscle in her direction, she'd stab the shard of glass into his body. "You should go back to bed."

"You should shut the fuck up." Meg reached over her shoulder and pressed a hand to the broken bone that was sticking out of her wing. It would never heal with how badly it was damaged. She glanced toward the bedroom door. "Let me out of here."

"No." Sparrow took another step backward.

Meg's stomach growled, and it echoed throughout the room. Sparrow glanced down.

"Don't look at me," Meg seethed.

"Lay down," he ordered.

"Fuck off," she snapped. She took a breath, collecting her energy, then pushed off the door frame and took a step toward the Raven King, murder in her eyes. "I want out. Now."

"Nope." Sparrow shook his head.

"I..." The hate in Meg's gaze vanished as her eyes rolled to the back of her head and she collapsed.

Sparrow waited, ensuring she didn't wake, burst to her feet, and stab him in the neck. She wanted to. That was easy to see. He toed her shoulder with his boot. She didn't wake, moved little more than shallow breaths. Sparrow crouched and peeled her fingers away from the shard of mirror. He took it to the sink and collected the rest of the broken glass, wrapped it in a towel, and set it outside the door to the room. He glanced at the bed, then to her limp body on the floor. She'd hate him for touching her, but he was going to do it anyway.

Sparrow stooped next to Meg and rolled her, protecting her broken wing. He slid an arm under her shoulders and another under her knees, then lifted. She was too light–nothing but bones, her cheeks gaunt. He wasn't so sure about Teari's recommendation of Tincture of Time for the dead blood to clear her system. Sparrow set Meg on the bed and looked her over. He got a cloth from the bathroom and cleaned the blood off her hand and wrist. He watched her thready breaths. A hand went to his pocket and fingers slid over the vial of blood. He'd been waiting for the right time to give it to her. He couldn't wait much longer for her to recover. Alastor was wreaking havoc on Hell and the Earthen plane. They needed to put a stop to it, but they needed Meg well.

Sparrow took the vial out of his pocket, flipped off the cap and dripped the blood into Meg's mouth. Then he turned tail and made fast work of getting out of her room. If she woke with fresh blood in her system, she'd probably have the strength to rip every feather off his wings. But Sparrow didn't feed her fresh blood. It was bagged like the Hellions would drink. Just enough to sustain her. He closed the door and locked it.

Picking up the towel filled with broken mirror, he made his way out of the bunker. He waited at the main door, listening closely to ensure no one was wandering the forest who might see him. Gabriel had taught Sparrow plenty, more than his own father. Always have a place to hide your people during disaster. When Angels had inhabited the Earthen plane thousands of years ago, they'd built shelter in the mountains to stay hidden and survive. The same kind of shelter worked well for Gabriel during the Fast-Zombie War, his kingdom surviving most of the massacre, when the other Archangels weren't so lucky. They didn't have a place to hide, thinking that the Seven Kingdoms of Heaven were completely safe. No realm was safe. And Sparrow was glad he'd heeded Gabriel's advice during the rebuild and had constructed the bunker in the small ridge of mountain at the edge of his Kingdom.

Not hearing a thing, Sparrow opened the door and exited the bunker. He made his way to the main house and made a mental note to remove everything sharp from Meg's room. The flash of her teeth crossed his mind. He couldn't remove those, unfortunately.

The Legion were in the training yard, the rest of his staff busy with daytime duties. The walk to the main house was uneventful. Sparrow was glad he didn't run into anyone. He surveyed the path in the distance, hoping not to see the dark flash of Nightingale's hair as she hounded him. He couldn't really explain the towel he carried, filled with bloody shards of mirror. He made quick work of returning home and disposing of the mess.

THREE

The sun was setting as Jed drove through the sleepy town of Perdido Key. The sky was painted in hues of pink and orange across the horizon, a stark contrast to the darkness they had left behind.

Tires crunched over a seashell driveway as Jed pulled up to the small beach house. It was dark and quiet. He'd had driven all day and night; over fifteen hours through the Carolinas and Alabama, states none of them had ever been to and didn't have time to peruse. Each time they used a rest stop, Jed drew more runes on the Jeep Grand Cherokee that they were driving. He'd darkened the windows and carved a shrouding spell into the roof. He could never be too safe after the disaster at the Peabody Library.

Shay reached for the door.

"Wait," Jed warned. "Let me check it out."

Shay sighed. "I'm sure it's fine."

"Listen to him," Chel grumbled from the cargo area where he was sitting. The Hellion barely fit. Shoulders hunched and wings awkwardly tucked away, Jeeps weren't designed for the comfort of a Hellion. "Believe me, if anyone wants out right now, it's me," he muttered.

Jed surveyed the beach house on Parasol Place. There were rocking chairs on the front porch and the yard was fenced. There was privacy and the soft sound of the ocean nearby was relaxing. He went to the front door, held his hand over the lock, and whispered a spell. The door opened. Jed flicked on the lights and searched the house. He found nothing surprising. The beach house was small and simply decorated. It seemed too quaint for Meg's tastes and the lack of books would have them all going stir crazy. They'd have to find a library or bookstore. Satisfied with his findings, he made his way back to the Jeep.

Shay was watching him as he walked closer.

Jed decided he liked the way his boots crunched on the crushed seashells and the smell of the ocean air. He opened Shay's door and helped her out. "All clear." He smiled.

They all piled out, the sea breeze instantly wrapping around them. Shay took a deep breath, savoring the salty air. It was a new beginning, a much needed respite from the chaos they had fled.

"Whoa," Jed stopped Chel. "We gotta do something about those wings."

"Who cares?" Chel looked around. "No one is here." He sniffed the air then his face twisted in confusion. There was no one for miles. He glanced at the nearby houses and apartments, not smelling any inhabitants.

Jed whispered a spell that hid Chel's wings from sight. "Come on, let's check out the beach," Jed said, a rare smile spreading across his face.

Rue and Remington ran ahead, their laughter echoing in the evening air. Chel followed, his eyes scanning their surroundings.

The light from sunset was so bright it hid their auras.

Shay and Jed walked hand in hand, the soft sand beneath their feet. The waves lapped gently at the shore, a soothing rhythm that calmed their weary souls.

Rue and Remington were splashing in the shallow water. Remington cupped his hands and shoveled ocean water at his sister as she shrieked in delight.

"This place is beautiful," Shay whispered, leaning into Jed.

"It is," he agreed, pulling her closer. "Their auras aren't like up north. The sun is brighter here."

"Hopefully the moon too." Shay kicked off her shoes and dug her toes into the soft sand. She'd never lived in a place that didn't require closed toed shoes or boots year-round. She had a sudden urge to buy flip-flops.

They stayed at the beach until the sky turned dark, the stars appearing one by one. And the moon *was* bright enough to hide the children's light.

Reluctantly, Shay called Rue and Remington out of the water and they made their way back to the house. Everyone was exhausted from the white-knuckled escape from Peabody Library. They had been afraid of being attacked while they drove.

They made their way back to the house, their earlier excitement giving way to yawns and drooping eyes.

Inside, Shay was glad to find a room for the children and a master suite.

"I'll take the couch," Chel said, bending to look out the windows.

Jed and Chel secured the house, making sure all was safe. They marked the doors and windows with runes of charcoal and salt.

Shay helped the children get settled.

"I'm hungry," Rue said.

"Well," Shay said as she searched the cabinets. "There's not much here." She found bags of expired chips and cans of expired soups. "This stuff might still be edible." She piled the items on the counter and found plates and bowls. "We'll have to go to the store in the morning."

Remington was standing in front of the pantry. "There's a lot of soda here."

Silence fell on the group. Shay glanced to Jed.

"Has our mother been here?" Remington asked.

"A long time ago," Shay said.

Remington turned with cans of orange soda in his hands. He gave one to Rue with a look, then passed the rest out.

"I'm sure she's okay," Chel said. "She has to be okay."

Cans popped open and Shay held hers up. "To bright sunshine."

"To sunshine," Jed echoed, a sense of hope filling the room.

For the first time in two days, they felt a sliver of peace. The road ahead was uncertain, but for now they had each other and a place to rest their heads. And that was enough.

"Where is Nero going to sleep?" Rue asked.

Jed nearly spit soda mid-swallow. "If I see that horse again..."

"Hey," Shay argued. "Be nice. There was a reason for what he did."

"To get us all killed." Jed slammed his can down. "There was no good reason for what he did."

"Don't judge him so harshly," Shay said. "We don't know."

Chel grumbled something about stupid animals.

———

THE MORNING BROUGHT heat and sun. Jed messed with the air conditioner, using more magic than handyman skill to get it working correctly.

"I want to go to the beach," Rue said. "It was so pretty last night. We've never been to the ocean before."

"Someone needs to go to the store," Shay said as she made a cup of coffee. Meg had an entire cabinet stocked with coffee. It was strange since she barely drank it in Hell.

"I can go," Jed offered. "You all can go to the beach."

The kids found shorts and T-shirts, Jed promised to look for swim suits while he was at the store.

"We are wholly unprepared for a beach," Shay said digging through her suitcase to find something. She settled on an old T-shirt and faded jeans and decided to sacrifice them to the cuts of scissors. "We need flip-flops, sunscreen, sunglasses, and hats."

Jed glanced at Chel. "I'm not sure they'll have your size in anything."

Chel looked up from his cup of black coffee and grumbled. "I'm not a beachy type of guy."

"You can't be going there in Hellion gear and combat boots." Shay was searching a hallway cabinet for towels. She found a stack, walked toward the front door, and motioned to the children. "Let's see if this daylight is enough."

Everyone filtered outside, shielding their eyes.

"It's a miracle," Jed said, staring at the children. "Not a speck of aura."

It was true. The Florida sunshine was so bright there was no aura visible. What little they'd seen last night was completely bleached out by the sun's rays.

FOUR

Alastor was covered in dirt, and as he dunked his head in the bathtub to silence the demands of Lucifer, the tiny finger bone slipped out of his shirt pocket and floated in the dirty water. Alastor snatched it up as though it were gold. He set it on the nearby table as the door to the ballroom creaked open.

An overpowering presence entered the ballroom and Alastor instantly recognized it.

"What do you want, Raven King?" Alastor wiped water from his face.

Heavy footsteps echoed as Sparrow made his way across the ballroom to the nook where Alastor was holed up.

"You could have chosen one of the smaller rooms," Sparrow frowned, taking in the disarray.

"That would seem too permanent." Alastor tore off his shirt, dried himself, then dug through a suitcase to find fresh clothing.

Sparrow rocked back on his heels. "Have you considered a deal with Babylon for the fallen Queen?"

"I will consider nothing until she brings me to Lucifer's

bones." Alastor plucked the finger bone from where he'd set it, tucking it in his pocket again. He made his way to the leather club chair and sat. "There was a horse here. A Demon horse. Shay's horse. Why was Shay's horse spying on me?"

Sparrow's brow rose. "The Crossroads Demon is a creature of Hell. I would know nothing about that."

Alastor smirked. "I think you know more than you let on."

"You took the throne. You should be aware of your realm." Sparrow took a step closer to get a better view of the map.

Alastor's mood shifted as he rubbed his face. "I want to be done with this." He knocked his knuckles against the side of his head. "I'm tired of Lucifer's voice in my mind, driving me insane."

"You know who is good at finding bones of family members? Meg, she found Clea's." Sparrow noted the new portals.

"You want her?"

"I've told you. Babylon does." The poor bastard couldn't remember much these days.

Alastor waved his hand to the sky. "Go find her."

Sparrow cocked his head, questioning. "She's not here?"

"Hellions scared her away. Said she disappeared." Alastor scoffed. "She can't be disappearing anymore since her Ouroboros has been cut off. The creature is stupider than a box of baboons." He turned to the window. "She's out there somewhere. Running."

"So you're ready to trade her?" Sparrow asked.

"With the agreement that she delivers the bones the next time I see her face."

"She may need some convincing."

"Do whatever you need. Take her soul. I'll increase your soul share ten percent." He exhaled a heavy breath. "I want to be done with this."

"Something new on your mind?" Sparrow asked.

"A Demon called Asmodeus is vying for the skin trades. I need to shut him down. Lucifer was nothing to me before this. I want him out of my mind, out of my life." Alastor suddenly screamed out in pain and fell to his knees, holding his head.

He didn't stop screaming. The sound echoed in the giant ballroom, making Sparrow's ears throb.

Sparrow stomped across the room and grabbed Alastor by the back of his shirt. He dragged the Demon to the bathtub and threw him in. He pressed a hand to Alastor's neck and shoved his head under as deep as he could.

Alastor's eyes flashed open with terror before slowly calming. Sparrow pitied the Demon; seemed the only time the guy had peace was when he was a few heartbeats away from death.

Sparrow held him under the water. The thought that he could end this Demon right now and take the throne of Hell crossed his mind. Wouldn't that be something special? Holding a throne in the Seven Kingdoms of Heaven and the throne of Hell. There were no Deacons to say anything about it. There was no balance. Only power waiting to be taken. The sensation of a thousand rocks dropping in Sparrow's gut startled the thought away. He gripped Alastor's shirt in his fist and pulled the Demon out.

Alastor leaned over the side of the tub, water sloshing onto the floor as he sucked in giant lungfuls of air. "Thank you."

"I'll find her," Sparrow promised.

———

Sparrow left the slowly breaking Demon in the ballroom and made his way to the winding stairwell. He climbed up the stairs, two at a time, and took a right. He walked down the hall until he found Meg's room. He kicked the door open and was greeted by a familiar scene. Sparrow knew Meg was always a bit of a mess, but she still lived life one heartbeat away from running for her life. She'd always been like that. Sparrow went to her closet and found the bugout bag near the door. He glanced at her clothing, grabbed a pair of boots, and then searched the room for her blade. He tucked everything under his arm and left, doing his best to focus on the door and not the bed.

He found her blade in the Hellion lair amongst the rotting bodies of her Hellions. Sparrow wrinkled his nose. Alastor was not doing the throne of Hell any justice by letting the castle deteriorate. He paused, recognizing the decomposing body of Skeele. No feelings passed through Sparrow. The Hellion was Sparrow's second in command when Sparrow was a Hellion Commander, and then Meg's lover, the father of her bastard child.

Sparrow left the lair and made his way to the closest portal, eager to leave the disarray that was now Hell.

Five

Gabriel paced the dimly lit chamber, his wings tucked tightly against his back. The room, a secluded corner in the heart of Gabriel's hidden catacombs, was filled with the flickering light of oil lamps casting long shadows on the walls. The last Deacon lay on a bed, his leg heavily bandaged. The air was thick with tension and the scent of medicinal herbs. Teari kneeled at the bedside, changing the gauze wrapping around the Deacon's leg.

"Alastor has officially taken the throne in Hell," Gabriel said, breaking the silence. His voice was a mixture of frustration and concern. "Things are bound to escalate."

The Deacon winced as Teari tightened the bandages on his severed stump. He took a deep breath, trying to steady himself before responding. "Alastor's rise to power was inevitable. But with Meg... she's more vulnerable than ever. We need to find her before he does."

Teari glanced up, her hands gentle but firm as she finished securing the bandages. "Meg is strong, she thinks she can face Alastor alone." Teari was shaking her head, hating that Meg had pushed everyone away. Nightingale had told her what happened. She hid her children, banished Noah and Nightingale and Thrush, and took on Alastor and his army of the dead with just her Hellions.

Gabriel rubbed his chin. "The balance of power in Hell is shifting and it's not in our favor."

"What about Babylon?" Teari asked.

Gabriel was silent for a moment too long. It didn't convey that Babylon was completely ignorant to the situation in Hell as he'd previously indicated.

Teari finished her work and stood, wiping her hands on a cloth. "Meg is missing." She reminded them.

Gabriel made a face.

"What?" Teari demanded.

"She's not really missing any longer." Gabriel looked away.

Teari was on her feet and in front of Gabriel in a heartbeat. "Excuse me?"

"She's safe," Gabriel said.

Teari hated that she was outside the loop of information.

The Deacon nodded, wincing as he adjusted himself on the bed. "Time is of the essence. Alastor can't wait. He'll be hunting for her, just as we are." The Deacon took a heavy breath. "I need her to find the feather of truth. I need it. We all need it to maintain some balance in this world."

"Where is it?" Gabriel asked. The last time he'd seen the relic was at Meg's trial, nearly fifteen years ago.

"It's at the Safe House in Auburn." The Deacon leaned back in bed with a heavy groan.

Teari crossed her arms to reassure herself. "We'll find her. And when we do, we'll make sure she understands the gravity of the situation." Teari knew Meg had secrets that needed to stay that way.

"Every moment we delay is a moment Alastor gains the upper hand," the Deacon said.

With that, the room fell into a focused silence as they began making their preparations, each aware of the immense challenge that lay ahead. The fate of Meg and the balance of power in Hell depended on her.

Six

"WHAT DO YOU HAVE UNDER YOUR WING?" Nightingale asked Sparrow.

"Mind your business, sister."

SEVEN

MEG

I FEEL HUNGOVER. Like, the worst hangover I've ever had in my entire life. I drag myself out of bed only to fall on the floor.

There's a tray of food and a glass of blood. Fresh blood. It smells decadent; better than chocolate, better than anything. The feeling of retching crawls up my throat, memories of the last time I had blood following it. Alastor had given me and Chel blood from the dead... I don't trust it. I don't know where it's from. I pick up the glass, take it to the bathroom, pour it down the toilet, and flush. My mouth waters. I hate myself for doing it.

There's no mirror in the bathroom. I lean against the doorframe and remember. Sparrow was here. Fucking Sparrow. I'm going to kill him. I glance back at the toilet. I should have drunk the blood. I cross the room to the tray and pick up a bottle of ginger ale. Gross. Inspecting the bottle, I notice it's sealed and not expired. Looks fine. I crack it open and take in the sweet hiss of carbonation. I drink it. No, I guzzle it like I've crossed the desert with no water. Ginger ale is far from my favorite but right now it tastes better than anything I've ever drank in my life. There's a bag of chips and a sandwich on the tray. It's been a long time since I've eaten real food. My mouth waters as I pick up the sandwich and sniff it. Turkey and cheese. Smells wonderful. I consider that it could be poisoned, but I'm starving and not queasy for the first time in ages. Food poisoning is easier to overcome than rotten-blood poisoning, or at least that's what I tell myself. I bite, devour the sandwich, and wash it down with the ginger ale. Then I break into the bag of chips and pour them into my mouth like an animal. As I'm chewing, something dark slouching against the wall catches my eye. I move closer and recognize my bugout bag. Wait... how did that get here?

I pick it up and go to the bathroom, checking the contents. I lock the door and turn on the shower and get clean. As I wash myself, I touch the scar on my upper thigh where my birthmark used to be. At least it's healed.

Wrapping myself in a towel, I take out a change of clothes, thankful for the T-shirt and jeans. After getting dressed in my own clothing and not the black sweats, I feel slightly normal.

I drape my bag over my shoulder and walk toward the bedroom door. My hand hovers over the knob. I could be anywhere. I glance down at my feet, wishing I had shoes. To my surprise, the doorknob turns when I twist it and the door opens.

There's a pair of boots in the hall. My boots. This is all very suspicious. I don't see anyone else. I don't smell anyone. As I'm stepping into my boots, I glance down the hall. It looks like I'm in some kind of underground bunker. It's massive with a dozen or more doors down one end and a large opening to the other end.

Why would Sparrow leave the door unlocked? Why would he give me food and my bag? Why would he leave the door open?

He's up to something. I'm still going to kill him as soon as I lay eyes on him.

My footsteps echo as I walk down the hall that opens into a great room. Not far away, I see a giant door that could only lead outside. As I'm making my way toward it, the metallic sound of locks opening echoes. I still and look around. There's nowhere to hide. There's only couches and end tables and a dining area.

The door opens and a dark figure steps inside. "See you're upright."

There's a lamp to my right. I pick it up and throw it at him.

Sparrow steps to the side and the lamp shatters against the wall, missing him.

"That was uncalled for." Sparrow says, a deep frown creasing his face.

"It was *very* called for." I search for something else to throw at him. If I had the strength I'd pick up a couch and whip it at his head.

"Are you going to beat me up and run off? You will not get far with that broken wing." He looks me up and down. "And you didn't drink the blood. Do you care about living? What if it wasn't me who opened that door?"

"I don't care."

"You need to care if you gave a fuck about surviving."

I scoff and take a step away from him. "My only plan is to kill you. I'll deal with surviving later."

Sparrow chuckles. "Save your energy."

"For what?"

"Babylon. The council wants to speak with you."

My mouth snaps shut. I wasn't expecting that. I'm in Heaven. Shit.

He kicks the broken lamp to the side and reaches for the door to the outside. "Follow me and keep quiet."

Sparrow holds the door open as I pass. We are standing in a dense forest. I turn and see jagged rocks of a mountain that go up and up and up. A soft metallic noise clicks and something sounds like fabric falling. I focus where Sparrow is standing and notice the door is now hidden.

"Keep up." Sparrow walks through the forest. There's no path and in the fading light I can barely keep up.

I stumble, my broken wing hitting a tree trunk, and I hiss in pain. It's quite brave of him, turning his back to me after everything we've been through.

He steps to the side as though he can hear my thoughts, then he picks up his pace. In the dusk, he doesn't look like much more than a moving shadow. We finally make it to a path.

I follow behind him, imagining all the ways I can kill him from this position. I wish I had my blade. It would be easy to stab him. He's so tall though, and I can't fly with this broken wing. I'd have to touch him–climb up his back and slit his neck. Or I could scrape his spine with a dagger at the base of his backbone. He walks like a God. Those big stupid black wings drag on the ground. Memories of featherless wings flash behind my eyes. An empty church. Glue. Feathers of every color. Sparrow's mouth on my body. My breath catches.

His head jerks to the side and I get a good look at his profile. Yes. He's just as handsome as he's always been. Moreso with the confidence he now carries. And that lingering darkness is about as tempting as a line of cocaine at a disco party.

Self-hate floods my body. I shouldn't be looking at him, not after Skeele sacrificed what was left of his short life to me. I look away, stare at anything but him. I do my best to find attractiveness in a stick on the ground. I pick up the stick and snap it between my fingers. Unfortunately, it doesn't compare to the Raven King and the thought of snapping his pretty neck.

Someone is on the path ahead. Sparrow steps to the side, blocking me from view. I keep my mouth shut like he asked–not because I want to follow his demands, but because I don't feel like fighting anyone. Whoever it is makes their way down another path, away from us.

The sky darkens and tiny lights illuminate the path. I notice a house in the distance but Sparrow leads me away from it. I recognize the house and the side lawn where we fought. I shiver and shake my head, chasing away the memories. I don't want to think of that now. I can't think about how the one man who broke my heart into pieces and nearly killed me is standing so close to me right now.

Instead, my thoughts turn to Skeele. My steps slow as pain aches in my chest.

"It's just a little bit further to Babylon," Sparrow says.

"Thanks for making me walk there," I mutter.

Sparrow makes a noise of exasperation. "If you think I'm getting in a vehicle with you, you're nuts."

"I'm nuts?"

"Yeah." He chuckles. "Way nuts."

"You're nuts." I jab a finger in his direction.

He shrugs. "Been worse."

We reach a stone wall with a gate. Beyond is Babylon.

Sparrow unlocks the gate and swings it open, motioning for me to pass.

I creep through and still. The canopy and forest that once camouflaged us is gone. The streets of Babylon are wide open. The walkway to the center looks like a park with perfectly manicured shrubs flowers. The path is lit with streetlamps and the splashing water of the fountain echoes.

"Walk faster," Sparrow says. "Or the Angels will start staring."

"How would they even know who I am?" I ask.

"Everyone knows the fallen Queen of Hell."

Ouch.

We make it to the courthouse where the Archangels hold their secret meetings about the world and lay down judgement and look down their perfect noses at everyone.

Sparrow opens the door and holds it for me. What a gentleman. His boot stomps down in front of me and I stumble to a stop.

"I swear to God if you try anything I'll stitch your lips shut. Do. Not. Bite. Anyone." Sparrow glares at me.

"Fine." It's not a promise but I'll try my best because I'd rather get the heck out of this place and get back to my children. I must tell them that their father is dead. They need to know Skeele died by my side, a hero; that's what I'll say. I'll spare them the gory details. They don't need the mental image of him being consumed by Alastor's chaos.

ALL THE ARCHANGELS ARE HERE: Michael, Raphael, Uriel, Raguel, Saraqael, and my father, Gabriel.

Sparrow moves away from me and takes his father's seat. That seat is empty because I killed Sparrow's father. Remiel was a bastard anyway, no great loss. He never did his time as a Hellion and as a result, Sparrow and Nightingale suffered. I have no remorse for putting an end to that Archangel.

I glance at Raphael and lick my lips, remembering how he screeched like a chicken and fainted when I bit him. Loser.

Gabriel stands. "Meg, it's wonderful to see that you are well."

"Am I though?" I ask.

"I pray." My father's blue gaze narrows on me, compelling me to mind myself.

"Thank you." I glance around the table. They're all staring.

"This is a bargain for your freedom." Gabriel sits and motions to the chair next to me. I sit, leaning forward so my broken wing doesn't catch on the back of the seat.

"Why should anyone be bargaining for my freedom?" I ask.

"You are a prisoner," Michael says.

"No I'm not," I say.

"You are," Sparrow says, his gaze narrowing on me. "You are my prisoner."

"I am?" I ask. He looks too dark amongst these assholes, the only one with black wings and dressed like he's black-ops. The rest are white-winged and dressed in flowing robes like a church choir. The contrast is astounding.

An awkward silence passes through the room. Gabriel clears his throat. "Without the Deacons, Babylon will maintain the balance between realms."

A laugh bubbles up out of me.

Gabriel glares and I go silent.

"What do I have to do with that?" I ask.

"You need to fetch the feather of truth from Hell and deliver it to us," Michael says.

"Then you'll have your freedom," Raphael adds.

"You want me to go back to Hell?" I ask.

"The feather of truth resides in the Auburn Safe House," Raguel says, his tone snide.

If I had a choice in who to kill next, I'd pick Raguel.

"Alastor is trying to resurrect Lucifer," I tell them.

"We are aware," Gabriel says.

I glance to Sparrow.

His gaze is empty.

"Do I get a choice?" I ask.

"Not really," Raphael says.

"Perfect." I stand.

"We'll escort you to the fountain so you don't get sidetracked by anything," Raguel says.

———

Being escorted by six Archangels and Sparrow is a daunting moment in my life. I was the Queen of Hell. I shouldn't be intimidated, but here I am with no throne, no Hellions, no family, a broken wing, and a dry throat–amongst other things. I feel like I'm walking the plank.

I stand at the edge of the Fountain of Eternity. My heart beats against my ribcage.

"It will take you to the Nightjar's pond," Gabriel says.

I nod. I've gone through this portal before; came through it to free Gabriel after the other Archangels turned on him.

"Don't jump without saying goodbye," Sparrow's voice is behind me.

I want to tell him to fuck off, but I can't find the courage.

"Take this." His hand touches mine and opens my fingers, he presses cool metal into my grip. I look down and recognize my blade.

I gasp and turn toward him, eye to eye since I'm standing on the edge of the fountain.

"One day," Sparrow says. "If you're not back in one day, I'll come for you."

I don't know what to say. But I don't have time to say anything because he shoves me into the fountain before I can stab him with my blade.

EIGHT

Sparrow stepped back as the fountain took Meg
to Hell. Unease flooded his chest. Sending her like this was not
right. He wished she'd drank the blood before leaving. She would
have been stronger. He felt the weakness in her back as he'd shoved
her into the fountain.

A heavy hand landed on Sparrow's shoulder. It was Gabriel.
The other Archangels had wandered away to their own kingdoms
after Meg disappeared beneath the water.

"You think she can do it?" Gabriel asked.

"She must," Sparrow replied without looking at Gabriel. It
was hard to say much to the Archangel he'd disappointed. Gabriel
wasn't his father but he was once Sparrow's superior. Sparrow was
Gabriel's Legion Commander for a time, before he was banished
for losing Meg and before he did his time as a Hellion to break the
family curse. But Sparrow had moved on to bigger things, like
nearly killing Gabriel's *special* daughter. Not one of the hundreds
of other children he'd helped give life to. Gabriel must've understood there was a deeper reason for all that had transpired, because

Gabriel threatened Sparrow's life once and then they never spoke of it again. Probably because Gabriel now knew the full story and he'd tried to intervene in their relationship before with disastrous results. The Archangel had received an omen just like the rest of them. And he'd tried to intercept fate.

Gabriel squeezed Sparrow's shoulder before moving away. They walked together for a few feet before Gabriel said, "How long are you giving her?"

"One day," Sparrow replied.

Gabriel nodded in agreement. "You let her go with that broken wing." His tone was concerned.

"She'd rather kill me than let it get fixed."

"Could see that," Gabriel said.

The dimly lit walkway was heavy with tension. Gabriel's presence cast a faint glow in the shadows. Sparrow gazed into the darkness, his expression stoic but his eyes betraying deep concern.

Gabriel faced Sparrow, his wings flexing. "Sending Meg back to Hell to find the feather of truth is reckless," he said, his voice tinged with worry. "The risks to her are unimaginable, especially if Lucifer is resurrected while she's there."

Sparrow pressed his eyes closed. "I know the dangers. We don't have a choice. Without the Scale, the balance of the realms is in jeopardy. The council will never give Meg a moment's peace. They will always be on her hide. You know this."

Gabriel's brow furrowed. "Hell is more dangerous than ever with Alastor on the throne. She might not survive. This could be the dire ending to Clea's omen."

Sparrow sucked in a breath, trying to steady his emotions. "You think I haven't thought of that? You think the worst outcomes haven't come to my mind?"

Gabriel's eyes softened. "You care for her deeply."

Sparrow spat out a horrified chuckle. "Don't let her know. She thinks I hate her. What can I expect after what I did?"

"It's been a long time. So what is your plan?" Gabriel asked.

"Alastor thinks I'm in Hell searching for her. If she's not back in one day, I'll find her." This was a dangerous game Sparrow was playing. One that could have dire consequences if Alastor figured out Sparrow was in on this for more than just souls and power.

Gabriel sighed, the weight of the situation pressing down on him. "If anything happens to her..."

Sparrow nodded, his blood had turned to ice with thoughts of her injured more, or dead. "I know."

"Keep your kingdom under shadow," Gabriel warned before veering toward his land.

Sparrow's lungs begged for air, he couldn't take a deep enough breath. At least she was safe in the bunker and he had control of the situation. Now he had control over nothing. He'd given her one day, but one day was too long. He didn't trust Alastor or the Hellions he employed. Hell was no longer Meg's safe space.

Sparrow launched himself into the sky and flew the rest of the way home.

He'd spent twenty-four years without her. Then nearly another fifteen. What was another twenty four hours? She might despise every fiber of his being, but he'd make sure she knew the truth when she came back. He'd sit her down and explain everything in a place with no weapons and... maybe he'd put tape over her mouth.

Without his grace, Sparrow was something different. And Meg had helped transform him when the Scarecrow convinced her to stab him in the heart.

NINE

J ED ROSE FROM THE BED. S HAY WAS SOUND ASLEEP AND didn't stir as he made his way out of the room. He moved quietly through the darkened beach house, careful not to wake anyone. The soft sounds of the ocean waves outside the window echoed throughout the house, a soothing backdrop. He reached the door, turning the knob slowly to avoid any creaking.

Just as he was about to slip outside, a voice cut through the darkness.

"Where do you think you're going?" Chel sprung from the couch.

Jed turned to find Chel standing in the middle of the living room, his silhouette barely visible in the dim light. Chel's eyes were sharp with suspicion.

"I have to speak with someone," Jed said, hoping his nonchalant tone would be convincing.

Chel crossed his arms. "At this hour? You're up to something. What is it?"

Jed met his gaze, determination in his eyes. "I need to talk to the Crossroads Demon."

Chel paused, tipping his head to the side as he realized what Jed was saying. "Just speak with Shay here."

"No." Jed was shaking his head. "I have to make a deal with them. With her."

Chel studied him for a moment, then sighed. "Alright. But if you're going to do this, you're not doing it alone. I'm coming with you."

"You can't," Jed said. "You need to stay here with the kids."

"I don't like this," Chel warned, glancing toward the closed door of the room where the children slept.

"You don't have to." Jed stepped out into the cool night air, the sound of the ocean growing louder as he moved away from the house. He didn't have to go far to find a crossroads; he walked down the street to find a paved intersection near the beach parking lot. He didn't want to be seen, but he doubted at this hour many would be awake. All the lights were off in the surrounding buildings. In the time that they'd been at the beach house, Jed hadn't seen another soul. There were people in town, at the stores and driving down Perdido Key Drive, but in the surrounding block and beach, no one. It seemed Chel was right when he mentioned the homes were empty surrounding the beach house.

Something tore in Jed's chest. He didn't want to put Shay in this predicament but something was coming, something dark and dangerous. This town was eerily quiet, barely populated and seemed to be stuck in a different era. Maybe that was the south since the Fast-Zombie War. Maybe people could feel the thinning of the Veil and that was the only explanation for what he'd seen while shopping. The empty beaches concerned him. He didn't trust Meg, knew that this was her hideaway all those years ago when she went missing for weeks and they'd sent Skeele after her.

She'd done something to this town and he was surprised she'd kept it a secret this long.

He took a piece of chalk from his pocket and summoned the Crossroads Demon.

———

NERO WHINNIED with delight when he saw Shay at the crossroads.

"Where have you been, boy?" Shay threw her arms around his neck and squeezed.

Nero neighed a response then went still as stone when he noticed who'd called them.

Shay turned slowly and faced Jed. Her eyes went wide. "You? No." She shook her head. "Jed, you can't do this. You can't make a deal with us." She settled a hand on Nero's neck. "I won't let you."

"I need to make a deal." Jed's hands flexed and he stepped closer to the rune circle.

"No." Shay couldn't control her shocked expression or the glare of betrayal.

"You haven't even listened to what I want." His voice lowered. "Please don't look at me like that."

"It doesn't matter," Shay said. "I don't want to make a deal with you."

"You've made deals with hundreds. Why leave me out of the fun?" Jed asked, a smirk dragging his lips aside. "Something is coming, Shay. And I don't want us to be without protection."

"You've protected us for this long." Shay tangled her fingers in Nero's mane and fought the emotions bubbling in her chest. She didn't want to lose Jed to a Crossroads Demon deal. Couldn't. Jed was all she had in this world. If she lost him, she'd be alone. "You don't want this," she warned. "We are strong together."

"We need to get home, so I'm going to make this quick," Jed said, tucking his hands in his pockets.

"Please..." Shay whispered. "Don't make me do this."

"I want to make a deal for power." Jed tipped his chin down.

"What kind of power?" Shay whispered, afraid of his response. Everyone wanted power or death, she just didn't think Jed would be the one to request it after all he'd been through, after all they'd been through together.

"Enhance my magic for whatever darkness is coming." Jed raised his hands and sparks crackled. "That's it. I don't want anyone dead, I don't want any souls. Nothing other than strength."

Shay bit her lip and met Nero's gaze. Silent communication passed between the two. It wasn't a difficult deal, they didn't have to kill anyone, but to enhance Jed's supernatural power, they'd have to do something unusual.

"Okay," Shay said. "You realize that we will call upon you."

Jed nodded. "I look forward to the day. I will always be by your side," he promised.

Shay's eyes flashed red. The tether that connected her to Nero went taut. The words that came out of her mouth were not of her own volition. They were compelled by the curse of the Crossroads Demon and Nero. "Out of the eater will come something to eat. And out of the strong will come something sweet." Shay smirked and held out a dusky hand with long necrotic fingernails and a transparent golden ring on her middle finger.

Jed shook her hand and the deal was done.

A shiver passed up Jed's spine. "Already?" he asked.

"Not yet," Shay said. "We must collect something first."

Jed rubbed his foot over the chalk line and tugged Shay into his arms. He kissed her, hard and desperate. "I wouldn't have made the deal if I thought we didn't need it." He searched her eyes for anger or hurt. He'd hurt her too much in the past and he never wanted to see that disappointment in her eyes again.

Nero made a noise behind them and Jed turned Shay to his side. "You!" Jed pointed at Nero. "Have some explaining to do."

"He didn't mean it," Shay said. "He was trying to find Meg."

"Did he find her?" Jed asked.

"Yes. He found her." Shay pointed to the marks on his back. "He was injured." Shay waited for more information to come through the tether that bound her to Nero. "Alastor and the fast dead attacked him. The Nightjar healed him. He brought Meg to the Auburn Safe House and left her there."

Jed rubbed a hand down the side of his face. "Shit. Where has he been?"

"At Peabody Library with the Angel." Shay smiled, glad to hear that Nero was some place safe.

"Warn him that there's not a lot of space where we are holed up," Jed said. "A horse on the beach will raise suspicion."

An ache lingered in Shay's chest. She didn't want Nero to be away from her. She moved away from Jed to stroke and hug Nero. "Will you stay?" Shay asked Nero. "There isn't enough room in the house but there's a backyard with a privacy fence."

Nero whinnied in agreement.

TEN

Nero lay on the warm but comfortable straw bed in the Nightjar's cabin. The clapboard house was dry and empty and the wounds on his backside were nearly healed. The scratches had progressed to dry scabs. The moon glow of Hellsky filtered through the small windows, casting an eerie light across the room. He shifted, turning his attention to the Nightjar's pond. Its surface shimmered darkly. The pond was a portal, but Nero had seen nothing come or go from it since he'd been taken in.

Nero knew the Nightjar was a haunting force, but she'd cared for him. Something tugged at Nero's heart. Perhaps that was all she ever wanted was someone to love, someone to love her. She'd never experienced that. Her unbaptized soul was doomed to wander the night sky because the Archangel Raphael discarded her in Hell. Nero nibbled at the clumps of sweet grass she'd collected. It was night and the Nightjar was out wandering the forests of Hell. He wasn't sure what she was looking for, but every night she left, every night she searched and mourned and moaned.

The Nightjar eventually returned, moving silently around the cabin. Her presence was both comforting and unsettling. She paused by the window, her gaze distant.

"Hell is changing, my baby. And it's not for the better. Not like with the Queen."

Nero's ears flicked forward, a soft snort escaping him.

"Alastor," she replied, her voice barely above a whisper. "He's grown more powerful, more ruthless. He's been digging around the castle grounds, looking for something. The new Hellions follow him blindly, causing chaos and destruction. Something is not right here," Demore sang mournfully. "Something is very very wrong with our home." She looked out the window, in the direction of the burning caves. "The dark days of chaos have returned."

Nero's eyes narrowed at the mention of Alastor's reign.

The Nightjar shook her head. "I don't know what he's searching for. But whatever it is, it can't be good. You must be careful. Alastor is more dangerous than ever. He's searching for you."

———

NERO WAITED for the Nightjar to fall asleep. She curled into a shadow, her form folding in on itself in the corner and disappearing with the sunlight. In sleep she was nothing, at dark she came to life like a nightmare. Or perhaps she went to haunt the Astral realm.

Nero stood and limped out of the cabin, his hooves crunching on the fallen leaves. He didn't want to leave the Nightjar without a goodbye of some kind. He made his way to the road then ran. He'd been running each day since the claw marks on his back started healing, stretching his muscles and gaining back speed he'd lost from the injury. The fast-dead seemed to be gone now. The only dead Nero saw were the slow, lumbering kind–the ones he could easily escape if need be.

He wandered the nearby forest, straightening his aching back and muscles. A noise broke his focus; he perked his ears and heard the sound of water dripping and sticks snapping as someone stumbled. He turned to the pond and saw a familiar form.

A sense of fear and joy flooded him. What was *she* doing here?

ELEVEN

MEG

I EXIT the portal and swim to the surface of the Nightjar's pond. I make my way to the shore, quietly, taking in my surroundings and wishing I wasn't soaked. I crawl out of the pond, water dripping from my clothing.

There's no sound, just evening crickets. I shrink back after stepping on a crisp twig. The snap echoes. Something feels strange here now. It's no longer my home, no longer my Hell. The brimstone that lingers in the air is more pungent than usual, no longer a familiar scent.

The weight of wet feathers makes my busted wing ache but I don't let the pain slow me down. I scramble up the shoreline and check the sky. There's nothing visible from the clearing over the Nightjar's pond. My eyes adjust to the dark forest. I have over a hundred miles to cover to get to the Auburn Safe House. I need a car or something fast.

A whisper of a whinny draws my attention. There's a black horse walking toward me.

"Nero?" I ask. "Is that you?"

A snort of steam answers as he trots closer and sniffs me.

"What are you doing here?" I ask. "You should be with Shay." I take off my shirt and wring it out, then put it back on. My jeans will have to dry on their own.

Nero turns, showing me the claw marks on his backside.

"Something got to you..." I gently touch the skin near the marks. "It looks like you're nearly healed."

I think of my hundred mile trek. My feet will be covered in blisters with these wet boots.

"Are you feeling well enough to give me a ride?" I ask.

Nero huffs and nods his head. "I need to get to the Auburn Safe House as fast as possible."

Nero tips his head and scrapes his hoof. I think that he's telling me to climb on his back, but he's pretty tall and I've never ridden a horse before. I look for something to stand on and find a fallen tree.

"I've never done this before," I warn him as I motion to the fallen tree I'm about to use as a step.

Nero moves closer.

Getting on his back seems impossible. The horse is huge and the fallen tree doesn't give me much rise. I try to jump and throw a leg over his back but I just wind up kicking him in the ass. He doesn't appreciate it and snaps his teeth at me.

"I'm sorry. I fucking suck at this."

I swear Nero rolls his eyes as he lowers himself to the ground and shakes his chin, motioning for me to get on. I straddle his back and hold on tight as Nero moves to his feet. He shakes his head, and I take it as a sign for me to hold on to his mane. I tangle my fingers in his coarse hair and hold on as he starts trotting.

Nero makes his way through the forest. The ochre moon in Hellsky casts long, flickering shadows that seem to dance and twist, mocking our every move.

I swear I feel eyes on me, the ever-present gaze of Alastor's Demons and dark creatures. A shiver runs up my spine as Nero makes it out of the forest to the crumbling roadway.

Hell didn't feel like this before, not even in the summers. The night air is oppressive, the heat and humidity making it hard to breath. Sweat trickles down my back. I should have drunk the blood.

Nero starts with a gallop. He whinnies and it sounds like a warning, so I lean down and wrap the strands of his mane around my hands.

"If you can get there before sunup, that would be great," I say.

Nero takes off, faster than anything I've ever experience. Wind blows in my ears. I pinch my thighs together and press my face to the back of his neck. Holy Hell, this Demon horse is faster than...

Before I finish the thought, he stops.

Auburn Safe House is directly in front of me. And my clothing and boots are dry.

I slide off Nero, feeling like I'm drunk or stoned or both. It takes me a minute to steady myself.

"Thanks." I pat his side. "You don't have to stay." I hold my stomach, ready to puke from the fast ride.

Nero whinnies a goodbye before trotting away to do whatever Demon horses do.

I walk toward the half crumbled Safe House. It's familiar, even in its dilapidated state. My boots crunch over crumbled concrete and the front gate squeals as I push it to the side.

As I walk inside, my old mantra surfaces, *never go back to the scene of the crime.* A bad feeling tickles my gut. I pause and grab a flashlight from my bag, the morning light not enough to see clearly yet. Every so often I hear a noise, a distant cry, wails that crate a haunting soundtrack to this task. I push the sounds to the back of my mind, concentrating on my goal: find the feather of truth.

Chairs and tables litter the open room. I recognize the visitation room, the doors that lead to quarantine and questioning. I step over a lonely shoe speckled with blood. Moaning echoes from the corner. I squint and see one of the walking dead headed my way. Damn. I grip my blade, thankful that Sparrow gave it back to me. I shouldn't kill the dead, but without the Safe Houses, they have nowhere to go. It feels wrong releasing their soul only for it to be stuck here, giving Alastor more power.

The dead man moves closer, moaning and shuffling. I take two steps forward and slice his head off. The body drops to the ground. I go still and let my eyes focus on the shadows to make sure there's no more dead.

I recognize the long hallway that leads to where the Deacons held my trial. I start making my way there, sure to be quiet as a mouse. I tuck my hair behind my ears and listen. There's more moaning down the opposite end of the hall. My damaged wing catches on a broken chair and I hiss in pain before crouching to pull the feathers out of the cracked wood. I need to get this fixed. I tuck the feathers in my pocket, not wanting to leave behind any evidence that I was here.

———

I FIND the door where the Deacons held my trial. As I approach the door, I glance around one last time, making sure I haven't been followed. Satisfied that I'm alone, I push open the door and slip inside.

The room is dimly lit. I collapse against the wall, finally

allowing myself a moment to breathe. I made it. I close my eyes and rest for a moment, my stomach still uneasy from Nero's speed.

A small scratching sound echoes. My eyes flash open. It could be a mouse or a dead person hiding under the debris. Or maybe those little burrowing owls moved in. I focus on the desk-of-questioning, the three chairs where the Deacons who judged me sat.

I close my eyes and remember... *the feather of truth is white with brown stripes. It's brought into the room on an embellished glass platter along with a gold scale.*

The scratching noise stops and the silence of the abandoned courtroom is unnerving. Dust motes dance in the dim, flickering light from a single broken window high up on the wall. I creep through the shadows, my footsteps echoing slightly on the cracked marble floor.

The once grand room now lay in ruins, the dark wood of the desk-of-questioning warped and splintered. The jury box stands empty, its seats covered in a thick layer of dust. I move cautiously, my eyes scanning every inch of the room for any sign of the feather of truth. This is like looking for a needle in a haystack. Who knows if I'll find a single feather in here, who knows if it will be the correct one? I glance at my wing over my shoulder. I could just give them one of my feathers. Would they even know the difference? How could Babylon do anything without the Deacons?

"Come on, Meg," I mutter to myself, my voice barely above a whisper. "Focus."

My heart is pounding in my chest as I approach the bench, my hands shaking. The knowledge of what this place once represented, the power it once held, the secrets it will now keep. I once hated this place, now I mourn its loss. The feather of truth saved me, it was the one thing that tipped the scales in my favor when I'd royally fucked everything up. A harsh, hushed laugh escapes my throat.

I search behind the desk, my fingers trailing over the rough, uneven surface. Nothing. Frustration nags at me; I can't lose focus. Where would I be if I were a golden scale and magical feather?

I move to the jury box, lifting the seats one by one, looking for any hidden compartments or clue.

A noise echoes through the empty room, making me freeze. My heart skips a beat as I listen intently. Is it my imagination, or is someone else here? I hold my breath, straining to hear anything out of the ordinary. After a few tense moments, the silence returns, heavier than before.

I continue my search, moving to the witness stand. I run my fingers along the edge, feeling for irregularities. There is a small indentation, barely noticeable. I press it and a panel slides open, revealing a hidden compartment. My breath catches in my throat as I reach inside.

My fingers brush against something soft and delicate. Carefully, I pull it out. The feather of truth. Its pristine white and crisp brown stripes are a stark contrast to the decay and ruin around me. Relief washes over me but is quickly replaced by a sense of urgency. I have what I need, now I need to get the heck out of dodge.

Clutching the feather tightly, I turn to leave, but a shadow moves in the corner. I spin, my heart racing. The courtroom seems to close in around me, the darkness suffocating.

"Time to go," I whisper to myself, steeling my nerves.

I tuck the feather of truth into my pocket, doing my best not to damage it. I make my way back through the courtroom, my senses on high alert. I can't shake the feeling that I'm being watched.

TWELVE

Nero wandered away from the Auburn Safe House. He was unsure of his next move, but he knew he couldn't stay in Hell. It didn't feel right. His flank shivered as the eerie feeling of being watched slid up his spine. It was time to move on. He'd been with the Nightjar long enough and he missed Shay. He was glad to have some answers on Meg and find her alive.

A flash of pink caught his eye, something half buried in the debris on the side of the road. Nero moved closer and nudged it, pushing the leaves and sticks away. A child's doll lay in the dirt. He knew what to do with this. He grabbed the toy between his teeth and made one last stop before returning to Shay.

Nero trotted back to the Nightjar's cabin and nudged the door open. He set the doll near her shadowed, sleeping form then lay in the straw and waited for a formal goodbye.

As night spilled through the windows, the Nightjar's form unfurled and came to life. She stretched her shadows, reaching out in tendrils to explore the cabin. She suddenly turned and focused on Nero as though she were spinning in dance.

"My baby, how are you feeling tonight?"

Nero nodded his head at the creature and neighed softly.

The Nightjar moved around the cabin, brushing away cobwebs and peering out the windows.

"Something has changed," she said. "Something feels off. Can you sense it?" she turned to Nero.

Yes, Nero could feel it. And he needed to leave, promptly. He couldn't afford another injury.

Nero stood and nudged the doll with his nose.

"What is that?" the Nightjar moved closer. "Oh!" her intake of breath sounded like howling wind. "A baby!"

The Nightjar reached down and picked up the doll with her long fingers. She held it to her chest before spinning in a circle. "A baby." She nuzzled the toy. "Finally. My own baby." She stroked its face, and delicately touched its nose, lips, and ears.

She turned quick as a whip to face Nero. "This is all I have ever wanted." Her voice sounded like a distant song, humming from the mountains. "Finally." She hugged it close. "Thank you."

Nero whinnied and nodded before glancing at the door.

"You must go?" The Nightjar's voice was distant. "I don't want you to go but you must." She was nodding in agreement. "Yes, you must. It's changing too fast, I fear. And I must keep my baby safe." She moved to the window, the doll nestled in the crook of her arm. "Alastor will search for those loyal to the Queen. He is twisted and sick." She opened the door. "You must go before he calls you back to the castle and injures you further. Hurry, the fast dead are coming."

Nero tilted his head and recognized the echo of fast moving feet.

He whinnied a thanks to the Nightjar before exiting her cabin.

"Be safe, my baby," the Nightjar called. "My friend."

Nero glanced back and found her rocking the baby doll in

folded arms. A memory of Shay rocking him the same way when he was all long legs and injured body flashed through his mind.

Nero nodded one last time before taking off. His hooves broke sticks and crunched piles of leaves as he made his way to the road and took off fast as lightning.

Nero ran until he saw the silvery break in the Veil between Hell and the Earthen plane. He picked up speed and jumped through.

The Peabody Library was different. Nero wasn't sure exactly what was different about it. Just, something. He wandered the edges of the lot, then around the building, unable to enter because of the wards. Someone was inside, he could tell. Nero made his way to the front door and tapped with his hoof.

The door cracked open and a man Nero had never seen before appeared.

"What are you?" the man asked as his face twisted in confusion. "You're not a real horse."

Nero whinnied before nudging the door open and stepping inside.

"Whoa, buddy." The man stepped back and Nero finally noticed that he was an Angel.

Nero reared up on his hind legs and neighed loudly.

"Quiet. Quiet!" the Angel said, shoving the door closed.

Nero galloped through the library, searching. He checked the rooms and the kitchen, then paused when he saw the destruction in the back corridor. He turned to face the Angel, wishing he could speak.

"Alright, you know this place." The Angel kept his distance, eager to avoid impalement by horse hoof. Or worse. "I know you. I saw you break the wards and run off."

Nero advanced on the Angel, neighing over and over again, nodding his head frantically. He was trying his best to express concern for his missing friends and threaten the Angel who didn't belong here.

"They're fine, big boy. They're alive just not here," the Angel finally said, holding his hands up in surrender. "They had to leave." The Angel's eyes searched Nero's. "I've heard about you. The Crossroads Demon horse." The Angel looked in awe. "The first of its kind."

Nero's steps echoed in the empty library as he roamed, moving away from the Angel. He huffed in disappointment. At least Jed and Shay and the children were okay. His back ached and Nero moved closer to the fireplace. He whinnied at the Angel, a demand to explain his presence in the library.

The Angel sat opposite Nero and crossed his legs. "An explanation, okay. I was drawn to this place by two beacons of light erupting into the sky. Being on the Earthen plane, I knew whatever it was didn't belong, but neither did I. There was a large collection of Demon-kind beyond the wards." The Angel was motioning with his hands, making circles and strange gestures, acting out his story. "I didn't want to get involved but then I saw you break through the wards and run away. Then I heard a little girl screaming." The Angel shook his head. "There was a lot of screaming and shouting and that half-Angel man who was here was drawing on a crap-ton of magic. I mean... ha... his aura was *lit* up brighter than the sun."

Nero showed his teeth, urging to the Angel to stay on track.

"Okay. Sorry I got sidetracked, it was just all very impressive. So, I entered the property and fixed the wards outside to stop the onslaught of Demons."

Nero nodded in approval. At least the Angel helped and wasn't the usual piece of shit he'd come to know.

"I met the blue-haired girl." The Angel shook his finger at Nero. "She's like you. Dark and powerful."

Nero nickered an affirmative.

"And there was a Hellion." The Angel chuckled and held his stomach. "I was not expecting that. A mish mash of creatures all being kept here in this library. The strangest were the children." He tapped his chin. "There's something about those two. I just can't place it. The boy looked slightly familiar." The Angel paused before shaking his head as though he were shaking away a bad dream. "Anyway. They packed their bags and left. Headed south. They said I could stay here and protect the place. Which was perfect because I needed a safe place to hide." He held arms open. "It was kind of a miracle, after all. I'm on the run myself." The Angel exhaled loudly, pressed his lips into a straight line and raised his eyebrows in an awkward expression. He shrugged. "That's it. That's my story."

Nero stared before whinnying in approval. Then he set his chin on the floor and gazed at the fire.

"Are you hungry? I have some fresh carrots from the farmer's market. They're organic. Locally grown."

Nero huffed.

The Angel shot to his feet. "I'll get you some. You can stay for as long as you want. It's kind of boring being in this giant place by myself. I leave every few days to get food but that's about all the excitement in my life." The Angel strode to the kitchen and got two carrots from the fridge. He returned to where Nero was resting, but the horse was asleep.

The Angel set the carrots next to Nero and moved to a nearby chair.

When Nero woke in the morning, he was greeted by a naked Angel sipping coffee in a club chair and reading a romance novel.

Nero nickered in disgust.

"Look, bro, I've been here for a few days now and I'm just enjoying the freedoms of the Earthen plane." He snuggled down in the chair and threw a blanket over his lap. "Nudity in Heaven is unheard of. Probably because it feels so nice to be naked." He pointed down the hall that led to the bedrooms. "I'm pretty sure your room is down there. One specifically smelled like a barn stall."

Nero showed his teeth and snapped them together in warning before moving to his feet and walking down the hall to his room. He nudged the door open and was greeted by the familiar scene. This was the room Jed had designed for him. A comfortable bed, plenty of space. He looked toward the bathroom. There probably wasn't fresh water in the tub. Nero settled down for a few more hours sleep and thought of Shay, hoping that she was okay and safe.

THIRTEEN

MEG

MY STOMACH GROWLS, echoing throughout the main room of
the Safe House. Something hears it and I curse my body for
requiring food and blood so frequently. There are shuffling footsteps from deep in the Safe House. I pick up my pace and get the
heck out of there.

Stepping outside, a strange sense of tension lifts from my
shoulders. I walk closer to the street signs, patting my pocket.
There was a portal in a graveyard not far from here. An arrow
points to Owasco Lake. Water is a universal conduit, the Scarecrow once told me. If there's water, I can whisper a little rhyme
and I could use the lake to make it back to the Seven Kingdoms of
Heaven. It would definitely be faster than trucking it all the way to
the graveyard.

I follow the signage to Owasco Lake and start walking down
West Garden Street. There are hotels on each side of the street and

big parking lots with potholes and crumbling asphalt. I keep my blade in my hand, ready to take on trouble. There's a sign for Holy Family Catholic Church and I notice the walking dead milling about in the parking lot. Maybe they're waiting for mass?

I move behind some broken down cars and keep moving. As the sun lights Hellsky, I make good time. I take West Garden Street until it comes to a dead end, then turn onto North Street and make my way to Osborne Street then East Genesee Street, then follow the sign pointing to Owasco Street. The lake is one mile away. I could run it in about nine minutes if I can still live up to my old high school mile run time. I didn't have to drag a broken wing on my back so I decide to take my time. The dead keep their distance and a sign for Fine Food and Gas catches my attention. My stomach grumbles again. My mouth waters at the thought of Hostess cupcakes and sugary soda. I smooth my hand over the feather in my pocket. I haven't eaten a real meal since that sandwich earlier. My gaze lingers on the gas station. The windows aren't broken and the door isn't chained, I can see the plastic packaging reflecting the morning light. It hasn't been twenty-four hours. I have time to get a snack.

I open the door to the shop slowly, reaching up with my blade and silencing the bell that would announce my arrival. The fluorescent lights flicker, casting a sickly pallor over the shelves of snacks and the grimy floor. My stomach growls as I take in the rows of chips and candy. I grab two packs of chocolate cupcakes and a pack of Snowballs. I linger in the aisle, opening one of cupcakes and shoving it whole into my mouth. I grab a Kit-Kat bar and tuck it into the side pocket of my backpack for later.

I gaze at the drink selection. I should choose a water but lemon-lime soda grabs my attention. I open a bottle and wash down the cupcake. I reach for another and tuck it under my arm. I'm almost done here, why not be greedy? I doubt where ever I go next they'll have snacks like this. I take another package of Snow-balls and head toward the door.

As I pass the counter, I feel a prickle of unease crawl up my spine. I turn, scanning the shadows in the back of the store but see nothing out of the ordinary.

I shove another cupcake in my mouth and push open the door. The moment I step outside, the air seems to thicken, becoming heavy and oppressive. I barely have time to react before Alastor and his Hellions emerge from a two black Jeeps. I stumble, shocked. I didn't even hear them pull up. Their eyes are gleaming with malice.

"Going somewhere, Meg?" Alastor sneers, his voice dripping with contempt.

The Demon looks like absolute dog shit. The throne does not look good on him. His clothing is disheveled, his hair messy and knotted. There's blood dried to his chin which tells me he's been drinking blood like a slob. I glance at his Hellions. Double shit, they look feral, which means they've been drinking fresh blood.

My heart pounds against my ribs as I flex my wings, desperate to fly away and divebomb into the lake in the distance.

Alastor glances at the packages in my arms.

"You were supposed to be finding Lucifer's bones, not shop-ping," he grumbles.

"Sorry." My eyes widen. "But," I clear my throat, "they're not here."

"Where have you been?" Alastor asks.

"Staving off death after you fed me that blood from the dead, dickhead." I'm not giving him any details, definitely not telling him that Sparrow had me locked up in Heaven until the rotten blood was out of my system.

Alastor glares at me as his Hellions pace like guard dogs. "What must I do to make you bring me those bones?" he asks.

"I'm clearly searching for them."

"You're shopping at a snack shop." Alastor points to the Hostess snacks in my arms.

"Fine," I lift my arms and everything falls to the ground. "I was hungry but I'll stop. I'll be on my way."

The soda bottle cracks and fizzles against the pavement, along with my hopes for making it to the lake and escaping.

"This is no game," Alastor says, his smile widening. "This is justice for Lucifer."

The Hellions lunge at me. I sidestep out of their reach. But a big one with a face like a boar grabs me. I punch his arm and kick his shin. I fight back with every ounce of strength I have left. My fist connects with demonic flesh. I grip my blade and slice one across the chest, then backstep to put distance between us. I didn't come into this fight at a hundred percent. One throws a fist that lands directly in my gut, sending me flying. I land on my back and hear the Kit-Kat bar snap like my last fuck.

That's it. I scramble to my feet and swing my blade, cutting off an arm. While that Hellion grumbles, I launch myself into the air and try to fly. With only one functioning wing, it's just enough rise to get a few stories up before they come after me.

We tangle in the air but I'm no match like this. One grabs onto my pack. I cut the strap and let it fall. Then I drop to the ground and roll to get out of their way. One grabs me by the throat and slams me against the wall of the store. Bone scrapes against brick wall and I hold in a hiss on discomfort. Nope, it's not a Hellion, it's Alastor.

"You've caused me enough trouble," he hisses, his face inches from mine. "Take me to the bones. Now."

"I've been searching, I don't know where they are."

"I don't believe you. What are you doing out here?" he slams me against the wall, harder this time.

"Checking the Auburn Safe House," I say. "Or what's left of it."

He looks down my frame to my boots and my blade. "Interesting."

He punches me in the jaw and I see stars before I can stab him in the gut.

"I'll tell you something, Meg." His grip loosens on my throat. "I think you're up to no good. I think you're being sneaky." He throws me on the ground. "I think you might have help. Where's that old Hellion I left you with?"

"Dead," I groan.

Alastor kicks me over onto my stomach. "And where are the chains?"

I don't say anything because I can't really think of a lie that would make sense.

His boot slams down on my spine, right between my shoulders.

"Tell me, Fallen Queen. Tell me the truth." He pauses and I hear what sounds like his head shaking. "Shut up!" he screams. "Shut up. Shut up. Shut up!" he slaps the side of his head.

"Are you fucked in the head?" I ask. "I used to know someone like that. It never ends well."

He drops to the ground, knees on each side of my back. "Those Archangels always said you had a fucking rich mouth. I'll give you something to flap your lips about."

The metallic zing of knife leaving its sheath echoes against the brick wall to my right. I struggle, trying to throw him off my back but he's too big.

"Hold down her arms," Alastor shouts to his Hellions.

Claws grip my wrists and pull my arms taut.

Hot breath brushes my face as he whispers, "Heard it took ages for you to get these."

I scream as he pulls my broken wing out straight. Bone rubs against the ground but it's nothing compared to the searing pain of his blade slicing through the thick tendons and bone of where my wings come out of my back. He cuts and saws with a serrated blade, slicing through my wing. Agony unlike anything I've ever known tears through me. I scream, the sound echoing through the empty streets as he cuts off the second wing. I scream, thinking it will never end. My voice echoes off the brick walls and my ears ring from the escalating sound of it.

I lay there, gasping for breath, my vision blurring from the pain.

Alastor moves to his feet, looming over me, his Hellions flanking him. "I'll leave you to die here," he says, ice in his voice. "Consider it mercy. Tell me where his bones are!" Alastor spits the words at me.

I press my lips together and hold in a cry of anguish. It hurts so bad. Blood is pouring down my sides, pooling under my chest. Through blurry vision, I recognize my lifeless wings on the ground. The Hellions release my wrists and I grip the dirt.

"Fine. Have it your way." Alastor picks up my wings and walks away, dragging them like palm fronds. "When you wake, bring me the bones. This is my last request. The next time I draw a blade on you, it will be to cut off your head."

As they walk away, I try to move, but every part of me feels shattered. This is worse than that day I killed those seven men. Worse than the day Sparrow stabbed me in the heart. Worse than anything. Darkness creeps in at the edges of my vision, and I can only hope that someone, anyone–maybe even Sparrow–might find me before it's too late.

Fourteen

Then

"Sparrow!" Meg called.

Sparrow was inspecting the burned ruins of his home. He'd returned to nothing, just ash and bone and sorrow. He'd been on the dark side of the walking dead for most of it. Meg had locked him up in the dungeon to keep him safe and figure out a way to cure him from the zombie bite on his leg. His ankle itched and he had a memory of Teari telling Meg to cut his leg off to stop the spread of the dead. She refused, thankfully. Part of him felt hollow for not fighting during the war. He spent his whole life training and preparing for battle, and he spent the time behind bars thinking of eating flesh. He was quite worthless for the whole ordeal.

The Archangel at his side wouldn't stop talking. "Your sister perished in the war alongside her husband."

It took Sparrow minutes to process what the man had said. Nightingale was gone. Jack was gone. He didn't mention the baby.

"What happened to their son, Thrush?"

"Can't find him. Either he perished by the Basilisk or that blasphemous trash from Hell took him. She was here. She brought the fast-dead. She brought the Basilisk. She brought death upon your family."

Sparrow glared at the Archangel, searching for truth. Angels couldn't lie but they could deceive. They could spread misinformation if they didn't know any better or if they chose to believe untruth.

"You must put an end to her. Purify your blood. You must set everything right again."

Sparrow tried to process everything but his brain was working in slow motion.

"You must do this to take your family's kingdom," the Archangel said. "You have to rid yourself of her filth. You are pure blood, your heritage cannot be tainted."

"She's half and half," Sparrow said, guilt and longing overriding everything. He rubbed his head, trying to rationalize what was right and what was wrong, what was true and what was deception.

"The rules of the Seven Kingdoms of Heaven are clear. You have seen darkness, you have seen light, you have been *tainted*. As long as your blood flows through *her* veins, you cannot take this land. You will not find peace. Your blood lineage does not need any more curses."

Sparrow glanced at Meg as Clea's omen ran through his mind.

WARS. *Blood and death. Good and evil. A dead Sparrow. A motherless child and a fatherless child. Light and dark. The*

Earthen plane and the ethereal realms. A burst of bright light. An explosion. Fear and pain. Emptiness. A dark, never-ending vat of emptiness that would suck every joyful moment right out of me.

"I saw a dark future, one where we are separate," Sparrow had told Meg.

"You will lose everything. Your family, your lands, your namesake. After all you've been through you can't walk away from your family throne." The Archangel said as he passed a knife into Sparrow's hand. "Straight through into the heart. If you don't do it, I will kill her where she stands. This is for your own good. For the good of Babylon. For the good of balance between realms."

"Sparrow," Meg called. "Will you talk to me?" Her voice sounded innocent, hopeful.

Sparrow took the knife. Grief gripped his chest. He didn't want it to end like this. He never wanted this. Damn he missed her, foul mouth and all.

Sparrow considered the first moment he'd seen Meg and lost her. He considered that lifetime banishment would have been better than this. He wasn't sure how they found each other in Noah's basement all those years ago, but with the task he now faced, he wished he'd never knocked on that door. He wished he'd wandered Hellscape alone into oblivion. Too many had intervened into their relationship.

There's joy on her face.

His heart shreds.

"Sparrow," Meg said. "You're back. "You're you." She smiled, hope lighting her face.

This was all they ever wanted. Freedom.

The blood running through his veins was like ice water. He

had to play the part, to make it easier for her. The only way she'd survive this was on pure unadulterated hate for him.

"Is that so?" Sparrow's voice sounded strange to his own ears.

He revealed the knife, and she saw the glint of sun on the blade. Teari's blood had given him strength, more than his years of training as Legion Commander and Hellion leader. He moved quickly and threw jabs to distract the Archangel and make him believe Sparrow wasn't holding back. Three to the stomach, to prevent any seed from taking. One to her thigh that he'd miss wrapping around his body. One to the arm that would never embrace his shoulders ever again. He held the blade against her breastbone. He had to do this. Had to. He hated himself for it.

She was pale with shock and pain.

He was the worst thing to ever walk the realms. A creature of death. A horrible creature that could never be trusted. Sparrow told himself what he was. He could have killed the Archangel and embraced the chaos. But then they'd never be free of this dance. This is what they needed, *freedom*. And there was only freedom in death and the spilling of blood.

"An eye for an eye. Grace for grace," Sparrow's voice was malevolent, filled with hatred. He'd never heard his voice like that. It was hatred for what they'd been through. Hatred for the laws of Babylon. It was all wrong. "Except you never had a speck of grace. I'll have to take something else."

He gazed into her blue eyes and saw the torture she'd endured at his hand. It was unexpected for them both. He would always hate himself for this moment. He hoped she'd hate him forever because there was nothing he could do to mend the sharp edge of betrayal.

He pushed the blade into her breast bone, past the cartilage, into the firm muscle of her heart. He glanced down, saw the blade was embedded in her watercolor tattoo of a sparrow in flight.

He couldn't explain the look on her face but he knew it was all he'd ever see for the rest of his life. It would haunt him forever.

Poof – she disappeared.

"Where did she go?" the Archangel asked.

"What does it matter? I did what you asked, now get off my land." Sparrow took in the scene–the rubble and the rotting basilisk carcass were all that remained of his father's house.

"You can rebuild." The Archangel was examining. "You'll need more souls since your kingdom lost nearly everything in the Fast-Zombie War. Congratulations on inheriting the weakest kingdom in the Seven Kingdoms of Heaven."

Rock bottom wasn't new to Sparrow. He just didn't expect the void within his center to be so deep. He had a dream of taking over these lands with Meg at his side. Now that would never be. He threw the bloody knife into the soil at the Archangel's feet.

"I SAW A DARK FUTURE, one where we are separate."

FIFTEEN

Sparrow moved cautiously through the darkened halls of the castle in the burning caves. His footsteps echoed against the cold stone floors. The oppressive atmosphere of the place, with its flickering torches casting eerie shadows, did little to calm his nerves. It had been twenty four hours and Meg hadn't returned. He hated himself for not leaving sooner, but he had to gain her trust somehow. He had to live up to his promises. Sparrow kept his expression neutral, hiding the unease that twisted in his gut as he approached the imposing doors to the ballroom which had become Alastor's chamber. He could smell the Demon from here.

With a steady hand, Sparrow pushed the heavy door open and stepped inside. Alastor was pacing near the balcony, stroking his chest pocket as though something beloved lay inside.

Alastor's eyes flicked to meet Sparrow's with a mixture of curiosity and suspicion.

"Raven King," Alastor greeted, his voice a low rumble. "To

what do I owe the pleasure? Have you found Meg yet?" The last question was delivered with a sly smile and narrowing of dark eyes.

"Just checking in before I start my searching for today." Sparrow forced a smile, masking his true intentions.

"Just checking in," Alastor mimicked.

As Sparrow scanned the room, his eyes fell upon something that made his blood run cold. Mounted on the wall behind Alastor's club chair, were a pair of familiar, mottled brown wings. Meg's wings. His heart thrummed against his ribs but he kept his composure and held in every ounce of reaction.

Alastor followed Sparrow's stare and chuckled darkly. "Ah, those. A little souvenir from our dear Meg. Seems you're not very good at hide and seek. I found her this morning."

Sparrow clenched his fists, every muscle in his body tensing. "Babylon still wants her soul. You bastard," he spat, the fury barely contained.

Alastor walked closer, the smirk never leaving his face. "Careful, Raven King. You wouldn't want to be caught double-crossing me, would you? I've been hearing whispers that you've been less than loyal."

Sparrow took a step forward, his eyes blazing and hand hovering over his blade. "I owe no loyalty to you, bastard princeling. I hold no loyalty to a *seat holder*."

"*Kill him. Kill him. Kill him.*" Lucifer's voice screamed in Alastor's mind.

"If you ever want to be free of your father, you should tread lightly around matters of Meg." Sparrow's eyes were blazing as he handed down the warning.

Alastor laughed, the sound devoid of any warmth. "Bold words from a King who has dabbled in darkness. Remember, Sparrow, I hold the power here. Step out of line and you'll end up just like those wings on my wall."

Alastor muttered something in Hellspeak and the ground cracked under his feet. Bugs and snakes and small Demons began crawling out.

Sparrow ran, leapt into the air, and twisted his body so his shoulder hit the glass window, breaking it. Glass shattered and rained down over the ballroom. He kicked off the frame and took to the air. Black wings spread wide, propelling the shards of glass back at Alastor.

"You're running?" Alastor shouted at him. "After all this?"

"This isn't running," Sparrow shouted back. "There is more at play than your simple chore of finding Lucifer's bones. You have caused chaos between the realms. Now I must clean up your filth." Sparrow flew closer. "And don't forget, you're still behind on your soul quota. We have a deal." Sparrow hovered in the air, pointing his blade in Alastor's direction. "Where is she?"

Something clicked in Alastor's gaze. The poor bastard. He had very limited control of his own mind. It wasn't enough to forgive, Sparrow would never trust the Demon even after he was free of Lucifer.

"Tell me now!" Sparrow shouted.

Alastor pointed to the North. "She's near the Auburn Safe House. If the dead haven't eaten her yet."

———

THE RAVEN KING took to the sky. He was a dark shadow that passed over the land of Hell. The Auburn Safe House was far and it would take him hours to get there. Each beat of his wings felt like a hammering reminder of urgency, pushing him forward. The hours passed by quickly, determination keeping him aloft and he cursed himself the entire way for letting her go alone. He knew she wouldn't allow him to go with her. He'd be more of a distraction than anything. They'd fight the entire time. She'd try to kill him and he'd be fighting himself not to spill the truth. The court of Babylon would be suspicious. He couldn't have risked it.

Sparrow scanned the barren landscape below, eyes sharp despite the weariness that gnawed at his muscles. Hellscape sprawled beneath him, a desolate wasteland spattered with hordes of the walking dead. Newly dead souls ran for cover when they saw his shadow pass over. He had to find her, quickly. The thought of Meg lying somewhere, injured and alone, spurred him on.

After what felt like an eternity, he spotted a dark silhouette sprawled on the ground. Darkness stained the space around her, spread out like wings of blood. His heart lurched as he descended rapidly, the coppery scent hitting him before his feet touched ground.

"No." His voice cracked with desperation. "No. No." Sparrow dropped to his knees. There was so much blood. Too much blood. She was laying on her stomach, the bloody stems of her wings leaking and saturating his pants. Dark hair covered her face.

Meg's eyes flickered open, a faint smile curved her lips despite the pain etched into her features. "Raven King," she whispered, voice barely audible. "You found me."

He never deserved her smile. She must be so close to death she couldn't remember her hate for him.

Sparrow gently cradled her body, trying to stem the flow of blood with trembling hands. The realization of her injuries crashed over him like a tidal wave, but he forced himself to stay calm even though his gut twisted. There was no time for panic. No time to think of what Gabriel would do to him. No time to think of Babylon's disappointment if she died.

She needed blood. Badly. "Tell me who you are bonded to," Sparrow demanded.

"I'll never tell you," Meg whispered.

"Tell me who holds the blood bond," Sparrow said. "I'll go get them. I'll find them. Tell me now."

Meg pressed her lips together. She seemed content with death.

"Christ, Meg, you're not going to make it."

She saw the glimmer of fear behind his steely gaze.

"Who?" he asked again.

She looked away from him. "There is no one. I haven't had a blood bond since Skeele died." Meg's throat felt thick and dry, her head full. Her vision was doubled and she closed her eyes because the sensation felt strange.

"Fuck." Sparrow moved to his feet and paced, tore his hands through his hair. The edges of his wings made a *shhhh* sound as they dragged against the pavement. It was soothing, making Meg want to fall asleep; a lullaby of feathers scraping. Meg closed her eyes, her body shutting down. She remembered this feeling, she'd felt it more than once, but there was always the warm press of Skeele's wrist to her lips to bring her back to life.

"Meg, can you hear me?" A swipe of blood stained his chin. He kneeled next to her again. He slapped her cheek lightly but she didn't respond. Not even a moan. She was pale as a ghost. "Wake up." He shook her harder.

She didn't rouse.

Sparrow turned her body and not even the discomfort of her wounds pressing against the pavement brought a flinch to her face. There was one thing he could do. One thing that would save her. One thing that would cause her to hate him forever.

"Give me permission," he begged. Sparrow didn't want to do this against her will but he was running out of options. Although, he didn't ask her permission before stabbing her. "Meg, tell me yes." He was running out of time. Fuck it. Fangs. He tore his own wrist before pressing it to her mouth.

Sparrow's blood dripped between her lips and down her throat. She was going to fucking kill him for this. Because now, they wouldn't be able to escape each other. Now they'd be blood bonded. Again.

Sixteen

Thrush tore through the drawers of the small cottage, his movements frantic and agitated. He was on a mission to find scissors. His body ached, his muscles ached, but worse was the damn white-blonde hair that kept falling into his eyes as his uncle's Legion beat him to a pulp every day under the guise of teaching him something. Everything felt out of control, and he desperately needed to change something – anything. His hair had grown unruly, a wild mess, just like his chaotic life. He needed to cut it, he needed some control.

Nightingale and Noah entered the cottage, sensing the tension even before they saw their son.

"Thrush, what are you doing?" Nightingale asked with a soft whistle, her voice filled with concern.

"Looking for scissors," Thrush snapped, slamming another drawer shut. "I need to cut this damn hair."

Noah stepped forward, his expression stern. "Thrush, calm down. Talk to us."

"There's nothing to talk about," Thrush shot back, his eyes

blazing with frustration. "I can't go back to Hell. I won't. I hate that we're all scattered, that my friends are suffering, maybe even dead, who knows... and I'm stuck here."

Nightingale sighed, reaching out to touch his shoulder. "We know it's hard, but running away from your duties won't help. You are part of a bigger plan." She lowered her gaze. "If you don't do your time as a Hellion, the family curse will return. You don't want that on your shoulders."

Thrush pulled away from her touch, his anger palpable. "I never asked to be part of this *plan*. I don't care about some obscure rules between the realms. I just want my life back. If there is no one else to curse, what does it matter?"

"If you have children–" Nightingale started to say.

"I'd never bring a kid into this mess," Thrush spat.

Noah handed Thrush a pair of scissors he'd found. "If cutting your hair makes you feel better, do it. But know that it won't change what you must face."

Thrush grabbed the scissors and moved to a mirror. With determined snips, he started cutting away chunks of hair, the pieces falling to the floor like snow. Nightingale stepped closer, gently taking the scissors from him and evening out his haphazard work. "I used to do this when you were a baby," she said softly. "Until you made me stop. You're not alone in this," she whispered, her hands steady as she trimmed his hair shorter. "We all have our battles, Thrush. But we face them together."

"We shouldn't be here." Thrush scowled. "We should be helping Meg. We should be with Remington and Rue. We shouldn't be separated."

"I miss them too," Noah said.

After a tense silence, Thrush pulled away from Nightingale and stormed out of the cottage.

"I'll go after him," Noah said.

"Please," Nightingale whispered, bending to scoop up the hair on the floor. It sifted through her fingers like snow.

Noah followed Thrush, the two walking toward the practice grounds. "I'll never get over this freaking sun." Noah pulled a pair of sunglasses out of his pocket and put them on. "Thrush, I understand you're upset. But avoiding responsibilities won't help."

Thrush scoffed. "You don't get it, Dad. I don't want to be a Hellion. I don't want to learn darkness." He used air-quotes as he mimicked Sparrow's words. "I miss my friends and I hate that we are all split up."

Noah placed a hand on Thrush's shoulder, squeezing gently. "It'll be okay. We'll find a way through this. But you have to trust us, trust the rules of the realms."

Thrush scoffed. "Yeah, like you and Mom? Following rules got you both killed."

"Hey," Noah tugged on Thrush's arm. "I died on the way to prison. And your mom died protecting you."

"I don't want to talk about this anymore," Thrush said as he stumbled to a standstill. "Holy shit."

Both were stopped in their tracks by a chilling sight. Sparrow, exhausted and distraught, was carrying Meg's limp body. Her wings were gone, her form lifeless and bloodied. Sparrow's pants were saturated in blood. Smoke rose from their bodies and the scent of brimstone wafted in the slight breeze.

"Oh my God." Noah ran toward them. "What happened?" he demanded, rushing to help.

Sparrow's eyes were hollow, filled with a mixture of rage and disappointment. "Alastor happened. We need to get her inside."

Thrush felt his stomach drop, the anger inside him turning to ice-cold fear. "Is she..."

"She's alive," Sparrow said through gritted teeth. "But barely. We need to move, now."

Noah ran forward and opened the door to the main house.

"Don't you have somewhere to be?" Sparrow snapped at Thrush. "Go!"

"We'll catch up later," Noah said, motioning for Thrush to head to training.

"There's an empty room in the back of the house," Sparrow nodded the direction so Noah could clear the way.

Meg's blood left a trail, dripping onto hardwood floors and smearing on the walls as Sparrow carried her.

Noah opened the door to the bedroom and pulled back the sheets.

"Get towels from the bathroom," Sparrow said.

Noah grabbed a stack from the bathroom closet and laid them out on the bed. "Do you have a healer I should call on?" Noah asked.

"I don't have a healer." Sparrow settled Meg on the bed and turned her so she was laying on her stomach.

"Christ." Noah rubbed his face, turned pale as dread threaded his veins. "Her wings."

"Get some water," Sparrow ordered, reaching for the hem of her shirt and tearing it off.

"You should get a healer in here to help." Noah said from the bathroom.

"I said I don't have one."

"Don't you have friends? Call Teari." Something fell on the floor.

Sparrow dabbed at the oozing bone. "She's not really my friend."

"Well maybe you should be nicer to her. To everyone." Noah

walked into the room with cloths and a wash bin of water. "You won't get far without friends."

"She'll live," Sparrow muttered as he cleaned Meg's back. Dried blood and dirt were crusted to her skin.

"How can you be so certain?" Noah asked, picking up a cloth and scrubbing. "I'm really tired of seeing one of my best friends nearly dead."

Sparrow paused for too long. "She's breathing." He motioned to the slight expansion of her rib cage.

"You have blood here?" Noah asked. "Blood would help her heal." He rubbed his face. "Last time she was injured like this, Teari said use blood from someone who had a bond with her." A million thoughts ran through Noah's mind and his hand that was cleaning her slowed. Everyone close to her was gone.

"She's had some already." Sparrow rinsed the cloth and resumed cleaning the red skin surrounding the bony protrusions.

"You found Skeele?"

"Skeele died weeks ago," Sparrow said.

Noah stopped washing her shoulder and stared at Sparrow, then glanced at the healing wound to Sparrow's wrist. "Please tell me you didn't do what I think you did."

Sparrow pressed his lips together in a straight line. "I didn't do it."

"Liar."

"I can't lie, I'm an Angel."

"No," Noah chuckled. "You're definitely not an Angel. You're not like the others. The rules don't seem to apply. I know a good liar when I see one. Meg's been my best friend for a long time." Noah pointed at the Raven King. "Angels can't lie, they can deceive. But you straight up lied to me just now. Liar, liar, pants on fire."

Sparrow muttered something about ghosts minding their own business and stupid child songs.

"Meg is my business." Noah picked up the wash bin and took it to the bathroom to get fresh water.

Sparrow kneeled next to the bed and continued cleaning blood off Meg. Her arm was hanging off the side of the bed and her face was relaxed in sleep.

Noah would never forget the scene; the way the Raven King looked kneeling beside a half-dead Meg, the look on his face, the emotion in the room, the tension, the knowledge that she'd live but they'd all have to deal with the repercussions of how Sparrow had saved her.

Noah set the wash bin down and water splashed. "Who else knows?" he asked.

"No one. As soon as I found her, I brought her directly here."

Noah and Sparrow cleaned her skin and dressed her wounds.

"Nightingale is going to want to see her," Noah said. "I can't keep this from her. You know she's been asking."

Sparrow nodded. "I know. Just... give me a few minutes."

Noah left the room with dueling emotions. He was glad to see Meg, but worried that Sparrow had clearly blood bonded with her after everything. He wasn't so sure Meg's heart could handle another blow.

She'd want to see her children. And judging from the clipped conversation with Sparrow, Noah assumed the war in Hell was far from over.

SEVENTEEN

MEG

I OPEN my eyes to a blur of darkness. My entire body aches, heavy with exhaustion and pain. I blink a few times, clearing the sleep. Panic surges through me as I try to move, a sharp, agonizing pain shooting through my back. It takes a moment for reality to sink in... my wings are gone.

"I'm sorry he took your wings," Nightingale's voice is soft. "It's not right."

"It doesn't matter. I've lived more of my life without them than with them. Where am I, Night?"

"Somewhere safe. Go back to sleep," she says.

"I don't want to sleep," I mutter. "Been sleeping for too long."

But my eyelids are so heavy I can't keep them open.

———

I TASTE blood in my mouth. Fresh, sweet, tangy. A sensation in my core throbs and burns. The images behind my eyes are nothing short of pornographic. A blurry face, his mouth on me; sucking, licking, fingers probing. Christ. I roll my hips, lick my lips. The blood stops flowing. The dream dissipates to darkness.

———

"GET UP, MEG," Nightingale's voice pierces through the fog in my brain. Her tone is urgent, laced with an edge of desperation. "You need to get up."

My eyes flutter open. I feel better–still tired but I can move my arms. I turn my head slowly, wincing with the effort.

"How long have I been sleeping?" I ask.

"About two days." I hear the familiar sound of Nightingale's roller skates as she comes closer. "You need to get up. Babylon wants to meet with you." Nightingale's face appears as she leans over me. "Come on, get out of bed." She grips my arms and helps me move.

"Why are you so bossy?" I ask, doing my best to ignore the sharp ache in my back as I sit up.

"Are you dizzy?" she asks.

"I don't think so."

"Good. You need to wash your hair. You stink." There's concern in her eyes. "The Queen of Hell can't be looking like this."

"I am no longer the Queen of Hell. Wait..." I go still as I piece together what she's said. "If you're here then I'm in Sparrow's Kingdom, again."

"Again?" Nightingale asks. "You haven't been here in ages."

"I was here before. Babylon sent me to get the feather of truth in Hell."

Nightingale's face twists in realization. "That bastard." Her hands clench to fists.

I don't argue with her. I can't; my mind is racing, trying to make sense of what happened. Alastor. The snack shop. The attack. Busted Kit-Kat bar. The feel of my wings being severed from my body.

"My... my wings," I choke out, my hands trembling as I reach over my shoulder to touch the bandaged stumps. A sharp ache radiates and my fingers snap away. "I'm useless."

"Don't say that," Nightingale snaps, her grip on my arms tightening. "You are not useless, Meg. You are strong." She bends to look into my eyes. "You can do this."

Somewhere deep inside, I know she's right. I have to keep fighting if my children will ever see peace. I can't give up.

"This sucks donkey balls," I say, my voice barely more than a whisper.

"Probably," Night agrees. "We must get you moving. Get up, get dressed." She steadies my arm as I move upright. "Thrush will be done with training soon. He wants to see you. He's worried."

"Okay." I nod.

Drawing on every ounce of strength I have left, I grab Nightingale's arm and try to stand. The pain is unbearable but with her support, I manage to get to my feet. I sway, my vision swimming.

"That's it," Nightingale encourages me.

I nod, clinging to her words like a lifeline. One step at a time. I can do this. I must do this.

Nightingale helps me wash my hair and get the rest of my body clean. She appears with my bugout bag, the straps cut and covered in dirt and blood. "You have clothes in here?" she asks.

I nod as I dry myself and run my fingers through my hair. She digs through the bag and finds clean clothing.

"This is all you've got," she says setting the clothes on the countertop. "We'll get you looking right and maybe Teari will bless us with her good graces and offer you some pain relief."

I reach for my pack, unzip the front pocket, and pull out the smashed Kit-Kat. I rip open the package and eat the busted pieces that are big enough to pick up. If I could, I'd lick the package. My stomach growls and Nightingale notices.

"We'll get you something to eat. The kitchen has really good food." Her eyes narrow in concern as I lick my fingertip then dab the tiny pieces of chocolate and press them to my tongue.

Nightingale helps me dress, easing my shirt over my back. The slits for my wings allow the bandages to poke through. I finger-comb my hair in the mirror, surprised that Sparrow let me keep it in this room.

"You want to dry it?" Nightingale asks.

"No. Take me to the kitchen." I release the counter and start walking, my legs wobbling.

Nightingale walks me out of the bedroom and down a long hallway to a kitchen. The style of the home is single level, pale colors on the walls, and lots of windows. I only notice two doors in the hall near my bedroom; an open room that looks like it could be a dining room but completely empty, and a living area with a black, overstuffed sectional sofa.

"Here we are," Nightingale says motioning for me to turn.

The kitchen is huge and bright and warm. Nothing in this place reminds me of Remiel's home that was destroyed in the war.

There are fruit and vegetables arranged on an island. Tall chairs line the counter, while a cozy breakfast nook nestles in the corner.

Nightingale helps me to a chair. "I'll get you a plate. What do you want?" she says.

"Everything." It's true, I could eat an ox and an entire restaurant, people included.

Nightingale finds a plate and fills it with premade foods from the fridge. She sets the plate in front of me and I start shoving it all in my mouth. She brings a soda, makes me sandwiches, brings ice cream and cake, chicken wings, pizza. I eat it all but it does nothing to fulfill the *hunger*.

She sits next to me, picks up an apple, and starts eating it.

"Well look what the cat dragged in," a familiar voice says.

"Noah!" I start to move.

"Whoa, whoa, whoa. Stay there." He rounds the island and stands next to me, giving me a side hug as I shove cake in my mouth. "Hungry?"

"Starving," I say around a mouthful.

"Maybe you need something more than regular food."

I pause. "That might be what I need." I haven't had blood since Alastor gave me the rotten blood.

I glance at Noah. He's no longer tethered to me and responsible for finding me food or whatever my heart desires. I look away.

"You don't have to worry," Noah says. "I'll get it." He crosses the room and opens a black fridge in the corner of the room. "Sparrow keeps a stash."

I am reminded of the day I flashed here, stole his blonde girlfriend, and bit her. I'm surprised he doesn't keep women around to feed off. I remember the two closed doors near my room. Maybe he does.

Noah brings me a bag of blood and pours it into a glass.

"I could have just drunk it out of the bag like a Caprisun," I say.

"Nah," he flicks out his pinky finger as he passes me the glass, "this isn't the place to be trashy." He winks, using his entire face to exaggerate it. "You're high class now."

I drink the blood. After, as I'm looking at my empty plate... I'm still hungry. Empty. Like I never ate a thing.

"Maybe I need more." Heat fills my center. I cross my legs and press my thighs together, trying to ignore the ache. Recognition flashes. "Is Skeele still alive?" I ask. "Did someone bring him back to life?" Hope flares in my chest. The image of his death flashes across my vision.

Nightingale shakes her head. "Not that I've heard. I could try searching the Astral realm or his sleep." She offers.

"I don't think so," Noah says. "We would have heard from him. We would have found him in the Astral," Sparrow said. "He's dead."

I nod and gaze at my empty plate, wishing something would fill the hunger in my stomach. The last time I felt like this I was traipsing through Hell with Sparrow at my side, always hungry because I didn't know blood would fill the hunger.

A sharp intake of breath disrupts the room.

Sparrow is standing in the doorway, staring at me. He looks disheveled, tired, hungry. Something twitches in my center.

"I should go," I mutter, standing.

———

I LAY IN MY BED, watching the curtains blow, remembering the fresh smell of Heaven from the first time I was here. My mind is a haze of pain and worry. I hope Teari comes. I'm not sure how much longer I can deal with the ache across my shoulders.

The door to the room flies open and I turn my head just in time to see Thrush rush in. He's sweating, covered in bruises and dirt. His eyes are wide with concern, his face etched with worry.

"Aunt Meg." Thrush's voice cracks with emotion. He hurries to my bedside and grips me in a tight hug. "I thought you were dead."

"I never stay dead for long." I chuckle. "How are you?" I touch his shoulders then press my hands to his cheeks. "What happened to your hair?"

He points to the sky. "Heaven sun."

I nod. "It looks good. Like a free dye-job. People pay a lot for that on the Earthen plane."

He's staring at me.

"I'm alright," I say, forcing a smile.

"Alright? How can you say that?" he demands. "Look at you. You're hurt. We should be fighting Alastor together, not like this."

I reach out and take his hand, squeezing gently. "I'm stronger than I look. And you... you're doing great out there. Nightingale says you've been training every day. It must be so different from the Hellions though."

Thrush shakes his head vehemently, tears glistening in his eyes. "I don't want to stay in Heaven. It's not home. But I can't go back to Hell either. I don't want to be a Hellion. I can't..."

His words hit me like a punch to the gut. I had always feared a moment like this, the day when the weight of his cursed lineage would bear down on him. The worry wasn't as dire when I sat at the throne. The thought of Thrush succumbing to his family curse, the madness that had plagued Nightingale and Sparrow for generations, terrifies me. And then... there's the thought of others yielding to the curse and suffering.

"Thrush," I say, my voice steady despite the storm of emotions inside me. "I understand how you feel. But running away from it won't make it go away. You have to face it head-on."

"I can't," he whispers, his voice breaking. "What if I end up like... like him?"

"Like who?" I ask.

"Like my uncle, the Raven King... there's nothing worse."

I pull him closer, ignoring the flare of pain across my back. "Listen to me, Thrush. You are stronger than you know. You have a good heart, and that will guide you through the darkest times. You won't end up like him because you have all of us. We're a family, and we'll get through this together."

He buries his face in my shoulder, his body shaking with silent sobs. I hold him as tightly as I can, my own tears emerging.

"Remington and Rue aren't here. We aren't together. I don't like this. It doesn't feel right," Thrush says. "I... I hate it here."

"We will figure this out," I promise. "We'll find a way to make Heaven feel like home. But you have to trust me, Thrush. Trust that this is the right thing to do."

"A long time ago I was here and I hated it too. I felt very wrong being in this place." Memories of waking up in Gabriel's home and attending that party they held to introduce me to the Seven Kingdoms of Heaven flash through my mind. I never felt right here. Not for one moment. "It's going to be okay," I tell him.

Thrush nods against my shoulder, his grip tightening across my shoulders. "I trust you. I just... I don't want to lose myself here."

"You won't," I assure him, my heart aching for the burden he's carried, the burden he will continue to carry. "None of us will let you. We'll find a way."

For a long moment, we stay like this; holding each other, drawing strength from each other. No matter how broken we both feel, as long as we stick together, we can face this. He can face his fate as a Hellion. I'll keep him safe just like the day Nightingale died and I kidnapped him. He may not be my own flesh and blood, but he is Noah's and that just might be closer than family.

EIGHTEEN

"This is nice," Teari's voice wakes me. "It don't smell like cockroaches in here or nothing." She closes the door then wiggles the handle to make sure it's latched.

"Sure doesn't," I say, sitting up. "You're a sight for sore eyes."

"Why did Sparrow wait so long to ask me to come?" Teari crosses the room and sits on the bed, pulling me close. "He said you nearly died. Again."

"It's not the first time." I shrug. "Look at me now, good as new."

Teari makes a sound as she holds me against her and touches the bandages on my back. "Damn, Meg, this looks awful."

"I can take my shirt off so you can get a better look." I reach for the hem of my shirt.

Teari moves away and waits as I tug it off, moving slowly as I get it over my shoulders then turn my back to her.

"I'm going to take these bandages off," she says.

The tape pulls at my skin as she peels it away. "Oh, Meg," she whispers. "Alastor is a bastard for doing this to you. I'd kill him myself if I had the chance."

"Next time I see him, I will," I promise. "I feel kinda bad for the Demon though, he's losing his mind with whatever Lucifer is doing to him from beyond the grave."

"Must be some kind of possession," Teari says absently as she removes the rest of the bandage. "I feel sorry for all the children of Lucifer. There's a reason why he was the original fallen Archangel."

"Can you fix it?" I ask, looking over my shoulder.

She presses her lips into a frown. "I can't make your wings grow back. But I can smooth the bone and stop it from oozing."

I nod in agreement.

"I'm sorry, Meg," Teari says.

"It's fine. I've lived long enough without them."

Teari rubs her hands together before holding them over my back. I feel the heat and sharp tingle of her healing magic going to work. "Do you want something for the pain?" she asks.

"It doesn't hurt," I lie. I want to remember it. Strength doesn't come from comfort.

"Cutting bone hurts like hell. I don't believe you." Teari's voice holds much concern.

"I can't feel a thing." I think about anything and everything else to distract me from the discomfort and the sound of shards of bone dropping onto the bed behind me. I think of Rue and Remington, Thrush, Sparrow's family curse, and the fact that I must return to Babylon and bring them this damned feather.

Teari's been working for a long time, and my spine aches from sitting upright for her. A cool sensation covers my back.

"I think I'm done here," she says. "Do you want to feel it?"

I reach over my shoulder and she moves my fingers over skin.

"You'll have scars and these bony ridges. But it should be more comfortable than how it was."

I can't help the twinge of disappointment as my fingers smooth over the scars.

"I've been told he made you cut off your birthmark," Teari says.

I nod.

"Show me."

I move to take off my pants. There's no shame in her seeing my body, she was there for the birth of my children. I've got nothing to hide from her. Not anymore. If anyone in the Seven Kingdoms of Heaven has my trust, it's Teari. Funny how it didn't start out that way.

She touches the scar on my thigh. "This was the source of you being able to travel like Gabriel?"

"As far as I know."

"Have you tried since it was removed?"

"No."

"Try," she urges.

I close my eyes and channel that power that helped me travel, I repeat the phrase *Angele Dei, illumina, custodi, rege et guberna.* Nothing happens.

"It's not working," I say as I move to get dressed again.

Teari paces the room, thinking. "I don't think this is the end of it all, Meg," she says. "I can find a way to fix this."

"Don't," I say.

"What? Why?"

"The only thing I care about is making sure my children are safe from Remiel's family curse and safe from Lucifer and whomever he decides to possess."

"You're giving up?" she asks. "You're giving up on fighting Alastor?"

"How could I win?" I ask. "I am half of what I was. No wings, no magical ability to travel." I shake my head in disbelief.

"I think you need more time to recover. You've gone through a lot. Losing someone you love and close friends," she sighs. "That's something no one can get over in a few weeks, not after all you've been through. I think you should rest. Take walks and get some sun."

I nod, wishing she'd stop talking.

"Maybe therapy..." she suggests.

"I don't need that. Therapy is for pussies." I lay back, grateful for the lack of ache and pain as I move.

"Consider it, Meg. None of us are immune to sorrow." She looks me up and down as my stomach growls loudly. "You should consider more blood. Probably fresh blood."

I shake my head. "I won't risk a blood bond," I say.

"It will make you stronger," she says.

"I can't risk it." I blink away tears and force my chin to stop quivering. "Never again."

"That's your choice." Something sounds off with the tone of her voice. "Consider eating more meat. Red meat. That might help your hunger. And the bagged blood."

"Sure," I agree.

She collects her bag and steps toward me. "Tell Sparrow to call for me if you need me again. Don't hesitate. He shouldn't have waited so long." Suddenly, she won't make eye contact.

"Teari..." I start.

"I've got to go. I have an appointment with Gabriel." She seems flustered as she tells me goodbye.

"Are you keeping something from me?" I ask.

"I've got to go." She rushes out the door and her footsteps echo down the hall as she leaves.

I stare at the door to the bedroom. Angels can't lie. They can deceive. But I think Teari just skipped out on the truth by avoidance.

———

TOO EARLY IN THE MORNING, a knock on my door wakes me.

"Meg," a familiar voice calls. "We must leave."

I open the door and find Sparrow standing there. He takes up the entire doorway, his wings spanning past the decorative casing. He tucks them closer to his back as though he's heard my thoughts. He doesn't look so good. He's pale, bags under his eyes and his cheeks look hollow. He looks... hungry.

"What do you want?" I ask.

"Babylon is calling us. They want the feather," he says. "Get ready." Dull green eyes flash to mine before Sparrow turns and walks away. I'm surprised he shows his back to me like I won't jump on him and slit his throat.

I shove the door closed and get ready.

I open the closet and see the black sweats and few articles of clothing that were in my bag. I need more clothing and instantly miss my closet in Hell. After getting dressed, I open the drawer and pull out the feather of truth. It looks so insignificant to hold so much power. I wonder what Babylon is going to do with it now that all of the Deacons are dead.

I tuck the feather in my pocket and grab my blade. The hall is empty when I open the bedroom door. My stomach growls and I veer toward the kitchen. It's rude that Babylon should call at this unholy hour. There's no time for a real breakfast. I grab fruit and two premade sandwiches. The motor of the black fridge in the corner hums, calling me. I bite a sandwich and cross the room, then pull open the blood fridge. I take out a bag of blood, rip the top with my teeth and down it without taking a breath. I take another bite of sandwich before the feeling of being watched tickles the back of my neck.

Sparrow is standing in the threshold to the kitchen. "Let's go," he orders.

I grab another bag of blood and drink it as I cross the kitchen, throwing the bags in the trash on the way out. I follow up with the next sandwich.

"Are you going to make me walk there again?" I ask.

Sparrow mutters something before saying, "I'm not getting in an enclosed space with you."

"Perfect." I eat the apple next, chewing slowly as he guides me across his property to the walkway under the canopy of trees. I shield my eyes, wishing for sunglasses. I toss the apple core into the bramble.

"Did you bring the feather?" Sparrow asks, his voice dull.

"Of course." I skip a few steps to keep up with him. "Why are we running there?"

"I want to get this over with," Sparrow mutters.

"That makes two of us." I adjust my bag and wish I'd brought more to eat.

We walk in silence and I stare back at the Angels who gawk at us. I flash a sharp smile at a few; they gasp and backstep.

"Stop tormenting them," Sparrow warns. "We're being watched."

"I don't care. I will tear out their necks. I haven't forgotten all they've done." Time can't erase the memory of them taunting me when the Archangels imprisoned me in Babylon. "If I ever find out who threw that tomato at me, I'll cut their arms off."

Sparrow opens the door to the courthouse and holds it for me like I'm a lady or something. It annoys me.

He checks the time as he leads me to the door where the Archangels meet.

"They need another moment," he says, leaning his shoulder against the wall. He looks like he could fall asleep standing.

I nod.

"Did Teari help your back?" he asks.

"Yes. She fixed it the best she could."

Sparrow nods, his eyes drifting over me and it feels like he's imagining me naked standing in front of him.

"What happened here?" Sparrow points to the black, fernlike scars stretching down my arm.

"I was struck by lightning while on the Earthen plane."

"You were cast out." Sparrow's eyes softened.

"Been cast out of plenty of places. They all left scars." I jerk the neck of my shirt down revealing the scar over my heart and the messed-up tattoo. Cast out of a realm, cast out of society, cast out of a heart. It all feels very similar.

Sparrow's mouth opens like he's going to say something but the door to the meeting room opens.

Sparrow enters first.

I follow.

Today the majestic courtroom of Babylon feels particularly oppressive. Golden light filters through the high windows, casting intricate patterns on the marble floors.

Sparrow stands to my right, his presence a mixture of support and silent concern. He doesn't join the rest of the Archangels like before. They watch us, their gaze overwhelming.

Gabriel is the first to speak. He stands, his eyes soft. "Meg, do you have the feather?"

I pull it from my pocket then walk forward and set it on the table.

"We are deeply grateful," Gabriel says. He looks like he wants to say much more but holds it in.

Michael opens his mouth next, his stern face uncharacteristically compassionate. "Your bravery and sacrifice have not gone unnoticed. Your injuries are a testament to the length you've gone for this mission."

"We are truly sorry for the pain you've endured," Raphael says.

I nod. "I'm glad it's over."

Gabriel walks closer and picks up the feather. "We need this, to keep the balance."

Uriel steps forward, his gaze piercing. "Meg, there is one more task that lies before you. To ensure the balance and prevent further chaos, you must return to Hell and give Alastor the bones of Lucifer."

The room goes silent. A hard chill runs down my spine. I glance at Sparrow, who remains stoic, looking ahead.

"Why me?" I ask. "Why not send someone else?" I scan the table, looking at every one of them. "Why don't you go?" I point at two of them. "Why me? I don't know where his bones are."

Silence.

"I'll go," Sparrow says. "I'll find them."

"No." I shift on my feet. "One of you go." I motion to the Archangels seated before us.

Gabriel sighs, his wings shimmering as he shifts in his seat. He glances at the feather laying on the table in front of him before saying, "Because you're the only one who can get close enough to Alastor. Your previous encounters have given you an understanding of him that none of us possess. And I have it on good accord that you might actually know where his bones are."

"I don't," I say quickly.

"She can't defend herself," Sparrow says.

Rage fills me at the implication of weakness. I tamp it down knowing I'm not what I was. No wings, no magical ability to *poof* and travel at will. I take a shallow breath and choose my next words wisely.

Michael adds, "And because of your unique heritage, you have a resilience that others lack. This mission requires not just strength, but the kind of determination that only you have shown."

Determination to stay alive and keep my children safe. That's all I have determination for these days.

"You found Clea's bones when we'd been searching for *years*," Gabriel says.

I nod, remembering the day I followed the strange inner tug to the location where her bones were buried in a shallow grave. Lucifer is my grandfather though, I'm not sure I could call upon the same power or even succeed.

"We must have balance between the realms," Raphael says. "The Veil is thinning. Chaos will overtake the Earthen plane again. The Fast-Zombie War was devastating. Their souls are trapped in Hell with the Deacons gone."

Sparrow seems strangely calm and impassive during all this.

"You want me to go," I say, the words feeling heavy on my tongue.

"Yes," multiple voices respond.

I clear my throat. "I'll go–"

"You won't go alone this time," Sparrow says again. "I will go, as will others."

"Good," Raphael says.

I raise my hand to interrupt. "I'm only doing this on one condition."

Everyone focuses on me. "Since I could die during this... mission... I want to see my daughter. It could be the last time."

"Where is she?" Raphael asks.

"The Earthen plane. Some place safe." It sickens me to announce what plane they're on.

The Archangels chatter amongst themselves.

"I haven't seen her in months," I say. "I need to see her. I might never see her again."

The strangest thing occurs. I notice Gabriel and Sparrow lock eyes. Sparrow tips his chin in the slightest of nods.

"Yes," Gabriel says before a conclusion is reached between the Archangels. It reminds me that he has held the power in Babylon for a long time with the largest number of souls in his kingdom.

Sparrow and Gabriel keep making eye contact like they're telepathic or have some type of an understanding. Or maybe they're just both fucked in the head for allowing this to go on.

"When?" Gabriel asks.

"Soon," I demand. "Tonight. In the morning. Whenever the portal is free."

"In the morning," Gabriel says. "We'll make sure it's clear for you and Sparrow."

"I don't need a babysitter," I say.

"You won't go alone," Gabriel says.

"Why? Afraid I won't come back?" I ask.

"You have a history of disappearing," Sparrow says.

My head snaps in his direction. The audacity.

"I will return," I promise.

"You can lie," Sparrow says with a smirk.

As we leave the courthouse, Sparrow asks me, "Where are Lucifer's bones?"

I shrug. "I don't know."

He sighs.

I ignore him.

Nineteen

I jolt awake, my heart pounding against my ribcage like a drum. *Thump-Thump-Thump.* The room is cloaked in darkness, a sliver of moonlight creeping through the curtains. It takes me a moment to remember where I am–Sparrow's house. The Raven King's prisoner. Heaven. I miss the smell of brimstone. The unfamiliar surroundings add to my disorientation. I shouldn't be here. I don't like that I'm here.

My stomach growls fiercely, the emptiness inside me gnawing with an insistent hunger. I feel like I haven't eaten in days but I remember eating roasted chicken and biscuits and pie before bed. And that bag of blood. Maybe the stress and pain are causing this. Although, the pain has been considerably less since Teari's visit. It could be all the healing catching up with me. My stomach growls again. This hunger is unbearable. I need to eat.

I throw off the covers and swing my legs over the side of the bed, wincing slightly as my feet touch the cool floor. Moving quietly, I navigate through the dark house, moving away from the two doors opposite mine. My footsteps are soft against the wooden planks. I find the kitchen by memory and the faint glow of the moon through the windows.

The kitchen smells like spices and herbs. My eyes adjust to the dim light as I scan the room, searching for something to satisfy the ache in my stomach. It's a bummer, having to find my own food instead of Noah bringing it to me. I open the fridge, grabbing whatever I find—cold cuts, cheese, bread, fruit. I place everything on the counter and start to eat ravenously.

The flavors of each bite burst in my mouth, grounding me to the present moment. The physical act of eating, the taste and texture of the food, it all reminds me that I am still alive, still fighting. And in a few short hours I will see my children. The thought of Sparrow seeing them crosses my mind and bile slides up my throat. I need to escape him. I can't have him go with me.

I move to the pantry, reach for a jar of peanut butter, unscrew the lid, and scoop it out with my fingers. I lick them clean, savoring the creamy sweetness. Next, I devour an apple, crisp and sharp. Tastes like it came from one of the apple orchards near Gouverneur. My stomach growls again, my hunger seeming insatiable, my body demanding more and more. After the apple, I could really go for some pumpkin pie with double whipped cream.

I glance at the black fridge across the room. Blood. No. Not yet. I press my lips together and hold in the urge to empty the fridge into my gut.

The room is silent except for the sounds of my chewing and the occasional clink of a jar or plate. The darkness feels less oppressive now, the act of eating somehow making everything seem more manageable. I sit at the barstools and lean my elbows on the countertop and take a few deep breaths. Something doesn't feel right. My stomach churns. My throat feels full. A cool sweat breaks out over my skin. Saliva floods my mouth. Christ.

The whisper of feathers dragging against the floor catches my attention. My gaze follows the sound to the threshold of the kitchen. A familiar shadow is standing there, watching silently.

"What do you want?" I ask, fighting the urge to purge everything I've stuffed down my throat the past few minutes.

"I was hungry," Sparrow says. "But it looks like you've eaten me out of house and home."

Gas bubbles up my throat with the burn of stomach acid. I stand, knocking the barstool over. I want to tell him I haven't emptied the blood fridge, but I'm afraid if I open my mouth again, everything I've eaten will be spilled across Sparrow's pristine kitchen floors.

I won't make it back to the bathroom inside my bedroom. I glance around the kitchen, searching for a garbage can. It's been moved. I can't find it. I start opening the lower cabinets, searching for one of those hidden garbage cans. I consider the sink, pausing to hold my stomach.

"What's wrong with you?" he grumbles.

I notice a door to the outside. I conclude I'd rather puke in the bushes than across the floor. I run for the door.

My hand hits cold metal. I shove it open, hearing heavy footsteps following me.

"Don't run, Meg," Sparrow's tired voice echoes across the yard. Sounds like he's not up for a race tonight.

I stumble down two steps, drop to my knees in the grass, and my stomach purges. It must be a scene; the fallen Queen of Hell puking her guts out under the icy moonshine of Heaven.

A bag of blood appears in front of my face, dangling.

"It probably won't hit the spot but it will help," Sparrow says.

I notice a cut on his wrist as I grab at the bag, greedy, and suck it down in a heartbeat. The need to vomit slows but the ache is still there.

"Here," Sparrow says.

I turn and find him holding out another bag of blood for me while he sips from his own. The moonlight is not gentle with his form. He looks gaunt, tired. Dark as a lake. Worse than earlier.

I drink the blood and take a few deep breaths. I should say thank you, but I can't trust opening my mouth again.

I try to move to my feet and Sparrow reaches down, gripping my elbow and helping me up. I don't want him touching me. I should pull away, but I don't.

When I'm on two feet, he steps away like I'm made of lava and might burn his hand. For a moment, I consider death by lava and add it to the list of ways I could kill him.

"Go back to bed, Meg." Sparrow frowns. There is something different in his green eyes. A familiar spark.

"You're not my boss," I argue.

"We have a busy day tomorrow." He finishes his blood but continues to gaze at me.

"Sorry I puked on your grass." I finish my second bag of blood, feeling stronger. I take a few steps away but familiar heat spreads through my lower abdomen. A twinge. An urge. Shit. This blood is not even fresh.

I hold up the bag. "What is this?" I ask.

Sparrow blinks, his head ticks to the side and he shivers. "Go back to bed," he orders through gritted teeth. His wings flash out, shielding the moonlight. It's impressive–always was. The wingspan, the flex of his muscles, the hunger in those green, green eyes. The gaunt stare.

I backstep. A familiar heat floods my core. No. What's wrong with me? Not today Satan. Not today, not ever again.

"What did you give me?" I demand. "What was in that bag?"

"Blood," he spits out. "Now go to bed."

"I am not a child." The scars on my back ache from the urge to spread my wings in an intimidating manner, just like he's doing.

"You are not a child." Sparrow's eyes roam over my body, head to toe, like I'm cake or a rare steak or whatever his favorite food is now.

Fuck.

I turn and reach for the door. A hand slaps down on mine. There is heat and darkness surrounding me. For a moment it feels comforting, like Hell, like... *home*. He twists my hand and the door handle, pulls it open and crowds me until I can feel the barest touch of his chest against my back as he inhales heavy lungfuls of air.

Then his breath is on my ear, stubble scraping against my cheek. I hate myself for not having my blade–it would be the perfect time to slit his throat and drain the blood from his body.

"Go," he demands.

I rip my hand from under his and run inside. I am not what I used to be without wings, without my ability to travel at will, without my blade. I'm nothing more than a weak human right now. Just sharp teeth but I won't risk that. I run through his house and slam my bedroom door closed. I stomp to the bathroom and find my toothbrush, then brush away the taste of vomit with pent up vigor. I could break something or I could fu–

My bedroom door slams open, then closed. I leave the bathroom to investigate. Sparrow is standing just inside my room. His eyes land on mine.

"I shouldn't be here," he whispers. Fists clench. His chin dips and there is something about the way his chest rises and falls.

"You shouldn't." I throw my toothbrush at him and it hits his shoulder then falls to the floor.

Sparrow moves fast as lightning, his hand gliding up the back of my neck then threading into the hair at the base of my skull. He presses his nose to my cheek. He takes a deep breath and closes his eyes. We just stand there for a moment, sharing air, bodies still.

Something dark and hot ignites inside me. "What do you want?" I ask. The room is starting to spin and my knees feel weak.

His eyes flash open and I notice the glint of sharp teeth. A drop of blood sits on his bottom lip.

That familiar ache returns, stronger than ever. I've never been one to make good decisions, or even smart decisions. I'll blame this lapse of judgement on the injuries, the lack of everything right in my life, my humanity. I reach up on my toes and lick the blood off his lower lip. I suck it into my mouth and taste the blood he drank earlier, nip it between my teeth.

A heavy hand falls on my hip and drags me closer.

"I hate you," I remind him. "I will kill you."

"I know." A groan escapes his lips, then a throaty chuckle that makes my insides light with fire. "I love it. Turns me on." And then his mouth is on mine, his tongue dancing in my mouth, hands gripping my flesh and pulling me tighter against his body. He moves to my jaw, then I feel the scrape of teeth over my neck and I tip my head further, a moan escaping my lips.

"Say yes, Meg," he begs. "You must give me permission."

I close my mouth, bite my lips together and refuse, not sure of what I'm giving him permission for. I won't ask his permission when I stab him in the back like he did me.

Sparrow grinds against me, fists gripping my shirt as he rips it down the middle. His hands smooth over my back, stopping at the scars, delicate fingers testing the skin before moving to my neck. Thumbs spread along my jawline and force my head back.

My eyes flash open and I take in his disheveled dark hair, the planes of his handsome face, the torment in his eyes. I wish he would smile. Laugh even. My hands move to the hem of his T-shirt and tug.

Sparrow clicks his tongue. "Tell me," he begs, breathless. He licks my neck, sucks on my collarbone, fingers sliding under the straps of my bra before pushing them away. "Please. Please. Please." He bends to trail kisses down my chest.

I touch him. My fingers slide up the dark marks tattooed on his skin, the tendrils of black that extend up his neck. My fingers slip into his hair as he sets his forehead on my shoulder and twists his head like a big cat being rubbed.

My heart is thudding against my ribs as my hands trail to his front and tug at his shirt, buttons falling to the floor. His touch is both familiar and foreign. Hot and cold. I want his hands on me, but I don't. I want to devour him and I want to slaughter him. There is a war inside my body.

"Meg..." he whispers.

At the sound of my name I am reminded that we shouldn't be here, doing this. But, I fought so hard to have him like this again and failed. Now he's here. What's wrong with one more time? One last time. Can't I finally have what I've wanted, what I've missed, what I've desired for years? Even drowning in heartbreak, I had hoped he'd come back to me. Even filling that emptiness with another, I've always wanted him to come back to me, no matter how much he hurts me. It's a sickness I suppose.

A sickness I fully embrace as I reach for the waistband of his pants.

Here I am, ready to go back to Hell and face my fate. I'm probably going to die for real this time once I hand over Lucifer's bones. I'm going to take one last moment for myself. I'm going to *take* just like the old Meg used to. Take and use and bathe in gluttony.

I push his waistband down and tear his shirt from his shoulders.

He must take it as permission because Sparrow grips me around the waist and throws me onto the bed. He grabs the hem of my pajama pants and tugs them down. His lips brush my ankle, then slide up my leg. He stops at the circular scar where my birthmark once was.

Suddenly I am in a church in Hell...

Sparrow turns, shifting me in his arms. "I didn't hurt you, did I?" he asks, his eyes heavy with concern as he brushes a thumb across my cheek.

My throat tightens and something beats heavy in my chest. "No, not even close," I manage to get out, not telling him that sex was never like that, not with anyone, not at any time, ever.

He looks down at me, his eyes focused on my tattoos. I suddenly feel self-conscious again.

"You don't like them?" I ask.

His eyes move to mine and he leans closer to me, pressing his lips to mine. "They're perfect. Just like you." He bends, pressing his lips to the feather across my collarbone. "This one." He rolls me to the side, pressing his lips to the stars on my shoulder. "These." He bends, pressing his lips to the heart on my hip and the anchor on my ribcage. I notice his eyes move lower. "And this one I didn't notice before." His fingers graze the inside of my thigh, up high, almost to where my leg meets my hip, but low enough for it to show when wearing a pair of short shorts.

I look down to see his eyes focused on the mark on my upper thigh. "That's not a tattoo," I tell him, my voice sounding thick and abnormal.

"It's not?" He sounds distracted, kissing and touching, his finger-

tips running across my legs, sending a sharp tingle to my lower stomach.

"No. It's a birthmark. Daddy always said it was my mark of the devil."

"Are you sure that's a birthmark?" he dips his head to inspect the patch of skin that looks like nothing more than an uneven-edged circle.

"Yes. Why?"

"Because... I think that changes everything." He presses his left thumb to the mark on my thigh, hard, mumbling words in a language I've never heard.

A bright white light erupts behind my eyes and a noise that sounds like an air horn fills my ears.

I SHOVE Sparrow's chest and scoot back from him. "Get away from me," I say.

Sparrow slides back, resting on his knees. His cheeks are flushed but his expression cool. "What?" he asks.

How do I tell him that I'm sad I've lost my ability to *poof* from place to place? I hate that I've lost everything. I finally had a home and now that's gone. I lost my children, my Skeele, my Hellions, my wings. I lost him and now he's here acting like a different person. Like he might actually want me.

Every insecurity I've ever possessed floods me. Teari was right, I need more time.

I pull my knees to my chest and reach for the blanket.

"Get out of here," I say.

Sparrow moves to his feet and... I'm not going to lie, it's impressive the way his abdominal muscles flex and arch, the way his wings drape, the way he crawls and shifts. He turns and walks toward the door without glancing back, without taking his shirt off the floor. When he slams the door closed with the flick of his wrist, I am reminded that I am nothing but his prisoner. I glance around the room and sigh. This is definitely the nicest cell anyone has ever locked me up in. Moonglow glints off the golden door handle. It's not locked. How am I prisoner if it's not locked? I pull the covers over myself and lean against the pillows. Nothing in my life has ever been black and white, it's always been shades of gray.

TWENTY

The sun was directly overhead, casting a hot glow over the sandy beach. The waves lapped gently at the shore, their rhythmic sound providing a soothing backdrop to the children's laughter. Rue and Remington splashed in the water. Having never been to the beach before, it was easy entertainment for them both. They dove for shells and chased small fish. Remington lifted Rue and tossed her into the waves. Laughter carried on the ocean breeze.

Shay stood a few feet from the water's edge, her arms crossed, eyes scanning the horizon. Chel sat beside her, cross-legged in the sand, looking thoroughly out of place. Jed had gone shopping for food again. Meg hadn't warned them that her children were bottomless pits when it came to food.

"They need this," Shay said, nodding toward the children. "A bit of fun and escape after everything they've been through. It's like a vacation here."

Chel's gaze followed hers, watching. "I agree. But we can't stay here forever. We've been lucky so far."

Shay shook her head. "I think Meg did something to this place. It's so empty. Where else could we go? It's not like we have many options." Shay bent to pick up a seashell. "Maybe a boat on the equator."

"Somewhere the Angels and Demons won't think to look," Chel replied, his tone determined.

"I think you're wrong," Shay said. "I think this place is perfect."

"I just have a bad feeling about it."

Rue and Remington's laughter grew louder and Shay smiled. For a little time, it almost felt like they were just a normal family enjoying a day at the beach. Shay scanned the water line. They were the only family enjoying the beach. They rarely saw another person out here.

"There's something out there," Chel jumped to his feet and pointed.

A gray fin appeared in the water.

A high-pitched scream shattered the peace.

"Rue!" Remington's voice was filled with panic as he swam toward his sister.

Shay and Chel ran into the water, their hearts pounding. Rue was struggling, her face contorted in pain, blood staining the water around her.

"A shark!" Remington shouted, eyes wide with terror and determination as he smashed his fist down on the shark's snout. The creature thrashed, sinking its teeth deeper into Rue's leg.

Shay plunged into the water. Chel was right behind her, his strong arms cutting through the waves.

Remington punched the shark again and again until it released Rue's leg. He gathered Rue under his arm and began dragging her to shore.

Shay and Chel reached the children in seconds. Chel scanned

the water for any sign of the shark and saw more fins appearing around the blood trail.

"Get out of the water," Chel shouted. "Now!"

Remington's feet dug into the sand as he ran, dragging his sister along with him.

Shay reached them in seconds. Blood continued to seep from the bite on Rue's leg, mingling with the saltwater.

"Hold on, Rue. We've got you," Shay whispered as she gripped Rue under the arm and helped drag her out of the water.

"Were you bit?" Shay asked Remington, frantically searching him for wounds.

"Just split my knuckles when I punched it." Remington shook his hand as they exited the water.

They moved as quickly as they could, adrenaline propelling them. Remington turned, noticing the blood trail behind them.

As Chel was running toward them, he tore off his shirt and ripped it into strips before dropping to his knees and applying a tourniquet above Rue's knee.

Deep puncture wounds decorated Rue's lower leg. Thankfully, the shark hadn't taken her flesh off the bone.

"Good job," Shay said to Remington. "It could have been a lot worse."

Rue was whimpering in pain. Her face was pale and pinched.

"Let's get her inside," Chel said, lifting Rue into his arms.

Shay grabbed Remington's arm. "Go get Jed."

Remington's eyes went wide. "Alone?" he'd never been sent off alone on the Earthen plane before. Jed and Shay forbid it. The boy never had a moment to himself unless he was in his room or asleep. The idea of going alone was crazy.

"He's not far. Just down the street at the store." Shay gave him a little shove. "Go."

Chel was running with Rue in his arms. Shay ran after him and opened the door to the beach house.

Chel moved inside and set Rue on the island countertop. Shay grabbed clean towels and began creating a makeshift bandage to staunch the bleeding.

"I'll hold pressure on it," Chel said.

Shay's hands trembled as she worked.

"She's going to be okay, Shay."

Shay nodded, her eyes locked on Rue's pale face. "Stay with us, Rue. Just stay with us. Jed will be here soon."

"I...I tried to touch it. I didn't know it would bite me." Rue confessed.

"Why on earth would you try and pet a shark?" Shay asked.

"I've never seen one before. It was curious. It looked friendly." Rue's voice was small. She'd lost a lot of blood and began feeling light headed.

"Sharks never look friendly," Shay said. "Not that I've seen many sharks in Montana, But they never looked friendly in the pictures."

—————

REMINGTON LEAPT off the porch and ran, taking a right on Perdido Key Drive. He could see the sign for the Publix grocery store where Jed was shopping.

He flexed his hand, hoping he wasn't dripping blood everywhere. Only two cars passed as he ran, neither seeming concerned about the tattooed teenager running barefoot in boardshorts down the sidewalk.

He was so close. He dug in and ran faster, stopping only to check the road before crossing the street. He ran into the parking lot and noticed the Jeep near the door. Jed was loading bags of groceries in the back.

"Hey. Hey," Remington shouted as he ran up behind Jed.

Jed turned. "Don't sneak up on me like that. You sounded like Nero coming full throttle."

Remington bent and gripped his thighs, taking deep breaths. "It's Rue."

"What happened?" Jed loaded the last bag and slammed the trunk closed.

"She was bit by a shark."

"You have got to be kidding me." Jed's heart plummeted.

"I'm not." Remington's face was pale, tears and sweat dripping down his cheeks. "There's so much blood."

There was blood on Remington's shorts and dripping down his legs, much more than would come from the cuts to his knuckles.

"Get in." Jed pushed the cart away and jumped in the driver's seat.

He peeled out of the parking lot, took a right, and accelerated down the street. He turned left, tires crunching on the narrow, crushed shell road. The Jeep jerked to a stop as Jed threw it in park. The drive had felt like an eternity.

"Get the milk in the fridge," he told Remington as he ran toward the door to the beach house.

Shay and Chel's hands were covered in blood as they held pressure on Rue's leg.

"A shark?" Jed exclaimed, as he slammed the door open.

Rue lay on the island, her leg a bloody mess and her face twisted in pain.

Shay looked up as Jed approached, her eyes filled with desperation. "Jed, please..."

He moved to the opposite side of the counter, his hands

hovering over her injured leg. The bite was deep, and the sight of all that blood made his stomach churn. There was no time for hesitation. He took a deep breath, summoning the magic from within him. His hands began to glow with a soft, blue light.

"Hang in there, Rue," Jed murmured, focusing on the wound. Magic flowed from his fingertips, knitting the torn flesh back together, stopping the bleeding.

Rue whimpered, her small hands clutching at the edge of the counter.

"Move the towel," Jed instructed.

Shay pulled it away and tossed it in the sink.

Jed chanted words that sounded like snow falling on rose petals. He poured everything he had into healing her. Slowly, the torn skin and muscle began mending. The glow from Jed's hands faded as the wounds on her leg turned to bright pink skin.

Rue's breathing steadied and she looked up with wide, grateful eyes. "Thank you," she whispered weakly.

"Great job, clotpole," Chel slapped Jed on the back.

Shay's face twisted in confusion.

"Old joke between us," Chel said with a wink.

Jed rested his elbows on the island countertop and bowed his head. "Christ, a shark?"

"It looked friendly," Rue said softly.

"Sharks are never friendly," Jed said.

"I told her that already." Shay reached toward Rue and helped her off the counter. "Go take a shower. I'll bring you clean clothes then we'll have dinner."

Chel helped Remington bring in the remainder of the groceries as Shay cleaned blood off the countertop.

—

As the adults fell into tense conversation, Remington wandered outside. He was looking for Nero, needing someone to talk to. All it took was a few minutes in the ocean to prepare Remington for the fact that they didn't belong on the Earthen plane. There hadn't been any Angel or Demon attacks since they'd arrived, but Rue and Remington didn't know enough about this plane. They didn't know about sharks or other creatures that could harm them. He wandered back to the beach and kicked sand over the trail of Rue's blood. He made it to water, stood with the tide lapping gently at his feet. The sound of the waves should have been soothing, but his mind was turbulent, swirling with the earlier events.

It was supposed to be a simple, peaceful day. The Earthen plane was a world of dangers they weren't prepared for, and today had been a harsh lesson. For a moment, he thought of Thrush, wondering where he was. All of this felt wrong. He'd tried to stay strong for Rue all these weeks, but something was going to need to change soon.

Remington let out a heavy sigh, running a hand through his hair. He turned away from the ocean, ready to head back inside when he heard a faint, distressed mewing. He paused, listening. The sound came again; a sad cry. He followed the sound and it led him back to the beach house. The mewing sound came again, and Remington thought it was from under the porch.

As his curiosity piqued, he knelt down and peered into the darkness. Two bright eyes stared back at him, and a tiny kitten edged forward, its fur matted and dirty. Remington reached out a hand, murmuring softly until the kitten crept close enough for him to scoop it up.

"There, little one," Remington whispered, holding the trembling creature against his chest. He knew about cats, they walked both sides of the Veil. Half in, half out. He straightened, casting one last glance toward the beach.

Inside, Rue was resting on the couch, still pale but smiling weakly at something Chel was saying.

Jed and Shay were preparing dinner in the kitchen and Remington's stomach grumbled at the smell of cooking meat. He missed having access to a fully stocked kitchen all day long. He was hungry here, a lot.

Remington approached Rue, the kitten clutched gently in his hands.

"Look what I found," he said softly, kneeling beside her. Rue's eyes widened, her face lighting up at the sight of the kitten.

"Oh, Remm," she breathed, reaching out to pet the tiny creature. The kitten mewed again, nuzzling into her hand.

Chel's brows rose in surprise. "They have those here too?"

Remington shrugged. "Guess so."

Remington watched as Rue's smile grew, some of the tension easing from her face.

"It's one of us," Rue whispered, rubbing her nose against the kitten's. "It smells like home."

Despite the chaos and danger, this small moment of joy felt like a gift. He knew they had a long road ahead, filled with challenges they couldn't foresee. But for now, this was enough.

"We might not be meant for the Earthen plane," Remington said, watching his sister cuddle the kitten, "but we'll make the best of it while we're here."

Rue nodded in agreement as the kitten licked at her fingers.

Chel patted Remington on the back. "Your father would be proud to see how well you've taken care of your sister today." Chel wished Skeele could have seen it, and that they wouldn't soon learn of their father's fate. Chel had a feeling it wouldn't be long.

Call it his Hellion intuition, he could sense something powerful headed their way.

Glass shattered in the kitchen and everyone turned.

Shay was gripping her stomach. She reached toward Jed. "The crossroads are calling," she warned.

"Be careful," Jed said as he leaned forward to kiss her quickly before she was pulled away.

TWENTY-ONE

Shay and Nero stood at the crossroads. One side of the road was open field, the other pine forest. The air was thick with anticipation, a foreboding sense of doom hanging over them like a shroud. Nero shifted uneasily, his muscles taut with tension. They both knew this wasn't just a routine summons, it had the stench of something far more sinister.

Asmodeus stepped out of the mist. Tall with dark, leathery wings and eyes that glowed like molten gold, his mere gaze made Shay wish Nero would take a step back.

"Hello, Shay," the Demon greeted, his voice a silken purr laced with venom. "So good of you to come when called." He smiled.

Shay squared her shoulders. "What do you want, Demon?"

"I told you we'd meet again." A predatory grin curled Asmodeus's lip. "I've heard rumors," he began, his gaze flickering to the ocean visible in the distance, "of Demons tasting the blood of something that doesn't belong in the ocean. Sweet, innocent blood." He sniffed the air. "It's a scent that's hard to forget. It's tainted the ocean."

Shay's heart skipped a beat. She felt Nero tense beside her, ready to spring into action if needed. "I don't know what you're talking about," Shay said.

Asmodeus tapped his chin. "First it was the auras, now the blood. Blood that has attracted attention. Demons are always hungry for something new, something powerful." He licked his lips.

"Get to the point," Shay growled as Nero snapped his teeth in agitation.

Asmodeus's smile widened. "The point is, I can protect whatever you're hiding. I can ensure your glowing, sweet-blooded creature remains safe from demonic interest... but it comes at a price."

Shay's eyes flashed with anger. "What do you want?"

"The same as last time we met. Alastor's skin trades," Asmodeus said, his eyes gleaming with ambition. "He's beyond simply being overdue and his failure is my opportunity. Give me a deal to take over his operations, and I'll guarantee your safety."

Shay felt a cold chill run down her spine. Making a deal with Asmodeus was a no go. There was already a deal involving Alastor's skin trades.

"The creatures who crossed the Veil will find you. They are *ravenous*." He looked over his shoulder and something growled in the dark shadows of the pine forest.

Nero stomped his front hooves before turning to gaze at Shay. He wanted to burn the Demon to ash.

"Do it," Shay said, gripping Nero's mane.

There was nothing Shay wanted more in this moment than for Asmodeus to no longer be a threat to them. He knew too much.

Nero whinnied vehemently and reeled back on his hind legs. Asmodeus's golden eyes went wide as the duo in the crossroads changed. Nero doubled in size, his long black tail and mane became stiff as needles and sharp as razorblades. Veins became giant ropes of obsidian, twining and swirling under his skin. Shay changed too. Wild, blue hair whipped in the night wind as she became something wraithlike and powerful.

Asmodeus stepped back, dust coating his leather wingback shoes.

Nero gnashed his teeth together before heaving forward and throwing flame from his throat.

Asmodeus shouted in guttural Hellspeak, one step ahead of Nero's flame. The Demon danced with fire. Nero took a breath, moved to the edge of the crossroads markings and breathed fire, this time igniting the Demon's pantlegs.

"You will regret this," he warned.

"Do not beckon us again," Shay shouted. "Or you will not enjoy the outcome."

Asmodeus disappeared into the mist without another word.

Nero strutted in the tight summoning circle, before dipping his head and burning the chalk line, releasing them.

"Good, boy," Shay said as she patted Nero's side then leapt down from his back. "Keep us this way," Shay said. "There's someone else we need to talk to."

Shay pulled a black feather from her pocket. She'd carried it for weeks and months, ever since that night the Raven King tucked it there. Shay didn't have Jed's magic, but he'd taught her a few spells she could use. She twirled the feather and whispered words that sounded like the chattering of a dozen birds, then waited.

Shay and Nero paced the roadway. She'd never summoned him before but he needed to know about Asmodeus sniffing around.

The air around them shimmered and crackled with electricity. The moon's silvery glow was suddenly shaded by a creature in the air. Shay focused on the form in the night sky.

Sparrow flew in a tight circle before plunging to the ground, his dark wings folding gracefully as he landed.

"The Crossroads Demons in full regal attention." Sparrow appreciated the duo but kept his distance. "Smells like char." He sniffed the air then glanced at the shadows and fog behind him.

"Nero nearly singed a Demon to death." Shay took in the hollows of Sparrow's face and the way his shoulders curved. "Are you sick?"

"No," Sparrow snapped. "What do you need?"

Shay took a deep breath, steadying herself. "We just had a meeting with a Demon named Asmodeus. He's making threats. He wants Alastor's skin trades." Shay paused. "This is the second time he's summoned us. He offered to take on all of Alastor's debts."

Sparrow's eyes narrowed, his expression darkening. "What else did he say?"

Shay took a few steps closer, nearly as tall as he was in this form. "Asmodeus offered my safety. What is going on in Hell, Sparrow? Have you heard from Meg? I know you'd rather kill her than help her, but this doesn't feel good." She glanced up and down his frame. "And you look like dog shit. I made deals with you. You get my soul in the end. You get Alastor's skin trades. What should we expect next? Am I going to die soon, Raven King?" Panic and rage were flooding Shay. She didn't want to die. She had too much to do and she wanted more time. Plus she had Meg's children to care for. She couldn't take care of them if she were dead.

Sparrow cursed under his breath, pacing a few steps away before turning back to her. "Asmodeus is a dangerous player. He's always been ambitious, but this... this is a new level of manipulation."

Shay's voice was barely above a whisper when she said, "What choice do I have? If he can guarantee my safety, I might have to make the deal." She glared. "And you... you look sick." Shay waved, motioning to his gaunt form. "Tell me what's going on."

"I'm perfectly healthy," Sparrow snapped. "Healthy as a horse."

Nero released a whinny of contempt, not believing any of it.

Sparrow side-eyed the Demon horse. "I am!" he argued. "I just need to eat something."

"You need to release some information to us, now." Shay was growing tired of Sparrow avoiding the truth.

"The Queen of Hell no longer has a throne but she's safe."

"Oh my god." Shay ran hands through her hair and glanced toward Nero. "She's alive?" Where is she?"

Sparrow was shaking his head. "I can't tell you everything."

"Then tell me *something*!" Shay said. "Let me know if I'm going to stay alive until the end of the week. Demons have been hunting us. We've been on the run. If Asmodeus offers to protect me again, I might take him up on it."

"Don't," Sparrow warned. "Don't you dare." His black wings spread.

"The Veil between Hell and the Earthen plane is thin. I can feel it," Shay said. "The dead will start walking soon. Why haven't the Deacons stepped in yet?"

"I can't tell you everything." Sparrow glanced at Nero. "Just trust me. Please." There was so much he couldn't tell Shay. There was too much resting on Sparrow's shoulders, too many secrets.

Shay studied him for a moment before nodding in agreement. "This war must end."

Sparrow closed his eyes and shook his head. "There are many moving parts which could too easily tumble down to nothing."

"Bring Meg to me," Shay said, clutching her hands. "If she's alive and no longer Queen, bring her to me."

"I'm not making that deal." Sparrow looked away. "There are others who need her."

"Who could need her more than her family?"

Sparrow's head tipped in question. "Watch what you say." He'd wondered where Meg had hidden her child, now he was quite suspicious of Shay's words.

"Me and Jed are part of her family. Just like Noah and Nightingale." Shay clarified.

"And her daughter?"

Shay's lips pressed into a thin line.

"Just as I thought." He glanced toward the shadows of the pine forest. "Plenty could be listening. Babylon wants her to find Lucifer's bones and put an end to Alastor's coup."

"What if he kills her?"

"I won't let that happen," Sparrow's tone was resolute.

"*You* won't?" Shay was watching him closely.

The moonlight cast long shadows behind Shay and Nero as Sparrow launched himself into the air without another word and flew away. Sparrow seemed rushed. Previously when they'd met he lingered almost as if he was bored.

Shay shivered as they returned to their normal forms.

"That was an interesting conversation."

Nero whinnied in agreement.

TWENTY-TWO

MEG

I STAND in the dimly lit room and pack my bag. Moving silently, I gather what little belongings I have. After strapping my blade to my thigh, I reach for the doorhandle. Every sound seems amplified by the stillness of Sparrow's house. I open the bedroom door and tiptoe to the kitchen.

I grab an apple from the countertop and the blood fridge catches my eye. No. I shake my head. No. I don't have time for that.

Standing by the door, I pause for a moment, my hand hovering over the knob. There's no noise. I open it. It seems too easy and makes me wish I'd left before this moment.

I leave before the first hint of dawn touches the horizon. The streets of Sparrow's kingdom are eerily silent, the usual bustle of activity still hours away. I move quickly, my footsteps echoing in the empty corridors, my heart pounding in my chest. Sparrow will be furious when he discovers my absence, but I don't want him by my side for this.

The chilly morning air bites into my skin and I zip my jacket and shiver. The path to Babylon is familiar, yet every shadow seems to hold a threat. I can't afford to be caught. As I walk, my thoughts are a whirlwind of memories and fears. I make my way to the forest path and jog toward the gate that opens to Babylon. The sun is barely up and I'm hoping I can get out of here without being noticed. I flip my hood up and keep it low, avoiding eye contact with the few early risers who glance curiously in my direction. Babylon is a city of secrets and I need to remain one of them.

The fountain finally comes into view, its waters glistening in the faint light of dawn. I approach cautiously, scanning the area for any sign of danger or attack. Nothing. It's a miracle.

I stand at the fountain, ready to jump in and finally see my children after all this time. I feel a shift in the air, a subtle change that makes the hair on the back of my neck stand up.

"Leaving without me?" Sparrow's voice echoes across the fountain with unmistakable firmness.

I look up and see him standing across from me. "I was trying to evade you," I say.

"I think that might be the first truth you've told." His expression is a mixture of concern and disappointment. He adds a cocky smirk after I've been staring too long.

"You wouldn't know," I say, adjusting my bag. My heart races in anticipation.

"Where are we going?" Sparrow asks.

"Peabody Library, Baltimore, Maryland."

Sparrow nods.

I jump.

The library looks abandoned, just like it's supposed to. The "Condemned" sign on the door is a nice touch. I walk up the stone steps and reach for the door.

"Let me," Sparrow steps in front of me and tries to open the door but it won't budge.

"It's warded against you," I say, moving to open the door.

"Not against you?" he asks.

"I own the place."

We step inside and close the door. I glance to the floor and step to the edge of the runes. The familiar scent of old books and polished wood is comforting, but an unsettling quiet fills the cavernous space.

"Where are they?" I whisper, glancing around nervously. The library is usually buzzing with warmth, Nero's hoof clops typically echo as he greets whoever is at the door. But he doesn't come. Everything feels eerily still.

Sparrow frowns, his eyes scanning the room. "Looks empty."

Suddenly, a rustling sound comes from behind one of the towering bookshelves. My body tenses, ready for the unknown.

From the shadows emerges an Angel, nearly naked, with disheveled hair and a look of surprise on his face. He clutches a towel around his waist, clearly caught off guard.

"Halt, who goes there?" the Angel exclaims, blinking in astonishment. "Oh, shit." The Angel drops to his knee and bows. "My apologies, Raven King. I never thought you'd ever walk in that door."

"Jasper?" Sparrow sounds surprised and the tone of his voice melts into amused recognition. "We thought you were dead. It appears you've simply run away."

The Angel moves to his feet and shifts awkwardly, his wings fluttering slightly. "Well, I was just, uh, enjoying the amenities of the Earthen plane. You know, hot showers, soft towels, the occasional... leisure activity. Nudity. Women." Jasper walks closer and scrubs his foot across the rune on the floor.

I step away from Sparrow and investigate. "What happened to Jed and Shay?" I ask, trying not to give away too much information. The floors are scratched from Nero's hooves. I notice burned books and a pile of broken shelves. Panic fills me. "What happened here?" I move toward Jasper, gripping my blade. "This looks like an attack."

"Whoa. Whoa." Jasper holds up his hands and glances at Sparrow. "I didn't do anything. I helped them. I killed the Demons that were attacking."

"Demons attacked my..." I hold in my secret, the word *children*.

Jasper is nodding. "There was a whole bunch. They came in the back. There was a break in the wards." He points to the back hallway. "I saw it from outside. I... I fixed it. I didn't hurt any of them. I promise."

"Then where are they?" I ask.

"Please, Raven King, tell her I wouldn't harm anyone." Jasper is looking terrified and keeps glancing in Sparrow's direction.

"It's true," Sparrow says. "Jasper is harmless. He's a healer in training from a... another kingdom."

"A kingdom that wants me dead?" I ask.

Sparrow clears his throat. "He won't hurt you. Tell us more."

"I was sent to protect someone. A human. I can't say any more about it." Jasper glances to the pile of rubble in the corner. "I've been cleaning up. Keeping the wards, although," he chuckles, "I'm not as good with magic like that half-breed Jed is." Jasper releases a breath, impressed. "Now that guy is something. You should have seen him when the Demons went after that little girl." Jasper looks at his own hands. "That guy has some power."

"What happened to the girl?" I ask, worried that Rue was injured–or worse.

"She's fine. They're all fine. Even that big Hellion. Wasn't expecting to see that guy on the Earthen plane." He motions to his wings then Sparrows. "But the Veil is so thin. Our wings are completely visible these days. I'm sure the dead will start walking again soon."

"Where did they go?" Sparrow asks.

"South. Florida. The blue haired girl, Shay, she had an address." He points to a hallway that leads to an underground garage. "They took one of the vehicles."

"Are you here alone?" Sparrow asks.

"Today I am. Sometimes that Demon horse Nero comes to visit. He likes the organic carrots from the farmer's market."

"Nero visits you?" I ask.

Jasper nods and tightens the towel around his waist.

The Angel just went up a few ranks in my book. Anyone who Nero freely hangs out with must be safe.

I head for the garage.

"Where are you going?" Sparrow asks.

"I'm picking out a vehicle and then I'm heading to Florida."

Sparrow and Jasper follow me to the garage. I flick the light and see that Jed and Shay took the Grand Cherokee. I open a box on the wall that contains all the keys and select the Jeep Commander. It's my favorite out of all of the vehicles I've stashed down here.

"Are we going to discuss this?" Sparrow asks.

"No." I unlock the Jeep. "I don't have much time before Babylon ships me off to Hell to die. I'm going to see my daughter now." I hate that I can't *poof* and travel there in a second.

"Wait, is that..." Jasper sucks in a breath. "Is that Meg? The Meg?"

"Not what you expected?" I ask, glancing back to Jasper to catch the surprised look on his face.

"I just thought you'd be," he clears his throat, "taller, maybe. Scary, or something more formidable."

I smile sweetly, innocently.

"Don't test her, bud," Sparrow warns. "She'll rip your throat out faster than you can say hallelujah."

I press the button that opens the garage door. "Are you coming?" I ask Sparrow.

"I'll drive," Sparrow says.

"You won't. You look like shit and you're moving slower than molasses in January." I point to the passenger seat. "Over there." I look at Jasper. "Just so you know, this library is mine. I'll allow you to stay here but fuck with me or my family or friends and I'll gut you in a heartbeat."

Jasper swallows hard.

"Was that necessary?" Sparrow asks.

"Absolutely." I slam the door closed and start the engine. I click my seatbelt before asking, "You're going to get in this enclosed space with me? After making me walk to Babylon?"

———

THE GPS in this old Jeep is pretty much worthless. I head for the highway, taking a turn onto Holliday street, then Baltimore street until I see the signs for Interstate 395 South. I drive too fast, take sharp turns that make Sparrow curse.

We drive the interstate through winding Appalachian mountains. As we approach a rest stop, I am reminded of taking a drive similar to this with Sparrow a long time ago. I remember him bending me over a guardrail in the middle of the night as shadows slithered in the forest below. I speed past every rest stop, refusing to let those memories resurface again.

The endless ribbon of asphalt stretches out before us as I drive into the night, the headlights cutting through the darkness. The hum of the engine and the occasional passing car fills the silence. Sparrow sits in the passenger seat, his usual confident demeanor replaced with a pallor I can't ignore.

"You're sick," I say.

Sparrow forces a smile that doesn't reach his eyes. "I'm fine. Just tired."

I frown, gripping the steering wheel a little tighter. "You don't look fine. If you're not feeling well, you need to tell me."

"I'm fine," Sparrow insists, his voice lacking its usual strength. "We should probably find a place to rest, though. You need a break."

"I don't need a break," I say. "Don't make this about me. I'm in tiptop shape."

He glances at me, unbelievably, from the corner of his eye.

"I can keep driving. We're not too far from Florida now."

"We need to stop for a few hours," Sparrow says, pointing to a sign for a nearby hotel.

"We'll be fine." I glance at the clock. We're only a few hours away from Perdido Key.

"You need to rest." He shifts in his seat. "And I need to get out of this confined space." Sparrow shakes his head slowly, wincing as if the movement pained him. "Meg, please. We need to stop. Just for a bit. Trust me."

My heart thrummed against my ribcage as I try to put the pieces together. Whatever was going on with him is slightly familiar. I search my mind, remembering when he was batshit crazy, when curses took his memories, when turning into a Hellion took his memories.

Reluctantly, I pull off the exit and drive toward the Microtel sign. The neon vacancy sign flickers in the night, casting an eerie glow over the parking lot. I pull into an empty space and turn off the engine. The sudden silence is almost deafening.

"Stay here," I say. "I'll get the room." I motion to his wings. "The poor schmuck working here won't know what the fuck is going on if you walk in there with those obnoxious wings hanging out."

Sparrow nods before closing his eyes and leaning back in the seat.

I hurry inside and talk with the woman at the counter. Her nametag says "Cherry" and she smells like an ashtray.

"Lucky for you we have one room left," she says, tapping on an ancient computer.

"One room?" I sigh. "There was no one on the highway."

She takes a puff from her burning cigarette. "Cause everyone is in bed. It's nearly midnight."

"Oh. Okay." I pass her my credit card.

"Need identification."

I dig in my wallet for the I.D. the Deacon gave me after my trial. The card sparkles and as I pass it to the woman, the image changes to a Florida State Driver's license.

"Hear the beaches are nice this time of the year," she says, passing my cards back to me.

"Yeah," I say. "The water is really warm."

"Okay we have room 7B with a queen bed." She passes me a key.

"One bed?" Something sinks in my gut.

"There's a couch. No pullout bed though." She looks away from me. "Enjoy your stay. Checkout is nine thirty."

"Is there free breakfast?"

"No," Cherry replies absently.

"Thanks," I mutter, taking the key and heading back to the Jeep.

Sparrow gets out of the vehicle as I get closer. We walk to the room, Sparrow's steps slower and more labored than usual. Something is up with him. Usually he's full of vigor and malice. Maybe he needs to eat. Too bad for him.

I unlock the door and go inside where I turn on the light and drop my bag in a dinette chair.

"You should lie down," I say.

Sparrow turns. "One bed."

"It's all they had."

He grunts before crossing the room to the couch and sinking down onto the cushions. He closes his eyes and tips his head back against the wall.

I sit on the edge of the bed, watching him with a mixture of worry and frustration. "Sparrow, what's going on with you?"

He sighs. "It's nothing. Just...I'll be fine after some rest."

My stomach growls. I wish I'd brought food.

Glass clinks.

"Here," Sparrow says.

He's holding out two vials of blood. My mouth waters. I cross the room to take one from him.

"Is this spoiled?" I ask. "I don't want to get sick again."

Sparrow opens the vial in his hand and throws it back like a shot. Blood stains his lips.

"If this is rotten, I'll slit your throat," I warn, cracking the top on the vial.

Sparrow rolls his eyes.

I sniff the blood, then taste it with the tip of my tongue. It tastes good; warm from being in his pocket and like something... familiar. I drink it all then fall back on the bed. So much for not taking blood from strangers. I kick off my boots and try to ignore the warm feeling blooming in my center. It intensifies. Shit. I sit up, gather a thick breath, and drag air into my lungs. Drinking blood with him was a bad idea.

But, I like bad ideas. Hell, bad ideas are my modus operandi.

Sparrow is staring at me, his cheeks flushed and looking a bit fuller now. Just one vial of blood made him look like he slept twelve hours. Interesting.

He shifts his hips, makes a growling noise like wearing pants is absolutely killing him.

"Come here, Meg," he beckons, reaching toward me like I am something delectable.

Hell, my legs move without my brain thinking logically. All I can think about is last night when his mouth was on my neck and his hands were on my body.

Sparrow's pupils are blown wide, like he's high as fuck. I glance in the mirror over his head and notice mine are the same.

"What was in that blood?" I ask. "Crack? Marijuana? Oregano?"

Sparrow is lounging in a whorish manner. I blink and put the image in a spank bank for later.

He reaches up, grabbing my hips, his fingers gripping the belt-loops of my jeans. "Just blood," he finally says, pulling me down to straddle his lap.

In an instant we're breathing the same air and his hands are on my neck, twisting in to my hair. His lips are on my jaw, the gentle glide of his tongue trails to my lips. "Kiss me, Meg," he begs. His voice is commanding yet gentle. "Don't push me away like before."

I do it because I'm too stupid to live. But the moment my lips press against Sparrow's, I don't regret it. I don't regret my tongue gliding against his, or the way my hips grind against the bulge in his pants. And then he's pushing me to stand and pulling my pants down my legs before dragging me onto his lap again. Large hands rub over my thighs and settle on my hips. I fall into him, kissing and grinding and enjoying the way his hands slide over my skin. Every breath is somehow sweeter, and I can't get enough of the feel of him, the smell of him, the taste. I've only waited forever to have him like this again. His hands slip into my underwear and I lean back, tugging my shirt off.

He's watching me, a lazy smile on his face, eyes dark. This is a cocky Sparrow. I've never seen him like this before. I smile back and let the ache in my center take over. I am being sucked into the vortex that is Sparrow. It feels familiar. Strong. It feels like... my stomach clenches as I realize it feels exactly like *bloodlust*.

My hand flies to his throat, gripping just below his jaw.

He smiles darkly.

"What the fuck did you do to me?" I ask, part of me knowing already and I feel stupid for not connecting all the pieces before this moment.

"I did what I had to do." He stares at me, unafraid, lifting his chin so I can get a better grip on his neck.

I squeeze, feel the pulse of his carotid against my fingertips.

"Do it if you want. How many times do I have to die for you, Meg? How many times before we can finally be happy?" Sparrow asks.

"I never asked you to die for me." I squeeze tighter, but grind against him like I can't control my body. I can't. I'm barely in control. "I could ask you the same question. How many times do I have to die? How many times do you have to break me?"

"I never wanted to do it," Sparrow says, hands rubbing my bare thighs. "I would do it again." The weight of his words hangs in the air, charged with an electric tension neither of us can ignore.

I squeeze my hand tighter around his neck until he closes his eyes. "You would kill me again. I knew it," I say. Something breaks in my chest. This was a bad idea. I should have run from him the first chance I got. I should have climbed out the window or hit him over the head with a shovel or... I should have done something different because now I'm trapped and I'm going to have to explain this mess to my friends and my children.

Suddenly I am in the air and being flipped onto my back. Sparrow is leaning over me, red lines across his neck from the grip I had on him.

"I meant the blood bond," he says. Sparrow's eyes are dark and intense. "I would do it again, a hundred times. I will always want you, Meg. We can't escape each other. We can't escape *this*. Soon we will go back to Hell and we'll need to be top of our game. It's about time you realized the blood bond took. At least now I can stop dripping my blood into a bag or a vial for you to drink from, and we can feed the old fashioned way. I've been hungry. Starving actually."

That's why he's looked like shit for days. He needs to feed from me with the blood bond. I swallow hard. If I feed from him I'll be feeling like a million bucks.

"When?" I demand.

"When I found you with your wings cut off. You were dying." A sadness slips into his voice. "You'd been poisoned and attacked. There was no healing from that without a bond."

I wrap my legs around his waist, moaning when he grinds his hips against mine.

"I know this is a lot to take in," he says, his voice a low, soothing murmur. "But I promise, you're safe with me. It won't be like before. You've suffered too much." His lips press to the scar over my heart. "I can never say sorry enough for what we've been through."

My heart races, a mix of apprehension and an undeniable pull toward him. We've always been connected, a magnetic force has always drawn us despite the chaos surrounding us.

His arms cage my head in place.

"I... I don't know what to say." My voice is barely above a whisper. "This changes everything."

Sparrow's fingers brush my forehead, sending a shiver down my spine. "It doesn't have to," he says, his touch igniting a fire within me. "It only makes us stronger. We will be invincible together. Everyone knows it. That's why they tried to keep us apart for so long."

I close my eyes and take in a deep breath, feeling the warmth of his skin against mine. The world fades away and it is just the two of us in a cocoon of shared history and unspoken desire. I look into his Ireland grass green eyes and find a depth of emotion I haven't seen before. It's all too real. Far too real and it feels like a dream to have him again like this but there's strings attached. A million strings.

"I'm scared," I admit, my chin trembling. "I've waited so long for this. For you. You broke my heart. Left me in pieces. I can't heal from that in a heartbeat. There's a reason why I don't trust a soul. That's baggage. I'll never trust you again."

Sparrow's gaze softens, a tender smile playing on his lips. He cups my face, thumbs gently caressing my cheeks. "I'll fix it. I'll glue it back together like you glued feathers to my wings in that church in Hell so long ago." He searches my eyes. "Please, Meg. Forgive me." He shakes his head as his eyes turn glassy. "I can't take you back to Hell and lose you again. We do this together. We do this strong."

My throat feels thick when I swallow. "And after, then you'll try to kill me again? How do I trust you? I can't survive you again, Sparrow. There will be nothing left of me."

He kisses me quickly. "No. The omens are done, they are fulfilled. We did everything. I did everything they asked."

"How can you be so sure?"

His hand moves behind my neck. "It's the only way. I'll kneel to you every day. I'll do whatever I can to win back your trust." He licks my neck. "Just say yes. Please."

It's the way he says *please* that melts my apprehension and replaces it with a fierce longing. I wrap my arms around his neck, pulling him closer into a deep kiss. "Yes," I whisper because I don't believe any of it.

Sparrow's hands roam over my ribs, his touch igniting every nerve ending. He breaks the kiss just long enough to whisper against my lips, "Meg, I need you."

"I'm yours," the words tumble out of my mouth breathlessly. My fingers tangle in his hair.

Our bodies entwine in a dance of need and desire. Sparrow's kisses trail down my neck and I cannot control the soft gasps as he tips my head to the side, exposing my neck.

"Do it," I say. "Drink."

"Not yet. Not like this."

Disappointment stabs me in the gut as he moves away and stands. Cool air rushes my heated skin. I prop myself up on my elbows and watch as Sparrow kicks off his boots, then tears his shirt over his head. He tugs his jeans off next. Naked Sparrow is a sight for sore eyes. I don't think I'll ever get tired of seeing him like this in all his glory.

He reaches forward, fingers looping in the edge of my underwear. He tugs them off then advances. His mouth is on my knee, my thigh, the vee between my legs.

My back arches, my head presses into the mattress as his tongue works my body into a tight coil. Soon I'm the one begging please and scratching at his shoulders until he kisses his way up my body, across my belly, his hot mouth stopping at my breast.

"Oh, god, Sparrow." The words come out of my mouth as a wanton whisper.

He rolls us and suddenly he's on his back, black wings spread across the bed, and I'm straddling his hips. Large hands grip my waist. He lines up our bodies and presses inside. It's too much, having him again. I can't control my body as the bloodlust takes over. My mouth falls to his shoulder and I bite. I savor the sweet taste of his blood on my tongue as he fills me.

He rises, sitting up as I ride him.

"Do it," I beg. "Please." His blood stains my lips.

He's holding back, his body tense, a string ready to be plucked. He knows we are both about to lose all control like never before. I feel his mouth on my shoulder, his tongue gliding up my neck, the sharp ecstasy of his bite.

We tumble away to bliss, to carnage, entwined and writhing as one. With blood on our tongues and a promise in our souls, we become one again like never before.

In that hotel room, with the night stretching out before us, we find solace and passion in each other's arms. The bloodlust has taken over. Sparrow will go to Hell with me and for the first time in my life I know in the center of my being that we will triumph together or we will die together.

Twenty-Three

"I saw Meg sneaking out this morning," Noah said as he poured a cup of coffee and stared out the window like a forty year old dad checking out the neighbor's grass.

"She's going to the Earthen plane," Nightingale said. "Sparrow told me. He's going with her."

"She was alone when I saw her crossing the yard." He sets a pan on the stove and starts cooking for Thrush; eggs and sausage and leftover biscuits. "She probably tried to leave him behind."

"I can't say I blame her," Nightingale said as she crossed the room to sit at the breakfast nook.

"What do you think he's hiding?" Noah asked.

"I have to do some digging. He hasn't exactly trusted me with any secrets after I chose Hell over my family's kingdom."

There was shuffling in the hallway as Thrush readied for the day. He made an appearance a few moments later, grumbling about them being too loud.

"Good morning," Noah said as he grabbed a plate from the

shelf and tipped the contents of the pan onto it. "You want coffee?" Noah asked Thrush as he sat.

Thrush nodded as he picked up a fork and began eating. He'd woken up with a sense of unease gnawing at him and spent the early hours of the morning staring at the ceiling, listening to the distant sounds of Sparrow's kingdom coming to life.

As he ate, he finally broke his silence. "I don't want to be here any longer," Thrush declared, his voice firm. "I can't stay here anymore."

Noah and Nightingale made eye contact, exchanging worried glances.

Thrush swallowed his bite of food. "I want to go to wherever Remington and Rue are."

Noah spoke first, his tone resolute. "Thrush, this is the safest place for you. Alastor's forces are everywhere in Hell."

Nightingale nodded in agreement, her eyes filled with concern. "We only want to protect you, Thrush. This kingdom has the strongest defenses. Leaving would be too dangerous."

"You died here, mother. How safe could it be?" Thrush's frustration bubbled to the surface. "I can't stand it here," he argued. "I need to do something, be somewhere I can make a difference. Our lives have been ruined by Alastor and we are just sitting here. Meg is going to go back to Hell to face Alastor and she's going to die."

"How do you know that?" Noah asked.

"I just know." Thrush stood up and left for Legion training. "I need to do something, be somewhere I can make a difference."

Without waiting for their response, Thrush went out the door. His mind was a whirlwind of thoughts, his focus scattered. As the day progressed, his distraction became evident. He narrowly avoided several accidents during battle drills, his mind consumed elsewhere.

The Legion Angels around him began to notice. They made

crude jokes. "What's got you so distracted, Thrush. Is it a girl?" one of them taunted, making horns with his fingers, and throwing kisses in Thrush's direction.

Thrush ignored them, pushing through the training with gritted teeth. By the end of the day, he was exhausted and bruised, his mind no clearer than it had been that morning. He missed training with the Hellions and learning spells with Jed. He missed Remington and Rue.

At dinner, his parents tried to engage him in conversation. Noah mentioned exploring more of the Seven Kingdoms and possibly visiting Gabriel's kingdom for a few weeks. Thrush didn't participate more than a few nods of his head.

After eating, Thrush excused himself and went to bed. He lay there, waiting for the cabin to fall silent. Sometimes his parents went to the Astral plane at night, but never for long.

Thrush quietly slipped out of bed. He moved through the darkened halls stealthily, his heart pounding in his chest.

He didn't see his parents anywhere. Returning to his room, he grabbed his bag and began packing. He found a change of clothes, weapons that he'd brought from Hell, and the books he'd dried out. That was all he had. His room was quite barren even though they'd been living in the cabin for weeks. This wasn't home to him, or his parents, no matter how much they tried to deny it. None of them had settled in. He'd heard his father mention Meg had left that morning and she could only be going one place, to see Rue and Remington.

Thrush made up his mind.

He tucked pillows under his blanket to make it look like he was sleeping in bed. Then he opened the window and climbed out.

Cool air brushed past his face. While the days had been hot, the night was cool and windy. There was a stone wall that bordered the Raven King's lands, so he stuck to the shadows of the tree line and made his way to the trail that led to Babylon.

He paused a few times, hearing voices in the distance. Angels from the Legion barracks were wandering.

"Sneaking out to see your demon girlfriend?" one of the Angels had seen him.

Thrush went still, gripping the knife in his pocket. "Yeah," he said with a light chuckle.

The Angel laughed, then muttered something about filthy blood and walked away. The guy didn't care that Thrush was sneaking out. It was just another reason to get the heck out of this place. This was not home. Not a soul cared about him here.

He jogged down the trail that led to the gate of Babylon. His heart was thrumming against his ribcage as he stepped across the threshold to his family's lands. He itched his head, thinking about the family curse of turning crazed if he didn't do his time as a Hellion. Thrush didn't care. He was going to find his friends.

He made his way to Babylon, navigating thought the park-like sidewalks with ease. The sounds of water splashing echoed through the night. The fountain was straight ahead.

Thrush took a notebook from his pocket. He'd started collecting spells just like Jed. While Thrush didn't necessarily have magic like Jed did, he had a tiny spark inherited from somewhere along his bloodline that allowed him to cast some spells. He flipped through his notebook and found the spell he was looking for.

Thrush stepped up on to the fountain, his boots hanging off the edge. He took a breath of the clean Heaven air and held a hand over the water while he chanted to spell which would reveal where Meg had gone earlier this morning.

The water bubbled and steamed for a moment before turning

smooth as glass. Meg's image appeared, and he saw her exit onto the Earthen plane.

Thrush closed the notebook and tucked it in his bag. Guilt flooded his chest. He'd never been without his parents, and he knew they'd be severely disappointed in him. But Meg had saved his life before, when he was an infant, and Thrush would always owe a life debt to her, even though she'd dismissed it as nothing. He couldn't stand by any longer.

His mother would find him in dreams. Thrush doubted he'd get far without them showing up. They'd just have to understand that he was ready to grow up.

Thrush took one last gulp of air before stepping into the portal.

He paused as the water stirred. And then, a hand appeared. Thrush waited as someone came through. There was nowhere to hide so he stepped down and waited, thinking of an excuse if whomever came through the portal asked who he was, or, worse, tried to attack.

Thrush tightened the strap of his pack and pulled the knife from his pocket. He took a defensive stance, just like the Hellions had taught him and waited.

"Holy crap," he said, joy and concern flooding his chest. Securing his weapon and reaching forward, Thrush grabbed the hand and pulled them to the edge.

Twenty-Four

The Jeep rolls to a stop outside the beach house on Parasol Place. Down the crushed shell road, white sand stretches out before us like a promise of peace. I take a deep breath, trying to steady my racing heart. The drive from the hotel was tense, filled with unspoken words and furtive glances. Now, as we sit in the Jeep, the weight of my secret feels heavier than ever.

"Well, here we are," Sparrow says, his voice casual, but I can hear underlying tension. "You ready?"

I nod, avoiding his gaze. "Yeah, just... give me a minute, okay?"

Sparrow frowns. "What's going on, Meg? You've been acting strange since we left."

"I want you to wait outside," I say. "I don't want you to come in with me."

Sparrow's eyes search mine, looking for answers I'm not

willing to give. He rubs his face. "Okay. I'll wait here. But not for long."

"Got it," I murmur, opening the car door and stepping out. The sea breeze hits me, bringing with it a sense of urgency. I have to get inside before Sparrow can see what I've been hiding.

The problem is, I don't get a chance to knock on the door and surprise my children in secret. They must have seen me from the window because they come bounding out.

"Mother!" Rue exclaims. "I was so worried." She throws her arms around me and I grip her tight. She's taller and thinner and I regret missing time watching her grow. But I don't regret hiding her away and keeping her safe. I notice her limp.

"What happened?" I ask.

"We were swimming in the ocean and I was bit by a shark." Rue twists her leg and shows me fading marks on the bottom of her leg.

Remington leaps off the porch and runs toward me. "You're finally back!" he throws his arms around me and Rue.

"Where's father?" Rue asks. "Is he coming too?"

There is a strange noise behind me, something that sounds like the garbled sound of a man being strangled. Something thuds on the ground.

"Who is that?" Jed shouts as he runs across the crushed-shell driveway. "No! No!" Bright light flashes from his fingertips. "How could you bring *him*?"

Shay and Chel run out of the house next, rushing toward us, ready to fight, ready to defend just like they've always promised they would.

"Wait," I shout, holding out my hand to stop Jed's attack. "Just... *wait*."

I turn and find Sparrow on his knees, his face pale, eyes watery. Shock and awe don't look so good on him.

I told him that I didn't want him to come and this is why. Rue looks suspiciously like me and... Nightingale. I spent plenty of time lying about genetics but there was no hiding Remington's heritage, because he was the spitting image of his father.

Sparrow.

Now I was going to have to explain the biggest lie in all the realms. The secret I've kept for nearly fifteen years. The secret Teari kept. The secret Shay and Jed have kept. The Hellions too. These are Sparrow's children. Not Skeele's.

I never told Sparrow. And I still don't want him to know. That's too late now. I can't lie my way out of this mess.

"Where is father?" Remington asks. "Did you defeat Alastor? Are we going home?"

I shake my head. "I must tell you both something." I take their hands. "Your father, Skeele, he died a hero. I did not defeat Alastor and I must go back and face him again. I wanted to come see you both just in case it's my last time."

Twenty-Five

Then

Teari was right. It was eighteen months. Eighteen months of apologies, forgiveness, and getting my shit straight.

When the birth finally came, there was no bloodbath like in the books she showed me. There was no gore or torn apart vaginas or vacant eyes. The birth was quiet. The parts of me that hurt during and after, Teari healed almost instantly. Skeele held me and fed me and brushed my hair out of my eyes when Teari set the naked baby on my chest.

"She has dark hair, like you," Skeele said.

I touched his horns and asked, "Not these?"

"No." He shook his head as the baby let out a blat. "She's mouthy like you too. Looks like she has your temper."

Now here's the part I didn't tell you. The part I hid because no one could know. The part that everyone close to me swore to secrecy.

Skeele is staring at the baby. He's in love, I think. Real love, true love. The kind of love only a father can have for his daughter. But the first wave of unease hits me when I see her eyes. I glance to Skeele. His eyes are black as night.

My stomach lurches then cramps start again.

"Teari..." I call.

"I'm here. It's alright." She moves closer and touches my leg. "It's the afterbirth. You have to deliver it."

"Okay." I nod and get ready. My abdomen cramps. "It feels like contractions again."

"Just push it out. Easy," Teari soothes. "This is all very normal."

I'm nodding even though something doesn't feel right.

"Push when you're ready," Teari says.

I'm nodding until the cramping is too much, then I'm pushing. I feel her hands on me.

"Oh Lord," Teari whispers.

"What is it?" She said this would be easier but it feels like I'm giving birth all over again. Sweat breaks out across my forehead. I find myself squeezing the baby on my chest.

Skeele is holding my hand. "Give her to me," he says, prying my fingers off her little shoulder. "Let go of her, Meg. Here, hold my other hand."

I glance at him, panic in my eyes. He's holding the baby girl with one hand, and my white-knuckled grip has his other hand. I don't know what to do or what to think. My blood feels like it's equal parts fire and ice.

"What's happening?" I ask, unable to hide the panic in my voice. "Am I going to die? Is this death? Is something tearing me apart from the inside?"

Teari's scrambling to collect supplies. "Everything is fine," she murmurs. "Just fine." She lays a clean towel over my stomach then opens a fresh supply kit. "You're going to have to give us a big push now, Meg. Bigger than before."

"Why?" It comes out as a whimper.

"Because there's another baby. I don't know how I missed this." She curses under her breath.

"Another fucking baby? No. No." I'm shaking my head frantically. "You're wrong. It can't be."

"It's okay," Skeele is saying from my side.

The baby he's holding starts to cry.

I start to cry.

"Teari, why?" I ask. "Why is there another?"

A contraction cramps my belly and I push as hard as I can.

"Good. Take a rest." Teari touches my abdomen, feeling for the next contraction. "The head is right there. This should be quick."

I'm nodding and sobbing and squeezing Skeele's hand as tight as I can.

The contraction starts.

"Now," Teari says.

I push, grinding my teeth together, pushing through the pain.

"Okay, take a rest. The baby will be out on the next push." Teari rubs her hands together then holds them over my abdomen using her magic to ease my pain.

"Why is there another baby?" I ask again, looking between Teari and Skeele. I didn't plan for this. I thought my belly was so big because of all the pizza and waffles I ate.

"Now," Teari says.

A contraction comes and I push. Things happen, the burning pain, the sounds of Teari's medical supplies. "Okay, relax. On this next contraction this one will be out."

My body pushes the baby out and my head hits the bed. "Please tell me there's no more," I mutter, holding my hands over my face.

Teari moves closer and sets a wet, calm baby on my chest.

"Congratulations, it's a boy," Teari says.

"Where did he come from?" I ask.

Teari chuckles. "You. He came from you."

I peer down at the baby boy. "Where did you come from? I wasn't expecting you." I laugh, exhausted and delirious.

The baby looks up at the sound of my voice and I bite my lips together. Something's not right.

I grip Skeele's hand.

"Teari, we have to talk," I say. "This baby is not part Hellion."

Teari moves closer and takes a better look. "Their faces can be swollen."

"Don't bullshit me," I say.

Teari pauses before nodding, knowingly. Something strange has happened. These babies are not part Hellion. Whatever books Teari was reading about my pregnancy were wrong. Completely wrong.

"It's fine," Skeele says, moving to set the baby girl next to her brother. He kisses me and looks into my eyes. "I know," he says. "I can see it in her." He motions to the little girl. "But they are yours and mine. Do you hear me? They are a gift. The halls of Hell have never seen such fortune. I am proud to call them mine." He kisses me again and nothing but pride washes over his face.

"I wish–" I start to say.

"Shh." Skeele shushes me. "I don't." He shakes his head before settling a large hand over the baby's backs. "I could wish for nothing more." He wraps his arm over us. He turns to Teari. "The second one never came. No one can know. It will be the best kept secret in Hell. He must remain hidden at all costs. Only the few closest to us will know. We'll make up a story. He is the spitting image of his father. He will be in much danger."

Teari is nodding, then shakes her head from side to side. "No one can know. He is a shadow heir." She swallows hard and her color changes to pale as a sheet. "No one."

The Hellions made a bassinet out of dark stained wood. And they quickly work through the night making a second one, sworn to secrecy. They will die with the knowledge of the shadow heir.

"How?" I ask Teari when she visits the next week. "I need answers."

She bites her lip. "I read every book in Babylon. But all I can think is that Sparrow is something different. Without his grace, I can't explain how or why. It can only be a miracle."

"That's not going to work for me."

Teari throws her hands in the air. "I don't have answers. I've never seen anything like this before. It's not like I can go to the Archangels and ask them if they've ever seen this before."

"I hadn't been with Sparrow for months," I remind her.

"You could have been pregnant the whole time." Teari shakes her head in disbelief. "The eggs could have been fertilized and embedded themselves late. Heck, maybe his sperm lives for a really long time."

I make a sound of disgust. "I can't believe any of this."

"All I know is that those babies are royalty, Meg." She sits next to me. "You are the Queen of Hell. He is a King of Heaven."

"Their father nearly killed me." Emotion swells in my chest. "He will try to kill me again. And them..." I glance at the sleeping babies. They do look angelic with their cherub cheeks and red lips. "How do I tell them their father is–"

"Skeele," Teari says. "Their father is Skeele." She nods matter-of-factly.

"Yes," I say. "I will tell them their father is Skeele."

TWENTY-SIX

Something broke within Sparrow that moment he saw Meg's children bound out of the little beach house to greet their mother. He'd never met the girl before, didn't care to know anything about the daughter of a Hellion. He'd always wondered why Gabriel kept his distance from his grandchild. But Sparrow's gaze flicked between the two teenagers. *Two.* They were either very close in age or... twins. The girl reminded Sparrow of his sister; long hair, green eyes, childlike joy–but she had a streak of Meg's darkness. That was easy to see in the tip of her chin and the dark glint in her eyes. But the boy... the boy was like going back in time and looking in the mirror.

Sparrow sat back on his heels and took a deep breath before standing.

"I won't hurt anyone," he assured Jed and Shay and Chel, who'd surrounded him with weapons drawn and magic flickering. "I promise."

Sparrow stepped back and blinked, waiting for Meg to explain. When she simply stared at him with a blank expression, he grabbed her arm and motioned toward the nearby beach. "We'll need a moment to talk," he told them before dragging her away.

Each crunch of the crushed seashell road under his boot was like another piece of his nearly cold, dead heart solidifying to ice. Meg didn't fight as he dragged her. It was unlike her.

Sparrow finally stopped and released Meg. He rubbed his face.

"Is there something you want to tell me?" he asked Meg.

She pressed her lips into a straight line and glanced toward the Gulf of Mexico.

"You can't run from this." He bent down so they were eye level. "Tell me."

Then it burst from her like a tornado, like a demon on fire. She had held so much in for so many years. Meg could not contain it any longer. "Tell you what?" she sneered. "You want me to confess to you that I've been hiding those children since the day they were born? You want me to tell you they aren't yours? What do you want me to tell you?" Meg's hands went to her hips. "Do you want me to tell you how I had to keep them a secret so *you* wouldn't kill them on the day they were born?"

"I wouldn't–"

"Be careful what you say, *Raven King*. Don't tell me you wouldn't have hurt them because you hurt me. You nearly killed me. And you threatened to come back and finish the job many times." Meg pointed a finger in his face. "You don't get to make me feel guilty for keeping them away from you, for keeping them *alive*."

Sparrow's hand closed around Meg's fingers that were pointing at him accusingly. He pulled her knuckles to his mouth and kissed them softly, eyes closed. No hate. The omen had always been true. So much of it. He cursed the Archangels for what they'd made him do. But, if he hadn't done it, if he hadn't set the slate clean, there would be no safe place for them anywhere on any plane.

"You'll all come back to my kingdom," Sparrow said. He demanded.

"No." Meg was shaking her head. "No, they will not step foot in the Seven Kingdoms of Heaven. They are not safe there."

"Did you see them, Meg?" Sparrow's hands moved to her shoulders. "Jed marked them with runes. Something happened. They are not safe here. They will have the protection of my Legion and Gabriel's. His lands border mine. There is no safer place for them."

Lightning struck the nearby beach and Meg was instantly reminded of the day she was struck not far from this very spot. There was a strange energy in the air that made her uneasy.

Sparrow looked up at the sky and the dark clouds headed toward them.

"There's too many of us here. Too many where we don't belong." He turned her toward the beach house. "We must leave the Earthen plane."

———

MEG AND SPARROW walked across the beach of white sand, then the crushed shell road. Everyone was watching them warily from the porch.

When Sparrow finally stood before them, his presence commanding and urgent, he said, "We must leave the Earthen plane. I will give you sanctuary in my kingdom within the Seven Kingdoms of Heaven."

Shay exchanged a worried glance with Jed. "Leave the Earthen plane? You can't be serious," she said.

Chel, leaning against the porch post, furrowed his brow. "What's happened now?"

Lightning struck on the beach.

"There are too many of us in one place. This is God's land. The balance is off." Sparrow motioned to Meg's lightning scars.

Jed shook his head, pacing. "This doesn't sound right. I can't go there." He pointed to his chest. "Those Angels have been trying to kill me my entire life. I'm a dead man there."

"They will leave you alone," Sparrow promised. "I said I will give you sanctuary. All of you."

Rue and Remington sat on the edge of the porch. Sparrow avoided their glances, unable to fully deal with the reality of the children.

"I am a Hellion. When has a Hellion ever been allowed in Heaven?" Chel asked.

"It will be allowed," Sparrow promised. "You'll be protected by powerful wards. No Archangels will cross into my territory. No Demons either."

Shay bit her lip, her gaze shifting to the sky. "What about Nero? I can't leave him here alone."

Sparrow shrugged. "What's one more?"

Meg, who had been silent, stepped forward, her eyes resolute. "Sparrow's right," she said firmly. "We can't stay here. It's too dangerous, more dangerous once I return to Hell. The Veil is too thin. My children are coming with me."

Lighting struck, closer this time.

"Please come with us," Meg begged her friends.

"Why should we trust him?" Jed asked, pointing to Sparrow.

"He's changed," Meg said. "He's going back to Hell with me."

Sparrow nodded, "You have my word. Noah, Nightingale, and Thrush are already there."

Remington's face lit up at the mentioning of his closest friend. "I'll get my things," he said before standing and rushing inside.

Shay glanced at Jed and then Chel, who both nodded in agreement. "If we're all in agreement, then we'll go," Shay said, her voice steady. "I'll need to find Nero."

"Where's the closest portal?" Jed asked.

"You're living right next to the largest portal on the Earthen plane." Sparrow pointed to the Gulf of Mexico. "Right there. Sounds like you've been swimming in it. No wonder the girl was bit by something. It was probably a Demon from another realm."

"Wonderful," Shay said with a sigh.

Lighting struck, closer to the beach house this time.

"We need to go," Sparrow urged.

Shay found Nero wandering the beach, and he galloped closer after hearing her frantic calls. She filled him in on the plan as though he spoke perfect English.

Remington had his bag packed and was standing by the door in half the time it took everyone else to pack.

Rue tucked the kitten into the half empty pocket of her bag, leaving plenty of room for air. The kitten was small and didn't take up much space. Rue held the bag across her front as though it contained the most precious cargo.

Jed and Shay gathered their belongings and closed up the beach house. Jed set wards of protection and set spells to the food so it wouldn't spoil.

Meg and Sparrow moved the vehicles into the yard and waited.

Chel didn't have much besides the few items of clothing that Jed had found for him. He carried the items in a plastic grocery bag.

Dark clouds had collected over the beach, promising a thunderstorm. Rain was falling in a gray sheet over the Gulf, headed their way.

"Now would be a good time to go," Sparrow warned.

The group walked to the beach and into the water, Demon horse included.

TWENTY-SEVEN

THE PORTAL SHIMMERED IN THE MORNING DIN, THE surface of the water rippling with energy. One by one figures emerged from the fountain. Remington came through first, someone grabbing his hand and pulling him to the surface. As his vision cleared, he recognized Thrush.

"Remm!" Thrush shouted, his voice cracking with emotion.

Remington's head snapped up at the sound of his name. He looked up from the hand gripping his wrist and his eyes landed on Thrush. A grin spread across his face, and he pulled Thrush in, closing the distance between them in a heartbeat.

"Thrush!" Remington cried, gripping his friend in a tight embrace. "I can't believe you're here!"

Sparrow watched the reunion with a guarded expression, his eyes flickering to Meg as she exited the fountain. He needed to get everyone back to his lands quickly, before too many of the Angels saw them and began spreading rumors. He needed to converse with Gabriel before the Babylon court began asking questions. He also judged his nephew's presence at the fountain.

No one knew that they were coming back, which could only leave one explanation for why Thrush was there. The little shit was about to run away. Sparrow's gut twisted as he glanced at the two children whom he shared blood with. The threat of their family curse reared its ugly head times three. The stakes were much higher now. He'd need to speak with Thrush and Remington.

Shay and Jed exchanged glances, the weight of their journey momentarily lifted by the joy of seeing Thrush and Remington together again. Chel clapped Thrush on the back, offering a smile and a joke.

Nero shook, spraying water drops over everyone before he strode out of the fountain and began inspecting the new realm.

"We need to move," Sparrow said, breaking the moment of the children's excitement over being together again. "Heaven or not, we're not entirely safe here."

Meg muttered something about fucking stupid Angels as she helped Rue out of the fountain and motioned for the boys to follow.

Thrush's earlier plan to run away dissolved.

———

Sparrow hurried the group to his kingdom and locked the gates behind them. He instantly regretted not building his home bigger when he considered where everyone would stay. He hadn't built a castle like most. There were the outlying cabins but he worried about the children being further away.

———

Sparrow stood outside the gates of Gabriel's lands and

waited. The Archangel was walking closer and motioned for the gate to open.

"Sparrow," he said, glancing over the Raven King's shoulder. "I heard a story about you coming through the Babylon portal with a gaggle of people." He held the gate open as Sparrow entered and slammed it closed.

Sparrow motioned to a clearing further away from the kingdom's border where they could speak privately.

"I took Meg to visit her daughter as we promised," Sparrow said, slipping his hands into his pockets and rocking back on his heels.

"Good," Gabriel nodded.

"There's just one thing." Sparrow leaned forward, eyes like daggers. "Have you set eyes on your granddaughter lately? She's about fourteen now."

"I've stayed away, at Meg's request." The old Archangel's eyes glistened. "I wish to know her and see her." He rubbed his white beard. "I wanted things to be different. I lost so much time with Meg."

"I brought her back," Sparrow said. "And others. There was plenty of lightning threatening us on the Earthen plane. Too many beings that didn't belong."

Gabriel made a questioning gesture, wanting more information.

"I need your allegiance now more than ever," Sparrow said.

"Of course," Gabriel agreed.

Sparrow knew Meg's father was the most open-minded of all the Archangels and sought not only peace but an end to the broken families of the Seven Kingdoms of Heaven.

Sparrow considered telling him exactly who he was hiding in his kingdom but decided against it. "Meg and I must return to Hell shortly, as soon as she reveals where Lucifer's bones are."

"I take it she is still your prisoner?" Gabriel asked. "And the others you've brought back. Are they prisoners as well?"

"She remains a prisoner," Sparrow said. "The others are... complicated."

"Once Lucifer is resurrected, a larger battle will be on our doorstep," Gabriel warned.

Sparrow nodded. "You should ensure my gates stay locked while I'm gone."

"Keep it under shadow," Gabriel said.

Sparrow thought about the bunkers in the mountain. There was space for plenty, but he didn't think mixing Angels and creatures of Hell was a good idea.

"I might need a few rooms," Sparrow said.

Gabriel was shaking his head. "I can't."

"Your kingdom is not under threat. There is no war at current." Sparrow thought for a moment. "What are you hiding?"

Gabriel's brows rose in non-answer before he motioned to the gate and for Sparrow to leave.

TWENTY-EIGHT

Nero explored the Raven King's sliver of Heaven.
He couldn't find any rips in the Veil that separated Heaven from
Hell and the Earthen plane. He considered how he would travel
between realms. He kept searching; there had to be a weakness in
Heaven's Veil.

Something didn't sit right in Nero's blood. He definitely
didn't belong here. There was a constant buzzing behind his neck
that reminded him. But, he did enjoy the sweet grass that grew
along the Legion training grounds and the fresh water of the
nearby pond. Everything tasted different here, better. The blasted
sun was hot on his back and he sought shade as he watched the
Legion of Angels train. It was a stark contrast between the
Hellions training with their leathery wings and heavy thuds on the
dirt. The Angels fought with an air of nimbleness and every so
often, a white feather would drift across the sky. Nero thought of
the Angel at Peabody Library, Jasper. He'd said his name but
didn't give much more information.

Nero wandered, searching for entertainment. He thought it

odd that there were no other horses here. Then he wondered what a heavenly horse would look like.

There was a noise at the forest fringe. Nero followed it, hoping to find a slit in the Veil for easy movement between realms.

The forest became denser, the shadows of ancient trees creating a maze of dark and light. The only sounds were the crunching of leaves under hoof and the occasional rustle of a hidden creature. Nero's dark eyes scanned the landscape, searching for any sign of movement. He sniffed the air hoping for the scent of the Earthen plane or the whiff of brimstone. He considered going back to the Earthen plane to find the wild horses again, although, they hadn't been very welcoming when he'd approached them last time.

Nero searched for hours. The ambling had driven him into the heart of Sparrow's kingdom. The forest was quieter here, almost unnervingly so, as if the trees themselves were holding their breath. Nero's steps slowed, his instincts telling him something was nearby. He let out a soft whinny, hoping for a response, but the silence persisted, thick and unyielding.

He waited longer. Probably too long. Just as he was about to move on, a flash of white caught his eye through the dense foliage. Nero froze, his breath catching in his throat as he saw it again–a gleam of pure white against the dark greens and browns of the forest. He stepped closer, careful not to make a sound, his heart pounding with anticipation.

As he pushed aside a low-hanging branch, the forest opened up into a small clearing bathed in dappled sunlight. And there, in the center of the clearing, stood a horse unlike any he had ever seen. Its coat was the color of freshly fallen snow, gleaming in the soft light as if it had been crafted from the very essence of purity. Its mane and tail flowed like liquid silver, and its eyes–large and dark—were filled with a calm intelligence that took Nero's breath away.

Nero stepped into the clearing, a soft whinny releasing from his throat. His movements were slow and deliberate. He'd come across wild horses on the Earthen plane and they were always skittish of him. The white horse lifted its head, meeting Nero's gaze with a quiet curiosity. There was no fear in its eyes, only a sense of understanding, as if it had been waiting for him all along.

He could feel magic in the air, a subtle hum that seemed to resonate from the white horse itself. It was a creature of some other kind, it was something more—something ancient and powerful hid beneath its gentle exterior.

For a long moment, the two horses stood there, silently acknowledging each other. Nero felt a connection, a bond that went beyond words or gestures. It was as if they had known each other for a lifetime, though they had only just met.

A sense of peace washed over Nero, easing the tension that had gripped him since he began his search for a split in Heaven's Veil.

Angels were flying overhead, blocking out the fading sun. Suddenly, the white horse huffed, then turned and took off at a gallop.

Nero whinnied and went after the white horse. He followed the flick of snowy tail weaving between trees and overgrown shrubs. The ground shifted so they were running uphill, the ground became rocky, the trees sparser, and the white horse was further and further away. Nero couldn't believe it. He was fast, the fastest creature on any plane. But this white horse was faster. Soon Nero cold no longer see any spec of white in the distance and he slowed as the forest fringe opened to a wall of rock. He paced the base of the mountain, saw no hooves, smelled no other horse.

TWENTY-NINE

MEG

IT FEELS good having everyone together again. It's like we're on vacation in a hot, sunny hellhole where none of us belong–AKA the Seven Kingdoms of Heaven. Thrush wasn't so wrong in his opinions about this place.

"Tell me about the boy," Sparrow says, closing the door and locking it.

"He is a shadow heir. Very few know of his existence." I take a few steps away from the looming form of the Raven King.

"Tell me why," he demands.

I let truth spill from my mouth like a river. "Every day I looked at my son and saw you and I loved him. I love him. Can you imagine staring into the face of your enemy every moment of your life and tucking away the hate and the fear? My son didn't make me feel that way, but you did. I had to raise him with love." I was shaking now, years of anger and sorrow that I'd tucked away rising

385

to the surface along with the distress of keeping the secret, of others finally finding out. I search Sparrow's gaze but I can't gain much. "But now you know. I'm guessing all bets are off. His life will be more at risk than ever." Emotion swells behind my eyes. "At least he has a chance to survive now that he's older."

"And the girl?" Sparrow says.

"She is a daughter," I point out. "No one will care much about her. She will be wed or bred." I hate saying the words. That sentence inflames my ears worse than all the times I've said fuck. "Or maybe I won't let that happen. Maybe I'll hide her away so none of you can hurt her. I'll take her somewhere safe so she can live a normal life."

"You're not going anywhere," Sparrow says.

"I have my freedom."

"No, you don't." Sparrow grabs my arm.

I wretch it away. "I delivered the feather of truth. I'm free. Babylon told me so."

"Where are you going to go, Meg?" Sparrow asks. "You can't go to Hell. You can't go to the Earthen plane for long." His fingers trace over the black scar down my arm. "God will cast you out again."

"I'll be good. Promise."

"You're never good. You're bad to the bone. Always have been. Always will be." His eyes drift from my lips to my neck. "You can't go back to Gabriel's kingdom; I know for a fact he does not want to deal with your bullshit."

"He's my father."

"That doesn't mean he must give you a place to live." His fingers drift to my wrist. "And we have the Bloodbond. You can't go far. You're mine. Your freedom is very limited."

"Bastard," I say between gritted teeth.

"We must deliver Lucifer's bones." Sparrow pushes away from

the wall. "Then we will discuss what happens next. But you are not free. You will stay here. As long as you starve yourself." He's too close to me. "Feed. Now. I will not have you going into battle at half a tank."

"I hate you," I say, knowing it's a part lie. I doled out my heart to him at that shitty hotel in the mountains.

"I know. I love it," he mutters with a smirk.

"You hate me."

"That's not true."

"The children?" Who could not hate me for keeping such a secret?

He's silent for nearly a full minute. "Just disappointed. I wish it could have been different."

"Are you going to tie me up then?" I ask. "Chain me in a dungeon somewhere?"

Sparrow smirks. "Why would I do that?"

"That's what kings do to prisoners."

"No, little Night Owl, you need this..." he closes his eyes and rubs his hand over his heart, "sickness inside you like your body needs a spine. You may survive without it, but how deformed and misshaped you'd become. I don't need chains when we have blood that ties us."

I scowl at the nickname once given to me by another. "I loved you and you devastated me," I remind him.

He licks his lips, shifts his wings. The sound of his belt buckle echoes in the sparse room. "You are mine. You will always be mine until one of us dies, again." He shreds his shirt and tosses the scraps away. "Call it what you want. Prisoner. Lover. Bonded. Until you come to terms with it, you will be a prisoner. That's not what I want for you, but you will not leave me again. I can't bear it." He reaches for me, pulls me forward, and our chests slam together. His hands slide into my hair and tip my head as warm lips press against mine.

It's all true. Every word of it. I don't trust him but these words are truer than rain.

"Don't forget," he whispers against my lips. "That I am your prisoner as well. And we have been chained when together and when without each other. It's been written in the stars, our souls perfectly formed puzzle pieces. No one else will do for either of us. We will be invincible together," he reminds me. "Where are the bones, Meg?"

I take a deep breath. "On route 37, there's an old barn with bones in the rafters."

Sparrow groans. "Of all places."

Then I feel his teeth on my neck and I tip my head away offering more.

Thirty

Sparrow was cooking. He'd never attempted to cook for others in his entire life. So far, he'd burned the pancakes, the eggs had a strange texture, and the only thing that seemed edible was the bacon, and that's only because bacon is good half raw or thoroughly burned. He considered making more bacon.

The first person to enter the kitchen was the girl. Rue.

She stopped in her tracks and watched him, warily.

"Are you hungry?" Sparrow asked.

"Kings don't cook." Her hand settled on her pocket protectively.

"Maybe I'm different," Sparrow said as he took a stack of plates out of the cupboard and set them next to the trays of food.

Rue moved closer, apprehensive. "My mother told me not to take food from strangers."

"Smart. I'd suggest the same."

"So I shouldn't eat this?" Rue pointed to the bacon.

"I'm not a stranger."

"Yes you are."

Sparrow pressed his lips together. Meg hadn't told her the truth, and as far as the girl knew her father had recently died in battle defending Meg against Alastor.

A soft mewling sound came from the girl's pocket.

"What is that?" Sparrow asked.

"My kitten." Rue held a hand over her pocket.

"Get it out of here."

"And bring it where? It's mine. I won't get rid of it. I love it." The small kitten meowed from Rue's pocket and its head popped out.

"I hate cats," Sparrow sneered.

"How could you hate a creature so innocent and sweet?" Rue's green eyes were judging him and her forehead wrinkled in scowl. She picked up a plate and began serving herself. "This better not make me sick," she warned.

Sparrow recognized that she sounded exactly like her mother.

Meg walked through the threshold next. She was wearing jeans and a wide-neck T-shirt and looked exactly like the first moment he saw her in Noah's grandmother's basement. So human without her wings. She glanced at Sparrow and proceeded to ignore his existence. Sparrow knew she had a lot to recover from and trust wasn't something he'd earn quickly, even if she needed his blood to survive. She defied him by piling her plate full of food and never looking at him once. Judging from Meg's vibe, she wasn't going to have much to do with him today. Sparrow knew this meant she'd deny him and herself blood until they were both so strained they would come together with the force of a tornado, spitting threats at each other and shredding clothes.

The boys wandered in with Shay and Jed.

"I'm starving," Thrush said.

Remington and Thrush joked and nudged each other as they filled their plates.

The serving plates were empty, all the food gone, and Sparrow decided to have bagged blood and ward off the hunger.

Sparrow opened the black fridge and poured the blood in a coffee mug. He microwaved it warm and went to the dining area and found a seat next to Remington. He wished he'd had time to speak to the boy, but Remington and Thrush had been inseparable. The boy didn't notice Sparrow sat next to him.

It was different having all the noise in the house. Sparrow glanced around the table, a warmth spreading through his chest. He looked down at his mug and thought about his and Nightingale's upbringing, the family curses, the threats from Babylon. He tapped his finger and pulled his wings tighter against his back and thought about the Christmases that were celebrated on the Earthen plane, and holidays with a full table of family and good food. He'd have a lot of work to do if that was his future. He wondered how they could hold this all together after returning to Hell to hand over Lucifer's bones. They'd have a war, instantly. Sparrow blinked and committed the scene before him to memory knowing that it might be his last and only one.

Something warm rubbed against his ankle. Sparrow looked down and saw the furry kitten that had been in Rue's pocket. He reached down and picked it up.

"Maybe you're not so bad." Sparrow muttered as he set the kitten on his lap. It licked his hand then put it paws on the edge of the table and stood up, sniffing his mug.

Sparrow glanced up and found everyone staring at him. He glanced to his left. Remington was staring. Green eyes, familiar eyes. Sparrow searched the boy's face and dark hair.

"You two look alike," Rue said.

"Me and the cat?" Sparrow asked, trying his best to deflect.

"No. You and my brother." She was pointing a piece of bacon at them.

A fork clanged against the floor.

Someone cleared their throat.

OMENS OF DARKNESS

About Veil of Shadows 13: Omens of Darkness

The Throne of Hell Awaits. The Final Battle Beckons.

Meg and Sparrow have faced insurmountable odds, but nothing could prepare them for the final descent into Hell. With Lucifer resurrected and chaos gripping the realms, they must rally their allies for one last battle to reclaim their kingdom and save their family.

But as the war unfolds, Lucifer delivers a shattering revelation: the curse Meg always believed marked Sparrow was hers to bear all along—a dark legacy that now threatens their daughter's life.

The stakes have never been higher, and as Hell's throne hangs in the balance, Meg and Sparrow must summon every ounce of strength, love, and sacrifice they possess. Because this time, the fate of more than one world rests on their shoulders.

The epic conclusion to the *Veil of Shadows* series will leave you breathless.

ONE

MEG

HEAVEN HAS NEVER FELT comfortable to me, and today is no different. It doesn't matter that I'm blood-bonded to the most powerful Angel in the Seven Kingdoms of Heaven; comfort has escaped me, and it seems I am back to searching for something that feels like home. Again.

I sit in Sparrow's living room, tracing the intricate designs carved into the armrest of an old wooden chair. I wonder if it's salvaged from his father's home–that would make it pre-Fast-Zombie War. This place is too quiet, almost eerie in its stillness. I wish Rue and Remington were here with me but they went to explore. I try letting the tension drain from my shoulders. Having my children nearby helps, at least we are in the same realm again.

I need to sit Rue and Remington down and discuss Sparrow with them. Maybe after that I won't feel so tightly wound. I've held on to this secret for too long and it's been eroding me from the inside. I just want to be free of it. The children are old enough to manage the truth. Although, I'm still worried about Remington's safety. He looks too much like Sparrow to keep his heritage a secret in this place.

The front door creaks open, the sound startling me out of my thoughts. A woman steps into the room. She is tall, her hair a cascade of golden waves that catch the light and make her look like the ethereal creature she is. She's wearing a white dress that clings to her curves, downy white wings stretching as she takes another step. A smile plays on her lips as her eyes scan the room, until they land on me.

"Oh," she says, her smile fading. "I didn't realize Sparrow had company."

My jaw tightens. Something about her presence ignites a fire within me, a possessiveness I've been trying my damndest to ignore.

"Who are you?" I ask, voice sharp. I don't bother to hide my annoyance.

She blinks, taken aback by the venom in my tone but she recovers quickly, giving me a smile too sweet to be genuine.

"I'm Lyra. Sparrow and I go way back. I thought he'd be here."

Lyra. Sounds like a strumpet.

"Well, Lyra," I say, standing and crossing the room until I'm just a few feet from her. Damn she's tall. "Sparrow doesn't need anyone from 'way back' at the moment."

She raises an eyebrow, her smile turning sly. "Really? Because last I checked, he and I have unfinished business."

The challenge in her voice is clear, and it sends a surge of irritation through me. Sparrow's old girlfriend is turning out to be a real bitch. I don't want her seeing my children. I don't want her around me. I want her *gone*.

"Whatever business you think you had, take it elsewhere," I say, my voice low and threatening. "Sparrow's not here."

She glances over my shoulder and down the hall. "I'll just go check his room. I know where it is."

"Don't," I warn. "Go."

Lyra chuckles, the sound grating my nerves. "Let me tell you something, sweetheart, you're not the first, and you won't be the last." She sighs, looking me up and down. "You don't look his type..." Her eyes narrow. "Wait a minute. Are you...?" she takes a few steps back.

I flash a smile. Sharp teeth.

"You're the biter." Her hands fly to her neck.

I smirk, remembering the time I flashed here and ripped Sparrow's *other* blonde girlfriend out of his bed and bit her neck. That was kinda rude of me. But I was searching for revenge at the time. Can't blame a girl for that.

I step closer, my eyes narrowing. "You're right. I bite." I snap my teeth.

For a moment we stand there in silence, the air between us crackling with tension. Doubt flickers in her eyes, her bravado faltering. I get the feeling she might have expected someone to be here but didn't anticipate me. Story of my life.

Lyra rolls her eyes as she steps back. "Fine. Whatever. He's all yours. But don't be surprised if he comes looking for me when things get boring. He *always* does."

That's it. I lurch forward and Lyra turns tail and runs out of the house. I chase her to the doorway, my heart pounding with the thrill of it.

Lyra takes to the sky and something sinks in my chest. A phantom ache stretches across my shoulder blades. I'll never fly again. I watch her go. He'd be better off with someone like her, someone whole.

.   .   .

"DON'T FORGET," he whispers against my lips. "That I am your prisoner as well. And we have been chained when together and when without each other. It's been written in the stars, our souls are perfectly formed puzzle pieces. No one else will do for either of us. We will be invincible together," he reminds me.

A DARK FIGURE with black wings appears, following Lyra off the Raven King's lands. I cross my arms and watch. Jealousy boils through my veins. Maybe I should have bitten her. I lick my lips. If she were royal lineage it would give me some more time before caving and dragging my sorry ass to Sparrow's room to beg for a meal. My mouth waters at the thought of drinking from him then instantly dries at the thought of him with another female.

I rub my eyes. Heck, I was with Skeele for nearly fifteen years; I'm sure Sparrow was with someone. I glance to the sky. Or many someones. Can't blame him too much.

When they are out of view I pace the porch. The thought of Sparrow's old girlfriends hanging around pisses me off. I don't want anyone snooping around. I step off the porch and start walking toward Nightingale's cabin in the distance. Jed might have to lay more wards or show me where I could bury a body on Sparrow's lands.

Two

"Lyra," Sparrow called as he landed, boots hitting the ground mid-step. The air around him crackled with dark energy. Lyra has always been slippery, finding her way into places she didn't belong. But this was different–this was personal. And he wasn't going to let it slide.

The woman was trying to avoid him now, walking with long strides until Sparrow caught up and grabbed her upper arm.

"Stop running," he called out, his voice cold and sharp, slicing through the silence.

Lyra stopped but didn't turn around immediately. She waited, plastering a smile on her face, refusing to let all of Babylon think there was a problem. When she finally faced him, she turned pale at the sight of him. "Sparrow," she greeted, her voice light. She glanced at where his hand gripped her arm until he released her. "I knew you were fucked up, but you're keeping that thing in your house." She pointed toward Sparrow's lands. "How could you? The fallen Queen of Hell. It's disgusting."

"I'm not going to answer any of those questions," Sparrow

said, eyes narrowing as he stared her down. "How did you get past my gates?"

She smirked, tilting her head. "You know me. I have my ways."

"That's not an answer." Sparrow growled, his patience wearing thin. "You've always been good at slipping through cracks, but you should not have been able to breach my lands. Someone helped you."

Lyra's spine straightened. "Your Legion let me in. I wasn't aware that I had been banished. I thought we had something." She reached toward him.

Sparrow caught her wrist before manicured fingers could touch him. "Things have changed."

"But she bit–"

"I know. I was there and it no longer matters. That was a long time ago." Sparrow stepped closer to her and squeezed her wrist. "Why did you come?"

"I wanted to see you." She searched his gaze. "I wanted to invite you out. We used to have fun."

Sparrow didn't trust her. There were plenty of female Angels he'd used for their bodies and their blood. He shouldn't have let his time with Lyra linger over the years. It had only created a problem. A promise she's assumed.

Sparrow said, "There's nothing between us. It's over. Ended a long time ago. Stay away."

Lyra batted her eyelashes before glancing up and down his body. "What will the girls think? They'll all be heartbroken. Some of us really thought you'd pick a girl to settle down with." Big eyes glanced in the direction of his kingdom. "It must be lonely in that big house all alone."

"That was never going to happen. You all knew it." He squeezed her arm harder and pulled her closer. "You have an agenda and I'm not going to let you get away with whatever game you're playing."

Lyra met his gaze; eyes like her father's pupils blown wide. Sparrow would warn the Archangel that his daughter had been snooping. She was probably spying for him. Sparrow was going to say plenty about it at the next council meeting.

"I have never trusted you." Sparrow's voice was dangerously low. "And I don't believe for one second that you came here just to hook up."

Lyra's expression hardened. "Maybe I was curious. Maybe I wanted to see what was so special about what you're hiding in there."

"This place," he said, tone icy, "is mine. And it's off limits to you."

"What else are you hiding beyond that gate?" Lyra tried to pull her arm back, but Sparrow had gripped her so tight it was causing bruises.

"None of your concern. Tell whomever you're working with."

"Protective, aren't we? What's the matter, Sparrow? Afraid I might tell the wrong people about your little secret? Afraid I might tell someone you have the fallen Queen of Hell hiding out in your kingdom? What other creatures are you keeping there? Babylon will have a field day with this. My father–"

Sparrow grabbed Lyra's throat and squeezed. Sharp teeth flashed as he dragged her close. "Now, listen carefully. You're never going to mention Meg being in my home. You're never to mention her name or presence to anyone. And you're never to come here again."

He squeezed her throat tighter until her breathing ceased and her eyes turned red. "Nod or die."

Lyra was still.

"This isn't a game. If you value your life, you'll heed my warning. Stay out of my lands. Stay out of my life. And stay the hell away from Meg."

She finally made the slightest nod of her head.

He released the Angel woman and pushed her away, disgusted.

"Fine," she spat.

And then she was disappearing down the pristine walkway toward Babylon.

Lyra was a problem he'd been able to ignore for years. He'd ruin her if she didn't keep her mouth shut. Or... Sparrow followed after her, palm tapping the blade at his hip, mind set. She would die today. Too much was at stake.

THREE

The sky was painted in shades of deep purple and gold as the sun began to dip below the horizon. Thrush led the way through ancient cobblestone walkways of the Raven King's kingdom. Remington and Rue followed closely, their eyes wide as they took in the scenery surrounding them. It was a place that felt both otherworldly and strangely familiar, like a dream they had almost forgotten.

They reached a secluded courtyard, where the scent of blooming night flowers filled the air. The courtyard was over-grown, the design quite different from the newer buildings and walkways. The children recognized it as something forgotten and discarded, the perfect place to meet in private.

Thrush turned to face the others, his expression serious. "What do you think of this place?" he asked, leaning against a marble fountain that burbled softly in the background. The marble had turned green with algae but the water ran clear.

Remington shrugged, his gaze drifting toward the sky. "It's nice, I guess. But it feels... heavy. Like there's a lot of history here."

Rue nodded, her dark hair catching the last rays of sunlight. She shielded her eyes. "It's so different from Hell. Not as chaotic but still intense. There's so much power in the air. The sun is too bright."

Thrush made a face before sighing and running a hand over his short, white-blonde hair. "Yeah, it's powerful alright. It doesn't feel like home. But all this... it's not enough to keep me here. Not when your mother is headed back to face Alastor. I want to go home."

Remington crossed his arms, his brow furrowing. "You think she's really gonna leave us behind again?"

Rue frowned, her eyes narrowing. "Mother has always been about protecting us."

Thrush's cheek twitched slightly, betraying his unease. "I don't want to stay here and be useless. We need to be ready, all of us together is our best shot at defeating Alastor. Look at your mother; Alastor cut off her wings. She's weaker than ever."

"Shay said she is formidable," Rue whispered.

"Not if she's dead." Thrush reached out to touch Rue's shoulder. "None of us have ever seen her like this. She's different."

Remington glanced at him sharply. "You think we have a chance against him? I heard that Alastor is going to resurrect Lucifer. Do you think we can win against him? Against the original fallen Archangel?"

Thrush hesitated, then shook his head slowly. "I don't know. But I do know we can't let him destroy our home. We can't let him kill your mother. We have to do something."

Rue glanced between the two of them, her expression conflicted. "I'm going to name him Lucipurr," Rue said, petting the tiny cat in her pocket. Talking about war and her mother made Rue uneasy. She'd been having nightmares about it all.

Thrush burst out laughing.

The kitten meowed in accepting retort to his new name.

A heavy silence settled over the group as they all considered the possibility of going to war. It was terrifying.

Thrush finally broke the silence, his voice quiet but resolute. "If it comes to war... we'll have to go. We can't let them kill her." He itched his shoulder. "If you'd seen how she looked when the Raven King brought her back the first time..." Thrush shook his head. "She looked dead in his arms, with her wings cut off and blood everywhere." Thrush paled at the memory.

"She's defeated Lucifer before," Remington said, "Noah told us the story of how she battled him in the sky before she had her wings. She doesn't need the wings to be strong."

"I don't want mother hurt again," Rue said. The kitten meowed in agreement.

The three of them stood in the courtyard in a moment of silence, the weight of their decision hanging heavily in the air. They were young, unsure of what the future held, but they knew one thing for certain–they would face it together. They would return to help Meg in Hell whether their parents liked it or not.

"They're going to try and stop us," Remington warned. He touched the runes on his chest before glancing at his sister.

"We'll have to prepare in secret." Thrush looked at Rue. "Can you do that without spilling the beans?"

Rue nodded.

———

"I've fashioned wooden swords from some sticks I found in the forest." Chel passed each of the children a weapon.

"What do you want us to do with these?" Thrush asked, his body bruised and dirty from a day training with the Raven King's Legion warriors.

"Continue your Hellion training." Chel gripped his blade. "There is no better time."

"I'm tired," Thrush complained. "I'm going to get something to eat." He walked away with plans of preparing to escape to Hell when Meg left.

"Wait." Chel grabbed Thrush's collar and dragged him back. He turned to Rue. "You've had the least training."

"Then she will join the Legion," a familiar voice said.

Chel turned to see Sparrow walking closer.

"The girl?" Chel asked. "She needs to learn the way of the Hellions. She is small. Weaker than the boys."

Rue gave him a dirty look and Lucipurr hissed from her pocket.

"All the more reason to send her to work with the Legion." Sparrow looked down at Rue, remembering how his sister Nightingale had never been trained in battle. She had been "too crazy," according to his father, and locked away. Sparrow wouldn't let his daughter suffer the same fate of being unprepared with what was coming.

Chel opened his mouth to argue but Sparrow said, "Come, follow me."

The Raven King's Legion training grounds were a sprawling expanse, filled with regimented rows of Angel soldiers running drills and sparring with one another. The air was thick with the rhythmic sounds of combat—swords flashing, wings flapping, and the occasional barked command from the Legion's seasoned trainers. Soldiers clad in gleaming armor moved in unison, their motions sharp and precise. Fresh dirt and sweat clung in the air.

The Raven King strode forward with purpose, his imposing figure easily commanding attention. Behind him trailed Rue and Remington, their eyes wide as they took in the sights and sounds around them.

Chel followed closely, his expression growing more tense with each step they took.

"I don't like this," Chel muttered under his breath as they approached. "Hellions and Angels do not train together."

"The rest of your Hellions died in battle with Alastor," Sparrow sneered. "It will do you some good to spar. You're the last that remains of her army. You don't want to be out of practice."

Chel snarled.

"They need to be ready," Sparrow replied, his voice firm but not unkind. "You know what's coming. We can't afford to be unprepared."

Chel clenched his fists. He knew the Raven King was right but he'd known these kids since they were babies. He'd seen the bruises all over Thrush. "Training with the Legion is too much for them."

"If we don't prepare them now, we'll be throwing them to the wolves. They need to learn," Sparrow insisted.

As they approached the central training area, the Legion Commander—a stern-looking Angel with scarred arms and piercing blue eyes—stepped forward to meet them. His gaze swept over Rue and Remington, and he recognized Thrush, then Chel, before settling on Sparrow with a mixture of respect and unease.

"Raven King," the commander greeted, inclining his head slightly.

"These two," Sparrow said, gesturing to Rue and Remington. "I want them trained."

The commander's eyes narrowed as he looked at the young ones, his expression hardening. "These are not Angels, Sir. They're children. We train Angels here, not... outsiders."

"Outsiders?" Chel snapped, stepping forward with a snarl.

Sparrow raised a hand to calm Chel before turning his attention back to the commander. "These 'outsiders' are the future. They're as much a part of this fight as anyone else in this Kingdom. I want them ready for anything. They've lost too much time already."

The commander hesitated, clearly conflicted. "They're not like us. Our training is... rigorous. They're younger than the fledgling." He motioned to Thrush. "It could break them. Especially the girl."

"Then let it break them," Sparrow said, his tone cold and unyielding. "Better they break here where we can put them back together. They break on the battlefield and it's too late. They'll train with the Legion, or the Legion can answer to me." Sparrow's brow rose as he waited for a response. He didn't rebuild his lands brick by brick to be argued with. He was the King. And if he had to, he'd remind his Legion that he was currently the most powerful King in the realm.

There was a tense silence as the commander weighed Sparrow's words, his jaw tightening. Finally, after one last glance at the girl, he gave a reluctant nod. "Very well. They'll receive no special treatment here."

"They don't need special treatment," Sparrow replied, his gaze steely. "They need to survive in a war against true darkness."

The commander pointed at Rue's pocket. "The animal can't stay."

Everyone turned to look at Rue as a tiny head popped out of her pocket and mewed.

Sparrow held out his hand. "Hand it over."

Rue sighed as she pulled the kitten out of her pocket. "You be good, Lucipurr," she whispered to the kitten. "Don't let him scare you." She kissed its furry head before setting the kitten in Sparrow's palm.

"Lucipurr?" he asked, holding in a chuckle.

Rue glowered at him, a threat if he ever saw one.

Sparrow held the kitten close to his chest and saluted Rue. "We'll be waiting for your return."

The commander turned and barked out an order, and a pair of Angels stepped forward to guide Rue and Remington toward the sparring rings. The two children exchanged a nervous glance but followed the Angels without complaint. Rue looked even smaller amidst the towering warriors. Thrush knew where to go and sighed as he walked onto the sparring grounds he so despised.

Chel watched them go, his heart heavy with worry. He turned back to Sparrow, thoughts of his sister coming to the forefront. Perhaps if Yelena had some training she wouldn't have been murdered. It didn't take him long to change his mind about training with the legion. At least they'd learn skills from each realm.

Sparrow walked away, his wings dragging on the stone walkway. He tucked the kitten into his shirt pocket and took to the air. He needed to speak with Jed. The half-breed was working on warding the Raven King's lands to keep wandering eyes out while Sparrow and Meg were gone.

The Veil was thin and while Sparrow and Meg would be returning to Hell shortly, he didn't want to risk the children being unprepared and unprotected. There were no allies left. While his lands were under shadow, Lyra had still found her way in.

FOUR

Teari kneeled next to the Deacon and began unwinding soaked bandages.

"There's something wrong," the Deacon said as he hissed in discomfort.

"The bandages shouldn't be soaked like this." Teari inspected the wound where his lower leg had been cut off just below the knee where he'd been bit by the dead while escaping Hell.

Gabriel was watching from a few feet away. He glanced at the Deacon's pale face and considered the ramifications of the last Deacon dying on his lands.

Teari's hands were glowing as she moved them over the wound. The Deacons were unlike Angels, Demons, or humans. There wasn't much on their biology in her books. She'd never seen one missing a limb–let alone injured–and wondered if that was the reason he wasn't healing properly.

Her hands stilled as she found a pocket of infection. Teari's eyes flashed open as she sensed the festering inside. She moved to her medical kit and chose a long scalpel and more gauze.

"Have you been changing the bandages every day?" she asked the Deacon.

"I try," was the reply.

"There's infection. I must drain it," Teari warned. "You want to be knocked out?"

The Deacon glanced warily at Gabriel then his stump. "Just give me something for the pain."

Teari nodded before going to work. She did her best to numb him with healing magic but was distracted by the infection. She cut skin and muscle until she found the pocket and drained it. When she looked up again, the Deacon's eyes were closed and Gabriel had a hand on the Deacon's forehead.

"Finish," Gabriel urged. "We have much to discuss with him."

Teari focused her energy on healing the surrounding tissue and closing the incision she'd made. There was still some healing to do but Gabriel stopped her.

"He's antsy," Gabriel warned. "I don't want him trying to get out."

Teari looked up and closed her hands, halting the healing. She grabbed rolled gauze and began wrapping the nearly healed stump. "It seems unethical to keep him injured."

"Everyone has their purpose. Being the last Deacon, we have to keep him safe and make sure others don't find him." When Teari was done, Gabriel removed his hand from the Deacon's head and the man woke.

The mood was somber as Teari packed her supplies, leaving fresh bandages on the table near the Deacon.

Gabriel dragged a chair closer to the Deacon and sat, his wings folded neatly behind him. His expression was one of deep contemplation, his brows furrowed as he traced a finger over the intricate carvings of the chair armrest.

As the Deacon woke, strange archaic energy gathered around him like shadows.

"She's been pushed to the brink," Gabriel began, breaking the heavy silence. His voice, usually steady and strong, wavered slightly. "Meg has faced trials that would have broken lesser beings. But this... this is different. Alastor will raise Lucifer... they are not mere enemies. They will be forces of nature against her."

"She is without wings," Teari warned. "Meg's strength is undeniable, but strength won't be enough. She can't poof to travel from place to place at will. She's still recovering from Alastor hurting her and Skeele's death." Worry lined Teari's face.

Gabriel nodded. "They will prey on her weaknesses, on her fears. The psychological toll could be her undoing."

"It's not right," Teari said.

"She is the only one who can bring balance," the Deacon said. He leaned forward, his voice a low, gravelly whisper. "You underestimate the depth of their malevolence, Gabriel. Alastor and Lucifer won't just battle her, they will seek to corrupt her. They know her vulnerabilities–the ones she keeps hidden from herself. They will use every trick, every whisper, every shadow to break her." The Deacon cleared his throat. "She has been very close to complete darkness before. It wouldn't take much to flip the switch."

"She keeps trying to go it alone," Teari said. "She's denying mourning Skeele. And I sensed a bond..."

Gabriel's hands tightened into fists. "The odds are against her but we must have some faith." Gabriel knew of the bond and it was one of the few things keeping her from running off to face the pending war alone.

"Indeed," Deacon agreed, his tone laced with sorrow. "But we cannot intervene directly, not without tipping the balance. The fate of many hinges on this battle. Meg must face it, but we must be ready... for whatever may come." He inspected Teari's work.

Teari's eyes glinted with something that might have been pity, or perhaps fear. Meg was an unexpected friend. They'd spent years growing and trusting each other. Even after Teari's first impression and judgement, Meg forgave her, somehow.

The Deacon said, "We must consider all possibilities. If she fails... if she is consumed by the darkness... we must be prepared to face the consequences. And they will be dire."

Gabriel stood abruptly, his wings flaring slightly as if to shake off the encroaching despair. "I refuse to believe that she will fall. She's come too far, fought too hard. If the worst comes to pass, we will do what we must. For her... and the balance of the realms. Babylon is prepared."

Teari was uncomfortably silent.

Gabriel took note and focused on her. "Tell me."

"Her children," Teari said.

"Child," the Deacon corrected.

Gabriel's head tipped to the side like he'd been told a secret he couldn't quite hear. "Repeat that." He held out a hand to pause the Deacon from interrupting again.

Teari took a calming breath before she spilled the best kept secret in all of the Seven Kingdoms of Heaven and Hell and the Earthen plane. She met Gabriel's gaze after.

"Heaven has never been so blessed." She paused, gathering her words on thick breath. "Thrush is not the only child born to the Raven King's heritage. It has been a long time since a child was born to the Seven Kingdoms of Heaven and now the Raven King's family bloodline has three."

"Thrush," Gabriel said. "And the girl. Rue." Regret filled his voice as he rarely saw the girl; Meg had kept him away with excuses. He blamed himself after his confessions during Meg's trial. He figured he was too desperate, too forlorn from the time lost during Meg's childhood.

"There is another." Teari smoothed a hand over her slacks, glancing between the Deacon and Gabriel. "There is a boy. Meg had twins."

Silence echoed.

"A boy..." Gabriel whispered. Large hands stretched across his knees and he gripped the fabric of his robe. "But he's half Hellion, like the girl."

"No," Teari said. "They are the Raven King's children. Both of them."

"This is... unexpected," the Deacon said.

"Sparrow has two children," Gabriel said, not believing.

"If you saw them, you'd recognize it. The boy is the spitting image of his father. It's like looking back in time," Teari said. "The girl resembles Nightingale."

"You never told me," Gabriel stood and paced, large hands tearing through white hair. "Why would you keep this from me?"

"She forbade me from telling a soul," Teari said. "It was not my secret to disclose. I feel badly telling you now. Meg doesn't want anyone to know. She fears for the safety of the children. She's kept them hidden all this time."

"Eventually they will have to send all three to do their time as Hellions," Deacon said. "Or the family curse will resurface."

Gabriel nodded slowly. "They must go."

"And if Meg fails against Lucifer..." Teari started to say.

"The children will be in Lucifer's grip," Gabriel said. "And this goes beyond retribution. You saw what he did to Sparrow. This is a war upon the families of the Archangels. Lucifer has always worked against us." He rubbed his chin. "He forbade my relationship with Clea. He was the reason she ran. The reason she died. The reason Meg was lost to us for twenty-five years."

"The Veil is thinning," Deacon warned and it seemed like a redirection of the conversation. "You'd like to blame Lucifer but Babylon has blamed Meg since the moment she stepped foot in Heaven."

"The Archangels have never been absolute in their theories." Gabriel stopped pacing. "The thinning will get worse. There are no Deacons in Hell. The newly dead souls will continue to collect. Hell's power will continue to strengthen. The Veil will continue to thin until it spills out onto the Earthen plane."

"And the Veil between the Seven Kingdoms of Heaven?" Teari asked. "There is a threat of thinning here."

Gabriel shook his head. "Our realm has never been breached. Our Veil is strong despite the imbalance."

Teari stood and lifted her medical bag. She turned to the Deacon. "I'll change the bandage daily, unless something more dire comes up."

"Thank you." The Deacon bowed.

"We'll have to get you walking again soon. I'll bring prosthetics. It will take some time to get you standing comfortably again." Teari adjusted her bag, waiting for Gabriel to *poof* her out of the mountain. He'd never shown a soul the entrance to this place, and she doubted he'd ever show her now that she revealed she'd kept the secret of his grandchildren from him.

"When will she deliver the bones?" the Deacon asked.

"Soon, they'll leave any day now," Gabriel said.

The fate of many rested on the aftermath of the coming battles, but none more so than Meg. Her children were at risk. Her soul was at risk.

As they left the chamber, the lights dimmed as if the heavens were holding their breath, waiting for the inevitable clash between light and darkness.

FIVE

Jed knelt in the frosty grass, drawing runes of protection and warding on the stone wall at the edge of the Raven King's lands with practiced precision. Each sigil glared briefly with faint light before sinking into the stone, extending the invisible protective web stretching across the kingdom. Jed was nearly done with the southeastern perimeter, the most remote of Sparrow's lands.

Jed felt a shift in the air and turned.

The Raven King was walking closer.

"Your work's coming along," Sparrow commented, his gaze sweeping over the runes. "Looks like you're nearly finished."

"Almost," Jed said shortly, his voice low. He trusted the Raven King less than most, but like before, Jed knew hiding in Sparrow's shadow would protect him.

Sparrow gazed over the northern perimeter and sighed. "Can you work faster?"

"I am only one man," Jed said, "in a territory that would rather see me dead than alive." Jed glanced over his shoulder. "I have no plans to die here. For every rune and ward I set, I must check my back for danger approaching."

"You're safe here," Sparrow promised.

Jed gave a sarcastic smirk. "You've a Legion of Angel warriors who have tried to kill me since birth. At any moment they could turn on me. My runes and spells only go so far when they can see my face and aura lit up from using my magic."

Sparrow tilted his head, the ghost of a smile tugging at the corners of his mouth. "Still don't trust an Angel?"

"Trust isn't the word I'd use," Jed replied dryly, brushing his hands off. "They've had eons to perfect a lot of things, including the art of deception."

Sparrow crossed his arms and pondered. "I could find someone to help you."

"No thanks. I work alone." Jed tapped the stone wall. "These will hold up against most intrusions. But I'd still keep an eye out for anything from these parts."

"Is it strong enough to stop anything coming from Hell?" Sparrow asked.

Jed raised an eyebrow. "Worried about escapees from the underworld coming for a visit?"

Sparrow's expression turned serious. "Things are... restless. Everywhere. Babylon has gotten curious. I trust no one. Already had someone sneak past the gates."

Jed was eyeing the runes he'd tattooed on Sparrow's arms years ago. "Did they ever work?" he asked.

Sparrow shrugged, but it looked like he was holding in a neck tick. "I can't remember."

Jed and Sparrow made eye contact for the briefest moment before Sparrow turned and walked away.

Six

Sparrow paced the length of his bedroom, boots scuffing softly against the hardwood floor with each agitated step. The room felt stifling, the walls closing in as his thoughts twisted and turned. The hunger gnawed at him; he'd drank half the stock from the blood fridge and left the rest for Meg. He knew she'd avoid him, just like she had the past few nights. She was stubborn, and avoiding the hunger would do nothing more than put them both at risk. There was a deeper hunger though, not just for sustenance but for something far deeper, something that clawed at his very soul.

Something–no, someone–who had dark hair, marked skin, blue eyes.

Sparrow's thoughts were a storm. He wondered if she had told the children the truth. The boy had avoided him since the morning he'd made breakfast and Rue pointed out they looked alike. Remington had simply stared at the Raven King, watching him thoughtfully as he chewed, then cleaned his plate and left with Thrush at his side.

The uncertainty of a future with the children gnawed at him, fueling his restlessness. If they knew, would they look at him differently? Would they hate him for the darkness that shadowed his past, or the curse that haunted their very existence? Would they hate him for what he'd done to their mother? Sparrow shook his head. There were no easy decisions between Heaven and Hell and he doubted the children of this kingdom would have it any easier.

Sparrow's fingers flexed involuntarily, itching to reach for the door, fly to Babylon, and jump in the portal so he could get this mission to Hell over with. Lucifer's bones were the last piece of the puzzle, the final task. The weight of it sat heavily on his shoulders, pressing down with the remainder that every moment he delayed was a moment Meg and the children were left vulnerable. They would go in the morning. They couldn't wait any longer.

Meg had been grumpy, withdrawn, ever since Lyra's unwelcome visit the previous day. Sparrow could sense the tension in the air whenever they were near each other. He had tried to approach her, but words caught in his throat. He didn't want to discuss what he'd done the past fifteen years and with whom. He didn't want to hurt her anymore.

Sparrow rubbed his throat. He didn't want to push Meg too hard, didn't want to make things worse, but the hunger was becoming unbearable. The blood bond was a double-edged sword; it tied them together in a way that was both exhilarating and terrifying. A strength and weakness.

Sparrow stopped pacing, his hand resting against the wall as he took in a deep breath, trying to steady himself. He had the children to protect now, the kingdom to rule and grow, and dark alliances to maintain that would bring him power.

Sparrow raked a hand through his hair, frustration tightening his chest. He wanted Meg, needed her, but knew he couldn't force her to open up and let him in. And the thought of her getting hurt, of losing her again–he couldn't bear it. The memory of losing her once before was too fresh, too raw. If something happened to her now...

No. He wouldn't allow it. He couldn't.

A familiar twinge started at the base of his neck and he couldn't prevent the spasm from taking over. Sickness filled his gut. The random twitches were few and far between, a muscle memory as Teari called them. His mind was intact but too long without his memories resulted in this. The jerks and tremors never left his body completely. His hand curled into a fist as the spasm in his neck stopped. He rested his forehead against the cool wall until the twitching dissolved completely.

With a final sigh, Sparrow pushed away from the wall and walked to the door. He couldn't wait any longer. He had to see her and find some way to make things right. The hunger was too strong to ignore. He didn't trust himself not to seek her out like the days when he was a Hellion, with urgency and little regard for her safety. No, Sparrow couldn't wait. He needed Meg *now*.

The flooring outside his door squeaked.

Someone was there. A spark of recognition flooded his veins. Sparrow whipped open the door to startled blue eyes.

"Finally," he muttered, grabbing her arm, and dragging her inside.

SEVEN

MEG

STUMBLING, Sparrow drags me into his room.

"I'm still mad at you," I say, pushing at his arm until he releases me.

"Stay mad then." His gaze drifts down my body. "Are the children asleep?"

"Yes."

I want to tell him that they know their real father is the Raven King. They seemed unimpressed, almost like they knew already. After, they settled into bed as though not much had changed. I'm not sure how to take it. Either they're resilient or smarter than I expected.

Sparrow's lips press into a thin line like he wants to talk more about them but decides not to. The discussion is due. Maybe I can ease him into it.

"Rue was grateful you didn't harm Lucipurr while she was

training with the Legion." I notice a scratch on his arm and press my fingertip to it.

"The kitten didn't like flying." He flexes his wings while stepping closer. "He will get used to it. If Rue plans on carrying him around in her pocket while she's flying."

"When will they get wings?" I ask.

"When the time is right," Sparrow replies. "There's no set age. They come when they've earned them."

I step away from him and rub my arms. My stomach growls loudly.

"You sent them to train without informing me," I say, holding back annoyance. "These are decisions you need to discuss with me."

Sparrow crosses his arms over his chest and looks down at me. "They must prepare. I will not have children of mine die at the hands of Lucifer."

I hold up my palm to stop him. "Slow down. Things are moving fast."

"They're about to move faster," he warns. "We must return to Hell in the morning. It's time to hand over the bones. This task is long overdue."

"Okay." I nod in understanding. "But don't think you're taking over raising my children. I make decisions about their safety."

Sparrow touches a rune on his arm. "Are you sure about that?" he asks. "Seems they've made plenty of their own decisions."

I exhale a breath and look up. Hair falls across his eyes but it doesn't hide the intense green stare. His wings shift. A man shouldn't look like he does. Handsome and dangerous, long lashes and high cheekbones. The dark runes tattooed over his arms and up his neck add to the dangerous aura of him. Who the fuck am I kidding trying to avoid him, he is everything I've ever wanted.

Batshit crazy or unnervingly sane, I cannot deny the attraction to all of his personalities.

Sparrow rubs the back of his neck.

My stomach growls too loud.

He glances down with a smirk. "It's been too long."

He tips his head, revealing throbbing veins.

I lick my lips and take two steps back. "I can go hungry for days," I warn. "But if you're hungry, you could call that bitch Lyra to come back. She looked your type."

It's not nice of me to hold it against him. But I'm still angry she barged in here unnoticed. Who knows what she's spread around the Seven Kingdoms?

"You told me we'd be safe here and she just walked in the door like she lives here."

"She's been dealt with," Sparrow says. He takes a step forward. "She won't return."

"How'd she get in?"

"That's been dealt with as well."

"Is that what you prefer now? Tall and blonde and winged?" My back aches. I've never been good at backing down, and it's worse now that I feel weaker than ever.

He looks me over and moves closer. "Do you prefer horns and rough skin and sharp teeth? Do you prefer leathery wings, the filth of Hell in your bed at night?"

His mouth is so close, his breath fanning my cheek then neck as he tilts his head.

"I prefer those who hurt me the least," I say.

I notice the smallest flutter of muscle along his shoulder. I touch the spasming muscle and notice as Sparrow holds in a twitch.

"It's come back?" I ask. Unease tightens my gut and reminds me that I truly don't know enough about Sparrow's lineage.

His gaze meets mine. "It never truly went away completely. I just learned to hide it."

My jaw drops as I try to think of a response.

"I see the way your expression changes. Maybe that's what you like? You want me so fucked in the head I can't think straight. You like the crazy. Every day is a battle keeping it at bay." His smile is kinda sad.

No, I never enjoyed one minute of watching him slip away and forget me, forget himself.

"I should have known. Nightingale still has her quirks," I say.

He whistles a soft trill that sounds like a Wood Thrush at dusk.

"The thing about learning darkness, is that it helps me hide the ticks in the light," Sparrow says. "The hunger makes it worse, harder to control."

He stretches his neck and groans. He licks his lips and I realize the hunger makes us both mad.

"We must return to Hell in the morning. This ends tonight." Sparrow's hand glides up my arm.

I shiver as his palm smooths across my back and pulls me closer against his hard body. "Just to be clear," he says. "I prefer you in my bed. Always have."

Firm lips press to mine and my hands smooth up his chest and behind his neck. My veins feel lit with fire as his hands slide across my back and under my thighs. He lifts me and presses my back against the wall.

"You're so bad. Little night owl. Swearing at me and being jealous of other women in my bed." He kisses my jaw before his tongue swipes over my neck. "You can hate me for it. I've given you enough reason. I can't apologize for trying to survive without you. I can never say sorry enough." We both know this.

I feel the sharp slide of his teeth sending a shiver up my spine, but he doesn't bite.

"You can bring it up a million times," he says.

Sparrow's thigh settles between my legs and I can't control my body as my hips grind on him.

"I can't make you forget, I can only repent," he says as he pulls away. Disappointment reveals itself as a sigh from my lips.

"I told you I'd kneel to you every day. I'm overdue." He moves lower, ready to drop to his knees.

I pull at his arms. Tug at his shirt. "Please. No."

He stills. Dark wings spread.

"Please," I beg. "Please…" My stomach rumbles.

He reaches for the button on my jeans, pauses. "You want me? This? Are you giving me permission?"

"No," I whisper before slapping my hands over my mouth. The lies fall so easily from my lips. I want him more than ever. More than anything. I always have.

"You don't want this just like you didn't hide Lucifer's bones." Sparrow chuckles as he drags the jeans down my legs and pulls my boots off.

I feel his warm breath on my thighs and squeeze my eyes closed.

"Maybe tell me some truth. Let's start with that, Meg." He throws my bottoms aside.

I suck in a shaky breath.

"You make me wait for days. You ignore me. You turn my world upside down." He rubs circles on my thighs with his thumbs. "You bring me two heirs to the throne out of thin air. I'm due for a truth." Teeth nip at my thigh.

I let my hand fall away from my mouth. "I don't like that you slept with tall, winged, blonde women." I am so judgmental.

He rises up on his knees, grips the neck of my shirt and pulls down until it rips. "They could never replace your addictive darkness." His fingertips trace the ink on my arms, my shoulder, the damaged one over my heart. "They were nothing." He glances up at me. "I quit them a long time ago."

Oh, this is a sight. Sparrow on his knees, touching me, wings spread, veins pulsing, begging for truth. Those green eyes looking up at me.

What he said doesn't sound like deception.

"Make sure they remain as nothing," I say, bending to drop my lips on his.

Kissing Sparrow is like kissing a bolt of electricity. His arm snakes around my waist and pulls me to sitting down onto his thighs. I feel a bulge in his pants. Frantic hands tug at clothing.

"Too hungry," he mumbles, his forehead pressed to my shoulder. He whistles something that sounds like a hungry chickadee.

"What are you waiting for?" I ask, tugging at the waist of his pants and tearing his shirt open.

"Permission."

"Do it. Please," I say as I lower my mouth to his chest and nip until a small drop of blood appears. I lick it away as Sparrow's hands slide into my hair, grip at the root, and tip my head away, revealing the side of my neck. He flicks his tongue over my blood stained lips before his mouth falls to the sensitive skin below my ear.

"Why do you wait for permission?" I ask. "I thought we were beyond that."

"For all the times I forgot to ask," he says solemn.

There are memories of him being loving and kind, memories of him forgetting who I was and taking at will only to leave me drained to a husk. There were times when he drew blood and never asked.

This is better. Much better. My hips grind against him and a coiling starts deep in my belly. "Yes," I groan, biting my lip. "Please."

It starts like a simple kiss to my neck, until I crave the pinch of teeth like he craves my blood. But he takes his time working me up. By the time he presses teeth to my skin, I'm nearly gone. The pinch sends me over the edge, gasping and throbbing...

———

"We leave in the morning," Sparrow says. We finally made it to his bed and I realize with both of us lying here, it seems kinda small for two people.

Belly full and legs weak, I move to return to my room across the hall. Sparrow grabs my hip and drags me across the bed, tucking me against him. His arm wraps around my waist, holding me against his body.

"What will the neighbors say?" I joke.

"They'd say finally, if they had any sense." He presses his lips to the scars on my shoulders. "But I don't care what those assholes say."

Something fades inside me.

"You are mine and I am yours," he whispers the familiar words. "Stay."

EIGHT

Nero had never been one for patience. What horse has patience? There are no virtues for horses to abide by or, at least, none that Nero cared about. Restless energy rippled within him. His black coat rippled as he galloped through the open fields of the Raven King's kingdom, wind tugging at his mane, whispering ancient secrets.

Nero had searched the forests, the rocky cliffs near the coast, and the winding riverbeds, but the white horse he glimpsed days ago was nowhere to be found. Nero wondered if the white horse roamed the hidden corners of the Seven Kingdoms of Heaven, slipping between realms like a shadow in the night, like Nero had done between the Earthen plane and Hell.

Nero didn't think the white horse was a ghost, but what was the reason he couldn't find it?

Nero's hooves pounded against the ground as he raced through the fields, eyes scanning the horizon, ears perked for any sign of life. He knew the landscape well, from the deep pine groves to the scattered rocks of a burial site. But there was something off about the air today, an uneasy stillness clung to him like an omen.

With a snort, he slowed his pace as he approached the outer borders of Sparrow's lands, Babylon visible in the distance. The towering spires rose like jagged teeth against the sky, their golden surfaces shimmering in the fading light. He had heard Jed and Shay discussing Babylon, sensed revulsion in Meg's voice when she spoke of the ancient city. It was not a place he ventured lightly, but if the white horse had passed through here, he would have to take the risk.

Nero stopped for a moment at the edge of Sparrow's territory, his gaze narrowing on the dimly lit pathways of Babylon. He could feel the power thrumming in the air, saw the cages where the Archangels punished sinners underneath the blistering sun of Heaven. Nero knew it was a bad idea to leave the misty cover of the Raven King's lands. But, desperate times called for desperate measure.

Nero backed up, then with a deep breath, he galloped forward and leapt over the stone wall separating the Raven King's lands.

As soon as his hooves touched ground, he felt the pull. Something ancient, older than anything he had ever encountered; older than the Demons he'd come across since he became a Crossroads Demon. It wrapped around him, trying to seep into his bones. Nero shook it off with a flick of his tail and continued forward, his gaze sharp and focused. He should have known better; a Demon horse can't walk the streets of Babylon unnoticed. He didn't belong here, and Sparrow had warned them all to lay low. He had offered them sanctuary, and Nero was sure he couldn't get back to the Raven King's lands should anything come after him.

His steps echoed as he moved through the deserted streets, the towering statues of Angels watching him from every corner. Despite the grandeur the streets felt empty, hollow, as if the city were waiting for something or someone. Most likely souls—Babylon was starving for them since the destruction of the Safe Houses and death of the Deacons. All souls were stuck in Hell and soon the dead would start walking on the Earthen plane again.

Nero pressed on. He saw a glimpse of white from his periphery, and it turned to nothing but a hint of mist. But then... there was the faintest trace of a scent. He wasn't sure it was real at first—something that smelled like freshly fallen snow. He followed it, galloped at moderate speed, and paused to hear something other than the echo of his own hooves. Something pulled him to the edges of the city. Maybe it was instinct or maybe the call of the white horse. Whatever it was, it led him toward the towering gates of the kingdom bordering the Raven King's.

Nero paused, taking in the grandiose gate that shimmered with celestial light. Nero paced and whinnied softly. He saw a flash of white again, raised his head, and watched between the gates. Something was running between the trees, teasing him, taunting him. "Chase me," he swore he heard the wind whisper.

Nero trotted in a tight circle. He didn't want to cause trouble, but the white horse was clearly beyond these gates.

Then, Nero remembered that he didn't care much what others thought. He backed up and sprinted forward, leaping over the wall.

Nero huffed, his breath coming out in a cloud of mist. This would cause trouble he wasn't ready to deal with. Trouble that would come to Shay and Meg. Deep down though, Nero knew that they'd want him to find the white horse. And if not, too bad for them.

There was a shift in the air, and a low growl made his skin prickle. Nero froze, muscles tense. Shay had warned him not to take his Demon form while in Heaven, but he was all too ready. Two Angels from the Legion approached.

"Never seen a black horse here before," one of them said, stepping forward.

Nero's lips curled in a snarl, but he remained still, hoping they'd spill some information.

Nero whinnied, tried to relay that he was no danger. He nodded in the direction of the white horse.

"Passing through?" the other Angel asked with a smirk. "You saw the white one, didn't you?"

Nero nodded.

"Ah the white horse," the other Angel said wistfully. "Usually the young ones search for it. It's a kind of enigma around here." The Angel secured his weapon. "Seen wisps of it myself. Never the whole creature out in the open. Lore says she sticks to the shadows and only watches from afar."

She? Nero held in all movement. He wanted them to keep talking. Wanted them to spill more secrets.

"I saw it once," the other Angel said, holding his hand out to Nero.

Wonderful. Nero didn't come here for pets and snacks. He was on the hunt and the longer he spent with these morons the further away the white horse would get.

Nero let the Angel get closer, then pulled away.

"Easy, boy. You want me to keep talking?"

Nero eyed the Angel, noticed the way the feathers of his wings fluttered with the night breeze.

"Okay. The white horse has been around for ages. Longer than anyone else."

Nero tipped his head and let the Angel pet his snout, then the sensitive scratching spot behind his ear. Nero was so invested in the story the Angel was spinning, he forgot to keep an eye on the other Legion guard. When Nero did glance over, the guard had a sinister smirk.

"Gotcha!" The Angel closest gripped Nero's mane.

Joke was on him. Nero reared up and kicked the Legion guard in the gut. The Angel went flying across the grass on his ass. The other one didn't dare approach after that move.

Nero took off in the direction he last saw the white horse. The faintest scent of snow hit his nose. He doubled down: Nero was faster than lightning, faster than the speed of light, faster than a black hole. Trees bent away from him before he passed them, hoofprints appeared in the soil before his gallop echoed. The ground in the distance shook before the black blur passed.

Suddenly, Nero was no longer in Heaven. He was on the Earthen plane.

He followed the smell of snow, ran across freeways and prairies and cornfields, until he saw *her* drinking from a half frozen lake in the middle of nowhere Utah.

The white horse.

"*Took you long enough to find me*," the white horse said with a voice that was soft and strong and very female.

Nero huffed in surprise and took a tentative step forward. The Angel was right.

"*Speak. Demon horse.*" She bent to gently lap water from the lake.

Nero stared, unbelieving. He'd never spoken, only had the inner monologue that lived rent free in his head.

NINE

Meg

THE PORTAL to Hell rips open in front of us, a swirling mass of black and crimson that feels like it could swallow us whole. Our hands brush for just a moment before I step forward into the abyss. Sparrow hesitates for the briefest second.

The instant we cross through, the air changes. Brimstone and pine and... something smells off. It's different than the last time I was here, or maybe I didn't notice the drastic change when I came searching for the feather of truth. The sky looks smokey, a red tint to the clouds that hadn't been there before. Maybe this is the imbalance the Deacons always warned about. I swallow hard and tamp down the unease threatening to take over my body.

I glance at Sparrow, noticing the brief second in which his jaw tightens.

"It feels heavy here," I say, rubbing my chest with the hope of releasing the weight of Hell.

I adjust the strap on my pack and shoot a glance at Sparrow. "We get in, we get out. No distractions."

Sparrow nods, his eyes scanning our surroundings. "No distractions."

We walk, our boots kicking up clouds of ash and dirt as we head toward route 37.

Alastor's reign has changed this place. I don't recognize the landscape much here any longer, but the one thing I do know is that there is a barn on route 37 with a snowy owl in the rafters. Except there's no snowy owl any longer. All I have left of her are feathers in a jar, hidden away for safe keeping. Now there's just the bones. The bones of Lucifer.

"Why don't you just fly us there?" I ask Sparrow.

"The tone of Hell has changed." He shivers. "Can't you feel it?"

I nod. "I can tell."

"Give it time," he warns. "It'll get worse. But, we walk." He points his blade toward the road ahead.

"Can't we hotwire a Jeep?" My thighs are already sore from the short distance we've walked. Or maybe that's from riding Sparrow last night.

"The noise," he reminds me. "I have to save flying as our last resort. We aren't that far."

The route is familiar because we've walked it before, side by side in a different life when we were different people. Sparrow asks about Rue and Remm, about Thrush and the childhoods he missed. I never apologize for it. I never will.

He mentions little bits, asks about moments he should know nothing about. Like when Thrush fell out of the tree in the courtyard and Nero watching Rue like a guard dog whenever she took a walk alone. He shouldn't know those moments and it leads me to believe he had someone watching us all along.

Eventually, we come to a stop in front of a dilapidated barn on Route 37.

"You sure you remember where you hid them?" Sparrow asks, his voice low.

I give a sideways glance. "I remember. Not the kind of thing you forget."

"Right." He nods. "Just checking."

Sparrow keeps looking around us like he hears something. Like he sensed something lurking just out of sight.

"What is it?" I ask.

"I can't tell if it's undead, Hellions, or bored Demons," he says, fingers flexing on his blade.

He glances at me and I notice his eyes linger to my back.

Rage instantly floods me and I can't control it. He thinks I'm weak. "The barn is up here. We can split up. How about I go left and you can go fuck yourself?" I walk faster, eager for this journey to be over.

Sparrow catches up with me in a few long strides. He grabs my arm. "What's that all about?"

"I saw you... that expression of regret and disgust."

It hurt. A lot. Dealing with my loss of power and ability to fly is enough but having him look at me like that was unbearable.

"I'm simply analyzing how to keep you safe. It's not like you can fly away. Not like you can just *poof* out of here like you used to."

Dark eyes glance down the length of me.

"Unless it's all come back." He waits for a response.

"It hasn't," I finally say. "And sorry I'm such a hindrance to this bullshit mission." I pull out of his grip and head toward the barn. He's so focused on my weaknesses. I should remind him I endured twenty-five years of abuse on the Earthen plane and survived. I didn't need wings then or the ability to travel from place to place at will. It would have been nice, but I survived without it. Just like I'll survive now. I count on my fingers how many times I've nearly died. Three sounds right. If I were a cat, I'd have plenty more lives left.

I take a deep breath and calm myself as we stand in front of the barn.

"Where would you like me to wait?" he asks.

"In the shadows," I whisper, fanning the fingers of my left hand like a magician.

Sparrow makes a deep hooting sound from deep in his throat. His head ticks to the side.

I go still as stone. "You okay?" I ask.

"Fine." His eyes darken. "Get the bones."

I get the bones all right. I know exactly where I put them. I enter the barn, the rotting wood shifting under my boots as I walk across the bottom floor. I pause for a moment to make sure the rafters aren't going to fall on my head. Then I make my way to the back corner. A beam of moonlight illuminates where I left them. Slamming my boot down on a loose floorboard, I bend the wood up and away. There it is. A bag of bones.

TEN

A chill ran down Sparrow's spine as he moved closer to the broken doorway of the barn. They weren't alone. He knew it; he could feel it. His fingers twitched on the hilt of his blade.

Suddenly a screech echoed in the distance, growing louder, closer.

"Come now, Meg," Sparrow called into the barn. Her shadow moved as she ran toward him, the hollow clank of bones in her bag echoed.

Both Meg and Sparrow halted, exchanging a knowing look before their eyes shot to the horizon. Shapes were moving fast, the unmistakable figures of Hellions.

"Run!" Sparrow shouted, grabbing at Meg's arm as they bolted away from the barn and through the nearby field. "Head for cover."

Sparrow was faster, nearly dragging Meg. He'd counted four Hellions. It would be an easy feat to take them on, but he didn't want to leave Meg on the ground and he didn't want her falling out of the air and getting hurt.

The Hellions were gaining speed, quickly closing the distance. Sparrow's wings flared, but there was no space to take off, not without leaving Meg behind. He gritted his teeth, using his strength to pull her along as they dashed through the dry, cracked field. The forest loomed closer, shadowed fringe calling to them—safety was within reach.

There was another building in the forest. They skidded around the corner, the sight of a door sending a surge of relief through Sparrow's chest. They could hide.

"In here," Meg said, yanking the door open and diving inside.

Sparrow followed, slamming the door behind them. The guttural calls of the Hellions lingered over the forest canopy. Sparrow hoped they were as thick as the Hellions of Lucifer's time. All brawn, no brains. He pressed his back against the door, chest heaving.

It was a smaller barn, a decaying remnant; rafters sagging, the smell of rot thick in the air. In the corner, something small like a rabbit or raccoon was rotting.

Meg stood, wiping her hand on her pants. Sparrow hadn't seen her fall and moved to help her.

"We can't stay here," Meg said.

Before she could finish her sentence, the barn door exploded inward. Wood shattered, and a hulking figure stepped inside. It wasn't a Hellion—not this time. It was something equally terrifying. A dark, monstrous creature, its body twisted and malformed: a Demon. Its eyes glowed red, claws dripping with black venom.

"Shit," Sparrow muttered, drawing his blade in one swift motion.

The Demon lunged at them, its roar shaking the ground beneath their feet. Sparrow shoved Meg behind him, swinging his blade in a wide arc as the creature's claws came down, barely deflecting the blow. The force sent him stumbling back, and the Demon's tail whipped out, catching Meg in the side, and sending her crashing into the barn wall. Her bag fell to the ground.

"Get out!" Sparrow shouted, but Meg was already on her feet, eyes blazing with fury.

"Not without the bones!" Meg gritted her teeth, her voice hoarse as she scrambled toward the dropped bag.

The Demon recovered quickly, roaring again as it barreled toward them. Sparrow darted forward, his blade slashing through the air, sparks flying as his blade collided with the Demon's thick, scaly hide. The creature was relentless, barely slowing as it swiped at him again, its claws raking across his arm. Blood welled, but Sparrow gritted his teeth, ignoring the pain.

"Go, Meg! Now!" he shouted, parrying another blow.

Meg didn't hesitate this time. She sprinted for the back of the barn, smashing through the rotting wood shoulder first, and disappeared into the night. Sparrow followed, barely dodging the Demon's massive tail as it lashed out. Sparrow created a bigger hole in the side of the barn as he followed Meg. They ran, the Demon close behind, the screeches of the Hellions echoing all around them.

There was no way they could outrun them all. They had to find another way out. Sparrow's mind raced, looking for an escape, any escape. He glanced to the sky. No. It was too early for that. The Hellions would take them both down before he could make it to Alastor.

"There!" Meg shouted, pointing toward a narrow crevice in the rock wall ahead.

It could work. Sparrow judged the width of his shoulders and wings. He'd make it work.

They dove into the crevice, squeezing through just as the

Demon reached them, its claws scraping against the stone, too large to follow. Sparrow collapsed against the wall, breathing heavily, the distant howls of the Hellions and the Demon fading into the background.

Sparrow glanced at Meg, blood dripping from his arm, his face pale. "Next time, maybe just bury those somewhere a little less conspicuous?"

Meg rolled her eyes but couldn't suppress a small grin. "Next time? There will never be a next time." She glanced at the blood dripping from his arm. "You're hurt." She moved closer.

"I'm fine."

Meg noticed the black venom pooling in the wound. "Shit," she muttered, taking off her belt and wrapping it tightly around Sparrow's forearm.

"What are you doing?" Sparrow asked, and Meg thought his words sounded a little slurred. He slid to the ground.

"We have to get the poison out. I've seen this before."

She didn't have time to tell him the story of Shay and the Demon poison trapped under her scarred leg. The last thing she needed was an incapacitated giant to drag around. She didn't have magic to heal him and had to revert to old school human first-aid.

"Are you going to pee on it?" he laughed. "Or thuck it out?" His lips were drooping. Shit.

"Yeah," Meg said cynically as she knelt next to him. "Or I could let it infiltrate your bloodstream and turn you into a Demon. Sounds tempting." She lowered her mouth over the scratch marks. "I think you're halfway there already."

Sparrow whispered something that sounded like a curse word, equal parts worried and turned on.

She sucked the diseased blood and venom out of his arm then spit it to the side. She did this until she could no longer taste the venom only blood that she'd much rather swallow than spit on the cave floor. Then she pulled a bottle of water out of her bag and rinsed her mouth before pouring some water on Sparrow's arm.

"Does it hurt?" she asked.

Sparrow licked his lips and made no effort to alter his expression. "That doesn't hurt," he motioned to his arm. "Something else does." He smirked. "I'm suddenly quite hungry."

Meg gave him a dirty look before moving away and searching her bag for bandages. She returned to his side and moved his injured arm to her lap. Sparrow's hand closed into a fist as Meg wrapped the cuts with a strip of gauze and tape.

"You should consider armor," Meg suggested.

"Never needed it before." Sparrow was watching her. "Maybe something cool like Basilisk skin."

"You heal quick." She started to move away but Sparrow's hand gripped her wrist.

"I could heal quicker." He dragged her arm closer. "Wouldn't even need the bandage you just wasted on me."

Meg's eyes went wide.

ELEVEN

MEG

HERE? In this filthy cave? I search Sparrow's face for clarity. Yeah. He's serious. Embracing the Bloodlust in a Hellcave isn't high on my list. But he does kinda look pathetic all bruised up. I consider all my options: I tell him no, and we carry on with his arm injury and hope it doesn't delay us. Or, I tell him yes and I keep my teeth to myself and suffer with blue balls the rest of the trip. I'm not sure which sounds worse. It all sounds shitty.

Sparrow is still waiting, holding my arm as his head tips back against the rocks. He takes a deep breath, and his finger rubbing my wrist sends a shiver up my spine. There is only a sliver of light from a crack in the cave above us and I can't gain much from his expression, only the pained sound of his voice.

"Anything involving teeth is a bad idea," I warn.

"I'll be good," he promises, voice low. "Just a sip. Just a few drops. Just the tip... of my teeth against your neck."

"I'm not fucking you in a cave in Hell after we just ran from an ugly ass Demon and Hellion." I gently pull my arm away but he grips tighter.

"Please," he begs. "It burns."

"Fine." I scoot closer as he moves my wrist to his mouth.

I look away as his teeth scrape and I hold my breath, tampering down the Bloodlust that's bound to torment me within a few moments.

"Better?" I ask as he settles my hand on his chest, holding my arm like it's a beloved teddy bear.

Sparrow smirks something dark. "It really wasn't that bad. But your mouth on my–"

I punch him in the gut.

Sparrow groans and tips to the side, holding his stomach.

"What the fuck is wrong with you?" I ask, shaking my sore hand. It feels wet. I move to the light shining down from the ceiling of the cave to get a better look at my hand. It's covered in blood.

Sparrow drops to his side and goes silent.

"What the fuck?" I mutter.

"I was hoping you wouldn't notice," he whispers.

"We have been here for five minutes..." I drop next to him and pull his shirt up. "Why didn't you wear some type of armor? Don't kings wear leather vests or some shit?" I sit back on my heels and take in the deep scratches across his stomach.

"I don't need armor. It's just a scratch. Suck out the poison," he says. "And then go a little lower." He shifts his hips and smirks.

I might kill him.

"Get your mind out of the gutter. If I didn't need you to fly me to safety, I'd slit your throat and leave you to rot in this cave." I reach for my bag. "I'm never going anywhere with you ever again."

The silence worries me as I search my bag for something

useful. I glance at his wound. The edges of his skin are turning black from the Demon's poisoned claws.

"You have a healer you can call on?" I ask.

"I don't have a healer." He groans. "You're going to have to suck it out again." He scrubs his face.

"I think you enjoyed that too much." I shake my head. "You disgust me." I move closer, bottle of water in my hand.

"I know," he says. "I am vile and despicable."

"Keep going." I bend and suck the poison out of the first deep gouge in his stomach. I spit the sour blood to the side, worried that I'm not hearing his voice. That he might be worsening. "I'm not hearing you," I say, ignoring the way his tense stomach feels under my lips. Damn.

"I am horrific. An abomination." Sparrow's hands remain over his face, muffling his voice.

I clear the next wound and become concerned with the amount of blood I'm spitting to the ground.

"A disgrace," he says. "Something loathsome."

I pour a few drops of water over his stomach then rinse my mouth. The edges of his skin are turning back to pale pink.

"Make it sound like a prayer," I demand.

"A stain upon Heaven's gates. Detestable."

I continue removing the poison, the sharp taste in my mouth becoming bothersome. I pause to rinse with the water. Sparrow's face looks pale. A fine sheen of sweat collects in the hollows of his neck. I gaze a little too long.

"Don't stop. I have more," Sparrow murmurs. "Wicked."

I press my mouth to the last wound.

"Revolting." His voice is so low.

I spit to the side and internally agree with Sparrow's assessment of himself. I've thought all the same things.

"Without my grace I am nothing. I am hollow. My heart is dead." Sparrow lowers his voice. "But... I have you again."

"Shut up." I rinse his wounds then press fresh bandages to them. He's so quiet I think he might be asleep.

Sucking out the poison wasn't enough. He can't be walking around with a torn up gut. I bite my wrist then hold it over his mouth. His lips seal around the marks. He holds my arm like it's precious. His hips shift. Wings scrape against rock. I want nothing more than to climb on top and quell the deep ache in my center. But this is not the time.

It's not long before he's had enough. I pull my wrist close, then scramble away from him and deal with the blood lust on the opposite side of the cave, pacing like a wild animal in heat until it passes.

———

THE CAVE'S mouth looms behind us as we make our way out of the forest. I glance at the sliver in the rocks and wonder how we even saw it in the first place while running from the Demon and Hellion. Must've been a miracle.

Above us, the sky churns with thick, swirling clouds, casting an ominous glow over Hellscape.

I glance at Sparrow; he's moving like he was never injured.

Sparrow notices me watching, giving me a sidelong glance before wincing dramatically and holding his stomach.

"Shut up," I warn.

"I suppose I should thank you," he drawls, his voice rasping from hours of silence as he slept while his body healed. "For healing me. Though it felt more like you were trying to suck the life out of me in the process. You know–"

I smirk, adjusting the strap of my bag. Lucifer's bones give a hollow knock. "If I wanted to suck the life out of you, Sparrow, trust me, you'd be dead by now."

Sparrow gives a low chuckle, though his eyes flick with the same unease that had lingered on me in the cave. There's a heck of a lot of heat in that gaze and all I can envision is the sight of him adjusting his hips like his pants were too uncomfortable on that hotel couch.

"Right. Always the gentle touch, Your Majesty."

"Don't call me that," I snap, the words sharper than I intended.

Sparrow lifts his hands, fake wincing at the movement in his arm and stomach. "Easy there. No need to get testy. Just trying to show some thanks."

I narrow my eyes at him, but the tension slung between us is heavy, unspoken. I wanted to do much more than heal him once I got a taste of his untainted blood. And he knows it. Not trusting myself, I move away from him. Nothing's better than distance in a situation like this. I know I'm short tempered, especially like this. Doesn't matter if we're dragging these bones back to face a war. I'd still knock him over in the woods and take what I want. So I move even further away.

We head deeper into the forest, following the path we ran to escape the Demon. The small barn is torn to pieces like a tornado hit it. Tree branches are broken and leaves disturbed. Hearing the snapping of sticks in the distance, we both stop and grip our weapons. We wait to see if it's one of the dead wandering, or something worse.

Through the trees, I can see the larger barn where I hid the bones, then the road beyond. Route 37.

Sparrow starts moving, blade out and wings lifted so they're not dragging in the leaves and creating more noise. A sharp feeling spreads across my shoulders. I never thought I'd miss having wings. Never thought I'd miss carrying their weight. I wipe at the sweat dripping down my neck and notice it's hotter here. Hell has never felt like this before; angsty and chaotic.

The ground rumbles under our feet.

Sparrow glances over his shoulder at me.

My mind races but I push all thoughts aside as I brush leaves aside with my boot. The ground is dry and cracked.

"You shouldn't have come with me," I mutter.

"You really think I'd let you deliver Lucifer's bones on your own? After what happened last time you were here alone? Who know what kind of royal disaster you'd stir up without me here to point it out," Sparrow says, shooting me a glance as he swipes at sweat beading on his forehead.

I huff a breath of laughter despite my annoyance. "That's assuming you survive long enough to make it to the castle."

"I've survived worse," Sparrow grins, his smile faltering when he looks ahead in the distance, a haze trickling down Route 37 like fog rolling in. "Thought I'd rather not push my luck today." His voice sounds far away.

"Do you see something?" I ask.

The ground shakes again.

"There's no earthquakes in these parts," I whisper to myself.

Sparrow sheaths his blade. "If I carry you into the sky, will you fight me?" his voice is suddenly serious.

I move my feet and notice the dry ground splitting apart, leaving a deep crevasse. The earth groans like a giant monster.

"Run!" Sparrow shouts.

The ground splits further. A molten river bubbles to the surface. Shit. I saw this in a movie once. I leap over the growing divide and start running, headed for the road.

"What's happening?" I ask.

"The land is changing into Alastor's Hell. That Demon is all chaos and fire." Sparrow's running next to me. The earth in front of us suddenly splits with vengeance, magma bubbles up and splashes onto nearby trees, setting them on fire.

I stop quick, splay my arms so I don't fall in, my toes on the edge of another split in the earth. Sparrow grabs my upper arm and we jump across together. He tugs me the last bit of distance—without him I would have missed my mark and fallen in.

Lava hits the back of my calf and burns through my jeans. I ignore it. I can only ignore it because the ground opens up and the barn on route 37 begins crumbling into a molten river. A puff of feathers erupts out of the roof as it cracks and breaks into fiery pieces. Two doves fly into the air but the cheeping of a nest echoes. A distraught expression flashes across Sparrow's face.

"Come on," I urge.

"It's not right," he says. "Harming the birds." He glances at me. "You never harmed the birds while you sat on the throne of Hell."

Memories flash to the front of my mind, memories of feathers in Sparrow's pockets and songbirds on my balcony. "Never," is all I can say.

"It was one of the reasons I agreed with the truce."

Something catches in my throat. Sparrow and his damn love of birds.

"I thought that was because of Thrush," I say.

"Sure." He shrugs. "But mostly because of the birds."

The ground quakes, the sound earsplitting. Sparrow grabs my hand and we run together. We leap over small rivulets of molten earth. We round giant pools of bubbling lava. Route 37 is in the distance but we are forever too far from it. Every step feels like a march toward something darker, something inevitable.

When we finally breach the canopy of the forest and our boots touch pavement, the quaking grows stronger. The asphalt splits in two, spreading our feet.

"Screw this," Sparrow mutters as he reaches down and hoists me into his arms. "Don't fight me," he warns.

Black wings spread and Sparrow bends his knees just the slightest before launching us into the air. I wrap my arms around his neck and cross my legs around his waist, not wanting to fall and burn to death in a pool of lava. On the list of dumb ways to die, that sounds like the most awful way to go. So I don't fight him. I hold on tight and watch Route 37 disappear over his shoulder.

Soon I recognize the beating of his wings is in sync with the blood rushing through the thick veins in his neck. My stomach growls for blood. I lick my lips, focusing on his neck.

"Just do it," he says against the wind.

I press my lips together because I left a hell of a lot of pride in that cave and I'm not about to have a day's worth of pent up blood lust hit midflight.

"I'm fine," I say.

Sparrow makes a noise that sounds like frustration.

I twist to focus on the distance and notice the castle in the burning caves. My stomach flip flops with the speed at which he's flying. I close my eyes.

"Don't puke on me," Sparrow says as he shifts, his arms wrap tightly across my back, securing my pack, and then he flies faster than I've ever seen a creature move.

TWELVE

Then

SHAY STOOD at the crossroads while Nero tipped his head curiously as a familiar face stepped out of the shadows.

Then, more followed.

The wind howled through the barren wasteland as Chel, Klaus, Tukka, and Skeele stood before the Crossroads.

Shay glanced over her shoulder. There was nothing for miles. No one was nearby to see or hear them. She shifted on Nero's back, uneasy as to what the Hellions were doing here, summoning them.

Chel tightened the hood of his cloak, eyes flickering with determination. "This is it. They'll come," he whispered, more to himself than the others.

Klaus stood beside him, stroking his white beard. "Do you think this will work?" His voice was hollow, laced with both hope and skepticism. "It's not like we're asking for a simple favor."

Skeele huffed, shifting his weight, the tension thick in his muscular shoulders. "We have no choice. Meg and my children are in danger. Lucifer's war will consume everything if we don't act. You heard the Deacon who came to us."

Tukka's eyes flickered with cold confidence. "We must endure that when the time comes, we can return to defend the throne. The deal is dangerous, but we'll already be dead. What more do we have to lose?"

Shay slid down from Nero's back and took a few casual steps forward, her toes stopping just before the runes on the ground that drew them. Sand brushed across her face from the night breeze.

"This is unexpected," Shay said, watching the Hellions and reaching out to touch Nero.

Nero moved closer with a whinny of agreement. A feeling of apprehension traveled down the tether that connected them.

"I don't like this," Shay said. "What are you planning?"

Skeele spoke first, "There is a war coming. The throne is at risk. We are here to make a deal."

"Have you informed your Queen?" Shay asked. "Calling on the Crossroads Demon might be a conflict of interest."

"She knows the war is coming," Skeele said. "Now. My deal." His gaze darkened. "Resurrection when the war comes."

Shay's expression twisted in confusion.

"I will die before the war." Skeele motioned to the other Hellions. "Most here will." He paused. "The deal. My soul to you for resurrection during the war."

Nero made a grumbling noise.

"I don't like this either, boy," Shay whispered as Nero nudged her shoulder.

"When you rise again, you will be bound to us. Your freedom

will be... conditional," Shay warned. "And in return, we will ensure you are strong enough to face whatever forces the war throws at Meg."

Skeele nodded sternly.

"Can you be sure this is what you want?" Shay asked.

Skeele moved closer. "The Deacons warned me."

"You can't trust them," Shay said.

Skeele held up a finger to pause her. "This isn't the Earthen plane, Shay," he reminded her. "This is Hell. We are not humans. You are barely human. *Trust* only goes so far here."

Shay nodded in understanding, but that understanding didn't help ease the tightening pull in her stomach as she thought of the future that might await her friend. Shay never envied Meg's place in Hell. Throughout the years she'd witnessed more danger threaten the Queen than she'd like to admit. The Hellions kept most of it at bay. Shay glanced between the warriors on the other side of the Crossroads Demon summoning runes. If they'd brought her here for a deal like this–death and resurrection for a future war–she couldn't deny them. Shay sighed internally.

"The deal," Skeele urged. "The Queen's bed is cold and she will come looking for me soon. My soul to you for resurrection during the war."

Shay's eyes flashed red. The tether that connected her to Nero went taut. The words that came out of her mouth were not of her own volition. They were compelled by the curse of the Crossroads Demon and Nero. "Out of the eater will come something to eat. And out of the strong will come something sweet."

Shay smiled and held out a dusky hand that was unfamiliar to her, one with long necrotic fingernails and a transparent golden ring on her middle finger. After all these years she still looked upon her hand as though it were foreign.

Skeele's eyes widened as he observed the change in Shay. He reached forward and grasped her dusky hand. They shook.

Nero whinnied softly.

Klaus came next. The same deal.

Then Tukka.

Chel was last.

"I can't," Shay's voice didn't match her current half-Demon form. Too much of her humanity was charging through, trying to stop something that could turn completely wrong. It could all go sideways. She'd seen it before. A deal didn't always work out as planned. The Deacons could be wrong. Something could change.

"Focus," Skeele warned. "Too much rests on this moment."

Chel had always been like a big brother to Shay. He protected her during the early days in Hell. Trained her. Forced Jed to buck up and face his feelings. Helped lead the rescue after Alastor kidnapped her...

Shay shook her head and pushed down the unease gathering in her chest. The ice that was flooding her veins threatened to take over. Chel should have a longer life than this; she shouldn't be outliving him, not on any realm.

A sharp tear gathered in the corner of her eye as Chel held out his large hand.

"My deal," Chel said, a smirk tugging on his lips. "I can still annoy you–"

"There is nothing funny about this," Shay warned, sensing something inappropriate about to exit his mouth.

Chel's head tipped in respect. "The deal. Resurrection after death. For the war."

Shay smiled sadly and held out her dusky hand. "Out of the eater will come something to eat. And out of the strong will come something sweet."

Nero whinnied in agreement with the pact.

They shook.

Chel kicked the runes and tugged Shay into his arms. She changed forms, turning much smaller and more human, barely visible within the tight embrace of his large Hellion arms.

"Can't have Jed seeing I made you cry," Chel muttered as he reached down, gently smoothing Shay's disheveled blue hair. His voice held its usual roughness, but there was something softer beneath it, something protective. He took a step back, narrowing his eyes as he tried to read her face, but the faint shimmer of tears in her eyes gave her away.

Shay bit her lip, her expression crumbling, and Chel quickly added, "That half-breed abomination will set my ass on fire if he thinks I upset you." He shook his head, a crooked smile tugging at the corner of his mouth, though the humor didn't quite reach his eyes.

Shay nodded, letting out a deep sigh. "I don't want you to die," she whispered, her voice trembling with the fear she was trying so hard to keep hidden. The weight of everything that lay ahead pressed down on her, making her feel smaller, fragile. It all felt so wrong. So far from that Montana ranch. A different world.

"You're one of my best friends," she said.

Chel's expression faltered for a brief moment, something unspoken flickering in his eyes. "We can't all live forever, Shay-baby." Chel's words were low, barely above a murmur, almost as if he didn't want the words to leave his lips. He cast a quick glance around, making sure none of the other Hellion guards were in earshot. He had a reputation to maintain, after all; he didn't want the rest of the Hellion guard knowing he might have a heart concealed deep inside his leathery chest.

Shay knew better.

"You say that like it's okay." Shay's voice broke as she looked up at him, her wide eyes shimmering with tears she refused to let fall. "But it's not. It's not fair."

Chel sighed and pulled her into a quick, firm hug, his chin resting against the top of her head for a second too long. He'd never been good with words–his family history was enough to prove that–but the embrace, fleeting as it was, spoke volumes. "Nothing down here is fair," he muttered into her blue hair. "You know that. This is Hell. We are all damned. Nothing is promised."

Shay clenched fists against his chest, holding on just a little tighter. "But this is different, Chel. I need you here. We all do. Meg does. Her children. We need all of you."

Chel stepped back, breaking the connection, and putting a few feet of space between them, his gaze hardening once more. "You'll be alright," he said, as if it were a simple truth. But even as he said it his eyes flicked away, betraying the weight of his own uncertainty. "Hell, Meg'll be alright. She's stronger than you think. You don't give her enough credit."

Shay wiped at her eyes, her breath shaky but steadier than before. "And what about you?" she asked, her voice barely above a whisper. "Who's going to make sure you're alright?"

Chel's lips twisted into a half-smile, one that didn't reach his eyes. "Don't you worry about me. I've survived worse." Oh the stories he could tell her growing up in Lucifer's Hell... he didn't though, because Chel knew a creature like Shay needed protecting. She needed the kind of protection his sister never had. And this was his second chance to provide it.

For a moment, Hellscape appeared to still around them, the heavy silence only broken by Nero's huffs and pawing at the ground. The Demon-horse was eager to end this deal. He didn't like the sensation of Shay's despondence shivering down their tether.

"Look, Shay," Chel said, lowering his voice further. "I don't plan on dying today or tomorrow. But if it happens..." He paused, the weight of those words settling between them like an unspoken promise. "If it happens, you remember this: you're stronger than you think, too. Don't waste time cryin' over me."

Shay swallowed hard, nodding even though her heart wasn't ready to accept it. "I'll try," she said, her voice small but determined. "But I can't make any promises."

Chel's eyes softened for just a second, a rare glimpse at the man beneath the Hellion armor. "That's good enough for me, Shay-baby. Now wipe those tears before someone sees you and thinks I went soft."

"It's too late," Shay warned. "We've all seen you with Rue."

Chel gave her a small, encouraging nudge before turning and walking away.

Shay watched the Hellions go, a strange mixture of sadness and strength settling into her chest. Nero nudged her shoulder and whinnied a noise of comfort. Shay turned and wrapped her arms around Nero's neck.

"Something bad is coming, boy," Shay whispered. "And I fear we will be caught in the middle."

Nero nodded his head faintly in agreement. The memories of the Fast-Zombie War had not escaped either of them. Years might have passed but the memories were still on their periphery. The death of her parents, the destruction of the ranch, the battle with Clyburn that would forever change their lives.

Shay stepped away, resting her shoulder against Nero's, relishing in the warmth of his body, the steady breaths that echoed across the desert wasteland where the Hellions had summoned them.

"We gotta go." Shay jumped onto Nero's back and clicked her tongue. "Fast," she urged.

Nero didn't need to be asked twice. He took off, his hooves hitting the ground like thunder. Shay's blue hair flowed in the night like hurricane wind, and they found their way back to the castle in the burning caves. They tucked their secrets deep down in their chests, never to speak of them again until the time was right.

Thirteen

Then

Skeele watched Rue and Remington as they sparred under the fading light of the evening. The clearing around them was quiet, the rhythmic sound of their blades clashing and the occasional grunt of exertion echoed. Skeele sat on a low stone wall nearby, his gaze distant but focused as if trying to imprint the moment into his memory.

Rue was small but lithe and quick. She moved with the grace of someone born to wield a weapon, her strikes precise and measured. She was always underestimated though, and Skeele took great pride in watching her defeat the giant Hellions who went easy on her in training.

Remington was taller, his fighting style more deliberate. The Shadow Heir countered his sister's blows with brute strength, his jaw clenched in concentration. There was a natural rhythm to their sparring, a fluidity that came from years of training together. It was hard not to admire how far they'd come.

Skeele smiled faintly, though the weight in his chest never lifted. Any moment could be his last with them. He knew that as his gaze spanned the edge of the clearing, watching for a walking corpse or other danger. The war was coming and there would be no avoiding it. His fate had already been sealed the moment he'd sworn his loyalty to Meg and the children. Their children. He wouldn't see them as anyone else's. Protecting them was the only thing that mattered now, even if it cost him his life.

Rue lunged forward, her blade narrowly missing Remington's side. She let out a triumphant laugh as he stumbled back, frustration flashing across his face. Skeele's smile deepened, but the shadow of what lay ahead crept into his thoughts again. These small moments, the laughter and teasing, the fierce determination in their eyes, this was what he was fighting for. This was what he'd die for.

"Dad!" Remington called out, snapping Skeele from his thoughts. "Who's winning?"

Skeele chuckled softly, shaking his head. "You're both too stubborn to lose. Just like your mother."

Remington rolled his eyes but grinned, wiping sweat from his brow as Rue smirked. She sheathed her blade with a satisfied flick of her wrist, then plopped down on the grass beside him, catching her breath. Remington followed, collapsing next to her with a heavy sigh.

"You never pick sides," Rue teased, nudging Skeele with her shoulder. "Afraid of hurting our fragile egos?"

Skeele chuckled, an ache behind the sound. "I think I'm more afraid of what happens if I *do*. Besides, the only side I can ever pick is your mother's." He winked and the children groaned and made gagging noises before falling into laughter, their voices cutting through the growing twilight. Skeele's thoughts drifted once more; it was harder to stop thinking of the future with each year they grew. Harder to ignore the omen that the Deacons had delivered to him.

Soon enough, their laughter would be drowned out by the sound of battle. Soon, his sword would be drawn not in practice, but to defend their lives. To defend Meg's life. To die was his duty, and he was just fine with that.

The war was inevitable. He could feel it in his bones, like the chill that set in before a brutal winter. He would fight to protect them even if it meant sacrificing everything.

Rue lay back, staring up at Hellsky, her fingers idly toying with the hilt of her blade. "You've been quiet today," she said, glancing over at Skeele. "Something on your mind?"

Skeele hesitated, then shook his head. "Just... thinking."

"About?" Remington pressed, ever the one to pry. He lacked trust; Meg had instilled that in him. He knew he was a Shadow Heir, he just didn't know of what exactly. He questioned every motive, knew one day it might save his life.

Skeele could have told them. Could have warned them of the darkness coming their way. But what good would it do? They were young, full of life and fire. They didn't need the burden of knowing what awaited them. Not yet.

"About how proud I am of you both," Skeele said instead, his voice steady but soft.

Rue sat up, her brow furrowed in confusion.

Remington's expression turned more serious. "Where's that coming from?"

Skeele smiled again, though this time it was tinged with sadness. "Just... reflecting. You've grown strong. Both of you. And you'll need that strength for what's coming."

Remington exchanged a glance with Rue, sensing the shift in

Skeele's tone. "We're ready for whatever comes, Dad. We've trained our whole lives for this."

"I know." Skeele nodded, the words catching in his throat. "But promise me... you'll look out for each other."

Rue's frown deepened. "Of course we will. We always have."

Skeele looked between them, his heart heavy with the knowledge of the omen. He wanted to say more, to tell them how much they meant to him, how he would give everything to save them. How he never expected to have children in his lifetime. But the words stuck, unspoken, as he looked away and rubbed an errant hand over his horns. He realized they'd never asked why *they* didn't have horns or scaled skin.

The sky had darkened, and the air grew colder as night settled in. Tonight he could pretend that they weren't on the brink of something terrible, that there wasn't a future battle waiting to claim them all.

Skeele rose to his feet, his movements slow as he extended a hand to Rue. "Come on. Let's get back inside before your mother starts worrying."

Rue took his hand, rising to her feet with a soft smile. Skeele thought she was lighter than a feather to lift. He shook his head and pushed the thought away. Feathers were not his forte, not his history. And he let the moment of sadness pass knowing that he'd never see them with their wings grown in.

Remington stood and brushed off his pants.

As they walked toward the castle in the burning caves, Skeele lingered just a step behind, eyes scanning for danger in the distance. He wasn't like their father. He wasn't a shadow in their lives, a ghost of what could have been. He would stand with them until the end.

When the time came, he would fall for them. And that, he accepted, would be enough.

Meg's Hell was unlike anything Skeele had ever experienced in his long life. The chaos was mild, the creatures of Hell were not oppressed like during Lucifer's time. He thought of the stories passed between him and the other Hellions. Chel always spoke of how Hell had changed for the better and how he wished his sister could see it. Something pinched in Skeele's chest when he thought of the ways Hell might fall if Meg lost the throne; if he couldn't protect her when the time came. There would be no wildflowers, no songbirds, no freely roaming horse-Demons wandering the royal grounds. No children giggling as they shoved each other during their walk back to the castle, trying to knock each other over.

Skeele sniffed to hide the emotion swelling. He wasn't a creature who should feel these things. Not a creature who should wish for better. Perhaps he'd read too many fairytales. Perhaps Meg had given him too much hope.

FOURTEEN

Now

THE HEAVY, brimstone-laden air pressed down on Meg and Sparrow, a suffocating weight neither of them could shake. Flames flickered from the cracks in the road, illuminating the stone path that wound its way deeper into the royal lands.

The castle loomed ahead of them, a jagged black fortress carved into the very rock of Hell, its spires disappearing into the swirling smoke above.

Sparrow's eyes were sharp, alert, darting from shadow to shadow as they neared the massive iron gates. His hand hovered near his blade and his wings were slightly spread, ready to take to the air if need be. He shot a glance at Meg beside him, her face set in a hard, unyielding mask. She hadn't spoken much during the journey as her mood grew darker with every mile. The tension between them simmered just beneath the surface, unresolved and thick as the ash that floated through the air.

They were both hungry. Moreso each time Sparrow was reminded of the feeling of Meg sucking the Demon poison from his arm.

"Stay close to me," Sparrow murmured, his voice a low rumble.

Meg exhaled a puff of annoyance, her fingers tightening around her blade. She pulled the strap on her bag, tightening it against her back, the bones poking against her spine.

"I'm not helpless," Meg reminded him, an edge to her voice.

"Not what I meant." Sparrow's gaze softened for a moment, but it quickly returned to the looming thread ahead. He was on edge, unsure of how Alastor would react to them since his last visit didn't go so well.

Sparrow was grateful the Hellions kept their distance. They were watching from afar like guard dogs. He noticed Meg shiver in response to seeing them. Sparrow was reminded of her past fear of the feral type of Hellions, Lucifer's type–they weren't that different from Alastor's Hellions. They'd hurt her. But Sparrow promised he'd die before he let them lay a finger on her.

"Let me lead," Sparrow warned as they reached the door.

"Because I'm your prisoner?"

"Yes."

"You're not going to knock?" Meg asked.

Sparrow paused before pushing the door open and said, "We have an understanding."

The giant wooden door groaned as it was opened, revealing a long, dimly lit hall.

Unease shrouded Meg's body. Once her home, the castle in the burning caves was darker than ever. It felt both abandoned yet occupied with decay. It no longer felt like home but a distant memory. Meg shrugged off the feeling. Before this place, she struggled to find home. She'd find another home, always did. Maybe she'd go back to the Florida panhandle and live at the beach house...

A horrible sound came from the Hellion's lair as they passed the slightly open door.

Meg refused to look inside.

Sparrow led her to the ballroom that Alastor occupied.

"What a pigsty," Meg muttered as she took in the chaos Alastor had created.

Chairs were broken and stacked in towering piles. Debris was strewn everywhere. Their boots crunched glass and a warm breeze blew in from the broken window Sparrow had dove through last time he confronted Alastor. The walls pulsed faintly with an eerie red glow as if the stone itself was alive, breathing in rhythm with the malice that filled this forsaken place.

They were greeted by the distant crackle of fire. A thin line of smoke rose to the ceiling of the ballroom as a pile of furniture burned.

Sparrow's fingers twitched with unease, though he kept his expression neutral. He glanced to the far wall and noticed Meg's wings still hung like a trophy, blood dried in drips down the wall. He hoped Meg didn't notice.

They crossed the room. Sparrow led her on the winding path that led to the cleared portion of the room Alastor inhabited.

The table was there. The map still spread.

"What the fuck," Meg muttered as she took in the scene before her.

———

Alastor was dripping with water, his lips blue. His burn scars had turned black from the lack of oxygen.

The Demon took deep breaths and pinched his eyes closed.

Find my bones. Find my bones. Find my bones!

Lucifer's voice was like an explosion in his brain. He dunked his head into the water-filled bathtub again and held himself under by sheer will until the voice stopped. And then he stayed a bit longer even though his lungs burned and his head felt dull. He pulled back, his body sliding against the side of the bathtub until his cheek rested on the cool ceramic. He blinked, thought the two shadowed figures in front of him might have been a mirage of sorts. Ghosts. Perhaps Meg's mother had come back to haunt him again. He'd feared her return since the moment he'd sliced her with that iron rod and sent her elsewhere.

He blinked. These weren't ghosts.

"Well, well, well," Alastor purred then coughed until he couldn't catch his breath. He leaned forward, spitting water. He stood and pain flooded his body. "I was beginning to wonder if you'd gotten lost. But here you are." His gaze flicked to Meg. "And I trust you've brough the bones? Finally."

Sparrow nudged Meg and a look passed between them.

Meg stepped forward, keeping her eyes on Alastor's face. She pulled the bag from her shoulders and it felt heavier than ever in her grip. She opened the zippered pocket and pulled out the dusty bag from inside. She shook it until the hollow knocking of bones echoed through the trashed ballroom like the sound of wooden windchimes.

Sparrow moved to her side, his body rigid, ready for any sign of treachery. He trusted Alastor less than as far as he could throw him. In this place, the shadows were as much a weapon as any blade. Sparrow had seen the things Alastor could pull up from under his feet.

Alastor moved forward, patting the fingerbone in his shirt pocket as he walked.

"Well done," he said softly, his voice dripping with satisfaction. "You've both done exceptionally well. How did you get your prisoner to break?" Alastor asked as his eyes roamed over her body. He licked his lips. "I could take her off your hands. I know some Demons who would pay well for access to her within the skin trades."

Meg stiffened.

Sparrow's hand edged closer to his weapon.

Neither answered. Sparrow prayed that Meg would keep her mouth shut.

Alastor glanced at the pack on the floor. He kicked it and heard a hollow knocking of dried bones.

Do it. Do it. Do it! Lucifer shouted in Alastor's mind.

Alastor rubbed the single finger bone that was in his shirt pocket.

The Raven King and Meg were watching, expectantly.

"End this," Sparrow urged. "Go back to your life."

"You've taken my throne," Alastor sneered. His eyes were bloodshot.

"You never wanted it," Sparrow reminded him.

"I will take something from you," Alastor threatened. "You've meddled in my trades business."

"Watch yourself, Demon. Without the throne you are nothing but a skin and soul trader." Sparrow stepped forward, his expression cold and dangerous. "You got what you wanted. We have a deal."

Alastor glanced at Meg. "You both will pay."

Alastor bent to open the bag containing Lucifer's bones. Dirt spilled out and stained the floor. As he stood, he reached into his pocket and pulled out the finger bone. He glanced at Meg, his lips pressed to a frown, then he dropped the last bone into the pile.

"We are not here to play games," Sparrow warned.

Alastor's grin only widened as he emptied the bones onto the floor then took the small finger bone from his pocket and held it up.

"You've both walked through fire, bled for this." Alastor smirked as he tossed the finger bone into the pile of Lucifer's bones.

Before Meg or Sparrow could react, the shadows in the room shifted. From the darkness, twisted figures emerged–creatures born of Hell's deepest pits. Their eyes glowed with malevolent hunger as they surrounded Meg and Sparrow, claws gleaming, teeth bared.

"Prove yourselves worthy to Lucifer," Alastor said.

"We have a deal," Sparrow interrupted. "You owe me too many souls. Our deal is binding."

The darkness surrounding them went still as Alastor pondered. "If you're dead, I owe nothing."

Sparrow drew his blade and pointed it at Alastor. "I am the Raven King. No one threatens me. Not an Archangel, not Babylon, and definitely not the bastard son of Lucifer. I will skin you where you stand."

Sparrow reached out with his free hand, gripping Meg's wrist and dragging her behind him.

"Send me the souls. Now." Sparrow stood a step forward, ready to gut Alastor where he stood.

"I need more time." Alastor tipped his chin and whispered something that caused Lucifer's bones to begin smoking.

Fifteen

Meg

WELL, that's disappointing.

I've known about Alastor's involvement in the skin trades since he kidnapped Shay. What I didn't know was Sparrow's involvement. I glance between the two men. Alastor is fucked beyond comprehension. Whatever Lucifer is doing to his mind has turned it to Swiss cheese.

I glance at Sparrow. He doesn't look at me and I take the time to examine his hardened expression and realize I have no clue who he is. I have no clue who he ever has been.

The smell of sulfur and decay is suddenly too strong to ignore. The stone walls echo with the hum of dark energy. I glance at Alastor, his figure half-obscured in shadow. He smirks, always too confident, too unbothered. Something feels wrong. A shifting tension thickens the air making my stomach twist with unease.

I turn to Sparrow. His arms are crossed defensively. His wings look dull in the dim light, feathers trembling with the vibration in the air.

"You're working with him?" I ask, my voice low and laced with disappointment. It's not a question. When I made the connection a few moments ago the realization fell like a stone in my chest.

Sparrow's eyes flicker with darkness but he says nothing, his lips press into a thin line. His silence speaks volumes. He's not denying it.

"Soul trading, Sparrow? You've been dealing with Alastor all this time?" My throat tightens as the truth sinks in.

Sparrow looks away, his jaw clenched, his silence a scream of betrayal.

To think I was stupid enough to start trusting him, to believe him, to believe in all those things he told me...

I PROMISE, *you're safe with me. It won't be like before. You've suffered too much." His lips press to the scar over my heart. "I can never say sorry enough for what we've been through."*

"WHY?" my voice cracks, anger builds. "After everything, after all we've been through... you're dealing in souls." All these years we tracked Alastor and anticipated an attack, Sparrow was working with him. My heart aches and the old scar throbs. I am reminded of the moment he tried to kill me; the questions he asked before we got to the barn on Route 37.

"There are things I cannot tell you," Sparrow mutters, not meeting my gaze. His wings flutter nervously, brushing against the stone floor. "We can talk about this later."

I've killed people for less betrayal. I killed his father for less. I killed Lucifer for less. The fury bubbles inside me, a raw mixture of hurt and anger boils inside me like molten steel.

Alastor chuckles from the corner of the room. "I told you she wouldn't understand, Raven King."

My gaze snaps to Alastor, my fingers twitching with the desire to reach for my blade and end this game once and for all. But something in the air shifts, a tremor ripples through the stone beneath our feet.

Suddenly, Alastor's smirk falters, his gaze drifting toward the bathtub where the ground begins to crack open. The fissures widen. Dark energy pours from the cracks like smoke, swirling in a suffocating haze.

The bones.

My heart pounds as Lucifer's bones start to move. Clinking and clattering, they begin to reassemble themselves.

Alastor shakes his head like a dog, dark hair flying wild, then he goes still. His eyes finally clear and a smirk lines his face.

"Finally," he says, voice strong. "He's gone. I can think clearly again." His smirk turns darker, more malicious. "Ah, the king returns." He steps back toward the growing rift in the floor. "And you, Meg, should get ready to bow."

"Alastor!" I yell, lunging toward him, but the ground beneath him cracks wide open. Shadows claw up around his ankles, pulling him into the earth. His eyes glint with a wicked amusement as he vanishes into the void, his voice lingering as he disappears, saying, "The souls have been transferred, Raven King."

I glance to Sparrow, dark energy emanating from him, his eyes brighten and widen as though he's received a power surge.

"We need to go," Sparrow says suddenly, his voice strained but urgent. He steps toward me, wings unfurling.

"Don't touch me!" I swat at his hands and step back. Anger flares. "After everything you've done."

"I'm not asking for forgiveness!" Sparrow snaps, grabbing my arm as the ground beneath our feet shakes harder. His grip on my arm is firm, desperate. "I will explain but we have to go. Now!"

I hesitate for a fraction of a second, anger battling the reality of the situation. The air around us crackles with dark energy as Lucifer's skeletal form begins to stir.

I have no choice. If I stay, if we stay, we will be killed–if not worse.

With a final, bitter glance at the bones assembling, I step closer to Sparrow. He wraps his arms around me, pulls me tight against his chest. His wings beat hard, sending a gust of air and debris around us as we lift off the ground.

The room collapses in on itself as Sparrow flies toward the broken windows near the balcony. I go stiff when I notice my wings tacked to the wall like a trophy. That bastard.

The ballroom crumbles under the weight of Lucifer's resurrection. Walls tip in and collapse, leaving a cloud of dust.

We rise above the chaos, the wind whipping at our faces as Sparrow flies out the broken window and hovers for a moment. I glance to the ruins below. My heart clenches as Sparrow's arm tightens around me. It looks like a bomb blew out the ballroom.

From the rubble, a voice echoes. Rich, deep and filled with malice.

"Meg..." Lucifer. His voice is chilling, sending a shiver down my spine.

Sparrow moves closer and we both see Lucifer watching us from the balcony. He points a bony finger at us.

"Granddaughter!" he shouts across Hellsky. "No hugs? No apology for killing me?" he laughs something maniacal.

The skin hasn't completely formed over his face and it looks like a half-skeleton man is yelling at us.

Unease is an icepick in my spine.

Sparrow's arms tighten around me.

"Go!" I urge Sparrow. "Get us out of here!"

"You cannot run. Not from me!" Lucifer shouts. "You took my throne, now I will take something from you!"

Sparrow flies faster, his wings straining against the howling wind of Hellsky. I wrap my arms around him, feeling the tension in his body, his guilt, his haste.

Lucifer is back and the world has just become a much darker place.

"Where are you taking us?" I ask.

"The closest portal is the Nightjar's pond," he says.

The ground cracks below us. Lucifer's rage is altering the landscape of Hell.

"Hurry," I urge.

They sky darkens and the Nightjar's call echoes. "My baby, I'll keep you safe," she sings into the howling night.

"Hang on," Sparrow says as he tips.

The pond glimmers from between the tree canopies. Steam rises. Ground rumbles.

I'm not the praying type, never have been––always lacked faith in a higher being–but in this moment I pray that he makes it to the pond before the water is gone and we crash into the boiling earth.

Our arms tighten around each other as Sparrow's wings stretch back and he divebombs toward the pond like a Kingfisher.

"Don't let go," he murmurs in my ear.

I close my eyes. His arms are so tight I can barely breath. My arms are so tight I'm ninety-nine percent sure he can't breathe at all.

Cold water hits my head and everything moves in slow motion. I swear I hear Nero's frantic neighing. I open my eyes, open my mouth, and water fills my lungs. Above us is the pond surface, fire erupting like an explosion beyond. Bubbles rise as I try to take a breath.

Sparrow makes a noise that sounds like he's yelling. Then blackness.

Sixteen

"*Speak. Demon horse.*" The white horse bent to gently lap water from the lake.

The air on the Earthen plane was unnervingly still. Nero's hooves struck a pile of rocks with a hollow thud as he walked closer to the white horse, her presence as silent and unsettling as the world around them. His eyes, dark and sharp, flicked toward her. Something had changed. He could feel it. The darkness inside him which he usually associated with the Crossroads Demon part of him, felt like it was ready to burst.

The white horse nodded her head and urged him to drink. Ice cracking echoed across the Utah abyss.

"*It won't be cold for long,*" she warned.

Nero moved closer and lapped at the cool water, watching the white horse warily.

"*Cold water helped me learn how to get the words out,*" she said, watching him closely. "*I'm not sure why.*"

Nero stopped drinking when his tongue was numb. A million thoughts ran through his mind.

The white horse's silver mane caught the faint sunlight, reflecting something beyond this world. She had been quiet for a few minutes now, her mysterious aura gnawing at Nero's patience. For a creature so calm, so poised, there was an unnerving power within her, one that Nero wasn't used to–one that rivaled his own.

Then, without warning, her voice, smooth and calm, broke the silence.

"*You're quiet, Nero.*" Her words sliced through the air, stopping him from drinking more. "*But you shouldn't be. Speak.*" She urged.

Nero raised his head, noticing that his entire mouth now felt numbed. He opened his mouth, gnashed his teeth, pursed his lips, huffed in annoyance until... "*How?*" came out.

"*Very good,*" the white horse approved. "*How, what? How can I speak or how can I be?*"

"*Speak,*" Nero said.

"*Come.*" She nodded to the frozen plain and waited for him to walk beside her. "*It took me years to recognize that I was something else. Something other. You see... I never died like the other horses did back in those days. I always lived. I always escaped. Always saw a glimmer in the distance and found myself elsewhere.*" She looked at Nero. "*I get the feeling something similar happened to you.*"

"*Yes.*" Nero nodded, his voice sounded jagged and harsh.

"*You can no longer remain silent–*"

The ground beneath them trembled.

The white horse's eyes darkened, and her expression became grave. "*You feel it, don't you?*"

Nero's heart pounded as the earth beneath them shook harder. The wind, once gentle and still and chilled, began to howl violently, whipping through the air like a warm curse. Ice cracked then melted. The once calm skies above them grew dark and twisted, angry clouds swirling and descending toward the earth.

The Earthen plane trembled as a loud ripping sound echoed throughout, like cloth being torn on a nail.

"*The Veil*," the white horse searched the horizon. "*Lucifer has returned.*"

The ground buckled, splitting open beneath Nero's hooves as the sky raged overhead. He staggered, his legs stretching wide as he struggled to maintain his balance. Lightning cracked across the heavens, illuminating the twisted storm clouds that now loomed ominously above them.

Then they saw it: a rip in reality in the middle of the thawed plain before them. The Earthen plane wavered, heat and fire blew in, the tear widened, and a handful of Demons charged through.

"*The Veil is torn*." The white horse nodded in the direction of the mountains.

"*It can't be*," Nero muttered, his voice rough with disbelief.

The white horse turned her gaze toward the chaos, her serene demeanor shattered by the sheer weight of what was happening. "*Lucifer's resurrection has thrown everything into disarray. His return signals the end of peace, the rise of darkness. The balance has shifted drastically.*" The white horse sighed. "*We worked so hard to avoid this.*"

Nero's eyes went wide. "*What are you?*"

The white horse began galloping. "*Come now, Nero, we must get to safety.*"

They ran past the lake which began to steam and boil. Past the plains where icy grass melted and turned brown. Past mountains that tremored and rumbled as rock tumbled down from the peak. Screams echoed in the distance.

They paused near an empty road. "*We must find a tear to*

Heaven. We aren't too late. There's still hope," the white horse said, her eyes reflecting the swirling darkness.

Nero looked at her, incredulous. *"Hope? You're seeing what's happening, aren't you? The world is falling apart. Exactly what the Deacon's warned."*

"Yes, they were a great help in keeping the balance. But now we have one last hope. There is something that can stop him. Something that even Lucifer fears."

Nero's ears perked at that. *"What are you talking about?"*

"I am thought to be lost, a treasure to find,
An ancient relic that transcends time.
They search for me where metals gleam,
But I walk the earth, not what I seem.
I am both the key and the guide." The white horse paused, her eyes distant as if searching through the vastness of memory.

"Where is it?" Nero asked.

"Hidden. Forgotten by most, but it exists. And we must find it if we're to stop him."

The earth rumbled again, louder this time, splitting the ground beneath them. Nero's hooves dug into the dirt, steadying himself as the world continued to crack and break around them. The storm raged and Demons roared as they poured out of the split in the Veil between realms.

The white horse turned toward him, her gaze fierce and resolute. *"It is more than an artifact. It is a key, a weapon, forged to contain darkness itself. But it cannot be wielded by just anyone. Only those who carry both light and shadow can unlock its power."*

Nero's breath caught and he stared at the white horse, realizing what she meant. *"Meg,"* he whispered, the truth sinking in. *"You're talking about Meg."*

"Yes," she stepped closer, her silver mane brushing against his

side. *"She is half-darkness and half-light. The key to saving this world lies within her."*

The storm roared louder, the wind tearing at their manes as the earth buckled once more.

"And the relic?" Nero asked.

"There is only one remaining. Hidden somewhere. We must find it and bring it to Meg before it's too late." The white horse whinnied and nodded toward a spec of light breaking through in the distance. *"There, a break. Run fast before it closes."*

Both horses took off, faster than lighting, faster than a black hole, faster than anything. Nothing had ever kept up with Nero's speed, not until this moment. Nero's heart beat kicked up a notch and he tipped his head down, running faster, challenging her. The white horse kept up, gallop for gallop, hoofprint for hoofprint. They stayed side by side. Black and white. If anyone could see them, they wouldn't believe it.

They leapt through the small tear and landed on the edges of Babylon. Nero paced, shaking off the adrenaline of the run.

Suddenly, his blood went cold. A scream traveled down the tether that connected his soul to Shay's. Nero took off in the direction of the Raven King's lands.

He didn't wait to discuss with the white horse, the pace of his gallop pushed his muscles to the brink. All he could think of was Shay and the terror coming from her.

I'm coming. I'm coming. I'm coming. He chanted, trying to send the message to her.

He leapt over the barrier to the Raven King's lands.

Seventeen

"Shay?" Rue was searching under the couch cushions.

"Yea?" Shay set down her book and watched the girl.

"Have you seen Lucipurr?" Rue kneeled on the floor to look under the couch. "I haven't seen him in a few hours."

"I'm sure he's fine. Kittens like to hide for their naps." Shay stood. "I'll help you find him. Where did you see him last?"

"He was in my room."

A small meow came from the front of the house.

"Did he go outside?" Shay asked, walking toward the door.

Rue followed. "He's never been outside without me."

"Maybe he was exploring. Kittens do that sometimes. He's a curious little thing." Shay reached for the door and opened it. "I had a barn cat as a kid and always found it sleeping in the strangest places. The chicken coop, under the porch stairs."

A man in a black suit was standing on the porch, holding Rue's kitten. For a second Shay's breath stopped thinking it was Alastor come back to haunt her. She blinked and realized it wasn't him. He was handsome yet... a shadow shifted across his face, darkening his features. Shay thought he might have been another Angel, but the scar on her thigh ached with familiarity. No, not an Angel. This man was something not of this realm.

He stepped down and back until his feet hit dirt.

A twitch of alarm hit Shay. "Who are you?" she asked.

"That's no way to treat a guest." The man stroked Lucipurr's head, his firm pets stretching the kitten's eyelids back.

"Stop," Shay said, reaching forward. "You're hurting him. Give him back to me." She grasped air, reaching for the kitten.

Something like fire and possession flashed in the man's eyes. He threw the kitten at Shay and reached forward, grabbing Rue's wrist.

The ground opened under his feet and in a split second, both the man in the suit and Rue disappeared into the ground. The only thing left in their place was a mound of dark dirt.

"No!" Shay screamed, dropped the kitten, and started clawing at the dirt. "Help!" Shay shouted as terror tore through her, dirt and rocks shredding her fingertips as she dug with her hands.

Nero was the first to arrive in a flash of black, a shadow zooming across the lawn. He whinnied a worried sound.

"Someone took Rue," Shay told Nero, the words came out like a scream. "Some man was here... he had to be a Demon. How did a Demon get here? They aren't supposed to find this place. They aren't supposed to be able to cross into this realm."

Jed was running toward her, Remington and Thrush not far behind.

Shay was still digging. Nero started pacing, he wanted to find the break in the Veil and go after whoever had taken Rue.

He whinnied and relayed the message down the tether that connected them. "Go!" Shay said, "Go find her. Please find her. Oh, God." Shay was trembling with fear as memories of her time in Alastor's hovel flooded her. She couldn't imagine a child with one of those skin trader Demons. "We have to find her!" Shay screamed.

Nero ran toward Babylon. The girl was too innocent to be in the hands of a Demon or worse, Lucifer. He leapt over the stone boundary that surrounded the Raven King's lands. He ran into the center of Babylon, not caring if anyone saw him and he leapt into the fountain.

Eighteen

Meg

I cough, light blasting my vision. Sitting up, I gasp in a deep breath then spit out a mouthful of water. The shimmer of the Babylon fountain ripples as I stand. The air surrounding me seems to hum with warmth but the subtle peace is fleeting.

The moment Sparrow tugs me out of the fountain and my boots touch the stone walkway I hear it, echoing throughout Babylon, coming from the kingdom in the distance. A faint, heart-wrenching sound carried on the breeze. My heart drops, the sound unmistakable, and my pulse quickens. Screaming.

"Sparrow." My voice doesn't sound right.

"We need to go," Sparrow says, his body vibrating with alarm. His wings unfurl and shake away the water before he grabs me and shoots forward. He races toward the noise. The closer we get, the sharper the screams become, cutting through the otherwise perfect stillness of Heaven like a jagged blade.

It's Shay's voice.

Something is wrong, very wrong. The type of wrong that buries itself in your gut and gnaws at you, urging you to move faster, to forego thought and only act.

From the corner of my eye, I catch a flash of movement. A blur of black and white. Two powerful forms moving with grace across Babylon. One leaps over the boundary to Sparrow's kingdom.

It's Nero. And... a white horse.

The screaming grows louder as we approach. My stomach twists with every single one of Sparrow's wing beats. I see the house in the distance. People are running. Something is wrong and it feels like a shadow is creeping over everything.

Shay is screaming and digging in the dirt with her hands like a crazy person. Her voice sends a cold spike of fear down my spine.

Sparrow lands, nearly dropping me, our feet skidding against the ground. The moment my feet touch grass, I feel it. Darkness. A flicker of Hell's influence coming from the hole Shay is digging.

Without another word, I push forward, Sparrow at my side, both of us racing toward the commotion.

Shay looks up and notices us. She's covered in dirt and tears drip down her cheeks. Everyone is shouting.

"What happened?" Sparrow roars over the voices.

Everyone goes still. There's a kind of fear in the air I've never felt before. They're all standing stone still, afraid. Shay, Jed, Nightingale, Noah, Chel, Thrush, Remington, and a soft meow from Lucipurr.

Shay stands, her hands bloody and dirty. "I don't know how it happened, Meg." She hiccups. "One minute we were looking for the Lucipurr, the next he was there. He just... he had the kitten and he was squeezing Lucipurr's head... and he... he threw the kitten at me. Then he... oh God, no..."

"What happened?"

"He took Rue," Remington says.

"Who?" I ask. "Who took her?" my heart starts beating too fast, the hairs on my scalp tingling. "Who was it?"

Shay is shaking her head. "A Demon in a suit. I've never seen him before. How did it get in? How?" Shay screams the question. "How can a Demon breach the Seven Kingdoms of Heaven?"

"Lucifer has been resurrected," Sparrow says.

"Where did he take Rue?" I ask, feeling like I'm losing it. My skin feels like ice, my blood like lava. "Where is she?"

Silence.

Shay looks terrified.

"I want her back!" I scream. "This wasn't supposed to happen!" I have never felt weaker, I have no wings, no ability to *poof*... I glance at Sparrow. I could drain him dry, it would make me strong. His blood would make me fast. I could take from him to find her. I glance at Remm and Thrush. When Nightingale and Noah arrive they pull the boys back, protecting them... from me.

"Stop," he warns. "We get her back together. If you kill me, we lose." He shakes his head. "Stop thinking about it."

Tears cloud my vision. "What do you expect me to do? I will kill every soul in Heaven and Hell and the Earthen plane to get her back. This was not supposed to happen. I was supposed to keep her safe!" Something dark is threatening to take me over. Black swirls in my periphery.

"Mom," Remington interrupts. "Rue is strong. She can hold her own until we find her."

"She's gone." The words hang in the air, heavy, suffocating, as if the weight was going to crush my lungs and choke the life out of me. I can't breathe. The ground tilts beneath me, the walls closing in, my mind spins out of control. Rue. My daughter. Taken. Just like... Elyse. My daughter. Dead. This is nothing but a family curse. All my daughters die. Not her. This ends now.

"No," I gasp, my voice barely recognizable, more of a rasp than words. "No, no, no!"

I stumble backward, my back hitting Sparrow's chest. My knees buckle, my chest heaving as a wave of panic surges through me. Raw, burning heat claws at my throat and my vision blurs with a mix of tears and rage.

"They took her!" The scream rips from my throat, ragged and desperate. My hands fist in my hair, pulling hard enough to sting, but it doesn't stop the spiral of terror. "I should've been here. I should've protected her. Lucifer's bones meant *nothing*! I should have burned them. You're all wrong. You've always been wrong. Handing over his bones was not what I should have done."

I can't think. My mind is a whirlwind of images; Rue laughing, Rue calling my name, Rue's face twisting in fear as a Demon drags her away. I need to find her. Now. I need to...

"They're going to kill her!" I shriek, my voice cracking. "They're going to kill my daughter!" Memories flash faster across my vision... falling down stairs, blood, Hellions, a snowy owl, a jar full of feathers...

I feel like I'm spinning, the world tilting on its axis. I have to get to her. I have to tear down every Demon, every barrier between me and her. I turn, stumbling to my feet, looking for something, anything to help me. My vision is blurry with panic.

I feel Sparrow's hands trying to steady me–someone speaking my name–but I barely hear their words. All I can hear is Rue's voice calling out for me, needing me. And I wasn't here.

"No!" I thrash, pulling away from Sparrow as he tries to hold me, my body lurching forward as I stumble and grab my blade from the holster on my thigh. "Let me go! I have to find her!"

"Meg, stop!" The voice is too distant, too far away to matter.

Another scream rips from my throat. "I can't–she's alone–"

Suddenly, I feel a strange pressure, a subtle warmth against the back of my head. Something soft but forceful, a whisper of magic winding its way through my skull until a blue light clouds my vision. It's calming, soft. I stagger, my breath catching as a thick fog begins to wrap itself around my thoughts. My knees buckle and the house in front of me sways. What is this? I've never felt anything like this before. I knew the rage, the sadness from a few minutes ago. Not this...

"Jed?" his name tumbles from my lips and whispers across my ears. The panic fades, dulled by creeping magic. It wraps me in a gentle, inescapable haze. There's no fighting it.

"Be still," Sparrow whispers in my ear as he lifts me.

I barely raise a finger to point at Jed. I'm gonna get him back. His hand swipes through messy hair and Shay gives a nervous glance. But then, everything goes dark. My body sags, I stumble back into Sparrow's arms.

NINETEEN

"I'm gonna kill Jed," I mutter as Sparrow tightens his grip on me.

Whatever spell he used didn't last long. I glance to the side and recognize the inside of Sparrow's house.

"Put me down," I say.

"No," Sparrow replies.

I struggle and kick.

"Stop it." Sparrow shoves open the bedroom door with his shoulder. He drops me to my feet and slams the door closed, backing against it, blocking my exit.

"Get out of my way." I stumble, feeling woozy. I shove at his big body, trying to get him to move.

"Calm down, Meg," he says.

"Move!" I shout.

"You want to be mad? Then be mad. Take it out on me."

Sparrow drops to a knee so he's below me. "I can take it. We need Jed. We need all of them to win this." He takes my hand and presses it to his neck. "Do it. I deserve it. Of all people. You can take your anger out on me."

I want to hurt him. I want to bite him. I want to tear him apart. But... the room starts spinning and my heart thrums against my ribcage.

Sparrow stands and I back away, still gripping his neck. My stomach flips in dread.

"You want to use your teeth?" He crowds me until the back of my legs hit the mattress. He pulls the collar of his shirt down. "You can do it. A hundred times if that's what it takes to sate your anger."

"They took my child." I grip his neck harder and swallow down the thickness gathering in my throat.

"They took my child," he says.

"This is different."

"I won't argue that." He nods before pushing me onto the bed. "You are a shade of moonlight. You need to eat and regain your strength. Because the next time your feet hit that floor, we'll be running into a war. And I'll be damned to lose you again."

I flash my teeth, pull him close and sink my teeth into his wrist, tears spilling from my eyes.

Something like fire rolls through my body and he senses it. He tugs at my shirt and I work the buckle of his pants.

Soon we are both breathing heavy, aching, distraught, trying our best to fill a void that cannot be explained.

Twenty

It was only moments after Sparrow had gotten Meg finally settled in bed, asleep, when the alert came through that the Archangels were at the gates to his kingdom.

Sparrow left the house and flew to meet them. Six Archangels in flowing robes were clustered near the gate.

"What has happened?" Gabriel asked.

"Did she deliver the bones?" Raphael's voice was hurried.

Michael was pacing and rubbing his chest, looking curiously past the barrier into the Raven King's lands. "There are creatures in there..." he seemed worried.

Sparrow smirked at the Archangel Michael, knowing he'd have the sense of kin being close. Jed was in there. Michael's bastard, half-breed son. Sparrow glanced at Raphael and wondered if the Archangel had the same feeling in his chest when he'd been near Demore. Sparrow only recognized the feeling after Meg had told him the truth about Rue and Remington and he'd made the connection.

"A demon broke through the Veil. It took the girl," Sparrow said, staring at Gabriel.

"Meg's daughter," Gabriel paled. "Not again." Rough hands tore through his hair before smoothing his beard. "Christ almighty. *Not again.*"

"They can get in," Uriel paled before blessing himself. His fingers trembled as he kissed a prayer against his hands. "It's all coming true."

The tension among them thickened. Gabriel's eyes flicked to Sparrow, desperation seeping into his expression. "You must return to Hell. You must find her. Now. Lucifer is growing stronger by the hour."

Raphael stepped forward, his eyes gleaming with urgency. "If Lucifer regains full control, the realms will fall into absolute chaos. You cannot wait any longer."

Michael had stopped pacing, his fists clenched. "The longer we wait, the worse it gets. We need *you* to act." His words were sharp, almost accusatory, as if Sparrow was deliberately wasting time.

Sparrow's jaw tightened. He knew what they expected of him. In fact, he knew more than most of them thought. His gaze drifted to Gabriel. Meg's father knew and was keeping secrets of his own. They saw him as the Raven King, the bridge between Heaven and Hell, the one who could stand with Meg against Lucifer's madness. But none of them knew the truth about the children. None of them understood why his every instinct screamed to stay, to protect what was his.

"The girl is my daughter," Sparrow cut in, his eyes hard as he stared at the Archangels. "There's a boy, too. A shadow heir that Meg has kept hidden."

Shock rippled through the group. Even Michael stopped, his

eyes widening slightly. Gabriel was the first to recover, his voice low. "Your children?"

Sparrow nodded. "Meg kept them a secret, said they were the Hellion's." He glanced to Gabriel. "She's kept you away for a reason. A good reason."

Voices chattered as the Archangels discussed the new information and how it would affect the coming war.

WARS. Blood and death. Good and evil. A dead Sparrow. A motherless child and a fatherless child. Light and dark. The Earthen plane and the ethereal realms. A burst of bright light. An explosion. Fear and pain. Emptiness.

RAPHAEL SPOKE SOFTLY, almost cautiously. "We didn't know..."

"Of course *you* didn't," Sparrow snapped, the words like ice. He took a breath, rage swirling. "But now you do."

Michael's voice cut through the silence, cold and matter-of-fact. "Every moment you wait, Lucifer grows more powerful. If you don't stop him now, there won't be anything left to protect."

Sparrow's wings twitched in irritation. "I understand the stakes."

Gabriel's eyes softened as understanding flashing across his face. "You are not your father, Sparrow. And you're not alone in this."

Sparrow's jaw tightened. "I know. But this is different. There is too much to lose. More than I ever imagined."

Gabriel nodded and pressed his lips together. He didn't need to say more because this was his family also, a family he wasn't sure he'd ever see again nor have a relationship with if darkness won.

"You'll take half of my legion," Gabriel said.

There was silence.

Gabriel turned to the others. "Hand them over," he commanded.

The others hesitated. Sparrow and Gabriel's kingdoms were the largest, the strongest. The other Archangels, while high on self-importance, couldn't match.

"Our kingdoms will fall," Michael finally said.

"Then so be it," Gabriel barked back. "You've taken enough from others. Taken from my family. Threatened my daughter for years. Imprisoned me on bad intel. Ignored omens you'd known about for ages. Even misinterpreted them." Gabriel's teeth were clenched as he took a rage-filled breath. "I have not forgotten whom you blamed for the Fast-Zombie war. I have not forgotten whom you locked in a cage. Hand over the troops."

Twenty-One

The air in the dimly lit living room was thick with tension. The walls seemed to close in as the group gathered, the flickering lights casting long shadows on their faces. Rue's absence weighed heavily on all of them.

"We need to move soon," Jed growled, pacing the room, his eyes darting to the map laid out before them. "If we wait any longer, who knows what that Demon bastard will do to her."

Remington, leaning against the wall, watched Jed with quiet understanding. "We'll get her back," he said calmly, though his voice was firm. "But we need to be smart about this."

Chel, arms crossed over his broad chest nodded. "Agreed. Rushing in could get Rue killed. Could get us all killed." His dark eyes shifted between the others. "We have to consider everything. These are no longer the Demons of Meg's rule. Everything will be different."

Sparrow stood by the doorway, his wings twitching slightly with nervous energy. He hadn't spoken much since the planning began, but his eyes were sharp, listening to every word. Thrush sat next to him, idly sharpening a blade, the steady rhythm of metal against stone the only sound for a moment.

"The landscape has changed. Lucifer tore apart the Hell you all once knew." Sparrow described the cracks in the land, the flowing lava, the shifting landscape.

"What about the black mansion?" Shay asked. "The hovels in the forests?"

Sparrow shook his head. "We weren't near those areas. But those Demons have always been sympathizers to Lucifer." Sparrow didn't mention with the transfer of souls and power he'd felt that the Black Mansion and all the Demons involved in the skin trades were more than likely still standing. Hell was greedy with Lucifer at the helm. The creatures would begin harvesting souls from the Earthen plane at a rapid pace for their new King.

Jed stopped pacing and planted his hands on the table, staring at the map. "That reminds me of something. Alastor's blade," he said, his voice low. "The Basilisk blade he used on me... it's unlike anything I've ever encountered. It nearly killed me. That kind of weapon... we need to prepare for it."

Shay, seated at the edge of the room, leaned forward, her brow furrowing. "The Basilisk venom in the blade... it's incredibly potent. If Alastor or another Demon has more of those weapons, we're going to need something to defend ourselves."

"Or better yet, fight back," Remington muttered from his seat next to Chel. His young face was determined, but there was a flicker of uncertainty in his eyes. "We can't go in there unarmed."

Sparrow's wings rustled as he shifted uncomfortably. He cleared his throat, drawing their attention. "I might know where we can get weapons like that," he said, his voice hesitant.

Noah's gaze snapped to Sparrow, eyes narrowing. "What do

you mean?" He'd been focused on Thrush, an arm wrapped around Nightingale to settle her nervous energy.

Sparrow rubbed the back of his neck, wings lowering. "There was a Basilisk here once, during the Fast-Zombie War. I had to bury it a long time ago."

There was a beat of uncomfortable silence because most in the room knew what Sparrow did when he returned to his kingdom during that war.

Shay's eyes widened. "You buried a Basilisk?"

"It was already dead," Sparrow quickly added, glancing down the hall where Meg was sleeping.

The room went silent as everyone absorbed Sparrow's words. Thrush stopped sharpening his blade, looking up with a thoughtful expression.

Jed straightened, eyes blazing with intensity. "If we can dig it up, we can make our own weapons. Use the same power that almost killed me and turn it on them."

Chel grunted in approval, his wings flexing. "It's dangerous, but if we can make weapons from the bones and the venom, it might give us the edge we need."

Remington, always ready for a challenge and ready to find his sister, stood up, the fire of determination in his eyes. "So we dig it up, forge the weapons, and get Rue back."

Jed slammed his fist down on the table, his eyes burning with renewed hope. "Then let's move. Every second we waste, Rue slips further out of our reach."

Chel uncrossed his arms, nodding. "We'll need to move fast. We've already lost enough time."

The room was a flurry of movement as everyone sprang into action.

"We don't need to dig it up," Sparrow announced. "I did that a few years ago." He cleared his throat.

"And?" Shay urged.

"I had the bones forged into a supply of weapons. Just in case." He glanced toward the front door. "Some of us have had warning of this war. There have been omens. Whispers. I've been preparing."

"Where are they?" Remington asked. "Did you know they'd take Rue?"

"I didn't." Sparrow pushed away from the wall he was leaning against and nodded toward a blank wall at the center of the house.

Everyone waited, expectantly.

"It's not a true wall," Sparrow said as he crossed the room, ran his fingers across the wood paneling until a faint click was heard. A door opened with a stairwell that went down.

"Hm," Nightingale resounded. "Always wondered if you'd rebuilt father's dungeons."

Sparrow glanced back at Nightingale. "It's not a dungeon. I am *not* our father." He flicked a light switch and began walking down the stairs. "Come on," he called.

They followed him down winding stone stairwell that opened to a large room that was empty except for weapons lining the walls.

"Holy crap," Thrush muttered as he moved toward an array of small blades.

"All this from one Basilisk?" Chel asked, remembering that Meg had sent the mother Basilisk to help clean up the Seven Kingdoms of Heaven. "She was a beast." He admired a long sword with a curved blade.

"Take what you can carry," Sparrow said. "The rest will go to my Legion."

"You're bringing them to Hell?" Nightingale asked.

"Nearly half," Sparrow said. "I can't leave this place empty. I don't know if the Veil will split and reveal the Seven Kingdoms of Heaven for the first time."

Noah made a noise of disagreement.

"If the Seven Kingdoms fall, and we fail, there will be nothing," Sparrow said. "This is not about my kingdom. This is about a safe stronghold against the darkness of Lucifer. There is a reason he was cast out."

There were footsteps on the stairwell and everyone turned as Meg muttered, "Holy fuck."

She was dressed for war. Leathers and holsters, her blade strapped to her thigh. She crossed the room with purpose, stopping in front of a giant blade with a black tip. It was a huge tooth fashioned into a wicked weapon. Meg recognized it instantly.

"Oh momma," Meg whispered. "You made the greatest sacrifice." She reached for what was left of the precious mother basilisk, the one who protected Meg's castle, who protected them during the fast-zombie war, who gave her life to save the Seven Kingdoms of Heaven when the dead breached their portals. It appears she would go on protecting Meg's life and family with her bones.

"Take it," Sparrow urged as he took the opposite tooth. There were two more; one he handed to Remington, the other to Thrush.

Nightingale made a noise.

"They'll go after the boys first," Sparrow said. "Shadow heir," he said softly, pressing the blade into Remington's palm. "If we don't make it, this kingdom falls to you." Sparrow turned to Thrush. "If he doesn't make it, the kingdom falls to you."

Nightingale gasped as Noah pulled her close.

Remington nodded sharply.

Thrush tipped his head in challenge. "Let them try."

Meg moved closer to the son whom she'd done her best to

shield and protect and hide. She touched his shoulder, squeezed slightly. "Let's go get your sister. Don't be afraid to let out the *darkness*."

The room was silent as Meg and Remington ran for the stairs. Thrush followed close behind. Then Sparrow. The others ran after them, ready for war.

Twenty-Two

Rue was screaming as she was pulled through the soil into darkness. The Demon was holding her tight like precious cargo. An arm around her shoulders and another around her middle, she couldn't escape even if she tried—even if she wasn't so afraid. She pressed her mouth and eyes closed, petrified of the dirt suffocating her.

Chel would be disappointed that she didn't fight harder but everything happened so fast. One moment she was reaching for Lucipurr, the next that man was pulling her away.

Rue squeezed her eyes closed and tried to hold back the lump in her throat. Her world was spinning. It didn't feel like traveling through a regular portal; being dragged through the ground was something disorienting and violent. Her ears popped, feet hit solid ground, and the arms around her released. Rue fell to a crouch, felt warm stone under her fingertips as she steadied herself. Blinking to force away the feeling of disorientation, she opened her eyes.

There was brimstone in the air, ash filtered through the dim light like dust motes. Rue knew where she was. *Home.* Or what used to be home. The castle in the burning caves felt different. The shadowed corners were darker, more creatures slithering and skittering in the spaces than ever before. She glanced at her feet and wished she'd put boots on that morning. She was only wearing socks, jeans, and a thin shirt.

"Get up." the man in the suit grabbed a fistful of hair and dragged Rue to her feet.

She inhaled a sharp breath and sprung up, the swift movement of her small fist followed her gaze. She almost clocked the Demon in the jaw, but he caught her hand, swallowed up by his much larger one. He twisted her arm behind her back. Rue glared at him. He was definitely a Demon, but more human-looking than any she'd come across before. She glanced across the room. They were in the dining room. There were so many memories of family meals here and she had a feeling the nostalgia for the dining room was about to be ruined.

"I never thought I'd see a Great-Granddaughter," a deep voice echoed.

Rue looked up and up and up. She gulped. She'd never seen a Demon so tall. Never seen horns so large. And if he was calling her Great-Granddaughter, then it could only be Lucifer.

He paced in front of her, hands clasped behind his back as he looked her up and down.

"You're too small," he said as he stopped in front of her. "A runt," he sneered. Lucifer looked disgusted. He paced again before turning to her and crouching. They were eye level now and she couldn't look away from his inky depths. Lucifer reached out and touched her hair, then a fingertip slid across her jaw. "Have you any powers?"

Rue shook her head.

"Can you not speak?" he scoffed, glancing at the Demon who gripped her hair.

The Demon let go and took a step back.

Rue's mouth opened but Lucifer spoke again. "Your mother is much taller. Stronger too." Lucifer took her wrist and stretched her arm out. "Any birthmarks?"

"No," Rue finally spoke but it sounded like a whisper.

"Maybe you're too young. How old are you?" Lucifer asked.

"Fifteen."

"No wings," he frowned.

"No," Rue replied.

He stared, seemed to be pondering her existence. "Your mother was older when her powers formed." He suddenly laughed. "But now she has none. You're both the same. Worthless. Useless. Weak."

Lucifer pressed his finger against Rue's shoulder and shoved. She stumbled back and fell.

Lucifer walked away. He made his way toward a window and gazed outside.

Rue noticed the landscape around the castle had changed; there was no grass or trees, everything was burnt, and rivers of lava flowed through the center of the royal lands where she'd played as a child. A shiver rolled up her spine. The Demon in the suit moved closer to her like he was a guard, like she might escape.

"No power, no wings, puny," Lucifer muttered. "The Deacons warned that my female bloodline would destroy me." He laughed. "But look at you all, weak or dead. The only one who gave me a struggle was Meg. I will kill her soon enough." He turned to face Rue. "But you... hm. You aren't much..." He squinted. "Your father was a Hellion. That shouldn't make you very dangerous. Your soul is still worth plenty."

Rue nodded, didn't dare tell him the truth.

"Doesn't matter, halflings are just as much trouble." He seemed to be conversing with himself. "It's the ones born half-darkness and half-light that have been the real issue. All the others were easy to kill."

"Her soul has value. We could use her to cultivate the skin trades," the Demon offered. "We lost many willing women during the transition of power."

Lucifer paused. Pondered.

"She looks very human. We could use her to recruit the human women from the Earthen plane," the Demon offered.

Lucifer waved the proposal away. "I will take over all the realms soon enough. The human women won't have a choice."

"Some prefer the willing, your darkness. Some will pay dearly for a willing one." The Demon bowed with the suggestion.

Lucifer growled, annoyed that the Demon dare speak out against his plan.

"Then she is your burden to use as you see fit for the skin trades. But," he raised a long finger. "She will stay here in the dungeons when you are not using her. And then, when I am ready, I will kill her. Just like I arranged for Clea to die, just like I will kill her mother, just like I killed that other halfling that turned into an owl. I will have no bringers of death in this bloodline. I will kill them all," Lucifer promised before disappearing from the room.

Rue shivered as she contemplated the truth she'd just heard; it felt like a thousand pounds of rocks had dropped in her gut. She hadn't seen her grandmother Clea in weeks, last she'd heard her mother said Clea had been sent to the Ether by Alastor. She wondered if her mother knew about the omen Lucifer had just mentioned. She'd learned about plenty of omens the Deacons handed down, most were poorly understood and interference by

Archangels and Demons made everything surrounding an omen worse.

"Come with me," the Demon standing near her said. He held out a hand.

Rue stepped back. "Get away from me," she said, glancing around the room, searching for an escape.

Rue's heart pounded in her chest as she stood frozen in the center of the dimly lit room. The flickering light from torches near the fireplace cast eerie shadows against the stone walls, each one shifting, stretching like something alive. Her mind raced, every muscle in her body screamed for her to move, to run, to escape this Hell.

The Demon who'd brought her here was watching, leaning casually against the fireplace, arms crossed over his chest as if he had all the time in the world. He was handsome. Too handsome. With sharp features and dark, unruly hair that framed his face perfectly. His eyes gleamed with something almost playful, a dangerous glint that made Rue's skin crawl then... she shivered hard.

"You don't need to be afraid," he said, his voice smooth, almost soothing, as if he were trying to coax a frightened animal. "You're not going to be hurt... yet." A faint smirk tugged at the corner of his lips, but there was something dark lurking behind the amusement in his eyes.

"I'm not going anywhere with you," Rue snapped, taking a step back until her back hit the dining room table. The stone floor was warm beneath her feet but that didn't stop the chill from writhing up her spine. She could feel tension tightening in her chest.

The Demon straightened, pushing off the fireplace with an effortless grace that made Rue's pulse quicken. "That's where you're wrong, princess," he said, his tone soft but dangerous. "The dungeon's close. We've been waiting for days. I just thought I'd give you the courtesy of walking there instead of dragging you." His eyes raked over her, lingering, settling on the mess of hair he'd pulled so hard earlier. Rue's stomach twisted with revulsion.

She glanced across the room, desperate to find an exit, a way to escape him. There was a narrow window on the other side of the room, but he was blocking it. She might be able to make it to the door if she could distract him.

"Why are you doing this?" Rue asked, trying to keep her voice steady. "You could have let him kill me and end it all."

The Demon laughed a low, amused sound. "There are secrets I won't spill. Even if you ask nicely." He took a step toward her, slow, deliberate, and Rue's breath hitched. "How cute."

She swallowed, her mind spinning. She needed to do something, anything. Her eyes flicked toward a small table with a heavy, iron candelabra. She knew it was heavy because it fell on Remington's foot when they were nine years old and it broke three of his toes.

Rue jumped up onto the table and rolled across, feet landing hard on the other side, socks sliding as she dove for the candelabra.

The Demon raised an eyebrow, amused. "I wouldn't try that if I were you."

Rue's hand wrapped around the base of the candelabra before he finished speaking. With a cry, she swung it toward him, the heavy iron catching the torchlight as it flew toward his head.

He was fast. Too fast.

Before Rue could blink, the Demon had ducked and surged forward, grabbing her wrist with a grip like iron. The candelabra clattered to the ground with a metallic ring as he twisted her arm behind her back, pulling her flush against him.

"Nice try," he murmured in her ear, his breath warm against her skin. "But you're not getting away that easily."

Rue struggled, thrashing in his grip, but it was like fighting against stone.

"No!" she gasped, twisting as hard as she could. "Let me go!"

She kicked him, trying to break free but he barely flinched, his hold unyielding. The door loomed closer and dread settled in her gut. He was going to take her to the dungeon whether she wanted it or not. And then... bile rose in her throat.

Rue thrashed harder.

"Stop fighting," he said, his voice growing darker, the amusement fading. "It's over, princess. You belong to us now. Until Lucifer decides to kill you."

Rue's chest tightened with dread as the Demon walked closer to the door, her feet dangling as he held her against his chest with one strong arm across her middle.

The door slammed open. The Demon set Rue on her feet and she made another attempt to flee, rushing to the side and out of their reach.

A giant Hellion stood in the doorway and roared like a boar. "To the dungeons!" The Hellion walked toward Rue–oily skin, horns protruding from its mouth, strange hair like slithering snakes. Rue backstepped, searching for a way to escape the monster. Her mother told stories about the Hellions of Lucifer's time. They looked worse in real life. The Hellion ran at her, grabbing her by the hair. Rue screamed. The Hellion slapped her so hard it knocked her unconscious. Rue's body slumped, nearly lifeless.

———

"Are you stupid?" the Demon yelled at the Hellion. "Don't damage her."

"She was loud." The Hellion swung Rue's body around like

she was a ragdoll, throwing her over his shoulder. "Come with me. I will show you to her cell in the dungeon."

"Let me carry her," the Demon offered, holding his arms out.

"No."

"You will break her. She is tiny. I can't make any money off her if she'd bruised up and has broken bones." He moved closer. "Give her to me."

The Hellion rolled his eyes before dragging Rue off his shoulder and holding her limp body and with a giant hand wrapped around her waist, he offered her to the Demon in the suit.

The Demon took her, gently draping her over his arms.

"Let's go," the Hellion muttered. "I have shit to do."

The Demon, Dacre, nodded and followed the Hellion to the dungeon.

The Hellion kept glancing back. He was keeping up so Dacre had to assume it was his looks that were making the Hellion suspicious.

Dacre was led down winding stairs. He'd heard about the dungeon here but had never stepped foot in it before. Giant looming shadows shifted behind dungeon windows and doors. Dacre held in a darkness that was swarming in his chest. He wouldn't reveal anything other than stoic strength or risk an attack. Most creatures of Hell didn't understand how he looked so human and most picked fights. He wouldn't risk it here, not with the princess draped across his arms. He tightened his grip on her.

"This one," the Hellion shoved open a dungeon door.

Dacre stepped inside and glanced around the damp chamber. "Get her a cot," he demanded, voice deep.

The Hellion scoffed.

"Do you know how much she is worth?" Dacre asked, glaring. "Lucifer is going to use her to recruit women into the skin trades.

She cannot be bruised. She cannot be sleeping on wet stones. She'll wake up with the damp cough and then no one will touch her."

The Hellion grumbled about runes on pale skin and weak children before leaving the chamber and returning a few minutes later with a small cot.

Dacre settled Rue on the bed. "Get out of here," he told the Hellion. "Wait outside."

Dacre inspected Rue's skin for injury; he didn't like the way the Hellion was slinging her around like a ragdoll. The girl exhaled a shallow breath and moaned like she was having a bad dream. She shivered and when the motion didn't stop, he pressed a palm to her bare arm. She was cold. Dacre shrugged off his suitcoat and covered her with it. He watched her sleep, moving the edge of her shirt to the side and read the runes that had been tattooed on her pale skin. Power. Protection. There was something he didn't quite understand, he read the rune a few times and eventually gave up after concluding it had something to do with her aura. He glanced at her dark hair. He hadn't seen an aura in Heaven or Hell but he had heard the stories about the beams of light on the Earthen plane months ago.

"I have shit to do," the Hellion bellowed from outside the door.

Dacre turned away from Rue, reluctantly. He didn't want to leave her here but he would not go against Lucifer's wishes and risk instant death.

"I will return in the morning for her. Lucifer said she is my burden." Dacre grumbled. The daughter of the fallen Queen was going to bring him riches like he'd always imagined. He had family debts to pay off, after all.

Twenty-Three

Teari knelt on the ground, her hands deftly adjusting the leather straps of the prosthetic leg she was fitting on the Deacon. Her brow furrowed in concentration.

The Deacon, sitting on a low stool, watched her with grim patience, his eyes flickering occasionally toward Gabriel who stood near the door like a guard.

His back was to them, his tall frame silhouetted against the dim lights of the shelter in the mountain. He was silent, shoulders tense as if bracing for an argument he already knew was coming. Outside, the wind howled through the cracks in the mountain stone, a chilling reminder of the storm gathering on the horizon, of the thinning veil, of the war that would soon tear their world apart. Of dark omens come to a precipice. He thought back to his one love, Clea. They'd started this against Lucifer's wishes. They'd been warned. Gabriel stroked his beard and thought on the omens delivered by Clea. Perhaps he'd interpreted them all wrong and everything he'd done to prevent this war was futile.

"It's time for me to leave this place," the Deacon said, stifling a groan as Teari tightened the prosthetic. "Lucifer has taken over. The Veil is dangerously thin."

Teari didn't look up from her work, but Gabriel's shoulders stiffened at the words. He turned slowly, his expression unreadable. "It's not yet time," Gabriel said firmly, his tone leaving little room for argument.

The Deacon clenched his jaw, frustration simmering beneath a calm exterior. His leg, or what was left of it, twitched involuntarily as Teari fastened the last strap. He flexed the prosthetic experimentally, testing its weight.

"How long?" the Deacon asked, his voice tighter now. "How long am I supposed to wait? Until Meg's fighting him alone? Until it's too late to make a difference?"

Gabriel stepped forward, his face hardening. "We wait until it's necessary, not a moment sooner."

The Deacon looked up at Gabriel, his eyes flashing with defiance. "You do not control me. Every day we wait, Lucifer grows stronger. Every day, Meg gets closer to that fight, and I should be there with her. That is the reason I was saved."

Teari glanced between them, sensing the tension. She tightened the final strap on the prosthetic, made sure the healed skin wasn't pinching, and gently patted the Deacon's knee, signaling her work was done. Rising to her feet, she wiped her hands on her pants, not wanting to get in the middle of the brewing argument.

She knew her place. She was Gabriel's healer and sometimes crossed royal lands to assist the Raven King, and sometimes crossed realms to assist Meg. She kept plenty of secrets for all of them, but this information didn't sit right in her gut. Still, she kept her mouth shut.

"When the time is right," Gabriel said, his voice measured and calm. "You can't run in there before all the pieces are in place, it's too much of a risk. You've barely been upright for a few days."

The Deacon stood, testing his balance on the prosthetic. He shifted his weight from side to side. The leather straps stretched, adjusting to his motion. The distraction wasn't enough to cool the fire brewing in his chest. The weight of the Deacon's existence had collected in his body creating an energy so strong it was hard to contain. Now that he was healing, it was only growing stronger. He knew what he needed to do, the urge to cross realms and fight for peace was stronger than ever. He glanced to the Archangel towering over him. Gabriel had always been the most open-minded of the Archangels, the one the Deacons had been watching closely. He was quick to think outside of the box and challenge Babylon. He stood up for what was right, even if it was wrong for the Seven Kingdoms of Heaven. He'd been moved by the peace his last daughter had brought to the realms. Years without war were difficult to come by when good and evil danced the tango under the shadow of the Veil separating realms. A white-flamed ember burned stronger in the Deacon's chest. Gabriel needed a push in the right direction.

"I'm tired of waiting," Deacon muttered, staring at the floor. "It's going to be too late. Much has happened already. You know this." The Deacon's gaze fell upon Gabriel. "You know Lucifer took the girl."

"What girl?" Teari asked, needing to know this instant who it was.

"Meg's daughter," the Deacon said.

Teari froze, knowing that if someone took Rue, Meg would kill them as soon as possible. "You didn't tell me," Teari said as she turned to face Gabriel.

"I shouldn't have told anyone." Gabriel frowned, glancing at the Deacon. "But those damned Archangels will spill the beans faster than a chickadee."

"I was not allowed to live to sit on the sidelines. Not when so much is at stake." The Deacon's leg was trembling.

Gabriel moved closer, his expression softening slightly but there was steel to his voice when he said, "We are all concerned about Lucifer and the thinning Veil. Rushing in alone and without a plan only puts everything at greater risk. What happens if you die before the battle begins?"

The Deacon glared, his jaw tight and fire threading his veins. He was on a precipice. He needed out but he needed strength.

Gabriel's eyes narrowed. "Deacons are quite invincible, but Lucifer will rip you apart if you're not careful, and then what? You think Meg would forgive me for letting you go now, knowing you'd die and never help her? She *doesn't even know you exist.* No one does. As soon as they find out you'll be at risk. Lucifer will slay you in an instant." Gabriel shook a finger at the Deacon. "Soon. Not tonight but soon."

The Deacon fell silent, his chest heaving as anger warred with the bitter truth of Gabriel's words.

Teari, sensing a lull in their arguing, spoke softly. "You're nearly ready, physically. The leg should hold well, you just need to get used to the prosthetic and work the new muscle." She gave him a small nod of assurance, though her eyes held a trace of worry. "But Gabriel's right. You can't do this on your own."

The Deacon's gaze shifted to Teari, then back to Gabriel. Lucifer's power was growing, he could feel it. If he went now, this early, he wouldn't last long.

Gabriel stepped closer. "When the time comes, you go. But until then, you need to be patient. This war will take more than strength. It'll take timing."

The Deacon closed his eyes for a moment, forcing the anger down. It still simmered beneath the surface. He nodded, slowly, reluctantly. "Fine. But when it's time, I won't hesitate."

"I won't stop you," Gabriel said. "I will go with you."

Teari exhaled quietly, relief washing over her. She gave the Deacon a neutral glance before gathering her bag. "Strengthen the leg," she said.

The Deacon nodded, his mind racing.

Gabriel held out a hand, ready to *poof* Teari out of the mountain.

"Healer," the Deacon called.

Teari turned.

"Why did you leave the Legion?" he asked. "You were a warrior once."

Teari glanced at the wall and collected her thoughts. "The true battle is not in taking lives, but in saving them. I seek redemption in healing rather than bloodshed."

The Deacon nodded in approval. "That's what I thought," he whispered.

Gabriel grasped Teari's hand and–*poof*–took her home.

Twenty-Four

The white horse watched Nero go through the portal in Babylon. She had a sinking feeling as she thought about what he'd meet on the other side. Portals were no longer a safe bet, especially if Nero was headed to Hell.

She sniffed the air and walked in a circle. From the corner of her eye, she saw Angels watching. She'd been standing in one place for too long. The white horse ran for the nearest tear in the Veil. She could smell it. Fire and brimstone and magma wafted from the cut between realms.

The white horse leapt through the tear, a shiver running down her spine as she anticipated the chaos which would spill over into Heaven soon enough.

She galloped away from the nearby steaming pool of magma. It had been ages since she'd stepped foot in Hell. In the distance, she heard a sharp whinny of distress.

"Nero!" the white horse yelled. She moved in the direction the sound came from and listened again. *"Where are you?"* Smoke was

rising from a crack in the ground and settled like a smog—visibility was low.

The noise echoed again. It sounded like Nero was sputtering or drowning.

The white horse dashed toward his voice; past tall trees, barren land, and cracked roads. The dead wandered close by. She crossed a road and what looked like a dried up stream. Nero's voice was louder now.

He whinnied a panicked sound.

The white horse saw the shimmer of his black coat. She came to a clearing in the forest. She'd been here before but it looked very different now.

A fine mist of rain fell over the once full pond. Now it was nothing more than thick mud. And Nero was stuck.

———

NERO'S HOOVES sank deeper with every desperate lurch. The more he fought, the more the mud gripped him, cold and unyielding, pulling him down. His nostrils flared and he let out a panicked whinny, twisting his head around, searching for any glimmer of hope beyond the misty pond.

The Nightjar fluttered nearby, its shadowy form darting anxiously from side to side. A whisper of cold air brushed over Nero's ear as the spirit coiled near his face, its voice low and hurried.

"He dried up my pond. Stop struggling, Nero! The more you move, the worse it'll be," the Nightjar murmured, its tones urgent yet strangely soothing. She darted down to examine his legs, flickering from one side to the other in restless motion. The Nightjar touched Nero, shoved at his rear, wrapped her arms around his neck and tugged, but she could do little to free Nero from the mud's merciless grasp.

Nero's muscles quivered with the strain, his breathing grew shallow, exhaustion dragged his head lower. He was sinking and could feel the cold seeping into his legs. The weight of the mud anchored him, draining his strength. For a moment he stilled, obeying the Nightjar's advice. Despair clawed at him just like the mud.

Then, from the mist, a soft glow emerged. Slow and steady the light grew brighter, slicing through the gloom, until the slender form of the white horse appeared. Her coat gleamed like starlight, her mane flowed like a river of silver as she approached with calm, deliberate steps.

"Nero," she called softly, her voice a warm contrast to the cold air and biting mud. She stopped a few paces away, assessing the situation with eyes full of patience.

The Nightjar fluttered toward her, casting a relieved shadow across the white horse's face. "He's sinking fast," the spirit whispered, urgency in her voice. "We don't have much time. The muck will swallow him soon."

The white horse nodded. She stepped closer, her hooves somehow gliding lightly over the mud's surface. She nudged Nero's neck, a gentle encouragement, and them positioned herself beside him, muscles tensing with quiet strength.

"I know you're tired, Nero," she murmured. *"We've got to get you out. When I say to move, push up with all the strength you have left. I'll lift as you press."*

Nero, filled with determination, gave a small nod. He braced himself, feeling the warmth of her presence beside him.

"Now!" she commanded.

With a final fierce effort, Nero heaved upward, his hind legs pushing through the thick mud as the white horse lifted him from his side, guiding his weight with surprising force. The Nightjar whispered encouragingly, its voice filling his mind with steady, rhythmic words as he strained forward inch by inch.

At last, with a mighty lurch, Nero stumbled free, his body collapsing onto firm ground. He lay there, panting, the mud clinging to his legs.

He inhaled deep breaths, legs twitching as he realized how close to death he'd just been. Drowning in mud was a fate he wished on no one.

"Gather your strength," the white horse said, taking in their surroundings.

"The dead will come soon," the Nightjar warned.

The white horse nuzzled Nero's shoulder gently. *"Why did you come here?"* she asked.

"A Demon broke through into Heaven. It took Rue." Nero coughed and moved his legs, getting ready to stand again. *"I must find her. She's just a child."*

"I saw a girl..." the Nightjar floated toward the road. She pointed. "A man took her from the castle to the Black Mansion. I followed them."

"Where is she now?" Nero asked, moving to stand.

The Nightjar worried her hands and glanced toward the cabin on the other side of the muddy pond. "Last I saw, he was bringing her back to the castle in the burning caves, she looked asleep in the backseat."

———

THE ENTRANCE to the burning caves loomed before them with the massive castle carved into the mountainside, molten lava now spilling down its craggy surface. Nero paused, his dark eyes narrowing at the sight. The castle's blackened towers twisted toward the sky like claws as flames flickered along the walls, casting an eerie glow on the ancient stone.

Beside Nero, the white horse stood calm but tense, her silver coat gleaming in the dim light. Together they moved forward, silent and alert, their hooves echoing on the rocky path.

Just then, Nero's gaze snapped to a figure approaching the castle gate. A Jeep stopped and a man in a suite got out before opening the back passenger door.

The white horse took a small step forward. *"Is that..."* she whispered, narrowing her eyes on the man in the suite.

A teenage girl jumped down from the passenger side.

"Rue," Nero whispered, nostrils flaring with a surge of protective anger. He took a step forward, muscles bunching, ready to charge, ready to change forms and get her.

The white horse blocked his path with a gentle nudge, her voice low but firm. *"We need to be careful, Nero. That castle is not what you remember."* She motioned to figures in the distance. *"Lucifer's Hellions have noticed us."*

"I don't care," he growled. *"Rue needs us, now."* He tried to push past her, his heart pounding, but the white horse side-stepped, her eyes filled with urgency.

"Nero—look!"

They both turned, and a shiver went down Nero's spine. Emerging from the shadows beyond the gate was a staggering mass of bodies, gaunt and hollow-eyed, each one moving with jerky, unnatural movements. The stench of decay filled the air, and the groans of the undead grew louder as more poured out from the surrounding forest.

Nero pawed the ground, a deep rumble of warning in his throat. *"The dead. Watch out for the fast ones."*

The white horse took a step back, ears flattened as she scanned the horde that stretched in all directions. *"We're outnumbered,"* she said, her voice tense. *"If we charge in now, we'll be torn apart before we can reach Rue."*

Nero's eyes stayed locked on Rue's distant figure as the man in the suite guided her through the castle door. His desperation flared as he looked at the white horse, determination blazing. *"I have to try,"* he said, but the sound of the zombies' footsteps closing in forced him to hesitate.

The white horse's gaze softened. *"There's a time for everything, Nero. Right now, we need to live to fight again. We can go back and tell Meg what we've found."*

The horde pressed closer, hands reaching, mouths open in silent cries. The undead surrounded them on all sides, their skeletal faces twisted in hunger. Nero's heart sank, the bitter taste of frustration mixing with the scent of death around them.

"So many do not belong here." The white horse glanced from face to face. *"The realms are drastically unbalanced."*

With a frustrated snort Nero backed up, and together they turned, galloping away from the swarm of zombies.

They sped up, but... the horde moved fast–faster than before.

"No," Nero whinnied. *"Run!"*

It was too late, the horde was a mix of slow and fast and the horses had waited too long to retreat.

Suddenly, the white horse's eyes went wide with fright. *"Go, Nero,"* she urged. *"Go back. Go back and find the relic!"*

She whinnied in pain as one of the dead scraped her flank.

Nero changed forms, full Demon. He shook his head as he doubled in size, his long black tail and mane became stiff as needles and sharp as razorblades. His veins became giant ropes of obsidian, twining and swirling under his skin like protective armor. Fire was collecting in his throat as another one of the dead scrambled toward the white horse.

"Go," she urged.

"I will not leave you to die," Nero said as he breathed fire and burned the walking dead to cinder.

"Don't waste their souls," the white horse begged. *"They are innocent. Lost. We must defeat Lucifer so they can be set free."*

Nero ignored her and burned the land around her injured body. When he was done, there was only a small white horse surrounded by char for a mile. He delicately picked her up in his mouth, felt the way her body sagged. He ran her back to the Nightjar's cabin, kicked open the door and set her inside.

"Oh, my baby, what have you brought me?" the Nightjar hovered over the injured white horse. "She's so damaged."

The Nightjar wasn't more than an anxious shadow at the moment.

"Watch her for me," Nero said.

The Nightjar's head turned quickly to face him. "You can speak?"

Nero nodded. *"I must find the relic. I will return for her."*

"You must be fast, Nero," the Nightjar said. "Lucifer's Hell is going to kill us all."

"I am thought to be lost, a treasure to find,

An ancient relic that transcends time.

They search for me where metals gleam,

But I walk the earth, not what I seem.

I am both the key and the guide." The white horse was mumbling softly, blood oozing from her wounds.

"What's that, baby?" the Nightjar gently set the doll in her arms down on a nest of leaves and sticks and moved closer. She bent to lean her ear next to the white horse's mouth. "Tell us again."

Nero shifted closer and nudged the white horse with his snout.

She repeated the phrase. Nero whinnied in agitation, language was not his skill, he'd only just learned how to talk. The white horse was speaking in riddles.

"An ancient relic that transcends time," the Nightjar set her ghastly hand on the white horse's head, touched her ear and wiped away a smear of blood. "Why don't you speak plainly and tell him what that is?"

Nero was looking between the two, confused.

"It's a Deacon," the Nightjar finally said.

"The Deacons are all dead," Nero said. *"Alastor killed every single one of them."*

"No," the white horse whispered. *"Gabriel knows."* Her eyes were closing, her muzzle sagged. *"Saw it with my own eyes. On the edge of his lands near the mountain."*

Gabriel. Nero snapped his teeth before glancing at the Nightjar. *"Keep her alive."*

The Nightjar shifted, floated around the white horse and inspected the wounds. "What is she?"

"A horse," Nero said.

"No. No this beauty is much more than a horse. She's already healing. She is so white and pure. Like the heat of the sun." The Nightjar touched the white horse's mane. "You've found a creature some have only ever wished to meet. Look how her hair sparkles. This is a pure soul. Something... *original."*

"Keep her safe," Nero said before turning.

"Stay out of my pond!" the Nightjar shouted after him. A warning. They had worked too hard pulling him from the mud.

Nero didn't need to be told twice. He'd nearly died in the mud, and he still had it stuck in his ears and hooves, making his black coat look mottled. He would never go near that pond again. Instead, he ran. Faster than lightning. He leapt over pools of magma and deep cracks in the ground until he saw a tear in the

Veil. It didn't take long, the Veil was ripping all over. In some places he could clearly see the Earthen plane like a picture between the pines. Demons crawled through. Nero didn't need the Earthen plane. No, he needed the Seven Kingdoms of Heaven. When he finally saw the slice ahead, he leapt through.

———

NERO PACED, cooling his hooves on the luscious grass of Heaven. He took in his surroundings, unsure of whose lands he'd came through into. There were Legion Angels in the distance who had noticed him. Nero began running. He didn't have time to fight. He scanned the landscape, recognizing the mountains in the distance that edged Gabriel and the Raven King's lands. He headed in that direction, outpacing the Legion in a heartbeat.

Nero slowed as he got closer to the mountain. He wove between giant oak trees and trotted toward Gabriel's house. But, something caught his eye near the base of the mountain. A figure moved slowly. Wood knocked against stone, leather squealed as it stretched, a man moaned in pain.

The man was muttering, pausing to catch his breath against a tree trunk before glancing up, eyes focused directly on Nero.

Nero couldn't ignore that the air around the man was humming.

It was a Deacon.

"You," the last Deacon said with a smile. "I knew you'd find me." The Deacon waved at the black Demon horse. "Come closer. I am not as nimble as I once was." He motioned to the prosthetic leg.

Nero trotted close to the Deacon then knelt so the man could get on his back.

"Take me to the fallen Queen." The Deacon wrapped his hands in Nero's mane and held on for dear life.

"She has crossed over into Hell," Nero warned. *"I must find the split in the Veil. Don't let go,"* he warned.

The Deacon smiled.

TWENTY-FIVE

Rue had been sitting in the dark for what seemed like hours. She shivered under the blanket and curled into a tighter ball. She was in a crap situation. Rue hoped someone would save her. She understood it had to be a calculated rescue. Her mother and the Raven King were planning on war. They couldn't risk a rescue mission and throw off their plans. Rue thought of her mother; she didn't seem that different without her wings. She still carried herself the same as she always did–tall, chin up, warm only to those closest to her. Rue blinked back the tears, hoped that one day she'd be as strong as her mother was... is. As strong as her mother is.

Rue's stomach growled. It made her think of the kitten and she wondered if Lucipurr was missing her. She hoped someone was feeding him. And cuddling him after the jerk who dragged her into that hole had tossed Lucipurr through the air like a stuffed animal. Rue wanted to go home. She sniffed back tears, noticing the blanket covering her smelled slightly familiar. A little bit like brimstone and pine, like how Hell smelled when her mother was Queen.

The door opened, its hinges squealing and echoing against stone walls. Rue scrambled to the corner of the cot and in the light she noticed she hadn't been covered with a blanket, but a suitcoat. She rubbed a finger over the smooth fabric. Strange.

"Get up." The handsome Demon was back, dressed in black slacks and a black button down with the sleeves rolled up to just below his elbows.

She wasn't prude. She'd read plenty of books and watched plenty of movies. She was a red-blooded teenager and knew a good-looking guy when she saw one. Why he was kidnapping her and then saving her from instant death was Rue's question.

Rue's eyes were wide as she stared at him. "I want to go home. Now."

The Demon chuckled. "Not today."

"My mother will come for me. She will kill you."

The Demon took a calming breath and waved toward the door. "Until she shows, we have things to do today."

Rue stared. The Demon's black hair was tousled, and his sharp features were unnervingly attractive. His dark eyes met hers with an unsettling calmness, betraying nothing of what he might be thinking. Dressed the way he was, he looked out of place in the grim dungeon, like a polished predator in a cage of filth. Rue was suddenly self-conscious.

"Get up," he urged, voice low and smooth but without warmth. "It's time to go."

"No," Rue rasped, fear lacing her voice.

"You're to be presented," Dacre replied, his gaze flicking over her with a hint of disdain. "The Black Mansion awaits."

Rue's heart sank as she scrambled to her feet. There was a sinking feeling in her gut. Dacre motioned for her to follow, and though her legs were feeling like jelly, she had no choice. She didn't want to be left alone in the dungeon with the door open. She knew the creatures that had been left to rot behind these doors–she'd listened to their guttural cries for hours throughout the night.

Rue followed the Demon down damp hallways dripping with grime and coated in lichen. Oil-like liquid seeped from under doors and down walls. Rue was relieved when they started walking up the winding stairwell and made it to the door to the outside.

The Demon held it open as Rue walked through. There was barely a glow from the sun as the sky was something darker than ochre. Ash filtered through the air, heat wafted off the pools and rivers of magma in the nearby royal grounds.

Rue sucked in a breath of surprise at what her home had become.

There was a black Jeep waiting. Something larger than normal, lifted and with big tires. The Demon opened the back door and motioned for her to get inside. Rue looked up and judged the distance from the ground to the seat.

"Need help?" the Demon asked, a grim expression plastered on his face as though helping her might disgust him.

"No." Rue straightened her shoulders and gripped the doorhandle.

"Might be easier with wings, princess." The Demon mocked.

Rue sprung up, grabbed the "oh-shit" handle over the window and swung her legs inside. She slid onto the seat and refused to look down at the Demon. He slammed the door closed, muttering something in Hellspeak.

Rue soon understood the reason for the giant tires on the Jeep. The road was bumpy, broken and there were deep potholes or sometimes no road at all.

Rue was starting to feel sick with all the jostling. She braced her arms against the door and seat and closed her eyes, holding back bile. She was thankful when the vehicle finally stopped.

Rue glanced out the window. The Black Mansion appeared as dark and foreboding as its name suggested.

The Demon opened her door and held out a palm to help her down.

Rue steadied her hands on the door and seat and jumped, ignoring him. She landed on two feet and then took a step away from the Demon. She smoothed dirty hands over her T-shirt and glanced at her socked feet. The driveway was crushed stone, sharp and glossy. It pressed through her socks threatening to cut her feet.

The Demon took notice and his eyebrow rose in offering to carry her across the sharp stones.

"Don't touch me," Rue warned.

The halls of the Black Mansion were cold and grand, every inch of the place dripping with malevolent elegance. It smelled like freshly cut wood and Rue noticed some rooms were being painted in black and silver. Elaborate wall paper was being hung, embellished with a matte black design. She decided the décor was actually pretty and if she were in a different predicament, she might have enjoyed it.

When they entered the main chamber, Rue's breath hitched. It was filled with Demons, all of them watching her with gleaming, predatory eyes. The room was lit by the eerie glow of fire pits casting flickering shadows on their sharp teeth, horns, and scaled skin. The Demons sat on dark elaborately carved chairs and lounges, like cruel kings.

The handsome Demon stood at her side, his presence both a shield and a threat. He led her toward the center of the room, where all eyes fell upon the small ex-princess with eyes unlike her mother's and long dark hair.

"One moment," the Demon said as he walked out, leaving her alone.

Rue swallowed hard. She glanced around the room searching for a weapon or a way out.

"She doesn't look like much," one Demon sneered, his crimson eyes narrowing as he leaned forward. "So small and fragile."

"No wings. Too human," another added, a smirk tugging at gruesome lips.

Rue went stiff, her heart pounding in her chest. She knew they could sense her fear. They were feeding off it, saying terrible things to make her scared. Rue couldn't slow her heart beat and calm herself.

"She won't last long on the bargaining table," the first Demon laughed. "Too weak."

"Let's see what she's made of," a third Demon growled, stepping forward with a goblet in hand. The liquid inside was thick and red.

"No," Rue whispered, her stomach churning as she recoiled. She didn't drink blood, she was too young to need it.

"Drink," the Demon commanded, his voice a growl of amusement. "It'll make you stronger."

"Rue backed away, but the Demon was too fast. He grabbed her arm and shoved the goblet to her lips. Rue gagged as the metallic taste filled her mouth, the blood spilling down her throat. She choked and sputtered, spraying droplets of blood on the grotesque Demon's face.

The other Demons laughed, taunting. Tears blurred Rue's eyes as she tried to spit out the blood coating her mouth.

"Enough!" The handsome Demon in the suit had returned, his face darkened with fury, fists clenched at his sides. His voice cut through the laughter like a blade.

Dacre remained silent, his expression unreadable. But there was a tension in his body, a flicker of anger in his eyes as he watched them.

The room fell silent as all eyes turned to him. He stepped forward, his cold gaze locking onto the Demon who'd forced the drink on Rue.

"You don't touch what belongs to me," Dacre said, his voice dangerously low.

The offending demon raised an eyebrow, unfazed. "Your little pet?" he mocked. "She's not going to last long anyway. What does it matter?"

Dacre's anger flared but before he could speak, another Demon chuckled from the corner of the room. "He always did have a soft spot for the fragile ones," he said slyly. "Maybe she reminds him of–"

"Shut your mouth," Dacre growled, stepping toward the one in the corner, hands curling into fists.

The Demon's smirk widened. "I wonder if she knows your name yet," he taunted, glancing a Rue. "Has he told you, little lost princess? Does she know who you really are, *Dacre*?"

Rue's head spun as the Demon's words set in. His name; Dacre hadn't wanted her to know. She didn't recognize it or him for that matter.

Dacre's eyes burned with fury, his jaw clenched. He took one menacing step toward the Demon, and for a moment it looked like he would strike. The Demon's eyes went wide and its goblet fell to the floor, staining the tile in thick red blood.

Dacre turned sharply on his heel and grabbed Rue's arm. "Come on," he hissed through clenched teeth.

Rue stumbled after Dacre as he dragged her from the room, her mind reeling. What had that Demon seen on Dacre's face? It was enough to scare him straight. Rue couldn't see a thing with

Dacre's back to her. Her short legs were running to keep up with him and her socked feet slid on the smooth, tiled floor.

They went up the stairs to a corridor that was decorated in peach and muted purples. The décor was a stark contrast to downstairs. Dacre's grip on her arm tightened.

When they reached a closed door at the end of the hall, Dacre released her roughly, his back to her as he stood with his hands braced against the wall. His shoulders heaved with barely contained rage.

"What just happened?" Rue demanded, still tasting blood in her mouth. "Why did they say your name like that?"

Dacre didn't turn around. When he spoke, his voice was cold and distant. "Don't ask questions you're not ready to hear the answers to, little princess."

Rue clenched her fists, anger simmering beneath fear. "What are you going to do to me?"

For a moment, Dacre was silent. Then, without looking at her, he replied, "I'll keep you alive." He knocked on the closed door.

The words weren't a comfort, not from him.

A female Demon opened the door and smiled at Dacre.

"Look what the cat dragged in," the Demon woman crooned. She reached out and drew across Dacre's chest with a red lacquered nail.

Dacre grabbed the woman's hand to stop her. "Not now." He motioned to the girl.

"Lucifer's balls," the Demon woman muttered. "What is that? A child? A human child?" The woman's eyes settled on the blood staining Rue's lips.

"Barely..." Dacre released the woman's hand. "She needs some... assistance." Dacre leaned closer to the beautiful Demon female and whispered something in her ear. The woman nodded, glancing at Rue a few times before she finally said, "I understand." They spoke in hushed Hellspeak for a moment.

Rue leaned closer, trying to eavesdrop. She knew little Hellspeak-only what the Hellions had taught her-but she wasn't fluent. Her mother feared that if she learned the language she might be tempted to run away when she got older and be lost to the realm of Hell. Or at least that's what she'd told Rue over the years.

Dacre stepped away and motioned for Rue to follow the woman. His eyes fell on her lips.

Rue licked them, tasted crusted blood. Her hands touched her face and scraped at the dried blood dripping down her chin.

Dacre frowned, his lips pressed into a thin line. He looked thoroughly pissed.

"Go, Dacre," the Demon woman said, waving him away before turning to Rue. "Come here, little thing." She reached for Rue's hand. "I won't hurt you." She glanced at Rue's socked feet. "We'll get you some shoes and clean clothes. Are you hungry?"

Rue moved so she could look past the doorway. There was an apartment beyond the threshold. It was tastefully decorated and it looked inviting. Warm and... safe.

"Are you hungry?" the woman asked again.

Rue shook her head. "Not anymore."

She frowned. "My name is Kit."

Dacre's footsteps disappeared behind them.

"Please come inside," Kit urged.

Rue was admiring the woman's sharp teeth, red lips, and curly hair when a strange sound echoed up the stairwell.

"Please," Kit reached out. "Now." There was urgency in her voice.

The stairs in the distance groaned as something big ran down them.

A guttural scream ricocheted against the walls. Rue turned,

ready to run down the stairs and out the door but Kit grabbed the girl by the back of her dirty shirt, dragged her inside the apartment, slammed the door, and locked it. She pushed a heavy table in front of the door.

"You weren't supposed to hear that," Kit said.

"What was it?" Rue asked.

Kit looked away, ringing her hands. The walls of the mansion shook and something boomed under their feet.

"The bathroom is this way," Kit waved for Rue to follow. "I notice you don't have wings yet." There was concern in her eyes. "You wear a size four? And it looks like size six shoes?"

Rue shrugged. "I'm not sure. I've just always had clothes and shoes that fit."

"Poor princess," Kit frowned.

"Please don't say that to me. I'm not poor. I was kidnapped. Threatened with death and now I'm going to be used by you people." Rue was annoyed and she didn't want pity from anyone, let alone this Demon woman.

"I apologize. I didn't mean it like that." Kit sighed.

Something slammed and the walls of the mansion shook again.

"Hurry. Get washed up. Get that blood off you." Kit led Rue into a tidy bathroom. She opened a cabinet and removed towels, setting them on the counter. "Help yourself to whatever you need. Take your time. I'll find you some clothes."

Kit closed the door and locked it from the outside.

Rue rubbed her arms and looked in the mirror for the first time since the morning she was kidnapped from the Raven King's house. She scrubbed her face, barely believing all that had happened. Her hair was a tangled mess. There was dried blood dripping down her neck and smeared across her cheeks. Something didn't feel right. Her stomach was aching and rolling like she'd eaten something spoiled. She didn't feel the need to vomit or sit on the toiled. It was almost as if she... wanted more.

Rue turned on the shower and peeled off her filthy clothing. She found pleasantly scented soaps and shampoo. When Rue was done, she was clean but her hair was more tangled than before. Rue wrapped a towel around herself and padded to the sink. She searched the drawers for a comb and heard a knock on the door.

"Can I come in?" Kit's muffled voice asked.

The floor rumbled under Rue's feet. Something was happening downstairs.

The door opened before Rue could answer.

Kit's large eyes looked the girl over. "You're looking better with that blood off your face."

Rue stared. She wasn't sure what to say.

"I found you some clothes. Jeans, a clean shirt, something warm to sleep in." Kit held up a pair of fuzzy slippers. "I don't have any shoes in your size so these will have to do. We'll get you more clothes from the Earthen plane."

"Why bother?" Rue asked.

"Dacre said the dungeon gets cold at night. He doesn't want you to get sick."

"The cold doesn't matter. Lucifer is going to kill me." Rue blinked then looked at her reflection in the mirror. Small fingers tried to detangle her hair as tears dripped down her cheek. "It's only a matter of time."

"Don't dwell on that." Kit shushed. "During Lucifer's reign, death comes for anyone and everyone. And now he's back." Kit picked up the comb. "Get dressed, I'll help you comb out the knots."

———

RUE WAS DRESSED in borrowed clothes and sitting at Kit's kitchenette table, a grilled cheese sandwich in front of her and a Coke in a can. Her toes finally felt warm in the fuzzy slippers.

"Don't waste the food," Kit warned. "Now that Lucifer is back, I don't know when there will be more."

Rue took a small bite as Kit sat behind her, methodically detangling the knots in her long hair.

"Who tattooed those runes?" Kit asked.

Rue pressed her lips together.

"Don't want to tell me?"

"Nope," Rue said.

"Why those runes?" Kit asked.

"I can't remember," Rue lied. She knew exactly why Jed had marked her skin with protective runes and strength spells. Too bad none of them seemed to work because here she was. But she wasn't dead yet, so maybe they did work a little bit.

When Kit was done removing the tangles, she went to the bathroom and came back with hair ties and pins. "Let's braid it to prevent more tangles tonight."

"No one has ever braided my hair before," Rue said, taking a sip of the Coke. She finished her sandwich and sat back. Having grown up in Hell, Rue was comfortable around Demons of all type. Kit was nice and was helping her for the moment. Rue relaxed against the back of the chair while Kit twisted her hair into four long braids, then wove them together before pinning them in plaited rows across the back of her head.

Rue had never needed braids before; her grandmother always said she sat by Rue's bed at night and combed her long hair so it wouldn't tangle.

"This should stay in place until morning," Kit said.

There was a knock on the door.

Kit cleared her throat and went to answer it. Rue didn't

bother turning around when she heard the piece of furniture scraping across the floor as Kit pushed it back into place. Instead, she finished the last bite of her sandwich.

Tension entered the room. She'd have to be dead not to feel it. Rue's spine went straight. She turned just enough to see the two Demons near the door. Dacre had changed his clothes. He was dressed in dark jeans and a jacket. His hair was wet. Rue looked him over, didn't see anything that would allude to all of the noise she'd heard since Dacre had left her here.

"Night is coming," Dacre said, turning dark eyes on Rue. "You must return to the dungeon. Lucifer's orders."

Rue stood and wiped crumbs off her fingers. She turned to Kit. "Thank you." Rue tucked the neatly folded set of pajamas under her arm.

Kit bowed her head slightly. "See you soon."

Rue was tired after the long day, she was grateful to be clean and fed. But she didn't like the sharp smell that wafted into the apartment. It smelled like cleaning supplies.

Dacre and Rue walked in uncomfortable silence. It seemed like the Demon wanted to say something but held it in. Rue had plenty to say but realized it was fruitless. She couldn't beg for her freedom–she'd seen Lucifer, the Demons wouldn't cross him. Rue knew she was shit out of luck unless she could find an escape and run for a portal.

They reached the stairs and began descending. The scent of cleaning supplies burned Rue's nose.

As she stepped off the last stair, Dacre's arm was forcing her toward the door and obstructing her view of the mansion.

"Only look at the door or close your eyes." Dacre was too close. The words brushed against her ear.

Rue turned her head to look down the hall. A hand slapped over her eyes. "I said no."

Rue froze. Before her vision went dark, she'd seen the blood splattered on the walls, floor, and ceiling. Dacre's arm snaked around her middle and lifted Rue off her feet. He carried her out the door like an insolent toddler. "You'll need to learn how to listen." He muttered in her ear before setting her on the stone driveway.

"I'm not a baby," Rue said as she turned to glare at him. "My mother was the Queen of Hell. I've seen things."

Dacre's eyes turned dark. "Do as you're told if you care to live." He brushed past her and opened the door to the lifted Jeep.

Rue climbed up and slid across the seat. "What happened in there?" she asked.

Dacre looked away. "Don't worry about it."

"There was blood everywhere."

Dacre slammed the door and paced behind the Jeep before getting in the driver's seat. Rue watched him warily. Something was off with the Demon. Heat was coming off him in waves. She didn't understand any of it.

Rue buckled her seatbelt, not wanting to receive a head injury from the jostling of the Jeep. She pulled her legs up and criss-crossed them, then held the folded pajamas against her middle like a pillow.

The dead wandered in the road and Dacre was quick to start the Jeep and pull away. Rue turned and watched them follow until they looked like small walking sticks in the distance.

Somehow, Rue drifted off to sleep. She woke to a warm breeze and the soft chirps of crickets. Someone was close, the soft click of the seatbelt releasing woke her fully. She felt an arm stretched across her lap and opened her eyes to the side of Dacre's face. He smelled good, like soap and apple scented shampoo. He went still, realizing she was awake, but that didn't stop Rue from inspecting him closely. There were no scales, no rough skin on his face or hairline.

"It's rude to stare." Dacre pulled away and held the door.

"It's rude to kidnap people," Rue replied.

"Touché." He motioned for her to get out.

"I don't want to go to the dungeon." Rue hugged the pajamas.

"Too bad."

Rue slid out of the seat. She tugged at the jeans that were as size too big for her. She glanced at the forest, didn't notice any of the dead lingering. Hellions caught her eye though. They were watching her. One sniffed the air and took a step forward like a bear ready to pounce.

Rue skipped a step to keep pace with Dacre.

He acted like she didn't exist until he held open the door to the castle and glared down at her.

Rue stopped, glanced over her shoulder at the nearby forest one last time. The Nightjar's cabin wasn't too far from here. She could run there in less than an hour.

"Don't run," Dacre interrupted her thoughts. "Your mother no longer sits on the throne of Hell which means the dead will go after you." He looked her up and down. "And you don't look like you'd survive five minutes out there alone."

"My mother will kill you," Rue muttered as she walked past Dacre and into the castle. The slippers on her feet making a scuffling sound as she walked.

Dacre muttered something in Hellspeak that sounded like, "Then I can finally rest." Rue wasn't sure if she had the translation correct but the way he sighed made her think it was.

Rue's chest tightened with fear as they moved toward the stairs that spiraled down in to darkness.

As they descended into the dungeon's shadowy depths, Rue's last hope of escaping today slipped away, and the cold, suffocating reality of her capture settled in. She rubbed the runes on her chest. Jed had tried to increase her strength, but she was no match against these monsters. She blinked back tears and wondered if this was how her mother had felt her first time in Hell.

She kept her chin up as she followed Dacre past oily dripping walls and thundering fists pounding on chained doors. Dacre held the dungeon door open, looking away as she walked inside, then he slammed it closed and locked it.

Rue paced her dungeon cell and sat against the wall. She wrapped her arms around herself, rocking against the stone wall until she drifted off to fitful sleep.

———

Everything moved like she was underwater; slow, and fluid. Rue was walking down a cobblestone street, autumn leaves of burnt orange and yellow crunched under her feet. Then she was sitting in a class with an animated professor lecturing on stones in the desert. Then ordering coffee from a cart near the library. She was moving through time in flashes. There was steam in the air and she stepped out of the shower to see a message on a phone but she couldn't make out the text. Anxiety twisted in her stomach. Something smelled like pumpkin coffee. Rue turned and then she was dressed in a costume, her periphery disrupted by the edges of a mask. She searched the cramped room, accepted a cup of beer only to set it down on a nearby table. Young people were surrounding her, dancing. Music boomed from another room. She was having fun, free and smiling behind her mask. She took a small bottle of cinnamon whiskey from her pocket and drank that because it was safe. She danced, felt the beat of the music deep in her chest. Someone touched her shoulder and Rue turned to find a man in a silver mask staring down at her.

· · ·

Rue woke up with a sharp intake of breath, shivering, despite the warmer pajamas Kit had given her. Rue searched for the cot in the darkness, patting her hand across the stone floor. She touched something soft, recognized it as the jacket she was covered with the other night. She pulled it close and draped it across her body before falling asleep again.

A deep roar woke Rue. She sat up, realizing she was in the cot and not on the floor.

Something shifted in the shadows in the corner of the room. Rue hoped it wasn't a snake or bugs. She shivered before squinting her eyes and focusing.

"You shouldn't sleep on the stone floor," a familiar voice said from the shadows.

"Why should you care?" Rue pulled the blanket around her, rubbed her lips against its softness before remembering it was Dacre's suit jacket. She released the jacket and let it fall to her shoulders.

Dacre stepped out of the shadows. "You sleep with your eyes open."

"No I don't." Rue blinked.

"You do." Dacre was dressed in a suit again. All black.

"No. I don't." Rue snapped. "And why are you watching me sleep like some creepy old man?"

Dacre chuckled darkly. "Get up. It's time to go." He checked his watch. "You've slept too long."

Rue shifted, moving to the edge of the cot, and setting her slippered feet on the damp floor.

From beyond her dungeon cell there was a howling scream. Rue covered her ears and shrank back.

Dacre grabbed her arm and pulled, unwilling to wait for her to get up. "Let's go. The longer you wait the more you'll hear. We need to leave."

Rue tugged her arm back and kicked.

"Stop," Dacre warned, shielding his thigh.

"It doesn't matter, I'm going to die here anyway. Just end it already." Rue punched him in the ribs then kicked his knee with all her might.

Dacre was spitting profanities in Hellspeak and hopping on one foot when a Hellion glanced into the dungeon and laughed.

"Get the fuck out of here," Dacre shouted to the Hellion. He turned to face Rue.

Rue's heart raced; she was breathing in sharp, quick bursts as she backed away from Dacre. The dim light of the dungeon flickered, casting ominous shadows on the stone walls. Dacre stood only a few paces away, his dark eyes fixed on her, unblinking and cold.

"What are you doing?" Dacre asked, his voice smooth, carrying a slight gentle tone, though the threat beneath was clear. The handsome Demon had a gift of threading fine words with threat. He took a step forward, hands raised in a mockery of peace. "Don't even try to fight me. It won't do you any good. You cannot escape this place. You cannot escape *me*."

Something had shifted in Rue during the night. That dream gave her some kind of home for the future which meant she did not stay here. "I'm not going to sit here and wait to be slaughtered by Lucifer. I won't be used by you in the skin trades." Rue shook her head. "That's not happening." Rue's hands trembled but clenched into fists, a fierce determination burned in her center. She had to get out. She had to escape. She had to leave. Now.

Dacre smirked, his head tilting slightly as amusement danced in his dark eyes. "Slaughtered? Is that what you think Lucifer will do to you? That's what he does to the Demons he rules over, makes us suffer. But you, he'll probably end quickly."

Rue didn't reply. Her eyes darted around, searching for anything she could use as a weapon. But there was nothing. Just him and the walls that felt as though they were closing in.

Dacre lunged.

Rue barely had time to react, diving to the side as his hand reached out to grab her. She stumbled, nearly losing her footing, but she caught herself and whirled around, her pulse pounding in her ears. He was fast.

"I don't want to hurt you," he growled, his earlier calm gone.

Rue's lip curled into a snarl, defiance surging through her. "I'm gonna hurt you."

Without thinking, she charged at him, fists swinging wildly. She knew she was outmatched. Dacre had the strength of a Demon, the speed and the power. But she wasn't going to go down without a fight. She'd fight him every day. Every step of the way.

Her first strike hit his chest, but it felt like hitting stone. A sharp ache spread up her arm. Dacre barely flinched, grabbing her wrist with inhuman speed and twisting it just enough to force a cry of pain from her throat.

"Stop," he ordered, his voice dark and edged with frustration.

Rue twisted in his grip, swinging her other hand up to strike his face. Her knuckles grazed his jaw and to her surprise Dacre stumbled back, releasing her arm. For a brief moment Rue felt the rush of victory, her heart soaring with hope.

But then he came at her again, faster, angrier. "If you are going to act like a child, I will treat you like one." He grabbed her by the shoulders, slamming her back against the stone wall. The impact knocked the air from her lungs and black spots danced in her vision. Dacre's face was inches from hers, his eyes burning with a dangerous mixture of anger and something else she couldn't place.

"You're wasting your energy," he snarled, his breath hot against her skin. "You won't get away."

Rue gasped, struggling in his grip. The stone at her back was cold, pressing into her spine as she fought to free herself, but Dacre was unyielding. His fingers dug into her shoulders, pinning her in place. Desperation flared in her chest as she kicked at him but it only made his hands press her harder against the stone. "You're in a time out." There was a lilt of humor in his tone.

"Let me go!" she screamed, twisting her body.

Dacre didn't move. A dark smile spread across his lips as if he enjoyed the struggle. "I could keep you here forever if I wanted. Do you understand that? You'd never see the light of day. Only darkness. Only the darkest version of the skin trades. I didn't want that for you."

Memories of yesterday flashed through her mind. He had taken her away from the damp dungeon for the day. The threat stung but fueled new anger. Rue's pulse quickened and before she could think it through, she lunged forward, sinking her teeth into the side of his neck with all the strength she had left.

Dacre froze.

For a moment, the taste of blood filled her mouth, metallic and bitter and... sweet. She bit harder, her jaw clenched, and Dacre's hands tightened on her shoulders. A guttural growl emanated from his throat, a sound equal parts pain and rage. His body tensed, his grip went so tight she was afraid he'd break her bones.

He shoved Rue away. Hard. Her head smacked against the stone wall and tiny lights danced in her vision. Rue licked her lips, noticed his blood tasted a lot different than what the Demon at the Black Mansion had forced down her throat. Her legs felt weak, her entire body was trembling. Rue wiped her mouth with the back of her hand, glaring at him, breathing heavily. She glanced down at the smear of blood across the back of her hand and licked it away slowly.

Dacre's hand was pressed to the side of his neck, his eyes wide with shock and fury. Watching her mouth, he moved his hand from his neck and glanced at his palm. Blood dripped. Rue focused on the small bite mark from her teeth. They weren't sharp and the bite was nothing more than blunt marks that had drawn blood.

"You have no fucking idea what you've done," Dacre glowered. "You're going to regret that," he hissed, his voice a low growl.

Dacre stormed out of the dungeon, slamming the door. A heavy lock slid into place.

"Don't let her out," he instructed the Hellion. "Ever."

Rue slid down the wall, her body sore and head aching. She had hurt him, maybe only a little but it was something. Rue touched her lips, watched the blood drip down her fingertips. She licked her lips, then her fingers. She swallowed down every drop of Dacre's blood and wished she had more. What was wrong with her? Her mother and the Hellions drank blood. Plenty of Demons did too. Children didn't. Rue knew why children didn't drink blood. Because it stopped their aging. A million thoughts clouded her mind but she couldn't focus on one of them. She was suddenly very thirsty.

The prisoners in the dungeon started going wild, banging on doors and walls, slamming furniture against the walls, howling and screeching like excited zoo animals.

TWENTY-SIX

Clea was somewhere dark. She tasted iron, though she hadn't tasted anything since she was alive. This was confusing. Plenty of omens had come to her over the years, visions of a future filled with chaos. She'd shared them but she had never seen herself turned so useless in any omen.

Alastor had done this to her, tried to banish her to the Ether after severing her form with an iron candelabra.

The problem with royal blood was Clea didn't disappear. She was still in the castle, invisible, unable to use her powers. Stuck. But, she'd heard every word from her father, Lucifer. She'd heard him reveal that he killed her, he'd tried to kill Meg and would end this war by killing her grandchildren.

Clea was filled with rage, and she was right to be filled with rage. She roamed the halls of the castle in the burning caves, watching as everything changed; the walls shifted, the grounds bubbled with magma, the Hellions and Demons transfigured into sinister forms. It was worse than before, much worse. Clea had spent enough time with her father to know that Lucifer was ready for war; she saw his tricks, too bad she could do nothing to help. She could only watch.

Now she was trapped between realms. Present in Hell but unable to speak with anyone or move anything. She'd watched hopelessly as Rue had attempted to escape the man in the suit. Something was off about that Demon, Clea could tell just by looking at him. She wasn't even sure he was a true Demon.

———

THEN

RUE SAT cross-legged on the bed, a blanket draped around her shoulders like a cloak, eyes wide with lingering traces of sleep. Across from her Clea sat in the same position, so pale that she might drift away into nothingness. Clea was a ghost. Rue didn't know any different-her grandmother had always been a ghost, it was the normal way of things in her world.

"Grandma, it felt so real," Rue whispered, leaning closer. Her small voice filled the quiet room, her words soft but urgent. "I saw you there, in my dream. You were... you were fighting. There were so many shadows, but you–" she paused, struggling to find the right words, "you were shining and then you disappeared. Forever." Tears glistened in Rue's eyes. "I don't want you to disappear forever."

"Oh, child," Clea's red lips curled into a slight smile, her gaze softened. "Dreams are strange things, my sweet Rue," she murmured, waving a graceful hand as if to brush Rue's recollection away like dust. "They're clouds; shifting, drifting, always changing shape. Just wisps of thoughts."

But Rue's brow furrowed in frustration. "No, this was different," she insisted, her small fists balling in her lap. "You were helping mother. You used your magic, and there was this... this light around you. And you were fighting–" her voice dropped to a whisper, "–you were fighting a giant bad man. I think it was Lucifer."

Clea's ghostly form stilled, though her gentle smile remained. "A giant, angry man?" she said, her tone casual, though Rue noticed the slightest flicker in her grandmother's eyes. "Oh, child. In the realm of Hell, there are plenty big, strong men and Demons who frighten the strong and tempt the brave. But that is a distant worry, far from us now. We have the Hellions who will do everything to protect you. And your mother. She is the strongest woman I've ever met. And she killed Lucifer a long time ago. He can't hurt any of us now."

Rue nodded, though a hint of disappointment glimmered in her wide eyes. "It's just... I felt like you were really there, like I was seeing something real. I could smell smoke and blood. There were so many people. Angels and Demons. Mother was there, fighting with... I don't know what he was."

"Tell me," Clea urged.

Rue blinked a few times, collecting her thoughts. "He was like an Angel but black wings. He saved her."

"Saved who, dear?"

"Mother." Rue swallowed and toyed with the edge of her blanket.

"You have more to say?" Clea asked.

Rue nodded, dark hair falling over her left eye. "I'm afraid."

Clea leaned closer, her gaze warm and unwavering. "Rue," she said softly, her voice lilting like a distant melody, "even if your dream were true, even if I could help in such a way–my time for such things has long passed."

Rue frowned, her small face set with stubbornness that made

Clea chuckle softly. "But you're still here," she argued, tugging her blanket tighter as if seeking reassurance. "You're still here with me."

Clea reached out, touching Rue's cheek. "For now, yes," she agreed, her voice softer than before. "But remember, my love, dreams have a way of playing with what we wish for. They show us glimmers, but we must live in the world we have."

Rue fell quiet, her little shoulders dropping under the weight of her grandmother's words. Clea gave a final, comforting smile before reaching forward and moving the child to her lap. "Don't trouble yourself over it, darling," she said gently. "Time will reveal what it wishes, and you will be ready, just as you need to be."

Clea smoothed her cold hands over Rue's dark hair. "Now, tell me more about the Angel with black wings. He can't hurt you. Skeele will keep you safe. And so will Chel. You know Chel thinks you are the sweetest little thing he's ever seen before, like a kitten. No one will let harm come to you." Clea adjusted the blanket to cover Rue's bare neck so she wouldn't catch a chill. "What did he look like?"

Rue raised one arm silently and pointed at the little boy sleeping in the bed across the room.

"Remm?" Clea asked. "The Angel with black wings looked like your brother?"

Rue nodded silently.

"Okay," Clea exhaled. "But you said he saved your mother?"

Rue nodded again.

"Good." Clea wrapped her arms around Rue and hugged her.

"You helped save them too," Rue whispered. "I saw you."

TWENTY-SEVEN

A sound like paper tearing echoed across the Earthen plane. Grandmother Crow looked out the window and up at the sky, not assuming the noise was thunder. That was anything but thunder. The sound came with the shuffling of heavy feet, hooved, padded, booted from creatures the Earthen plane had never seen before.

Grandmother Crow knew demonic forces gathering. She'd seen the stories in the papers of storms and illness the past few days. Diseases that had been long forgotten had suddenly returned. Floods in the mountains and heat like never before struck the coastline. Strange creatures caused destruction in small towns. Something dark was taking over and spilling onto the Earthen plane.

Hosa's eyes narrowed at the sky. "Ah what has the Allegewi done?"

"No, not him," Grandmother Crow reached for a shotgun and locked the kitchen door. She shivered, noticing a shadow that looked like a hyena ran across the yard. "This is something darker. I fear this Earth is melding with something treacherous."

Elsu and Jacy set down their cards and focused on the sound of the wind whistling through the pines. There was plenty more movement they could discern besides the pine needle-hush.

Grandmother Crow turned to her sons and cocked the shotgun. "This will be difficult without Iye. We will be fully outnumbered very soon."

She glanced at the picture of her long dead son, killed by Demons while rescuing Nicholas and Janet's daughter who'd been kidnapped years ago. None of them had seen Shay since, but every so often she'd send a postcard or call.

Elsu stood, downed the last of the whiskey in his glass and slammed it on the table. "We've been waiting for retribution for a long time." Elsu glanced at his brother's picture and the empty seat at the table that had collected dust over the years.

"I told you the Allegewi would bring war," Hosa said with an anger filled voice.

Grandmother Crow was quick to slam her fist on the counter. "This is not the war of one Allegewi. Jed did not bring this. You forgave him once. He might be the only one who can save us." She pointed out the window. "Or maybe Shay."

Hosa bit back words he wanted to spit in vengeance. He knew Jed wasn't the cause, but he wanted to blame his brother's death on someone.

Wind slammed against the door, threatening to blast it open. Nails scraped against glass. A cluster of moving shadows scrambled toward the single light in the backyard. A crashing sound echoed like a shutter stuck in the wind. The light in the backyard went out with the shattering of glass.

"Now, boys," Grandmother Crow warned as she picked up satchels of powder, tucking them in her apron. "We need to leave this place." She felt the darkness encroaching, knew the sound of claws scraping against the windows of their secluded house in the Montana reservation.

"The others–" Jacy started to say.

"They're dead." Grandmother Crow's voice was dire. "There is no one but us." She filled her apron pockets with shotgun shells. "This is worse than when the dead walked. The devil has sent creatures not of this realm."

Elsu, Hosa, and Jacy canvassed the old house, collecting every stashed gun and knife.

They met at the door that opened to the driveway.

Grandmother Crow was chanting, her hand filled with dark powder. She nodded to Hosa, who opened the door. Hot air blasted into the house, and with it came a high pitched squeal of excited creatures ready for their next meal.

Hosa turned to Jacy. "You make sure she gets to the truck."

Jacy nodded and moved closer to his mother.

Something from the shadows was running full bore toward the door. They all saw it, a creature like a hyena with blackened skin and sharp teeth. It yapped as it leapt toward the door opening. Grandmother Crow threw the handful of black powder at the creature. It dropped to the ground with a whine that could be heard for miles. Elsu shot the creature, blasting it's head off the neck.

"Now," Grandmother Crow said, running out the door behind Hosa.

They made it to the truck, the shadows keeping their distance after seeing what happened to the creature at the door.

Hosa got behind the wheel and started the engine. Jacy opened the door and helped Grandmother Crow into the backseat.

Elsu was last after letting off a few blasts from his shotgun. He opened the passenger side door, black ichor dripping down his arms. "Go. Go. Go!" Elsu shouted. His face was pale as though he'd seen something not meant for human eyes.

Hosa kicked the truck into gear and sped away.

"Where do we go?" Hosa asked as they cleared the reservation and made it to the highway, swerving around broken down vehicles.

Grandmother Crow was wringing her hands. She had a bad feeling. The worst feeling. Their home was being destroyed quickly. Creatures of all sizes ran in the shadows like packs of venomous dogs. Every so often, they saw one of the walking dead ambling on the side of the road.

"Mother?" Hosa urged after she hadn't replied to him for minutes.

Grandmother Crow cleared her throat. "Get to a crossroads. We must call upon Nero and Shay." A hard shiver ran up her spine and across her shoulders. "I fear that we may meet Iye very soon."

Twenty-Eight

The Basilisk stirred, curling its immense, scaled body along the parched riverbed, where dry cracks spiderwebbed across the mud. The Black River, once coursing thick and dark through the Adirondacks of Hell, lay silent. The Basilisk slithered between pine trees, watching. Its glossy black scales reflected the faint, ever-bleeding red of Hellsky as it raised its massive head, forked tongue flickering to taste the stale, smoky air.

Then, a scent—a faint, familiar trace woven through the air—made the Basilisk's nostrils flare and its pale eyes narrow with recognition. Meg. She had returned.

Slowly, the Basilisk began to move, each ripple of its muscular length carving a path through the brittle forest floor, splintering dried branches and scattering leaves like ash in its wake. The trees twisted away, bowing to the creature's passage. The Basilisk emitted an odd, almost eager energy, gliding in winding curves that quickened as it scented Meg closer with each mile through the dark woods.

It slithered through forests and open roads, through fields

turned to ash and around pools of magma. The sharp silence of Hell in waiting was broken only by the soft, rhythmic scrape of scales over stone. The Basilisk was headed somewhere with a purpose–its singular purpose since Meg's presence had returned to Hell's tortured land. Lucifer might have reclaimed the throne, but it was Meg the creature sought, a beacon that called it like a master's whistle.

Twenty-Nine

MEG

THE BABYLON FOUNTAIN stands before us, glistening ominously under the dim light, its waters an eerie mirror to the dark realm we are about to enter.

I glance over my shoulder at the others–Chel, Nightingale, Noah, Jed, Shay, Thrush, and Remington–all resolute, faces set with grim determination. My eyes fall on Sparrow, clad in shadowed armor, his eyes sharp and ready. The Legion of Angels are behind him. All this time we fought against his family curse and never focused on the reality: my bloodline is cursed just as deep. My mother, dead. My first child, dead. My daughter, kidnapped. I can feel in my bones that death will come for me before this battle is over. It has come for me many times. On that stairwell in Gouverneur. In that little hospital when John Lewis held a pillow over my face. The moment when the Raven King stabbed me to death. I glance at my son; all these years I kept him hidden away, protected, his true identity concealed... I should have done the same for her. I grip the Basilisk blade at my side. She will not find the same fate as the rest of us.

"No one separates unless necessary. Rue's priority. We get her and get out," Sparrow says firmly, tracing the plan in the air as he speaks. He turns to his Legion Commander who bows his head in silent understanding, stepping back to prepare.

I take a deep breath, my heart beating loudly against my ribs. My gaze shifts to Remington. Reaching out, I pull him close, holding his face in my hands, memorizing each line. "Be careful," I whisper, my voice only loud enough for him to hear. "Stay close to me. Promise?"

Remington offers me a half-smile, filled with familiar bravado, his eyes serious. "I will. I promise. A promise is a promise."

My breath catches before I repeat the phrase. "A promise is a promise." I glance at Sparrow and nod.

With a unified, collective, steeling breath, we plunge into the fountain.

———

THE PLUNGE into Hell is instantaneous. The fading light blinks out as the heavy atmosphere swallows us. But... something is wrong. I am not met with the cool water of the Nightjar's pond, instead something dark and thick coats my body. Remington's hand slips out of mine as we try to swim through the thickness. There's dirt in my mouth, grit in my eyes. This is not the murky water of the Nightjar's pond. It's mud. Clinging to us, dragging us down. My lungs burn as I try and swim through it, grabbing handfuls and pulling myself up. I finally break the surface, wipe the mud off my face, and gasp. Thicker than pudding it clings to me, my feet sunk deep–but I can feel the bottom. I'm near the shore at least. I stagger, gasping, the mud pulling at my ankles, it's cold grip relentless. Around me, the others break the surface, gasping and moaning. They are trapped, the mud spread out like a vast mire, swallowing everyone.

I struggle to the shore, stretch out flat and grab a tree root, then pull myself in. The mud threatens to keep my boots as I pull my feet free with a sucking sound. My eyes dart around and I catch the panic in Remington's face as he fights to free himself. Thrush is nearby, calm as he scans the shore and moves to his back to float.

"Remm," Thrush calls. "Don't struggle, it will pull you under."

Remington freezes still and glances to Thrush, then tries to maneuver his body to float on his back.

Sparrow is a short distance away, his movements growing sluggish as the mud pulls him deeper.

With one final heave, I manage to wrench myself free and scramble forward onto firmer ground. I look back, heart hammering. This is a shit show. An absolute shit show if I ever saw one. The Basilisk tooth blade is gone, sunk in the mud.

I glance to Remington, then Sparrow, swallowing. Dread is slicing through me.

Sparrow holds my gaze, his expression with steady assurance. "Get the boys first," he rasps. "I'm not going anywhere." He stops struggling in the thick mud, sinking to his jawline.

I search the area, looking for a way to get them out. There's a fallen sapling, half burned. I grab it, maneuver toward Remington and drop it, holding the shoreline end.

"Pull yourself in," I say. "Hurry."

Remington rolls to his stomach and I am filled with relief as he grips the end of the sapling and begins pulling himself to shore.

I stand on the end, holding it down, and take in the scene.

Sparrow is slowly drowning. There is no sign of Noah or Nightingale, but since they are ghosts they might have traveled to another realm to escape the mud. Chel is wading in the middle, giving orders to the Raven King's Legion. There's too much panic. Some are already dead, their faces blue and frozen in time. Shay comes through, her blue hair coated with mud. Panicked eyes take in the mess we've stepped into.

"Float on your back, Shay," Chel says as he reaches for her. "Don't struggle against it. Where's the half-breed?"

"He was right behind me," Shay's voice is strained as she struggles against the mud.

A head breaks the surface not far from Chel. Chel reaches out and grabs the back of the man's jacket, lifting him above the surface.

It's Jed. I glance at Shay who is taking a sigh of relief.

Remington makes it to shore.

The mud is up to Sparrow's ears. He points to Thrush, eyes dark.

I move the sapling closer to Thrush and he grabs the end. Remington helps me hold the opposite end as Thrush drags himself in. My arms burn with strain.

"Hurry up," Remington urges. "My dad is dying. Again." He chuckles as Thrush swears and drags himself faster.

"You're a real sick fuck," Thrush snaps.

Remington shrugs. "Learned it from you."

Thrush makes it to shore and catches his breath as Remington moves the sapling closer to Sparrow. I am glad to see the bow and arrows didn't get lost.

The mud is over Sparrow's ears. Over his mouth. He only has one hand above the surface. The sapling lands just out of reach of his fingertips.

Panic rises in my chest as his fingertips reach and miss and reach again. Pained eyes glance at me. I don't think he ever considered death by mud. But who would? It's a shit way to die.

We move the sapling closer, Remington and Thrush stepping into the mud, their feet sinking.

A set of green eyes are watching me. The mud is slowly consuming him as he sinks further, the surface coating his cheekbones, nearing the crescent of his lower eyelid.

"Grab it!" Remington shouts.

"Reach for it, Sparrow!" I shout. "Grab the end."

Slowly, achingly slow, his hand moves and he grips the end of the sapling just before closing his eyes and going under.

"Pull!" Remington shouts.

The three of us pull him in. Sparrow's grip remains strong as we drag him through the mud. As he gets closer to the shore, he is nothing but a giant mass of mud-covered Angel slowly being dragged in.

THIRTY

At last, through the thinning line of dead trees, the Basilisk spotted her, a familiar figure standing against the burnt landscape. There were flickers of firelight from the distant, smoky horizon. She was covered in mud. The Basilisk slowed, lowering its enormous head to meet her gaze, a strange glint of devotion shimmering in its pale, unblinking eyes.

With a gentleness belying its monstrous form, it curled around her feet, body looping in heavy, rippling coils, waiting for her acknowledgment. Its large head rested mere inches from Meg's hand with its long fangs sheathed and jaw relaxed in a rare display of trust and submission, an unspoken loyalty in the creature's silent, expectant stare.

Meg's hand hesitated only a moment before resting lightly on the Basilisk's head, feeling the cool, ridged scales beneath her palm. She gave the Basilisk a small, steady nod, and it responded with a soft rumble, almost a purr, vibrating through the ground beneath them.

"You came," she murmured. "Can you help the others?" She

pointed to the Legion warriors sinking in the mud of the Nightjar's pond, so thick it was, like a bog or quicksand; bottomless, wanting to consume.

The Basilisk unfurled from around her feet and floated toward the warriors that were still alive. Chel grabbed on with a hearty groan, one arm circled around the Basilisk's middle, the other he used to grab hands and tug up. Then the Basilisk pulled them free and deposited them on the burnt land near the pond. The creature made three passes over the mud, pausing for those stuck to grab onto it or for Chel to help. He even dragged in a few of the dead ones.

"No. No. He's dead!" Shay screamed.

Chel grumbled something in Hellspeak before dropping to his knees next to Jed. "A little mud can't have killed you, weak fuck."

Shay was crying, wiping mud from Jed's face.

Chel slammed his fist down on Jed's chest in some form of archaic and violent resuscitative effort.

It worked.

Jed gasped, sitting up with wide eyes and rubbing his chest. "What the hell was that for?"

"To bring you away from the light, clotpole." Chel stood, the giant Hellion taking a look at the Angels cleaning their wings and making it to their feet. Half were missing their weapons. "Goddamn," Chel muttered. He ran a hand down his leg, relieved to feel his weapon in the holster.

THIRTY-ONE

MEG

As Sparrow's body is dragged in completely, I dash closer to him, grabbing onto his arms with desperate urgency. I wipe the mud from his mouth and nose and eyes.

"Please be alive," I mutter. "You can't die now you big stupid bird." I shake his shoulders.

Bright green eyes flash open. "It's our wings," he says softly, dirt caking his lips and sticking to his teeth. "Lucifer knew we'd die in the mud. Never stood a chance." Sparrow struggles to sit up, reaches over his shoulder, and spreads one of his wings out to drip the mud off. "It coats the feathers." He points at Chel. "The Hellion doesn't have feathers so he made it to the surface." He nods to me and the boys. "You all don't have wings. I'd say, no more travel by water."

"Yeah, sure, whatever," I agree. "Because I'm not traveling fucking anywhere until I get my daughter back."

Sparrow stands and shakes his wings. "Let's move. Rue doesn't have time for us to slow down."

I catch his gaze, my chest tightening at the near miss. A quick nod from the others communicates that they are shaken but intact. The bodies of the dead Angels will have to stay.

We take a few steps, scanning the landscape, shadows thickening around us as we start for the burning heart of Hell.

Heavy footsteps from the nearby forest draw our attention. A sickening feeling fills my stomach as we brace ourselves for what is about to come through.

———

"Nero!" Shay announces.

The giant horse gallops closer. There's a man on his back, missing a leg, a pointed prosthetic in its place. His face looks vague, like everyone and anyone. I can't place him.

Sparrow reaches for me. "How are you here?" Sparrow asks the man.

He's looking down at us, face pale and pained. He struggles to get off Nero's back and lands with an indignant thump.

"I knew the horse would bring me to you," pegleg says.

"There is no way you are real." Sparrow is glaring now.

The man smiles slightly before wagging a finger in our direction. "That's true. I shouldn't be alive. But there are forces at work here. Something bigger than just us and I was saved."

"Who is he?" I ask.

"A Deacon," Sparrow replies.

"Not just any Deacon," the man says. "The *last* Deacon." He claps his hands together. "Now." He looks around us at the Legion. "I was hoping for more troops but it shouldn't be a problem." He groans, walking closer. "Let's go to war." His common face splits into a dark smile.

"Nero," Shay is out of breath after helping Jed to his feet. "Destroy the portal." She points at the muddy pond.

Nero shakes his head, his entire body shivering and shuddering as he changes forms.

None of us want to risk death by mud if anyone comes through that pond again.

Nero gallops toward the pond then blows fire over it until it is nothing more than baked dirt, hardened and cracking.

"Could've used that trick while heating up your pizzas," Noah's voice breaks the silence.

I turn to find Nightingale fussing over Thrush and Noah taking in the scene and the dead Angels.

"Good, you're back," I say.

"Good. You're alive." Noah brushes a hand through his hair. "We got really worried about that mud. Couldn't make it through." He looks me over. "Seems you made it out okay."

Breath escapes my chest as a half laugh. "Yeah, I made it out just fine."

Noah nods, cautious eyes search my face. "Let's go get your girl."

THIRTY-TWO

HELL STRETCHED OUT BEFORE THEM, A LANDSCAPE twisted by Lucifer's return. The sky burned crimson, split by blackened lightning, and the ground was a shattered wasteland littered with cracked and oozing molten rivers.

Meg moved swiftly with Remington at her side and Sparrow on her left.

The Basilisk slithered alongside them, its scaled body whispering over rock and ruin, eyes glowing with a predatory light.

Ahead, the familiar path was littered with the dead stumbling through the debris, drawn to the pulse of life that dared to invade their corrupted domain.

The Deacon was riding Nero and raised a hand, veering them away. The dead had collected to the greatest numbers ever. Hell had all the power without the Deacons to sort souls and send them to their rightful place.

Several of the undead sensed their presence, emitting hollow, gurgling cries as they lunged forward.

"We can't avoid them all," Sparrow muttered, drawing his

weapon. The Legion behind him followed suit, their weapons raised, sending the walking dead to a future of eternal darkness.

Magic crackled in Jed's fingertips. Shay touched his side and whispered, "Save your energy."

Meg waved everyone forward, eager to find her daughter and end this war. They left crumbles of mud as it dried and flaked off them like evening snow.

The group pushed forward, exhausted but determination burning brighter than ever.

Sparrow and Chel watched the sky for Hellions and Demons, but it was eerily silent.

"He's expecting us." Sparrow's voice is deep with worry. He gripped his weapon, the Basilisk tooth blade strapped to his thigh, ready for use.

They waited at the sparse treeline, the castle in the burning caves ahead. It loomed above them, a fortress of stone and flame. A broken home. The air was thick with heat, shadows dancing along the cave walls whispering chants of the devil who now ruled.

Meg stepped forward into the clearing, heart thundering in her chest. She may not have wings, she may have lost her power to travel and *poof*, but she had none of that when she killed seven Hellions who came to slaughter her on the Earthen plane. She had none of that and she survived true evil and darkness.

This. Was. Nothing.

———

"LUCIFER!" Meg shouted. "Grandfather! Come out and face us! Come out of that cave and bring me my daughter!"

There was a beat of silence, the kind that stretched too far and too long. A hush of wings echoed across the royal grounds. A dark shadow circled overhead.

Sparrow took the Basilisk blade out of its holster and passed it to Meg.

Everyone readied themselves with the Raven King's forged blades. Or at least, those who hadn't lost them to the pond.

A dark chuckle echoed before the shadow landed on the balcony of the ballroom, crumbling walls as his backdrop. Lucifer's form was radiant with an unholy light. His dark hair framed a face that was both beautiful and monstrous, his eyes holding a fire that promised destruction.

"Granddaughter!" Lucifer shouted across the grounds as he leaned casually against the balcony baluster. "You always did have a flare for dramatics. Your mother too. But, what makes you think you've earned an audience?" His smile was sharp. "Rue is... indisposed at the moment."

Meg's grip tightened on the Basilisk blade, rage boiled in her veins. "Give her to me!"

Lucifer straightened, clapping his hands mockingly. "Oh, you want a fight." He leaned to the side, eyes narrowing at the forms in the treeline. "What have you brought me? More souls? Is this a trade? I've plenty without the Deacons but my strength can only grow. I'll gladly take whoever you are hiding behind you." He laughed.

Meg held her ground, never taking her eyes off Lucifer, but she heard the footfalls as those she brought began stepping out of the treeline and revealing themselves.

"Oh!" Lucifer clapped his hands like a kid at Christmas. "You brought me a *Raven King*. Oooh, he's worth *millions of souls*. A perfect sacrifice." He swung his legs over the baluster and balanced on the edge of the balcony. "What else have you got there? Children? What the fuck is wrong with you, Meg? Bringing children to a war."

Remington and Thrush stepped forward, weapons gripped in

strong hands. They were far from young boys–they were nearly men now and they'd come for vengeance. They'd come to reclaim their home. They'd come to protect those they loved.

Lucifer held his hand over his eyes as though to shade out the ocher sunlight of Hell. "What is that?" he pointed at Remington. "Is that... oh, it can't be. I never even heard a whisper about *that one*. I would have taken that one too. Hm. Too bad really. He would have looked nice in my dungeon. He's still young enough to mold into something else. He's still young enough to turn to *destruction*. I never thought you'd do that, Meg. Never thought you'd bring a Shadow Heir straight to my door. This is the best sacrifice I've ever received." He laughed excitedly.

"You will not have him. You will not take any of them!" Meg bent her knees, ready for whatever came next. "Now shut your filthy fucking mouth and give me back my daughter!"

Lucifer straightened, clapping his hands mockingly. "Oh, you really do want a fight? Well, you shall get one."

He gestured, and from the shadows emerged an army of Hellions and Demons. Creatures forged from infernal magic with twisted form and eyes aflame with malice poured out in a flood of darkness, weapons raised, and the battlefield quaking beneath their advance.

Sparrow stepped beside Meg, ready.

Meg's throat felt thick as she envisioned all of her children dying today. She glanced to Sparrow, and he shook his head.

"You've battled worse. This is nothing." He smirked, winked, showed sharp teeth. "These are weapons as well."

Meg nodded in understanding.

A row of Hellions charged, roaring and growling like wild things. Footsteps came from behind Meg and Sparrow as the Raven King's Legion moved ahead to fight.

Smaller, lesser Demons scrambled toward Meg, Sparrow, and

the others. Their clawed feet scraping against the ashen ground. The horde moved like a swarm, their twisted forms distorted by the pulsing Hellfire that sprouted up around them. Their eyes glinted with a frenzied hunger, their jagged teeth gnashed as they closed in, eager to rend and tear.

The Angels fought expertly, their movements a blur of grace and lethal precision. Wings unfurled in flashes of white and gold and mud as they cleaved through Hellion flesh. Similarly, Hellion weapons cleaved through Angel flesh, each strike sending a ripple of light through the air, momentarily illuminating the battlefield.

Sparrow's sword sliced through the small Demons that lunged for his legs, their bodies disintegrating into ash as they hit the ground. He kept moving, each step careful but forceful, as he shielded Meg's side. His blade glowed as it cut through another Demon, the ichor sizzling off its enchanted edge.

"Keep close!" He shouted, his voice strained with effort.

Meg nodded, her weapon arcing through the air as she brought down a Demon that had managed to slip past Sparrow. Her breath came in short gasps, but she forced herself to stay steady, to remain a pillar of strength for the others. She gritted her teeth and pushed forward even as more Demons poured from the shadows.

Thrush and Remington fought alongside them, a deadly pair with skills honed by countless days of training. Thrush's blade struck a demon with flawless precision. Demons crumpled and dissolved, but for every one they struck down, two more seemed to take its place.

Jed's hands were aglow with battle magic as he sent bolts of fire and electricity to the surrounding Demons and Hellions, holding back the line.

Thrush and Remington stood back-to-back, covering each other's blind spots. A Demon with wings of leathery sinew swooped toward them, but Thrush sheathed his blade then ducked low, readying his bow and sent an arrow straight into its eye. It let out a shriek before crashing to the ground.

"Is it me or are these things multiplying?" Remington grunted.

Thrush shot him a grim look. "It's not just you."

Nightingale and Noah fought around the boys, taking down bodies with blades and astral magic of firebolts and fire.

Meg moved forward, but a Demon sprang up from the ground, claws reaching for her face. Before she could react, Sparrow was there, cutting it down with a swift, brutal strike. He glanced over his shoulder, sweat and ash streaking his face.

"You good?" he asked, voice tight with worry.

Meg swallowed and steadied herself. "Still standing." Her blade swept out to catch another Demon.

Meanwhile, Chel fought like a whirlwind, his weapon spinning deadly arcs. He parried a blow from a Demon wielding a jagged spear, then countered with a strike that sent the creature sprawling. Nearby, Shay reloaded her pistol, and took note of how many bullets she had left. She glanced to the Deacon hanging back with Nero. The urge to change forms tingled the back of her neck. The Demon poison in the scar on her thigh burned with fury. She wasn't sure how long she could hold off.

Jed's battle magic left the ground scorched and smoking.

Despite their fierce resistance, the lesser Demons kept coming, their screeching cries echoing in the fiery darkness. The group pressed on, knowing that every second counted to Rue. They must reach the castle.

But the deeper they fought into Hell's twisted battlefield, the more desperate the Hellions and Demons became, as if driven by a force greater than themselves. Too many replenished. Too many Angels were dying. It was easy to see, they were quickly losing this battle and yet they were so far from the castle in the burning caves.

The last row of Angel Legion faced off with endless rows of Hellions and Demons.

Meg glanced to Remington. A sickening feeling gnawed at her gut. "You run away. You live in hiding if we fall," she mouthed to her son.

Remington coldly shook his head no.

Lucifer laughed over the battlefield before taking flight. He circled above the fighting.

Angels dropped and soon there were no more than a few dozen standing between Meg and hundreds of Hellions.

Just as the Hellions charged, a beam of light split the forest behind them, and the losing edge of the battlefield was bathed in brilliance. Gabriel stepped forward, wings outstretched and armor gleaming, his expression a mixture of fierce resolve and holy wrath. Behind him, a Legion of Angels advanced. Their ranks stretched as far as the eye could see.

Gabriel's voice boomed across the battlefield. "That is no way to speak to a lady!"

Lucifer smiled darkly, lifting an arm and calling upon hundreds more Hellions and Demons.

"She is far from a lady." Lucifer landed on the battlefield. "A lady wouldn't kill her grandfather. A lady wouldn't take all she'd been given and destroy it. A lady would not give these creatures hope that they deserved something better. A lady of darkness would not turn Hell into some... refuge."

Gabriel shrugged nonchalantly before turning to Sparrow. "We are late because the Nightjar's pond is gone. Completely disappeared."

Sparrow motioned to the dried mud on his clothing. "There was an incident."

Gabriel motioned for the army to move forward. "We had to use a portal halfway across Hell."

He took in Meg's form, coated in battle fluids, sweating, rasping breath. He nodded. "The Seven Kingdoms of Heaven have sent warriors."

"All seven?" Meg asked, unbelieving.

"All seven," Gabriel said. He glanced to Thrush, then the young man who looked very much like the Raven King. He paused a moment too long before joining the army of Angels.

It wasn't long before the battlefield was coated in a thick sludge of blood and ichor from Angels and Demons alike as they perished in battle. Everyone surviving was covered in a film of sweat and gore. Meg was closer to the castle than ever before, Hellions charged her only to be struck down by her Basilisk, who'd joined in the fight.

———

THE LAST DEACON gripped Nero's black mane, heart thundering against his ribs, stump aching as it rubbed against the wooden prosthetic. The battlefield before them was a seething chaos of fire and shadows, the sky above streaked with crimson as if Hell itself was bleeding. The Deacon's ancient magic pulsed through his veins, the weight of centuries pressing on his soul, but he drew strength from it. This was his purpose, his final stand against the darkness that threatened to consume them all. He had to maintain the balance.

He leaned forward and whispered in Nero's ear. "I think now is the time."

Nero snorted, his nostrils flaring, sensing the tension and power in the air. The Demon horse's hooves thundered against the scorched earth as he charged forward, slicing through the thick clouds of ash and smoke.

Nero didn't like watching Shay risk her life like she was. He wanted to be by her side but the white horse had given him duty. He had the key and the guide; the secret to defeating Lucifer.

"Giddy up," the Deacon patted Nero and twisted his hands in Nero's mane, holding on as Nero ran into the battlefield.

The Deacon's cloak billowed behind him as he whispered an incantation older than time itself. The air around them hummed, vibrating with the potency of his magic.

Nero jumped over fighting warriors, weaved around charging Hellions, moved so fast the only one who kept a close eye on him was the fallen Archangel who'd been consumed by darkness.

Ahead, Lucifer stood at the heart of the battlefield, his presence an unholy beacon. His form radiated malevolence, a towering figure of black wings and burning eyes. He watched their approach with an expression of twisted amusement, as though the Deacon's defiance was nothing more than fleeting entertainment.

The Deacon lifted one hand, symbols of ancient power glowing around his fingers. He was prepared to unleash power that could unmake the fabric of reality itself, power born from the dawn of creation. His lips parted, ready to release that incantation that would strike at Lucifer's very core and end this war and seal the shredded Veil between realms.

But Lucifer moved with a speed that defied belief.

In the space between one heartbeat and the next, he crossed the distance. Nero reared, trying to throw himself backward, but Lucifer's hand was already there, gripping the Deacon's throat. The Deacon continued his chant, voice scraped, air barely moving through his windpipe. Lucifer took the Deacon to the air for all to see and the battlefield went still.

The Deacon's eyes widened in shock, and the power he had

summoned dissipated, leaving him defenseless before he ever had the chance to use it.

"No," was the Deacon's last gasp.

Lucifer's lips curled into a mockery of a smile. "Did you really think you could stop me?" His voice was velvet; cruel and dark and full of mirth. With the flick of his wrist, he drove his other hand forward, a blade of pure hellfire piercing through the Deacon's chest.

The Deacon's vision blurred. Pain seared through him as his life force slipped away like sand through fingers. He tried to speak, tried to call on the magic of the Deacons one last time, but it was too late. The light in his eyes dimmed and his body went slack. Lucifer held the Deacon's body out for all to see, shook him like a fish on a pole. Then Lucifer released him and the Deacon fell lifelessly to the charred battlefield.

Nero's eyes went wide with disbelief. The white horse had told him. The key and the guide would save them...

The Deacon was the answer. But now he was dead. Nero trotted backward, gathered fire in his throat, and made his way to Shay. There was no way out of this war now. No way out besides death and he was not going to let Shay die amongst Demons and Angels.

THIRTY-THREE

MEG

I watch, horrified as the last Deacon falls from Hellsky. Shit. There goes our secret weapon. There's still too many Hellions between me and Lucifer. Definitely more than seven. Too many bodies between me and the castle.

It all feels so defeating, watching that blasted Deacon fall from the sky like a sack of shit.

"We didn't need him," Sparrow says. "We will be invincible together." He wipes gore from his cheek but I catch his absent gaze as he internally recalculates how close to defeat we actually are.

"I don't think this is the time for omens delivered by feather." I wipe my hands on my dirty pants and try to quell the growing unease in my center.

I glance over my shoulder and take inventory. Shay is moving toward me, a smile on her face.

Nero gallops close to her.

"Don't worry, Meg," Shay smiles before brushing blue hair out of her face. There is a strange twinkling in her eyes. "You don't need a Deacon, you've got a Demon-stained girl and her trusty Crossroads Demon-horse."

"I don't understand." I search her face for a clue but I get nothing.

Sparrow slashes at a tiny Demon biting the toe of my boot. I kick the carcass away.

Shay nods to Nero before her body flickers and wavers. She changes before my eyes. Suddenly she's tall, hair so blue and wild, eyes darker than night. She isn't a terrifying Demon like Nero, no, she is a warrior; intimidating and absolutely stunning.

"Oh my god," I whisper. "You're amazing."

Shay smiles before chanting, "Out of the eater will come something to eat. And out of the strong will come something sweet."

The ground smokes. Brimstone fills the air. The ground vibrates under our feet.

"Out of the eater will come something to eat. And out of the strong will come something sweet. Out of the eater will come something to eat. And out of the strong will come something sweet. Out of the eater will come something to eat. And out of the strong will come something sweet." Shay chants it over and over again, her eyes glinting.

Nero whinnies something dark and guttural before pointing his muzzle to Hellsky and releasing a steady stream of fire.

My pupils blow wide as I take in the scene before me.

Figures begin appearing behind her. Hundreds–no, thousands. Some, I recognize. Some I've never seen before.

"I have my own army," Shay says proudly. "Thousands of souls from Crossroads deals."

Nero snorts.

"And a dragon horse," Shay says, patting his flank.

"Okay." I nod, barely believing.

"Oh, one more thing." Shay holds out her hand. "Out of the eater will come something to eat. And out of the strong will come something *sweet*."

The Deacon appears next to her; the one whom we just watched fall from the sky like a sack of shit. He looks at me, then in the direction of Lucifer.

Nero whinnies and stomps his hooves with joy.

The bodies don't stop appearing. Men and women. Demons. Angels. And... Hellions. Oh my god, Hellions! My Hellions.

A lump forms in my throat. I swallow it down because girls like me don't cry. We don't cry when the Hellions who gave their lives to save me come back from the dead.

Klaus smiles and waves. Tukka salutes me. And then...

"No," I whisper, walking closer.

He moves forward, men and women and Demons parting to let *him* through. I hold my breath, recognizing the curled horns, the broad shoulders, the sharp-toothed smile.

"Skeele!"

Skeele walks toward me, arms out. Last time I saw him he was dying. Skinned. Bloodied. He was one breath away from the Ether and begging me to feed from him. I couldn't do it.

"Night Owl," Skeele says. "You're looking... dirty."

A strange noise escapes my throat, both a cry and soft laugh. I run toward him and throw my arms around his neck. He hugs me back, cold arms and all.

"I can't stay," he whispers. "I knew I could never stay forever." He presses cold lips to the side of my face.

I nod, noticing he doesn't smell alive. No brimstone and smoke. He doesn't smell like the Skeele I spent all those years with.

"Don't cry, little Night Owl," Skeele says, cool lips against my ear. "We are in the middle of a war."

"They have Rue," I say.

Skeele's expression turns to stone. "Then they must die. Now, tell me how we win this thing."

I release him and turn to face the battlefield. Angels and Hellions and Demons are still fighting. Lucifer is watching us from the sky where he circles like a seagull ready to pounce.

I glance to Sparrow, who nods while pressing his lips into a thin line. I try to think of the best approach but brute force seems to be the only answer.

"Clear us a path to Lucifer," I say.

Shay has a Deacon. Which means I have a Deacon. But this one is different. This one can't die because he already did. I've never loved double jeopardy more than in this moment.

Hope floods my veins like hearing there's a snow day and no school in the morning.

Lucifer lands. Dark eyes focus on me. "I'm waiting, Granddaughter," he shouts over the sound of battle. "If you want your child, come and get her."

Thirty-Four

Jed reached in his bag, scraping off thick, dried mud. He pulled out the jar of feathers Meg had left in his and Shay's safe keeping when she brought Rue and Remington to the Peabody Library.

"Hmm," Jed shifted the jar of feathers, holding it up to Hellsky and letting the ochre din filter through.

"I wonder...." Archaic light twisted from his fingers. He whispered words that sounded like the sweetest lullaby, like the guttural moans of a woman giving birth, like the crackling of sunlight at first dawn.

"What are you doing?" Shay asked, towering over him in her Demon form.

Jed didn't reply. He was too focused, drawing on magic he'd only used once before. Something that was both dark and light, both beautiful and ugly. His aura was glowing Cherenkov radiation. Bright and blue—so bright Shay had to shield her eyes and back away.

Shay had an uneasy feeling. "I think you should stop, Jed," she warned.

He didn't acknowledge that he'd heard her. He'd only done something like this once before when he brought back Nightingale. But it seemed he might have a gift for bringing back the dead. He continued his spellcasting until the jar of feathers transformed into the form of a snowy owl.

The raptor settled on his arm, her dark eyes gazing into his.

"Hello, Elyse, I've heard a little about you," Jed said. "Your mother needs you." He shifted his arm and the owl took flight.

THIRTY-FIVE

Having spent half her life alone and unloved, Meg was having a hard time comprehending the scenes that had unfolded moments ago. Her father, her Hellions, the Crossroads Demon army... it was too much and everything. It filled her with hope. She was not alone in this. She had so many who had come to defeat evil and save Rue. Meg didn't have time for tears now. She reached down for something she'd buried, something she'd held back for years. It was a quick anger, a rage, a hate for those who had wronged her, it had grown even stronger knowing they'd wronged her child.

The battlefield parted, pushed back by Shay's army and Meg's Hellions. Meg went straight for Lucifer who had landed in the clearing, wings spread wide.

"Where is my daughter?" Meg screamed at Lucifer, face twisted in hate. "What have you done with her?"

Meg's heart pounded against her ribs as she raced across the war-torn battlefield. The ground trembled beneath her feet, fractured and steaming from the infernal heat that emanated from the heart of Hell. Crusted mud fell from her body and Sparrow's as he ran beside her.

The clashing of weapons and roars of Demon, the cries of Angels faded into a distant roar as Meg's focus narrowed on Lucifer.

The battlefield spread, leaving a straight path. Shadows twisted away, recoiling from the power that radiated from her, and the jagged earth pulled back, forming a corridor that led straight to Lucifer himself.

Meg's boots pounded against the scorched earth, each step driving her forward, closer to the embodiment of Evil that had stolen her daughter and shattered the fragile hope she'd fought so hard to protect. Her fists were clenched weapons, nails biting in to her palms but she welcomed the pain. It anchored her, fueled the fire burning inside her chest.

Lucifer stood at the far end of the battlefield, his dark wings spread wide, his eyes twin infernos of crimson light. He waited, unbothered, his lips curved in a mocking smile. His presence dominated the world around him, warping the air with raw, suffocating power.

"Come then," he called, his voice echoing with sinister allure. "Face me, little queen. Let's see how strong you really are without your wings."

Meg didn't falter. She drew in a breath, tasting ash and magic, and felt her own power surge to the surface. Her determination crystallized, a molten resolve that burned hotter than Hellfire. This was for Rue. This was for every sacrifice, every piece of herself she'd lost along the way. She would not bow. She would not break.

The path before her began to close, jagged shards of stone rising up as if to trap her, but Meg kept running, defiant. Energy crackled around her, a wild unchained force that lit up the battle field.

Suddenly, there was a movement in the air, the sound of beating wings, the whisp-hush stroke of feathers, a shallow hoot.

Meg glanced to the side, nearly stumbling when she recognized the snowy owl. Elyse. Fire flooded her veins.

As she drew nearer, the world seemed to hold its breath, a stillness descending over the battlefield that made the hair on the back of her neck stand on end. This was it. She raised her Basilisk tooth and leapt over the debris with a battle cry that echoed for miles.

———

Lucifer was relentless, his dark wings slicing through the air like jagged shadows. He lunged, his hands crackling with Hellfire. Meg barely managed to dodge it, rolling across the cracked earth. Lucifer stomped and magma broke through the ground with a crack, heat searing her cheek, leaving a blistered line of red.

"Is this all you have, little fallen Queen?" Lucifer taunted, his voice a rich, mocking drawl. He glanced at Sparrow, who had been intersected by a huge Hellion that looked like a boar crossed with an elephant. "So much for the help. Your cursed bird-man can't help you now." He advanced, eyes alight with cruel fire. "I was told an omen ages ago. The Deacons told me the females of my bloodline would kill me." He reached for Meg, grabbed her leg and dragged her closer. "So I've killed them. One by one. But for some reason, you just won't die."

The snowy owl swooped down, talons spread and clawed at Lucifer's face. He dropped Meg's leg with a howl and batted at the owl. But Elyse was quick this time–she remembered the quick swipe of Lucifer's blade and dodged it, flying out of reach before planning her next attack.

Meg gritted her teeth, anger surging through her veins. She lifted her Basilisk tooth blade and lashed out, firelight glinting off the edge with desperate brilliance. The strike connected, cutting Lucifer's arm and sending a spray of dark ichor into the air. But Lucifer only laughed, the wound sealing as quickly as it had opened.

"That tickled," he chuckled.

Meg's eyes went wide as she realized the Basilisk poison did nothing to him.

He retaliated with a brutal backhand, his strength sending Meg crashing to the ground. Pain erupted in her ribs and the impact forced air from her lungs. Stars danced across her vision as she struggled to rise.

A strong hand reached down and dragged her up. It was Skeele, but he was a momentary blur as he went on battling the Demons surrounding them. He moved like a dancer, agile and nimble. The way he pulled Meg to her feet was nothing more than a heavily practiced segment of his routine, reminiscent of the smooth and steady years they'd spent together.

"Stay down," Lucifer commanded, his voice booming. "Your defiance is pathetic. Your unwillingness to die, uncouth."

Meg refused.

Above her, Lucifer loomed, a dark fallen angel? of power and malice. His wings unfurled like a shroud, casting her in shadow. He summoned a spear of black flame, the weapon pulsing with deadly intent.

Meg's legs shook but her will was unbroken. The war raged around them, her allies battling for their lives. For Rue. She couldn't give up. Not now. Not after all she'd been through. Lucifer was nothing more than a dog on a chain with a peanut butter and jelly sandwich.

Lucifer sneered, his eyes narrowing. "Very well. If you wish to die on your feet, so be it."

He lunged, faster than lightning. Meg brought her blade up to meet him. The clash of their powers sent a shockwave through the battlefield, scattering lesser Demons and Angels alike. Lucifer's might was overwhelming, his strength too much for Meg. He drove her back, blow after crushing blow.

Meg's grip on her blade weakened. She stumbled, barely keeping herself upright. Each strike from Lucifer sent agony shooting through her limbs. She spit blood into the dirt.

Meg glanced toward Sparrow, afraid. She was losing, and quickly. This was defeat. All these years she thought she could do this alone. She couldn't. She needed him.

"Meg!" Sparrow's voice cut through the chaos. "Watch out!"

Meg's gaze flicked away for the briefest moment. She only wanted to gaze upon her family and friends one last time before death was delivered to her.

Lucifer struck, his fist colliding with her chest. She was thrown backward, her body slamming into the ground. The world spun as pain reverberated throughout every bone in her body.

Lucifer approached with merciless, dark aura suffocating the air around her. Meg's hands twitched, struggling to grasp her fallen sword. The edge of despair crept into her heart.

"The Deacons were *wrong*." Lucifer raised his flaming spear.

Meg closed her eyes, bracing herself for the end.

"There isn't room in my back for any more knives. If you're going to kill me, you're going to have to look me in the eyes while you do it," Meg whispered, blood dripping from her mouth. Pain radiated in her ribs. She widened her eyes in challenge and Lucifer paused.

Sparrow grabbed Meg in a violent maneuver, but he couldn't stop the haste. He wrapped her close then knelt, forcing her to the ground underneath him protectively. Then, he collected the darkness within, letting it boil until it was ready to burst. There would be other injuries, maybe even deaths, but he had to do something.

He wasn't going to watch her die again. The feathers burst from his wings, a million black razors filled the air directly over them.

———

THE DEACON WATCHED Meg and Lucifer battle with bated breath. He noticed when a cool burst of air approached his side. He turned, detecting the flickering of a ghost breaking through. He recognized the dark hair and red lips. The Deacon smiled. Clea had arrived.

"Now, specter, now is our time," the Deacon said as he raised his hands.

Clea drew upon rage, one that boiled within her when she saw all the ways her father tried to kill the female blood line. She drew upon ancient power, something deep from under the realm of Hell. Something she never knew existed.

She screamed. The Deacon was staring at her, but it didn't stop her as she raised her arms and gathered wind from Hellsky.

The Deacon matched her energy.

Clea and the Deacon blasted the wind in the direction of Sparrow's feathers that were hovering in the air.

The razors from Sparrow's wings hit only one target, the one Clea directed them at, She forced the wind to drive every feathered blade into her father's chest: deep. Into his heart. Into his bones. Into his blackened soul. So deep they would never be removed.

The Deacon smiled proudly. "There you go."

"Grandmother," Remington whispered as he ran toward Clea's flickering form.

But then she was gone. She'd used every ounce of energy that had kept her soul there. She was gone for good, no longer trapped after Alastor had sliced her with iron. The prophecy was half fulfilled.

Sparrow stood, wings nothing more than a skeletal scaffold, watching as Lucifer roared and bled. Meg made a noise, unable to contain the desire to end him once and for all.

Sparrow gripped her arms, he gave her a hard stare. "Your teeth are *sharp*. Your eyes are *luminous*. Everyone will whisper your name in hushed tones after *this*." He nodded then picked her up and ran with her, straight toward Lucifer. Sparrow threw her through the air, launching her like a missile.

Meg didn't have wings but the flight was graceful and strong. The way Hellsky lit up in the background, the way the lightning cracked and energy lit the air, she might as well have had wings burst from her back in that moment.

Meg's feet hit gore-stained dirt. She ran three steps, leapt, climbed up Lucifer's tall body like he was a tree and *bit*. She didn't leave one drop of blood. She drank until he was a husk and his skin turned to ash. She broke his bones, cracked his femurs over her knee, and drank the marrow until they crumbled to dust. She drank until the blades from Sparrow's feathers fell to the ground in a metallic clatter.

"Fuck your omen," she muttered with blood stained lips.

The battleground went silent. The Hellions and Demons that were once noble to Lucifer paused to face their new Queen.

Meg closed her eyes and turned to find every soul on the battleground staring at her. She wiped blood from her mouth and searched the field for her son, then Sparrow. After setting eyes on both of them, she said, "I'm going to get Rue." And turned, running toward what was left of the castle.

Sparrow darted after her, bone tips of what was left of his wings scraping on the ground.

Thirty-Six

Rue lay motionless in the dark, cold dungeon of the castle in the burning caves. Her skin was pale, her breaths shallow.

Dacre knelt beside her, his heart pounding with something he wasn't used to. He couldn't explain it. He knew from the moment the little princess had sunk her teeth into his neck that everything had changed. The handsome Demon, who usually wore arrogance as effortlessly as his black suite, looked uncharacteristically vulnerable. He brushed a strand of hair from Rue's face, his hand trembling. Something had happened to her while he was gone. Dacre scanned her body for injury and concluded, perhaps, it was the blood she'd taken from him. It was changing her and had sent her body into some kind of hibernation state.

The battle above raged on, the sounds of Hellfire and war echoing through the stone walls. He had to get her to safety, incapable of denying the pull to keep her safe. It was too strong, overwhelming. It had kept him awake all night, made him unable to sit or calm his thoughts.

"Come on, Rue," Dacre whispered, his voice horse. "Wake up."

She didn't stir. Her eyelids remained closed, her lashes casting shadows over bruised cheeks. Dacre's jaw clenched. The castle shook. He glanced at the door, remembering the empty cells he'd passed on his way to Rue's. The creatures of the dungeon had been let loose by Lucifer and they were battling above. Rue was alone. The heat from the caves was growing more oppressive as Lucifer's dark force pulsed through the air. Dacre doubted the castle would remain standing much longer.

He stood, carefully gathering Rue in his arms. Her small form was fragile against his chest and he felt a surge of protectiveness that made his blood boil. The battle outside wasn't over yet, but he had a duty now. He had always teetered between alliances. His family was devout to nothing more than the shadows and debts. But all that had changed now.

Dacre made his way out of Rue's cell and through the dungeon's dim corridors. He was wrong when he thought all the creatures had joined the efforts on the battlefield. Demons and hellish beasts lunged at him, desperate to tear them apart. Dacre's eyes flashed dangerously, his nearly human features twisting with fury. Dacre didn't need to fight with a weapon; the claws that appeared from his fingertips was enough to scare the creatures away. The way his face transformed told the story of *what* he was, more formidable than anything housed in the dungeons of the castle in the burning caves. He held Rue close, clutched her small form to his chest until he could feel her shallow breaths against his ribs. He didn't dare wake her now, didn't want her to see him like this.

A monstrous creature with jagged horns leapt from the shadows. Dacre spun, lashing out with one clawed hand, relieving the creature of its head with one rake of his talons. The creature dissolved into ash, leaving the air heavy with the stench of sulfur. Dacre gritted his teeth, his muscles straining as he continued forward, doing his best not to lose control while he held something so precious in his arms. He'd never forgive himself if he harmed her. He had to keep the darkness in check.

Dust sifted through the air as the castle shook again. Stone crumbled. The hallways behind them began collapsing in on themselves. Dacre clutched Rue tighter and moved faster. He ran past stone walls bending and dripping ichor. It was as though the castle itself was bleeding, wounded. The balance between realms was so off that it threatened to destroy everything. Dacre imagined buildings were crumbling in the Seven Kingdoms of Heaven as well. He already knew the Earthen plane burned and shifted with chaos.

Dacre saw the winding stairwell a few feet away. A stone from the ceiling fell, hit his foot and caused him to stumble. He shook off the pain, one goal on his mind.

"Hold on, princess," he murmured, not caring that she couldn't hear him. "We're almost there."

He ran up the stairs that crumbled under his feet. More stone fell. Windows broke and glass sprayed. Dacre ignored the fresh cuts to his face and arms, only glanced down at Rue to ensure she remained unharmed. The glass had cut her cheek. A small dot of blood began to seep out. Dacre shook his head to focus, reached the landing, and began sprinting toward the door that led outside.

The battle outside the castle was a nightmare of chaos and destruction. The landscape of the royal lands had changed, warped by Lucifer's reign and fury. The sky burned with dark flames. Dacre waited in the shadows, Rue cradled protectively in his arms. He watched as Hellions and Angels slaughtered each other. He smiled as the Crossroads Demon girl revealed her own army and the Demon-horse set fire into the sky. His head snapped, refocused on the female voice who cried over the battlefield and demanded Lucifer give back her daughter.

Dacre's chest was heavy. He didn't want to let Rue go. He wanted to take her and run away. He glanced down, focused on the drop of blood on her cheek. A deep growl emanated from his chest.

"Just this once," he promised himself as he dipped his head and licked her wound, savoring the taste of her blood. "Never again."

The cracking of bones echoed across Hellscape and Dacre looked up to see Meg standing over Lucifer's carcass. It was time, she would come for Rue next and nothing would stop her.

Dacre recognized the skeletal wings of the dark Angel who followed Meg. He straightened his back and began walking toward them.

Dacre exited the shadows, carrying Rue toward her mother at an even pace. His arms aching only because he knew he couldn't keep her. He didn't want Meg to see him as threatening, knew that might certainly end his life prematurely. The battle for Hell and balance was over, the war ended, but the tension didn't leave him.

"Give her to me," Meg shouted as she ran closer.

Dacre didn't back down, he did his best to communicate that he was not going to harm Rue.

"She's okay," he said. "I didn't hurt her. I got her out. The castle is going to collapse."

Meg glanced to the burning caves, the smoke replaced with rock dust as the building slowly collapsed in on itself.

"If you hurt her, I will kill you," Meg promised.

Dacre knew she would. "I would never," he said.

The Raven King was eyeing Dacre suspiciously.

Dacre carefully lowered Rue into Meg's waiting embrace. Then he stepped back and dropped to his knee. The Demon's usual cocky demeanor was nowhere to be found. He looked at Meg, his eyes shadowed.

"She'll be okay," he said, though the assurance felt hollow. "I kept her safe." It was mostly true.

Meg didn't reply, her attention wholly on her daughter. She held Rue close, tears streaming down her face, but a flicker of gratitude shone in her eyes as she looked down at Dacre.

"I won't forget this," Meg promised.

Dacre finally let his exhaustion show, his shoulders slumping. The weight of everything he'd done, every choice he'd made, pressed heavily on him. But as he watched Meg hold Rue he knew he'd made the right choice, and for once that was enough. He hated that he'd never see Rue again. She was something he couldn't keep, something not meant for him. Like so much in his world.

THIRTY-SEVEN

Shay stared at the ones whom she'd made Demon pacts with. They were all whole, they hadn't turned into walking sacks of flesh. They were certainly dead but wandering this realm. They were newly dead. The realization came as Shay's figure returned to normal. They'd died. *And out of the strong will come something sweet*. She'd used the power of their souls to change forms, her and Nero both, the pact fulfilled.

"Send their souls away," Chel ordered.

"No," Shay said. "They're *mine*."

"You can't keep them," Chel warned. "They must repent in a Safe House and go to whichever plane they belong on. This is not for you to decide. You'll disrupt the natural order of things. The Deacons will put a bounty on your head."

"Your natural order of things appears to be quite fucked. They are mine. I won't send them away." Shay wasn't about to bow down to Hell or the Seven Kingdoms of Heaven or the Deacons. None of them had done much for her. She glanced around.

"There are no Deacons. No Safe Houses," she sneered. "It no longer matters."

"Shay-baby," Jed's voice broke through the chaos of her mind. The Demon poison was spreading the longer she remained in this form. It was changing her, erasing her humanity.

Energy crackled in Jed's fingertips. "You don't want to do this, Shay-baby," Jed said softly. "Remember who you are."

Shay glanced between Chel and Jed. Thousands of waiting faces focused on her, waiting for her next move. The war between Meg and Lucifer was over but a new war raged on in Shay's center. Her soul battled the Demon-poison that had taken over her body.

Shay only saw blackness, power that had boiled to a char during the darkest parts of the war and refused to leave her veins. She wanted to keep it, wanted to marinate in it. She had a power like never before. No one could hurt her now. No one could hurt Nero. The horse whinnied wildly, sensing her thoughts. She was remembering all the terrible things that had happened during her life on the Earthen plane. The taunts from Clyburn, the kidnapping, the death of her parents, the devastation of the family ranch in Montana. Dark power surged through her body. She'd never be weak and human again, never find herself in those situations ever again. Shay smiled darkly.

Nero nudged her shoulder and whinnied softer. He sent a plea down the golden thread that connected their souls. Shay shivered, hated that it was so hard for her to *want* to return back to her human form.

"Shay-baby," Jed said calmly, moving closer, fingers glowing brighter. "Remember who you are. You aren't this."

Shay gripped her weapon and glanced toward the thousands of souls who waited for her next move. A familiar face stepped forward. Grandmother Crow.

The old woman's expression was one of concern. "Your Daddy wouldn't want this for you," Grandmother Crow said.

She remembered the old woman from her childhood and life in Montana. It seemed so long ago. Grief surged; she didn't want Grandmother Crow to be dead.

Shay rubbed her face and fought the forces warring within her chest. But then, something strange happened. The thousands of souls that stood steady, awaiting her decision to release them or hold them, parted. A white horse walked toward her. Sparkling white. Its mane was glossy and twinkling as though specked with diamonds.

Nero whinnied softly and Shay felt something pure emanate from him.

The white horse stopped in front of Shay. *"So, you are Nero's human."* The white horse tipped its head to the side, inspecting her. *"You're not looking very human right now. I've been watching you, Shay. Watching you for a long time. You've been very brave. But this is not what your soul wants. You know this, cowgirl."*

Shay's eyes were wide, she'd never heard a horse speak before. Something throbbed in her chest trying to get out. It clawed at her throat.

"I can't let them go," Shay whispered, her eyes wide.

"You want to let them go, Shay-baby," the white horse said. *"You don't want this darkness. You are good."* The white horse searched Shay's blackened eyes. *"You are the wind that races lightning over the Montana prairie. You are sunlight and wildflowers. Not this."*

Jed was close enough to stop her; a spell was waiting on his tongue, his fingertips glowing with magic.

"Shay-baby," the white horse said, *"Come back to us as you were."*

In the space between heartbeats, Shay changed back into her

human form and collapsed on her knees. She was crying—exhausted, but free.

Jed picked her up and held her close. Nero nuzzled Shay's shoulder.

"I'm so sorry," Shay whispered. "I don't know what happened."

"You helped save us," Jed said.

Everyone turned as the castle in the burning caves came tumbling down in a thundering roar.

Thirty-Eight

"I kept her safe, like you asked," Skeele said, voice full of emotion. "But it was so much more. More than I ever thought I'd have. More than I ever thought I deserved. A Demon from the hovels..." he shook his head, a tear beading the corner of his eye.

Sparrow's expression was blank and he only glanced at Meg exactly once, his arms tightening on Rue as he passed the unconscious girl to her brother. Remington carried her with ease and Nightingale fussed, delving into her dreams to wake her.

"She'll be mad that you asked me to watch over her," Skeele continued. "But it was my duty." He patted over his heart. "It was my greatest honor."

Skeele turned to Rue and Remington. "You've both grown so much in such a short time. Too much, really. And I'm sure by now you know the truth. I'm not your father." His expression faltered to one of regret.

"Yes, you were," Remington said as he set a now awake Rue on her feet.

Rue threw her arms around Skeele, unsteady on her feet after being woken from such a deep sleep. "Of course you were," she whispered. "We never got to say goodbye."

Something meowed from Skeele's pocket. "Oh," he smiled. "I found this." He pulled Lucipurr out and handed the kitten to Rue. "He told me he belonged to you. I found him biting a little Demon. Seems he wanted to join in on the battle."

"You can speak to cats?" Rue asked, tucking the kitten in her pocket.

"Cats walk the edges of the realms. They talk in an old dialect of Hellspeak. They're half in." Skeele smiled.

"You're going away?" Remington asked.

"Yes," Skeele nodded. "I can't stay here." He hugged Rue then Remington then Thrush. He shook Sparrow's hand and patted his elbow. "Take care of them." He stood in front of Meg and smiled softly. "Be nice." He kissed her cheek, his eyes falling to the missing wings behind her shoulders. "You're looking very human these days. It suits you. The wings were kinda preposterous." He smiled.

Meg's face was twisted in sorrow. She scanned his face, unbelieving he was there. Unbelieving that she had another moment with him. There was so much she wanted to say but none of it would pass her lips.

"I love you too, Night Owl," Skeele smiled. "I wish we'd had more time." He glanced to Sparrow. "But you were never fully mine. We both know that."

A whimper escaped Meg's throat as she reached for him, one last hug for the man she knew she didn't deserve. Every memory flashed through her mind as though she were dying right along with him. But, this wasn't death, no this was rebirth. She kissed the corner of his mouth, scratching at his clothing as it began slipping through her fingertips.

"I'm going now." Skeele waved and winked, then faded away to nothing.

Meg threw herself at Sparrow, sobbing like never before crying like she'd never ever let herself do. The deep sobs wracked her ribs and made a terrible sound in her throat and echoed over the silent battlefield.

Sparrow rubbed her back and buried his face in the crook of her neck. He folded skeletal wings around them both, bent his knees and took her to the ground on his lap. He held her tighter than ever before. He would never let her go. He would spend the rest of his life keeping her safe, protecting her, groveling for the hurt he'd caused in the name of balance for the realms. He hated that he'd hurt her to protect her. Never again.

"I told you...," Sparrow whispered in Meg's ear, "I told you we'd be invincible together." He wiped ichor from her shoulder and kissed the soft space over her collarbone.

THIRTY-NINE

The hallways of Sparrow's house were quiet, the echoes of recent battles still lingering in everyone's minds. For days everyone had slept and ate and hid in shadows.

Meg moved silently though the corridor, her steps heavy, heart caught between a pang of sadness she couldn't quite shake and relief.

Jed walked beside her, his expression shadowed and conflicted. He didn't like what Meg had asked of him, and though he'd agreed, the unease in his eyes was hard to miss.

"She's sleeping," Meg said as she reached for the door handle to Rue's room. "I checked on her earlier." She opened the door.

Rue's dark hair spilled wild over the pillow, her forehead creased in dreaming. Rue's breaths were rapid as though she were running. Meg couldn't shake the memories of Rue's broken sobs and her wide, haunted eyes. The darkness that lingered in Rue's gaze was something Meg couldn't bear to see.

Teari had seen the girl and uneasily blamed the crying and haunted expression on the war and the kidnapping. But Rue continued to walk the halls of Sparrow's house with haunted eyes, waking the house frequently at night with screams from nightmares that no one could wake her from. It needed to end. And Meg only knew of one way to help her daughter.

Jed moved closer to the bed, his hand hovering uncertainly at his side.

"Are you sure, Meg?" His voice was rough. "What if she asks questions? Figures out something's missing?"

Meg's gaze didn't waver. "I'd rather she has a gap than live with those memories. Look what it's doing to her. She's too young for that darkness." Meg's eyes softened as she looked back at Rue, sadness clutching her throat. She'd promised herself that her children wouldn't see trauma like she'd endured in her childhood. Meg had promised to keep her children safe and she'd failed with Rue. She needed to fix it.

"Please," Meg begged Jed. "Just since the kidnapping, that's it. Leave everything else. We can work around a few days missing from her memory."

Jed swallowed and gave a slow nod. He'd seen memories etched in blood, trauma carved into minds so deeply that no spell could ease them. Rue was young, her spirit hadn't taken in that darkness fully. He hoped, at least, that it hadn't.

Jed stepped closer to the bed and lifted his hands, his fingers glowing faintly as his magic rose from his center and began to pulse through the room. Since the war, he'd become much stronger. The air felt heavy, charged. Jed closed his eyes and whispered words that sounded like the falling petals of a rose, the gentle lapping of dark lake water in the moonlight, the foggy sunrise on an autumn day. He found the memories that tormented Rue's mind; the cold stone of the dungeon, the chains, Hellions, the Demons that had looked at her with hungry eyes, the taste of blood on her tongue, and... a handsome Demon. Jed wiped it. Memories gone. Blank slate.

As the spell settled, Rue shifted slightly in sleep, her small hand clenching and then relaxing as Jed's magic wove gently around her mind. Rue's breathing relaxed, the creases in her expression faded to a peaceful, almost angelic expression.

Jed lowered his hands, the glow around them fading. He took a step back, exhaustion settling into his features.

"It's done," he said quietly, his voice thick with the strain of the magic he'd used. The aura around him pulsed blue light. "She won't remember any of it. All she'll remember is looking for the kitten that morning and waking up on the battlefield after the defeat."

Meg nodded. "Thank you."

Jed paused, before telling Meg about the handsome Demon and the blood-drinking that had been forced upon Rue at the Black Mansion.

Meg's features shifted as anger threatened to overtake her. She closed her eyes and took a deep breath before saying, "Never tell a soul. Erase your own memories of this moment if you need to. But never, ever speak of this."

They left Rue to sleep undisturbed and walked back to the living room where Teari and Shay waited.

Teari looked worried. "Did you do it?"

Jed nodded.

Teari sighed and walked toward Meg, pulling her into her arms. "I'm sorry we couldn't find another way to help her. I think this is the right thing to do."

Meg smiled softly and gripped her friends' hands. "I know you tried. You always have."

FORTY

Early dawn stretched across the vast, untouched grasslands of the Earthen plane, the world now quiet and still. Sunlight seeped over the horizon, casting hues of amber and soft pink across tall grasses creating a warm glow. All of it undisturbed by darkness, finally. Nero stood poised, muscles coiled and tense as though he still had to prepare himself for the weight of the past. Nearby, the white horse watched, her gaze serene.

For the first time in what felt like ages, they had no destination, no battle calling them, no shadows tracking their every move. They no longer moved through the realms like wisp on the periphery.

For Nero, calls to the Crossroads had slowed. For the white horse, the pursuit of others trying to find her dissipated like the wind. There was open sky and endless earth before them. The tears in the Veil had become so small, they had to search for hours before finding one for crossing into the Seven Kingdoms of Heaven or Hell.

Nero took a step, feeling the softness of the earth beneath his hooves. He surged forward, his mane streaming behind him like a dark banner, hooves thundering against the earth as he raced nothing more but the sunlight. The white horse bolted beside him, graceful and sure, keeping pace with an effortless stride. Her whinny of joy echoed in his ears.

They ran as if they were the wind, two figures who belonged wholly to the wild. Nero veered toward a hill and the white horse followed, their breath visible in the cool morning air. When they reached the summit, Nero halted, looking over the stretch of land that lay below; the valleys and rivers winding toward the horizon like threads in a vast tapestry. He recognized this place, wandered until he found where he had been left by his mother. Tucked away under scrub brush, this was the tiny corner of land where Shay had found him covered in bees and barely alive.

The white horse nudged him, her eyes gleaming with quiet understanding.

"It was not chance that she found you," she whispered as though it were the simplest truth. *"It was not chance that she nursed you back to life."* The white horse circled him.

HE'D ONLY BEEN BORN a few hours earlier, dropped in the prairie grass by a mare who wasn't sure raising a foal in the offseason was such a good thing. When the bees came out of the ground and swarmed on her, she ran. She left him to die, wet and cold. But the warm Montana sun dried the wetness from his coat and mane, and he rose up on knobby-kneed legs only to be stung over and over again.

Shay wasn't much more than a teenager when she pointed to the black foal in the distance. It didn't take much to convince Nicholas to take the foal home. Shay lifted him, draping the small horse over her lap as she rode back to the ranch.

What Nero didn't know was that Shay saw the white horse first. She'd followed the white horse like a mirage and was led to Nero.

Nero broke into a gallop, the white horse matching his speed. They splashed through a river, cold water spraying around them before veering into a thick grove of pines where shafts of light filtered down, illuminating their path like a blessing. They didn't stop; they ran until the landscape blurred, until every memory felt like a distant dream. Each step took them further from the darkness that had once bound them.

And as the sun rose higher, they continued, two spirits, wild and free, their whinnies echoing through the fields, untouchable and unconquered. The white horse was now able to carry on in the realm that was her land. Her peace. There was finally balance.

"Do you want to go home?" the white horse asked.

"Yes," Nero said, finally tired of running.

"Let's go home to Shay," the white horse said, and they turned toward Montana and the ranch that Shay and Jed were rebuilding.

FORTY-ONE

MEG

WALKING through these hallways has become familiar, calming. There are no shadows for dark creatures to hide and slither. No Hellions roaming the halls looking for danger. I pause outside Sparrow's bedroom door. We've been discussing rebuilding Hell and in the coming days we'll need to return. Thankfully Sparrow has experience rebuilding a kingdom even if it's on a different realm. Heaven isn't that far from Hell.

I look forward to building a new home, something that suits us both. I smile to myself. What chaos we will bring to the realms; half-darkness, half-light, intermingling in realms we don't belong in. Too bad. Those Archangels will have to eat a dick because after fighting for our lives against Lucifer, I'm never listening to a single one of them ever again. My stomach grumbles and the door whips open.

Sparrow glances down at me, grabs my hand, and drags me inside his room.

"You're hungry," he mutters.

"I was gonna make some spaghetti," I say.

Sparrow smirks. "I'm hungry."

"I didn't know you liked spaghetti."

"Maybe get some Twinkies." He smiles. "Or pizza. Or those blasphemous snowball things you eat that make a holy mess."

"Those are delicious. Don't hate on the snowballs." I shake my head and consider biting him for talking shit about my junk food. "You don't keep that stuff in the house and Noah refuses to find me food after what we put Thrush through. Especially since I gave him freedom."

Sparrow's brow rises. "Thrush did what he wanted to do. We couldn't have stopped him. He hated it here and told us so each and every day."

I shrug. "I know. I just hope he's feeding the Basilisk."

Sparrow shakes a finger at me. "That is why Noah is mad at you. He hates those things."

"They're good to have around."

He scans me for a moment, licks his lips, and says, "I guess I'll just have you then."

I glance at Sparrow's bony scaffold of wings. Small, black feathers are starting to grow in.

Sparrow shudders, holding in a tic of madness that threatens to wrack his whole body.

"Is it back?" I ask, worried.

Sparrow holds up his finger, his jaw clenching and eyes closed as he tries to control it. He sits on the edge of the bed and grips his knees, leaning forward. His teeth grind.

"I'm fine," he finally says.

Green eyes flash open and the dark haze clears.

"Is it bad like before?" I ask.

"No." He grabs the waistband of my jeans and drags me closer, between his legs, trapping me.

I thread my fingers through his hair and massage his scalp.

He kneads my back and hips, wraps his arms around my waist and presses his face to my stomach. We just hold each other like this for minutes. And I remember how he looked in battle... graceful and elegant and absolutely fucking lethal. He is mine and I am his. Both of us half-dark and half-light; mine born and bred, his by torment and curses and honor. We have been broken and reborn. Hated and loved. The cycle of chaos ends here, like that birthmark. Little did I know Alastor was doing me a favor when he made me cut the birthmark off my leg. When I find him again, I might thank him.

Sparrow's arm snakes around my waist, pulling me closer, nuzzling his face into my stomach.

"I hear you," he whispers. "Are you ever not hungry?"

I grip his hair and pull at the roots until his head tips back and we make eye contact. I lick my lips. He's never looked better than he does right now, staring up at me.

"I still haven't forgiven you for what you did to my book." Sparrow blinks slowly.

"Which book?" I ask.

"Birds of Paradise."

Damn. That was a long time ago. I stole it from his house and dragged it all over Hellscape. It was dropped in the mud and covered in food. Hmm. It's probably gone for good, destroyed when the castle in the burning caves collapsed.

"Well..." I release a small huff that sounds like a laugh. "I guess you have the next best thing."

"Oh yeah, what's that?" he asks.

"We are birds of paradise."

He smiles and nods, slowly agreeing before he presses the side of his face to my belly again, wrapping his arms so tight I can barely breath and begins to hum *Bed of Roses*.

There he is. There's my old Sparrow Man. I've finally got him back.

———

There is a feather, sparkling and golden. Of all places, it's resting inconspicuously on the bathroom countertop. I hesitate. I haven't received a feather in years. It could be nothing. It could be *something*.

I reach forward, finger pointed. An arc of electricity connects with the tip. My eyes widened and I suck in a breath. My knees buckle. I grip the counter. Blood turns to ice in my veins.

There is a thud from the bedroom. Maybe he senses the feather. He's always had a knack for that. Sparrow tries the handle, then bangs on the door.

"What's happened?" he asks, breaking the handle and shoving the door open, eyes wide in fear. I guess that's what happens after all we've been through.

I fake a smile and brush the feather down the drain. I turn the water on for good measure and drown it.

"Nothing." I smile. "Everything is fine. Just fine. Never better."

I'll be damned if I let a fucking feather ruin my life ever again.

-The End-

AFTERWORD

From the Author.

Wow. I can hardly believe I just typed "The End" on Meg and Sparrow's story. After 10 years of writing this, it is bittersweet giving them an ending. After all I've put them through, I think they deserved it. After Veil of Shadows 4: Raven King and Veil of Shadows 6: Night Owl, we were so disappointed in Sparrow and his separation from Meg. But, they had things to do, people to see, lives to live/ruin, and hearts to break.

Even though this is the end, you might still have some questions about people we've met. While Meg and Sparrow's storyline is done, the Veil of Shadows world will live on in at least 4 planned spinoff standalone books. The first will be Rue and Dacre's story. This will be a standalone New Adult Dark Fantasy Romance titled: "The Sky is Starless." It is scheduled to release in the spring of 2025. Follow me on the blog and/or social media and never miss a release!

Special thanks to my editor Kristy, who has been through the thick and thin of it with this series. She's seen all the "neck ass" and "eye shits" and improperly used "?" and repeating repeating repeating words/phrases, yet, she's stuck with me! Thank you Kristy, for all your editing prowess through the years!

Preview: The Sky is Starless by M. R. Pritchard

Her memories were stolen.
Her nightmares won't let her forget.
And now, the shadows are coming for her.

Caught between worlds, Rue fights to unravel the truth of her past while resisting the dark pull of Dacre, the one man she shouldn't trust—but can't stay away from. Love was never meant to be easy, but for Rue, it could be deadly.

You can't outrun your bloodline... or the shadows it casts.

Rue is determined to live a normal life, far from the dark legacy of her family. College is supposed to be her fresh start—a chance to blend in, bury her secrets, and maybe even discover who she truly is. But when shadowy figures begin stalking her and nightmares plague her nights, normalcy slips further out of reach.

Her parents' solution? A bodyguard.

Nothing could be more infuriating than Dacre, the mysterious, maddeningly handsome man assigned to shadow her every move. Rue's stubborn streak refuses to make it easy for him—until she notices her nightmares quiet when he's near, and when shadow demons attack, Dacre sends them back to the darkness with startling ease.

Rue's missing memories hold the answers she needs, but everyone —including Dacre—seems determined to keep her in the dark.

Dark secrets.
> **Forbidden love.**
> **A battle for her soul.**

The Sky is Starless is a spellbinding dark fantasy romance perfect for fans of supernatural intrigue, steamy tension, and heroines fighting for their destiny.

———

CHAPTER ONE

Early morning light was creeping through the blinds like

unwelcome fingers. Rue watched the coffee maker brew, steam rising from the dark liquid as it streamed into a Hedwig mug. It made her think of smoke and dark magic. Of fire and brimstone. Her vision blurred. Rue blinked a few times but it was too late, her mind was going elsewhere... drifting. The stream of coffee turned to thick blood. It dripped in slow, deliberate rivulets, each drop echoed in the small kitchen. *Drip. Drip. Drip.* Rue's throat felt dry. Sweat beaded her forehead as last night's nightmare's resurfaced, she was drowning, gurgling on blood but so *so* thirsty. Rue gripped the edge of the counter, willing the memory to pass.

"It's not real," she whispered, her voice soft, her heart thumping against her ribs. Rue squeezed her eyes shut and shook her head, trying to erase the phantom sensations: the taste of iron, the warmth spreading down her throat, filling her stomach until it no longer ached. It was all so real and it felt *too* good.

Rue rubbed her eyes until she saw stars. When she opened them again, the coffee maker had stopped and the mug sat innocently on the counter. The owl stared back at her, unmarred. The counter was dry and there was no blood in sight. The mug was filled with dark brown liquid, not red. Rue licked her lips and her stomach growled in protest.

Her hands trembled as she reached for the mug, but... she paused, couldn't shake the feeling of being watched. A shadow passed the edge of her vision. Turning slowly, Rue scanned the empty kitchen, her heart racing.

Nothing.

She blew out a nervous breath and muttered to herself, "There is nothing here. No Demons. No Angels. Just you, Rue. Nothing else. No blood. No monsters."

She took milk from the fridge and a spoon from the drawer. She sat with the coffee mug near the window, opened the blinds and watched the sun rise the rest of the way. Rue's leather messenger bag was in the chair next to her. She opened it and took out her planner. She had class in a few hours. Midterms later in the week. She turned the page as she sipped the coffee and glanced out the window again, watching the oak tree drop orange leaves.

She shivered. Although she wasn't cold, it was the understanding that she'd have to leave this world soon and visit home for the winter break. She just wondered if it would be Heaven or Hell and if the dreams would follow her.

———

CHAPTER TWO

Shower steam fogged the tiny bathroom of Rue's apartment. She stepped out, wrapped herself in a towel and reached for the door to let the steam out. Something written on the mirror caught her eye.

A message: *Meet me at the Coffee Connection at two.*

Rue swiped her finger over the message and got ready. She chose jeans, sneakers, and a chunky black cable knit sweater. She loosely braided her hair to keep it under control with the wind.

Rue slung her leather bag over her shoulder and locked the door to her apartment. She lived in a little brick Tudor style house, that had been converted into two apartments. One above an done below. Her parents had bought the house for Rue to live in, but when Rue argued that it was too much space for just her and the kitten, it was magically renovated. Rue took the upstairs one since she liked the view of the trees and surrounding Loyola campus. The downstairs one was rented quite possibly to a ghost because she never saw the person, only heard the occasional creaks and door squeals. She never saw anyone coming or going, never saw packages get delivered, never heard a vacuum running. She had hoped the person living down there wasn't a complete pig. But, she figured she'd smell something if they were.

Rue jogged down the stairs and passed her car, opting to walk to class since the weather was nice.

*

Rue slid into her usual seat near the back of the lecture hall. The room was already buzzing with conversation, students flipping through notebooks and idly tapping on laptops.

Professor Camden, a wiry man with round glasses and patches sewn over the edges of his brown suitcoat strode into the room. He clapped his hands together, voice booming with too much energy for the hour. "Good morning, everyone! Today, we're diving into the mysteries of the Zapotec civilization!"

Rue opened her notebook, clicked her pen but the tip hovered over the page. Professor Camden's voice became a distant drone as her mind wandered.

A soft tap on her arm pulled her back. She turned to see Evelyn, her perpetually cheerful classmate, grinning like she had a secret.

"Hey, Rue. We're all going to Justin's party tonight. You should come." She swiped at blonde fringe before pressing a Chapstick to her lips.

Rue hesitated, grip tightening on her pen. "I don't know." She hated parties, she found it too hard to relax and have fun. She blamed it on the way she was raised which was not on the Earthen plane.

"Oh, come on!" Evelyn pouted. "You never come to these things. Just for a little while, okay? It'll be fun."

Rue forced a small smile. "I'll think about it."

"No," Evelyn pressed. "You will come. It's the last Halloween party of the season. You haven't seen any of my costumes this year."

Rue's cheeks flushed. "But... I don't have a costume."

"Good. I'll bring one for you." Evelyn winked. "I've got the perfect one. See you at six."

Rue grabbed Evelyn's sleeve and looked her dead in the eyes.

"What?" Evelyn asked.

"It better not be... slutty," Rue warned.

Evelyn smiled widely. "No promises."

Rue slipped out of class as soon as it ended, her bag slung over her shoulder. The campus buzzed with the energy of students heading to lunch, Rue felt like she was moving through a different world. One she didn't belong in. The feeling was what held her back from campus parties and dates and fully putting herself out in the world. The thing was, she didn't belong in this world. She didn't even belong in this realm. She watched people walk by her, none of them had any clue that they were so close to a princess of another realm. Rue shuddered at the thought. She had stopped thinking of herself as a princess a long time ago. Now she was simply Rue. Rue the runaway. Rue the atypical who chose a life in the Earthen plane amongst the normies. She fidgeted with her dark braid and raised her face to the cool breeze. Even if she didn't belong here, it did feel like home.

The Coffee Connection was a typical college town coffee shop with alternative music playing low on the sound system and a sagging couch in the back corner that no one in their right might should ever sit on.

A bell hanging over the door jingled as Rue stepped inside, greeted by the smell of roasted coffee beans.

"Welcome to the Coffee Connection," a barista called from behind the counter.

Rue waved and smiled before scanning the shop.

There she was. Short-cropped black hair and bright blue eyes hidden behind big sunglasses, and legs twice as long as Rue's. One thing Rue didn't inherit from her mother was height.

Meg, her mother, waved and motioned for Rue to come to the small table she'd chosen near the window. Rue went and Meg stood and pulled her in for a hug.

"Rue, I've missed you," she whispered like it was a secret.

"We met here last week," Rue reminded her.

She sat, crossed her long legs and took off her leather jacket. She was wearing a wide necked T-shirt, scars and tattoos marred her arms and shoulders.

A man walked by and did a double take, spilling hot coffee on his hand.

She received looks and stares a lot and Rue was unsure how she ignored it all.

Meg slid a mug toward Rue. "I got you the pumpkin spice latte. I hope that's okay?"

"It's perfect. Thank you," Rue said as she sat and scooted closer. The woman was slightly overbearing at times, but she was Rue's mother.

Rue sipped at her coffee and remembered why she'd limited the meetings and moved away from home. They were too close, she needed distance. Rue needed to get out and find her own place in the world. She had to stop living in the shadow of her parents. She had to get away from the secrets and lies.

"Have you been drinking the bagged blood?" Meg whispered and touched Rue's face. "You look pale."

"I don't need it. I'm fine." Rue plucked the menu off the table and considered a pecan muffin.

"I thought I was fine when I was your age too." Meg frowned. "Your father is worried. He wants you to come home."

"And you?" Rue asked.

"I want you safe. Hidden. But... happy." She stared at Rue. "Would you tell me if something was wrong?"

"Sure." Rue rubbed her arm and pushed away the thoughts of the song from her nightmares that had interrupted every moment of peace.

"You seem distracted."

"I have exams this week." Rue sipped at the coffee. "It's just stress. I promise"

"Did you pick a major?" She asked.

"A long time ago." Rue chuckled. "Archaeology."

"Oh, you did say that. I forgot. Sorry." Meg nodded. "Just don't... do anything dangerous. I'm glad you didn't choose criminal justice or healthcare." She shook her head. "I don't want you in more danger."

"Mother." Rue rolled her eyes. "I can handle myself. I'm fine. Nothing has happened for years and years and years. I'm not in any danger."

There was a pregnant pause. She didn't bring up Angels or Demons because it would be wrong to discuss them in a coffee shop amongst normal humans. But, it wasn't that long ago when her mother sent Rue away to live with her Aunt Shay and Uncle Jed while she saved the world as they knew it. No one here would know anything about that though.

The man was still staring. He'd sat at the table behind them, his eyes focused on Meg's back and the two vertical scars that marred her shoulder blades.

Meg touched Rue's long, braided hair. "I know you can take care of yourself. Remm wants to see you."

"I'll be back for holiday break," Rue reminded her.

"Maybe call him?" she suggested. "I think he likes talking to you. Maybe you could convince him to find a girlfriend."

"I have called him. He never answers." Rue sipped at her

coffee. "Why does he bother having a phone if he never answers? Plus, he could come visit me."

"He's been busy..." Meg bit her lip and looked away. "I'll tell you more about it when you come home to visit. This isn't the place to discuss such things."

"Sure." Rue checked her phone, nope not one reply from her brother to any of the text messages she'd sent him last week. She showed Meg, then lowered her voice before asking, "Where are we having the holidays this year? Heaven or Hell?"

Meg smiled wide. "Hell, of course. You know those fucking Angels will ruin every peaceful moment with some shit-fuckery."

Rue laughed, seeing her mother's sharpness reveal itself. She always tried to hide it but every now and then it escaped when everyone least expected it. Dry humor and lots of swearing, she always made Rue laugh.

"What?" Meg scoffed innocently. "You know they will. How is Lucipurr?"

Lucipurr was Rue's cat. A little black kitten with green eyes that her brother had found and brought her when they were kids. The kitten never seemed to grow much, but was smart and friendly and everything Rue needed in a companion.

Rue was still nodding in agreement at the shit-fuckery comment when she replied, "He still acts like a kitten, hiding and escaping." Rue glared at the man behind her mother's shoulder and he noticed, his eyes went wide before he looked away.

Too late. Meg noticed. She leaned back and sipped at her coffee before saying, "You know, this city isn't what it used to be. People used to have respect." She shifted in her seat, turning to face the man and smiled, flashing sharp teeth.

He startled, spilling his coffee. Dark liquid spread across the table and into his lap. "Jesus Christ," he muttered, looking around.

"Meg?" a barista shouted from behind the counter.

She stood and walked toward the counter. The barista passed her a bag.

"Thank you. My husband really loves these," Meg said.

"You tell us every week." The barista was smiling wide, smitten with her. She must've left a big tip.

Rue sighed, assumed that's what a Queen can do. Throw money around willy-nilly, dress like a biker instead of royalty. Rue smiled as she sipped at the pumpkin spice latte and watched the orange and yellow leaves tumble across the sidewalk. Her gaze drifted across the street. The shadows moved just a little too deliberately. She squinted her eyes as it lingered just long enough to send a shiver down her spine.

This Title Releases Spring 2025

About the Author

M. R. Pritchard delves into the profound clash between good and evil, the mystical realms of gods and monsters, and the intricate transformations of ordinary people into beings of immense power. Her gripping narratives often unfold within the haunting backdrop of apocalyptic or post-apocalyptic landscapes, offering a unique blend of suspense and wonder.

M. R. Pritchard is a two-time Kindle Scout winning author, her short story "Glitch" has been featured in the 2017 winter edition of THE FIRST LINE literary journal. Her short story "Moon Lord" has been featured in Chronicle Worlds: Half Way Home (Part of the Future Chronicles) and will be time capsuled on the moon on the Lunar Codex in 2024.

Visit her website MRPritchard.com and Subscribe. You'll get subscriber only content, deleted scenes, updates, special previews of new projects, and book deals.

ALSO BY M. R. PRITCHARD

Other Books by M. R. Pritchard

<u>Science Fiction/post-apocalyptic:</u>
The Phoenix Project
The Reformation
Revelation
Inception
Origins
Resurrection
The Phoenix Project Compendium Edition
The Safest City on Earth
The Man Who Fell to Earth
Heartbeat

Asteroid Riders Series
Moon Lord
Collector of Space Junk and Rebellious Dreams

<u>Steampunk:</u>
Tick of a Clockwork Heart

<u>Dark Fantasy:</u>

Veil of Shadows Series:

Sparrow Man

Nightingale Girl

Scarecrow

Raven King

Nightjar

Night Owl

Etched in Darkness

Embrace the Night

Shadows of Destiny

Midnight Serenade

Echoes of Treachery

Omens of Darkness

Thread the Bone

<u>Fantasy/Fairy Tale Love Story/Romance:</u>

Muse

Forgotten Princess Duology

Midsummer Night's Dream: A Game of Thrones

<u>Poetry/Short Stories</u>

Consequence of Gravity

www.ingramcontent.com/pod-product-compliance
Lightning Source LLC
Chambersburg PA
CBHW061529190726
48289CB00004B/984